Cursed with a poor se[...] propensity to read, **An[...]** her childhood lost in b[...] Literature followed by a career in computing didn't lead directly to her perfect job—writing romance for Mills & Boon—but she has no regrets in taking the scenic route. She lives in London: a city where getting lost can be a joy.

Hopelessly addicted to espresso and HEAs, **Kristine Lynn** pens high-stakes romances in the wee morning hours before teaching writing at an Oregon college. Luckily, the stakes there aren't as dire. When she's not grading, writing, or searching for the perfect vanilla latte, she can be found on the hiking trails behind her home with her daughter and puppy. She'd love to connect on X, Facebook, or Instagram.

THE GP'S
SEASIDE REUNION

ANNIE CLAYDON

A KISS WITH THE
IRISH SURGEON

KRISTINE LYNN

MILLS & BOON

First published in Great Britain 2025
by Mills & Boon, an imprint of HarperCollins*Publishers* Ltd,
1 London Bridge Street, London, SE1 9GF

www.harpercollins.co.uk

HarperCollins*Publishers* Macken House, 39/40 Mayor Street Upper,
Dublin 1, D01 C9W8, Ireland

The GP's Seaside Reunion © 2025 Annie Claydon

A Kiss with the Irish Surgeon © 2025 Kristine Lynn

ISBN: 978-0-263-32497-6

02/25

This book contains FSC™ certified paper
and other controlled sources to ensure responsible forest management.

For more information visit www.harpercollins.co.uk/green.

Printed and Bound in the UK using 100% Renewable Electricity
at CPI Group (UK) Ltd, Croydon, CR0 4YY

THE GP'S SEASIDE REUNION

ANNIE CLAYDON

MILLS & BOON

CHAPTER ONE

THE EXPECTED KNOCK on the door came at ten past eight. Dr Hope Ashdown looked up from her desk, a welcoming smile already forming on her lips. Dr Jamieson, the senior partner of Arrow Lane Medical Centre, had mentioned that the doctor who'd be filling in while Dr Anna Singh was on maternity leave would be starting work today.

'Meet Dr Lewis...' Sara Jamieson was clearly busy this morning, and taking the orientation tour at breakneck speed. Dr Lewis had better keep up or the chance for the briefest of hellos, or even a swift looking-forward-to-working-with-you, would be missed.

'Dr...' The word died on Hope's lips as the new doctor caught up, appearing in the doorway.

'Theo?'

'Hope!'

What were the chances? Recognising someone that you hadn't seen for eighteen years, straight away. Having them recognise you back and, against all the odds, remember your name... Hope couldn't calculate the exact likelihood of that, and settled for *highly unlikely*.

She'd been in the third year of her medical degree, and a little lost in the complexities of a large teaching hospital. Theo had been three years ahead of her, in the first year of his foundation training, and part of a scheme that helped third-year students make the transition from non-clinical to clinical study. He'd come to her rescue, tipping her off about the best way to approach the lead consultants on each of her rotations and telling her what to read up on to impress.

They'd become friends, and...they'd kissed. Once, at a Christmas party in the fourth year of Hope's studies. They'd laughed that off as the kind of thing everyone did at Christmas parties, and when she'd gone home for the holidays, Hope's father had died suddenly. She'd postponed her return in the new year and when it had become obvious that her mother couldn't cope alone, Hope had transferred to a medical school closer to home. They'd corresponded a lot at first, but slowly she'd felt she had less and less in common with Theo and their texts and messages had petered out. The kiss had been forgotten.

And she'd felt forgotten too, because Theo hadn't come to rescue her this time. She'd been mired in loss and regret, slowly coming to terms with the idea that her mother was going to need ongoing care and that all of her own plans needed to be put on hold for the foreseeable future.

But, somehow, Hope could still taste his kiss. Maybe because of the look in Theo's dark eyes...

'You know each other?' Sara Jamieson never much liked being out of the loop, and Hope smiled up at her.

'We were at medical school together for a while. Theo was a few years ahead of me.' Hope had to admit that he was wearing those years well. 'We haven't seen each other for...'

'Eighteen years.' Theo smiled. Apparently their old habit of finishing each other's sentences hadn't reached its expiry date yet.

'Well... Should I leave you to catch up? I have a few phone calls to make.' Sara clearly needed to be somewhere else at the moment.

'Yes. Thanks, Sara, I'll finish showing Theo around.'

Sarah flashed Hope a smile and hurried from the room. Hope got to her feet, staring at Theo, which was okay because he was staring at her. He wasn't quite the same, his dark hair had a streak of grey at the temples, and his manner was a little more measured. But he still had that certain something. Her head couldn't quantify it, but her thumping heart seemed to know just what it was.

Then he broke the silence. 'Is Dr Jamieson always that brusque?'

'No. She usually has a great deal of time for everyone here, and I imagine those phone calls she needs to make are urgent ones, on a patient's behalf.'

Theo nodded. 'I wish she'd mentioned it. I would have been more than happy to find my way around the place and introduce myself.'

Hope sat down, waving him towards the seat on the other side of her desk, and he settled into it. Still staring at him, as if taking her eyes off him for one moment would make him disappear.

'I'm sorry I didn't keep in touch, Hope.'

That was Theo all over. Taking the initiative and saying the things she didn't dare say.

'It takes two to lose touch. I should apologise too.'

Suddenly, everything came flooding back, more potent than it had been before because Hope didn't take it for granted, now. The exchanged looks that told them both they were thinking the same thing. The warmth that didn't need words.

'It takes one to keep in touch.' He grinned at her.

'Then I suppose we'll both have to share the blame,' Hope shot back at him. 'It was a long time ago, Theo.'

She didn't want to think about it any more. He'd just walked back into her life and she wanted the adventurous pleasure of his smile. That still had the power to put the everyday hum-drum of regret behind her for a while.

He nodded. 'So. What have you been up to in the last eigh-teen years? In three sentences or less...' Theo's tone intimated that he expected that to be a challenge.

Two sentences would probably cover it, just as long as she didn't try to justify not getting around to all of the things she'd planned to do. 'You remember I came back here to be near my mum?'

Theo nodded. 'How are things there?'

'Mum needed a lot of support after my dad died. She had a number of medical issues and never really got back on her feet again. She developed symptoms of dementia soon after I qualified as a doctor, so I moved in and looked after her until she died, four months ago.'

That covered it. Hope was staring the big four-zero in the face, and that was all she had to say about her life so far.

'I'm so sorry to hear that. It's a special kind of achievement, building a career and caring for someone.'

It was a nice thing to say. Hope gave a small shrug and Theo raised an eyebrow.

'You don't think so? You made a difference for your mum and she was lucky to have you.'

Making a difference had always been the highest praise that Theo could give. Eighteen years ago, he'd been sure that work-ing in the community was his way of making that difference. Hope doubted that his path from there to here had been quite as straight and uneventful as hers had been.

'How about you, then? Eighteen years in three sentences.' She threw the question back at him, knowing that Theo couldn't resist a challenge.

'I trained for general practice, then decided to specialise in addiction issues, which have taken me abroad for most of the last fifteen years. I was married for a while, but it didn't last. My daughter has a university place in Brighton, and so I'm looking to establish a home base back in the UK now.'

'Wait…' Travel. Marriage. A child. Clearly the last eighteen years had been more eventful for Theo, and Hope wasn't sure which to ask about first. 'You have a daughter?'

'I've had my three sentences, haven't I?' Theo grinned.

'Your rules. You can break them.'

He nodded. Theo still had that streak of mischief running through his veins, and the thought sent shivers running down Hope's spine. 'Willow was twelve when I married her mother, and when she was thirteen she agreed to my adopting her formally. Carrie and I had talked about setting up home here in England after we got married, but she said she wanted more from life and was keen to travel. It turned out that I couldn't give her the *more* she wanted, because she found someone else and moved on, leaving me and Willow behind.'

'You sound bitter.' Hope hadn't meant to be that forthright, but it came so easily with Theo. He shrugged, puffing out a breath.

'Nah. Not for myself, at any rate. But Carrie shouldn't have walked out on Willow like that, and she was terrified. It took me a while to convince her that she didn't get rid of me so easily. She dropped behind with her schoolwork, but she worked hard and made that up. We were in Kenya for her gap year and then she landed a really good place at university and we came back to England two years ago. I did my GP's return to practice course up in London, and…here I am. Being here in Hastings is perfect for me, not too far from Willow if she needs me, and not so close that she feels I'm crowding her.'

His face was shining with pride. Theo had been there for his daughter when she'd needed him, and now he was going through the process of letting go. Hope had done her share of letting go, and Theo seemed to be making a better job of it than she was.

'So where have you been, for work?'

'Europe, Asia, Africa… The challenges are different in different places, but the answers are surprisingly similar.'

'And what made you decide on those challenges?' This was beginning to sound as if she were subjecting him to a second interview. 'I'm just interested. You never mentioned specialising in addiction issues at medical school.'

His face darkened. 'You remember Andrew Locke?'

'Of course I do. You and he were close friends, weren't you?'

'Yes, we were. And yet I missed all the signs, the same as everyone else did. A year after you left, he wrapped his car around a tree and was killed instantly. Toxicology showed that he had a high level of cocaine in his system.'

Hope's hand flew to her mouth. 'Andrew? He's the last person… Had he been taking drugs for long?'

'None of us thought he'd been taking them at all. That was the hardest thing—he had a lot of people who cared about him, but he'd never told anyone. His family were just as shocked as we were and we got together to try and find out what had happened. It turned out that he'd been using cocaine for almost three years, and that he'd been forging signatures on prescriptions to finance his habit. I got involved with a charity that aims to help people in the early stages of substance abuse— hopefully before their lives start to fall apart. I realised very quickly that I'd found my vocation.'

It was a lot to take in. *Theo* was a lot to take in. So much like the young man she'd known, and yet somehow more. A little more assured, maybe, but his dark eyes still glimmered with endless possibilities.

'How about you? You have a significant other? Or children?' Theo asked.

That would have been nice. Hope's parents had married relatively late in life, and she'd been their only child. There had been a lot of love in their small family, but she'd lost her father too early, and then found herself looking after her ailing mother. Hope had returned home willingly, but it felt a little as if the opportunity for making her own life had passed her by.

'I never really had the time. Dating's not that easy when you have to be home by seven because that's when Mum's daycare finishes.'

Theo nodded. He seemed to understand, although he couldn't possibly know all of it. The large house, full of secrets. Boxes upon boxes of things, which now made clearing the place and moving on an insurmountable task. But suddenly it seemed that there *was* a new life out there, even if it couldn't break through the all too physical barriers that had separated her home life from the world outside, ever since she was a child.

'You know Hastings?' She tried to make the question sound casual.

'I know my way from where I'm staying to here. And back out to the motorway, in case I ever need to escape. Since we're old friends, I was wondering whether you might give me a map reference for your favourite restaurant, so that I can buy you dinner sometime and quiz you on some of the best places to go.'

Theo had ticked all of the boxes. A dinner invitation could be many different things, but the addition of *old friends* and *sometime* put everything in its right place.

'That sounds good. How about next Saturday? We can take a stroll around the Old Town or along the seafront first.'

Theo's broad smile spoiled it all, by reminding Hope once

again that she was a woman, and he was a very desirable man. 'I'd really like that. And in the meantime, if you could show me the way to my desk…'

In Theo's experience, moving on had always provided perspective, allowing him to cope with the pressures of a high-stress job. But seeing Hope again had been the exception to that rule. Everything he'd felt eighteen years ago was still sharp and clear, preserved unchanged through the passage of time, and it had hit him like a sledgehammer.

Her green eyes were still captivating, and her auburn hair shimmered in the sunshine, even if it was shorter now and her curls a little neater. He could feel the warmth of all the good times they'd had together, and the sharp pain of his heart breaking when she'd left. The realisation that he'd been a little in love with her had come too late, and the one kiss they'd shared had become the last of a whole catalogue of missed chances.

It had been a shock to see Hope again, but Theo had somehow managed to distance himself from the moment. He couldn't help his questions, though, or the careful probing for some hint that she'd been happy.

Neither of them were kids any more, starting out on an adventure that couldn't possibly fail. He'd had his share of bad times and Theo was in no doubt that Hope had, too, but he had no regrets. He'd loved his work, even though there was a high failure rate, and the pain of his broken marriage was long gone. Willow had been an unexpected but precious gift.

And now he was back in England, starting again. An old friend had asked him to take his son on as a patient, and when the young man had died the family's grief had broken Theo. He'd returned to general practice, and somehow life had brought him around full circle. Seeing Hope had suddenly made him feel the thrill of an unknown future, beckoning him on.

Maybe Hope would understand that and maybe not. Her neat consulting room, decorated with plants and pictures, felt so different from the string of anonymous workplaces he'd inhabited over the years. She showed him to a room, just along the corridor from hers, opening the blinds to let the sunlight in.

There was a large desk, the surface clear except for a computer and telephone. A comfortable chair for him to sit in, along with patient seating and a curtained area that contained a couch. Everything was clean and tidy, and Hope looked around, wrinkling her nose.

'I think we can do a little better than this.' She marched through the open doorway, leaving him to look around and try the chair out for size. Then she reappeared, holding a couple of potted plants, which Theo guessed were from the exuberant greenery in her own consulting room.

'Will these do?'

Theo couldn't help smiling. Hope could always be trusted to bring a little colour to a room. 'They're great. Sure you won't miss them?'

She shook her head. 'You'll be doing me a favour. It takes me ages to water them all. Has someone given you a log-in for the computer system?'

'Not yet.' Theo took the plants from her, arranging them carefully on the deep windowsill behind him, as if they were precious jewels.

'I'll see if our practice manager knows.' Hope leaned over, picking up the telephone handset and dialling. 'Rosie, I'm with Dr Lewis. I don't suppose you know whether anyone's created a user profile for him on the system yet?'

She listened for a moment, quirking her mouth down. 'Oh. Okay, I'll tell him. Thanks…'

'What's the verdict?' Theo couldn't help grinning at her as she replaced the phone in its cradle.

'Well… Our IT guy will be here in an hour, and he's not allowed to give your password to anyone but you. And in the meantime, you're on vaccinations. The practice nurse usually does them but there are a lot to get through and she needs a hand.'

'Sounds good. I'll make a list.' Theo opened the top drawer of the desk, and found that it was empty.

'That's okay. Rosie's already printed out the list. She's ferociously efficient, and if there's anything you ever want to know, she's your first port of call. I'll get you a pen, and you can ask her to show you the stationery cupboard when you get a moment. That's as long as she hasn't beaten you to it and already brought you everything you'll ever need.' Hope frowned. 'Sorry there isn't anything more exciting to do on your first morning.'

'Vaccinations can be exciting. Remember that bag of oranges you found yourself in a life-or-death struggle with?' Maybe she didn't. He shouldn't expect those memories to be as clear in Hope's mind as they were in his.

'You'll be happy to know I've improved a bit since then. No thanks to you and your "mad scientist" impressions, I'll have you know…'

She *did* remember. Better than he did. 'I'd forgotten all about those. Not very tactful on my part…'

'I survived.' Hope grinned, looked round as the practice manager appeared, holding a sheaf of paper. She ducked out of the room while Rosie took him through the list, explaining that he just needed to add his initials, the date and the batch number for each patient.

'Thanks, Rosie. Where can I find…?' Theo smiled as Hope

reappeared in the doorway, holding up several brightly co-
loured pens. 'Ah. Never mind.'

Rosie looked round and rolled her eyes. 'I could bring you
something from the stationery cupboard, if you'd prefer grey?'

Hope chuckled at the thought, and Theo shook his head.
'Nothing says *welcome* quite like a handful of pink pens.'

'Fair enough. I'll leave you to it, then. Extension 204 if
you want anything.' Rosie shot Hope a smile on her way out
of the room.

'You could have blue…' Hope's green eyes were daring him
to stick with the pink.

'Nah. Blue's so mad-scientisty.' Suddenly Theo *was* at
home. He had plants, and pens and an extension number to
call. And Hope, to share jokes and memories with.

She nodded. 'True. Well, I'm within screaming distance so
if I hear any cries for help, I'll be right back…'

CHAPTER TWO

BREATHLESS. IF SHE'D had any warning of Theo's arrival then Hope might have predicted a whole assortment of reactions, but there had been only one. She felt breathless.

Not the painful wheeze that she listened out for when examining a patient, or the panicky gasp for oxygen when life suddenly threw too much at her. This was as if she'd suddenly been set free, and could stretch and run again.

Hope sat in her consulting room, waiting for her next patient to make their way from the waiting room. The stretching and running were probably all an illusion—nothing had really changed and Theo had just reminded her of a time when she'd been young and thought that anything was possible. She turned down her mouth, reaching for the phone as it started to ring.

'Hope...' Rosie was muttering quietly, clearly not wanting to be overheard. 'Theo's finished the vaccination list, and the IT guy's given him access to the system. Can I get him to see Mrs Patel?'

'Yes, of course. She's just come in for a chat about the results of her latest cholesterol test and he can handle that. Is there something you wanted me to do instead?' This kind of phone call from Rosie rarely came without an ulterior motive.

'Mrs Wheeler's here. She doesn't have an appointment but she's in a bit of a state. I can't get the full story out of her, but something's happened with her daughter.' Rosie repeated Mrs Wheeler's patient number, knowing that looking her medical record up on the computer would be the first thing that Hope would do.

'Okay. Send Mrs Patel through to Theo. Could you tell him, please, that the only thing I wanted to see her for was the blood test. There are no other concerns. I'll come down to the waiting room to collect Mrs Wheeler. Thanks, Rosie.'

Hope scanned the screen quickly. She hadn't seen Joanne Wheeler for a while, and there were no outstanding issues, no clues about what had prompted today's visit. She made her way downstairs, and found Joanne sitting in the corner of the empty waiting room wiping her eyes with a handkerchief.

'Hello, Joanne.' Hope sat down next to her.

'I'm so sorry...'

'That's okay, you obviously need help with something. Before we do anything else, I need to ask you what's happening right now. Is there an emergency that we need to address? Something to do with your daughter, maybe?'

Joanne shook her head. 'No, Doctor. Amy's all right, although she's in hospital at the moment...' She dissolved into tears again.

'I'm sorry to hear that. Let's go upstairs and talk about why you're here, then.'

Hope waited while Joanne gathered her coat and handbag, nodding as Rosie quietly suggested that a cup of tea might be in order. By the time the receptionist arrived with it, Joanne was settled in a seat by Hope's desk, and seemed to be rallying.

'I shouldn't have come without an appointment.'

'That's okay. Just take a breath or two, and tell me what's bothering you.'

The story came spilling out. Joanne's seventeen-year-old daughter had gone to a party on Saturday evening, and been rushed to hospital in the early hours of Sunday morning, suffering from a drugs overdose. She was stable now, and the hospital would be sending her home the day after tomorrow.

'I don't know how to cope with it all...' Joanne turned the corners of her mouth down. 'My husband, Joel, and I... Joel said that we should search her room and we found three little bags of pills, hidden away.'

'I can see this is a really frightening situation for you. Can you do something for me, Joanne? I want you to take a breath.'

'I can't...'

'I know it's not easy. Just do your best.' Hope filled her own lungs with air, and Joanne followed suit. A few deep, steady breaths and she began to calm a little.

'That's good. Have you eaten today?'

Joanne shook her head. 'Neither of us can sleep, either.'

'When are you next going to see Amy?'

Joanne turned the corners of her mouth down. 'This evening. They're keeping her pretty busy during the day, with tests and talking sessions.'

'Those are the three things I want you to do this afternoon, then. Breathe, eat and sleep. And concentrate on doing all three of them as well as you can, cook a nice meal and sit down at the table to eat it. Make yourself a hot drink, close the curtains and just lie down for a little while. It's okay if you don't go to sleep, just try to get some rest. And if you feel yourself panicking, take a few breaths.'

Joanne frowned. 'That's not going to solve anything...'

'No, it isn't. But if you can keep your own strength up, then you'll be able to support Amy better. What's going on with your husband?'

'He's taken the week off work, as compassionate leave. This has just floored him. He wants to protect Amy but neither of us know how.'

'Okay, perhaps you can do what I said together, then.'

Joanne shook her head. 'But... We have to find someone for Amy. There's a drugs counsellor at the hospital and she's talked with him, but we don't know if that'll be enough.'

It was the start of what might be a long road. But Joanne was too fragile to hear that at the moment. 'Have you been able to speak to him? What's the situation with aftercare?'

'He says that there will be some, when she comes home. But I don't even know what she needs. This is all so new for us.'

'Leave it with me, just for this afternoon. There are a lot of different resources, and support's available for both Amy and for you, as her family. I'll be thinking about different options this afternoon, and come back to you with some choices that are available locally.' Hope knew that the hospital's drugs team would be following up on Amy's case, but ongoing care for the whole family was her responsibility. 'What time will you be going to see Amy this evening?'

'Six o'clock.'

'Then I'll call you at five, if that's okay.'

'Thank you, Doctor. I just don't know what to do for the best.'

'Right now, you need to take a few hours off. You can take this time to relax, knowing that I'll be doing some of the heavy lifting, eh?'

Hope recognised Joanne's sigh. She'd heaved that sigh herself a few times, when someone had told her to just stop and leave her mother's care to them for a while. 'Okay. We'll try.'

'Trying is good enough. What did you do with the pills you found, by the way?' Hope had set that question aside for the moment, but it was one that should be asked.

'We destroyed them.' Joanne pursed her lips. 'We could hardly put them back where they were, but Amy's going to realise we searched for them sooner or later. I'm not looking forward to that conversation.'

'I'll put that on the list of your immediate concerns. Leave it with me.'

* * *

Hope left the door of her consulting room ajar, waiting until she heard Theo bid Mrs Patel a cheery goodbye. Then she counted to ten, and made her way along the corridor. Breathless, again. In a good way, which seemed to lighten the load of the worries that patients left behind them.

'Can I ask a favour?'

He leaned back in his seat. 'If you want your pens back, I'm afraid I've already given one away.'

Of course he had. Hope had seen how Theo was with kids, and even as a young doctor he'd usually had something in his pocket to give a crying child. 'Nothing's changed, then.'

'Quite a lot's changed. Just not that.' A shadow seemed to form across his face, and then dispersed again as he smiled. 'What can I do for you?'

'I've just seen a lady who has a seventeen-year-old daughter in hospital—she's on the mend apparently, but she was rushed in over the weekend, after a drugs overdose.'

Theo nodded. 'And she turned up here, needing some help.'

'Yes. Maybe I should have taken Mrs Patel and left you to talk to her.'

He shrugged. 'You're the boss.'

No, not really, although she supposed she was senior to him now. Theo had never been her boss either, but he had known a great deal more than her when she was a third-year medical student, so she'd generally done whatever he'd told her to do. It seemed that they were still feeling their way in this new version of their relationship.

'I imagine you've dealt with a lot more situations like this than I have. And since I'm not in the habit of wasting what resources I have available…'

He grinned. 'I can speak to some of my contacts, and get a

list of people in the area who'd be able to help. What are the specific concerns?'

'Just…a few ideas about where to start would be helpful. Although Joanne did mention to me that she and her husband had searched their daughter's room. She said that they found some pills, hidden away, and destroyed them. She knows she'll have to tell her daughter that they've been through all her belongings and that it's not going to be an easy conversation.'

Theo shook his head. 'No, it seldom is. Give me an hour and I'll put together a few thoughts on how to approach that.'

'Would you? You have time this afternoon?' Hope's satisfaction wasn't all on Amy's behalf. It was so good to be working with Theo again.

'I was thinking I might water my new plants, and then find out where the stationery cupboard is, but this sounds a lot more useful. Anything else to concentrate on…?'

Theo had always accepted that general practice was going to bring him into contact with patients with drug issues. No one had ever asked about the experience listed out on his CV, but Hope always asked when the welfare of a patient was at stake. And now he felt her guiding hand hovering over him, keeping him on track. He spent a busy afternoon, making calls to patients on the review list that Rosie had given him, and then completing his research on local resources for Joanne Wheeler and her husband.

Hope had set up a video call with Joanne and her husband, and invited Theo to join them. They spent nearly half an hour talking and Hope's support and reassurance, along with the information that Theo had compiled, had helped with that first, important step in the process of turning a teenager's life around.

'Thanks, Theo.' Hope leaned back in her seat, smiling.

'Your advice made all the difference. Joanne seems more con-fident that they can tackle this as a family now.'

'Sometimes all a teenager needs is a wake-up call and a supportive family.' Theo shrugged. He'd seen kids with ev-erything going for them, who couldn't get themselves back onto the right road. Others who'd turned things around against all the odds.

'How do you deal with it? The uncertainty?'

'That's one of the reasons I don't do this kind of work full time any more.'

'What are you doing for dinner?' She was moving on now, with the practised ease of someone who knew she'd done her best and had to leave it at that. 'There's a nice eatery down by the seafront…?'

She left the invitation hanging. Casual and friendly, some-thing that could be taken up, or turned down, with ease.

'I was thinking a takeaway, since I haven't got around to even switching the fridge in my flat on, let alone putting any-thing in it. But a little eatery down by the seafront sounds a much better option.'

A late spring breeze tugged at their jackets as they left the medical centre, becoming stronger as they reached the hotels and restaurants that lined the promenade. Hope turned into a doorway, leading him upstairs to a bright, busy seating area, and made a beeline for an empty table by the windows that faced the sea. Theo watched as she took off her coat, plump-ing herself down in a seat.

'You like looking out to sea?' He sat down opposite her.

'Yes. When I was little and we used to come down to the beach, I used to think of all the places that you could go, if you just put out to sea and sailed away. I lost sight of that over the years, when my mother became ill.'

'And now you see it again?' The open sky made Theo feel

slightly weary, as if he'd already travelled into enough sunsets. 'Or is it too soon for that?'

'It's…' Hope spread her hands, shrugging. 'My mum's death wasn't unexpected. I'm still not quite sure what I want to do next, though. Everyone says *give it time*.'

'Sometimes things get to be clichés because they're true.'

She nodded, her eyes filling with tears. Hope brushed them away impatiently, as if they were something to be ashamed of. 'Sorry…'

'Don't be.'

'There's a lot to do… It's a big house.' Hope seemed keen to explain what didn't need to be explained to anyone. Theo leaned back in his chair, waiting for her to say whatever it was she wanted to say, and she smiled suddenly.

'Are you making me into a therapy project?'

Never. Hope wasn't a problem to be solved. Right now she seemed like the ultimate solution. The sunshine she carried with her, the sense of belonging… It all felt as if he'd found the home he craved.

'Force of habit.' He allowed himself to meet her green-eyed gaze with a smile. 'Whatever you do, don't talk about it. I won't be listening.'

That made her laugh out loud. She picked up the menu that lay in front of her, glancing up at him every now and then as she studied it carefully. Theo laughed and did the same, covertly surveying her from behind his menu. By the time the waitress arrived to take their order, they were chuckling together, catching each other out, like a pair of incompetent private eyes.

Hope chose ravioli with a side salad, and Theo was hungry and went for a large portion of lasagne. He suggested a half-bottle of house red, and Hope nodded. Old friends, who didn't need to negotiate too much over their likes and dislikes,

Only they weren't. Theo hadn't known Hope for eighteen years, he'd known her eighteen years ago, and there was a difference. If he felt at home with her, then that was all an illusion, which he had to step away from. He was beginning to see that Hope was working through the process of spreading her wings, while his own mission in life was to find a place where he could settle.

'Where are you staying?' she asked.

'I've got a small flat, on the edge of town. A bed, a shower and an empty fridge. That's enough for me for the time being.'

'Until you find somewhere to call home?' Hope had always had a talent for the unspoken.

'Yeah. I reckon somewhere within easy reach of London as it'll be easier to find a permanent job there. Close to Willow, but not too close. A place she knows she can come back to, whenever she wants.'

'And where *you* can put down a few roots?'

'I'd like that. I still want to make a difference, but I want a life that isn't governed by work, as well.'

Hope nodded. 'The elusive work-life balance. Let me know when you find it.'

Didn't she have that already? She appeared to, but then Hope was still making the journey towards living without her mother. Coming to terms with the fact that everything might change if she wanted it to, and deciding what she wanted to change.

'What happens if Willow decides to move away, after she's graduated?'

Theo chuckled. 'There are buses. Trains. Planes... It's about having a place, not where that place is.'

'And...someone?'

Theo had wondered about that, and realised that it wasn't too late to satisfy the obscure longing for someone to share

his life with and that things didn't inevitably work out the way
they had with Carrie. Now that he was settled he wouldn't face
the same problems that had always put a time limit on his relationships. But he didn't want to talk about it with Hope, because right now it felt as if *she* was all he needed.

'I can handle Willow having boyfriends.' He deliberately
misinterpreted the question. 'Just as long as they submit to
a full blood work-up, a credit check and an enhanced DBS
check. Along with in-depth counselling, to sort out any baggage they might be hauling around.'

Hope's outraged laughter was just as he expected. 'So you're
a dad who worries, are you?'

'Of course. I try not to behave like one, though.'

'And what about her? Does she return the favour?'

Hope must know that it was an obvious question. A child
who'd been abandoned in her teens would be forgiven for being
a little possessive of the only carer she had left.

'Willow takes a keen interest in my love-life. I only need to
spend ten minutes chatting to a single woman, outside work,
and she's dropping hints about my giving her a call.'

Hope winced. 'Do I have to worry?'

Not about Willow. Maybe a little about Theo, but he was
keeping those thoughts under wraps, at least until he knew
more about the things that Hope very pointedly *hadn't* said.

'Nah. I won't tell her if you don't…' His phone rang and
he took it from his pocket, a guilty grin spreading across his
face. 'Hi, Willow… Yeah, everything's good… I'm with one
of the other doctors at the practice at the moment, can I call
you back later? Yeah, thanks for calling. I appreciate it.'

Theo stared at his phone for a moment, and then decided
to put it back into his pocket. 'I don't *think* she's installed a
tracker on my phone.'

'Would you know if she did?' Hope teased him.

'No, I don't have a clue about how these things work. Let's put it down to coincidence, she must have reckoned I'd be home by now and called to ask how my first day was.'

Hope nodded. 'Okay, we'll go with that. It would be awkward if you felt you had to throw your phone into the sea...'

It had been a great evening. A really good day, too. They'd walked back to the car park at the medical centre, and she'd watched as Theo had driven away.

Hope had thought about Theo so much during the last eighteen years. Woven a perfect life around the handsome, talented young man, which her own achievements couldn't possibly measure up to.

He hadn't changed so much. He still had that easy charm, and his eyes still held the promise that whatever the future held it would be a challenge to embrace. And now was really no different from when she'd first known him, Hope wasn't sure what her own future would be, but she knew it wouldn't be all about putting down roots. She had enough of those already, and was trying to disentangle herself from them.

Which was why she wasn't going to think about the look in his eyes, or his smile. Wanting Theo was too hard to bear, because if she allowed him too close she ran the risk of disappointing him, just as she'd disappointed herself.

It was only a ten-minute drive home, and Hope got out of her car, surveying the large family house that was now hers. It looked good from the outside, with fresh paint, neatly trimmed bushes and spring flowers already in bloom. The shutters at the upstairs windows allowed in the light, but protected the rooms from anyone's prying gaze.

She usually went around to the back, entering the house through the kitchen door where the stairs weren't right in front of her, seeming to mock her. But this time she walked to the front door, sliding her key into the lock. It was a little stiff, from lack of use, but the door swung open to reveal the long hallway.

There was one door to the right, which led to a light, airy sitting room, and another to the left, which she'd helped her mother turn into a bedroom after her father died. Further back, a smaller family room that Hope had been using as a bedroom ever since she'd moved in here, a bathroom and a large kitchen diner, which looked out over the back garden.

This had been Hope's domain, a clean, tidy and above all rubbish-free zone. Upstairs were stacks of old furniture and boxes, which made the rooms unliveable, but which her mother had guarded fiercely. She'd cry, and then linger in the hallway for days, to make sure that nothing else was taken away, if Hope tried to remove as much as a carrier bag. The two, completely different, floors of the house had been an uneasy solution, but the only one that had allowed Hope to ensure her mother's safety without breaking her heart.

Four months ago, Hope had inherited her parents' hoard of belongings, the boxes of newspapers, old clothes that were no longer wearable, every toy she'd played with as a child... Three old gramophones that her father had picked up at junk shops and brought home meaning to mend them and polish them up, but which still stood silent, crammed in with everything else.

She'd set out with good intentions, and made a start on emptying a few of the boxes, but she'd found herself in tears, putting everything back exactly where it had come from. All the things that her parents had saved so carefully over the years had grown in importance now she'd lost her mother. And she was caught now, pinned down by the weight of the hoard. Keeping it a secret, and never asking anyone back to the house, in case they climbed the stairs and saw what she was most ashamed of.

Hope ventured halfway up the stairs, wondering if this evening she might see the hoard in a different light—something that she *could* deal with. Then she chickened out, making a dash for the kitchen to make a cup of tea. It was no use. Theo couldn't come here and see this. Outside, in the sunshine, they could be friends, but she could never risk asking him back to see her home.

CHAPTER THREE

THEO HAD SPENT the week settling into the busy medical centre, finding his way around and learning how everyone liked to do things. Even his temporary assignment here, filling in during Dr Singh's maternity leave, was different because when that was over he didn't face moving again. He was a free agent, who could find another job in the area and stay as long as he wanted.

And it was good to have a friend, someone who'd known him for longer than six months. He had to be careful not to take up too much of Hope's time, because she had her own issues to deal with. She never spoke about her mother, but her silences, the abrupt changes in direction of a conversation, told him that her grief was still fresh.

'I spoke with Sara Jamieson about Amy and her family.' Hope bowled into his consulting room, still full of energy after a very full week's work.

'Yeah? How are they doing?' Theo had deliberately stepped back a little, reckoning that he'd done as much as he could to set everyone on the right track. The family were Hope's patients, and he knew she'd find him if she wanted to discuss anything.

'They're…' Hope shrugged. 'Amy's home, and physically she's recovering well. On an emotional level, Joanne tells me that some days are better than others.'

Theo nodded. 'Just having some better days is something to build on.'

'Yes, that's what I told her. She's joined one of the groups on your list, for parents of kids with drug problems. Amy didn't like that very much. Joanne went once and she made such a fuss that she hasn't gone again.'

'Doesn't like being a problem who gets talked about behind her back?' Theo suggested.

'Yes, that's pretty much it. Sara and I were wondering whether you might like to take the family on as your patients, since you have particular expertise that might help them.'

It sounded like an obvious move, but Theo hesitated. 'I'm a GP now. And I'm committed to that change.'

'Understood. But this is all part of a GP's work, isn't it?'

'I don't know the family as well as you do.'

'What's your *real* reason?' Hope was clearly not in the mood for excuses. He'd only ever spoken to one person about this, not family or friends, just his therapist. But he could give Hope the bare facts and leave out the part about his own life crashing and burning in response to one too many young lives lost to drugs.

'Coming home to England and becoming a GP wasn't one move, it was two. Willow had a place at university and I told the drugs agency I was working with that I needed to be here for her. They understood that—everyone gets to the point where travelling loses its charm—and I started work in London.'

'Doing the same kind of work that you'd been doing abroad?'

'Largely, yes. There was less emphasis on setting up brand-new facilities, and a little more on casework. An old friend contacted me. His son had become involved with drugs, and they'd been trying for years to help him. Several stints in rehab had failed and nothing seemed to be working. I said I'd do my best, and I got too involved.'

Hope's face darkened. She seemed to know what was coming but said nothing.

'Jonas was an amazing young man, had everything going for him. I'd seen cases like his before but this time… When he died from a drugs overdose, I knew that I needed to go back into general practice, to regain some balance.'

'I'm so sorry, Theo. I shouldn't have asked you about Amy, without knowing the full story.'

'It's okay… I'd just rather not be too closely involved. Maybe I could help out, rather than take Amy on as a patient?' It was a risk, but one that Theo felt able to take. He'd put some distance between himself and what had happened with Jonas, and done some healing. And this time he had Hope on his side.

She hesitated for a moment, clearly not completely buying into the idea that Theo's decision had been as easy as he made it sound. 'So I'll keep Joanne and her family on my list, but you might be able to give some input now and again. Are you sure that's okay, Theo?'

'It's fine. If I get too involved, you'll drag me away into a corner and give me a talking-to?'

Hope laughed, giving him a nod. There had been times when Theo had done the same—explaining the limitations and what they could and couldn't do for their patients. And times when he'd held her, when she'd cried over a particularly challenging patient. That seemed far more special now than it had then.

'I'll be glad to return the favour. I've promised to pop in early this evening. Would you like to come? You don't need to pretend you're busy if you don't want to, a *no* will do.' She shot him an impish look.

Theo chuckled. 'In that case, it'll be a *yes*. Thanks.'

* * *

The family lived on the outskirts of Hastings, half an hour's drive away. Hope had decided to keep things brief for starters, and just introduce herself and Theo to Amy, and let her know that they were both there to listen and answer her questions. Theo seemed relaxed and rather less worried about the meeting than she was.

'How did I do?' Hope asked as she settled herself back in the driving seat of her car.

'Fine. Great, actually. You didn't come across as judging Amy, and you made it clear that we were there for her. You ran through the options available to her, and emphasised that what she wanted was important to you.'

Hope puffed out a breath. 'She didn't seem terribly interested in any of them.'

'Well, she's been through a lot in the last week, both physically and mentally. I suspect that her one aim in life at the moment is for everyone to leave her alone. Let her think about it a bit, and we'll see if she comes to any conclusions.'

'Thanks, Theo. I really do appreciate your help.'

He nodded an acknowledgement. 'Do you fancy a coffee? My place is on your way home, and I have an ulterior motive.'

'You do?' Hope would bet her last shilling that Theo's ulterior motive was entirely honourable, and bit back her disappointment. 'In that case, you'd better give me directions.'

The flat was on the top floor of a small block, set back from the road slightly. Neat and utilitarian, it was the kind of building that would be easy to walk past without even noticing it was there.

'It's a bit… I haven't got around to many home comforts yet. I do however have milk and coffee…' Theo let her walk ahead of him into the sitting room, clearly expecting that Hope wouldn't much like the place.

But she did. Cream walls, wooden blinds at the window, and a timber floor. Not a great deal of furniture, there was a sofa, a TV and not much else, but that made Hope feel somehow lighter.

'I like it. It's uncluttered.'

Theo looked around. 'Yes, I suppose that's one thing it has going for it.'

'Don't knock it, Theo. I have a bit of decluttering to do at home.' Decluttering sounded rather more everyday and civilised than…whatever it was that needed doing to her place. That probably involved a lot of heavy lifting, both mentally and physically.

He chuckled, walking through the open archway that led to the kitchen. White kitchen units, with a wooden counter top, which was completely clear, apart from a coffee machine. 'You brought that with you?'

'Yeah. How did you guess?'

It wasn't white, for starters. And it was a little more complex than the kind of kitchen equipment rental properties usually provided. What would it be like to just leave everything behind, and come and live in a place like this? Somewhere that faded into the background, and wasn't constantly tearing at her.

'So what's your ulterior motive? Do I need coffee first?'

'Yeah. Maybe.' Theo took two mugs from a half-empty cupboard and set about making the coffee.

'You're planning on staying here?'

'In the short term. It's a bit basic, but it suits me at the moment. I guess if I'd brought a bit more than a carload of things with me, it might be a bit more welcoming.'

'Surely you have furniture, though. Is that in storage?'

Theo shook his head. 'When I was abroad, the agency used to deal with accommodation. We stayed in some really nice places, and they were all fully furnished. It's not really practical to have furniture when you're moving around so much. When I was in London I rented a furnished flat and when I came here I had to organise this place in a hurry, so I took what I could get.'

'Well, this is great, Theo. You can really make it yours, and if you move on and buy a place then you'll have some bits and pieces to make a start with. You said you wanted somewhere that you could call home, didn't you?'

'Yes, I did say that, didn't I?' Theo frowned, and suddenly the penny dropped.

'That's the ulterior motive, isn't it?'

He nodded. 'Not so much here...' He beckoned for Hope to follow him, and walked out into the hallway, leading her past the open door of a bedroom, which contained a bed and a wardrobe. Opening a door further down the hall, he stood back so that Hope could enter first.

'This is nice, too. It's really light in here.' Hope looked around. In addition to the bed and wardrobe, there was a large old-fashioned leather trunk in the corner of the room. 'Is that yours?'

'It's Willow's. After her mother left, the thing she needed most was security and continuity, and one of the things I did was to get her this. Having her own things around her made her feel safe and I told her that she could put whatever she wanted in it, and that it would always travel with us and be in her room wherever she went. She doesn't have room for it in her student digs, so it's here.'

'This is Willow's room?'

'Yeah. She'll always have her own room, wherever I go. That was part of the bargain as well.'

'It's a beautiful thing. I bet you can get quite a lot into it.'

Suddenly, clutter took on a whole new meaning. It held memories, kept them safe from the passage of time and the pain of loss. Maybe Hope should think about her own problem that way, although the difference in scale made the hoard confronting rather than comforting.

If full spaces were a challenge, then she could tackle empty ones. Hope looked around the room. 'So you want to make this nice for Willow?'

He nodded. 'She loves colour and light. Remember the room you had when you shared a house?'

She remembered. Hope hadn't been there long, but she'd loved that room. It was still the only place she'd lived that felt truly hers.

'That had cream-coloured walls, as well.'

Theo chuckled. 'Yeah, and you filled it with colour. Willow's taste is a lot like yours and I was wondering if you had a spare afternoon to come shopping with me. There's no particular rush. She won't be coming to stay here until the end of term.'

'Won't she want to choose her own things?'

'Oh, she adds to whatever I do. But I want to show her that I've made an effort, at least. And a bit more furniture wouldn't go amiss. Somewhere to put her shoes—she has lots of them.'

'You mean more than two pairs? That's a very positive thing, Theo.'

'See. You *do* have a much better handle on this than I do.'

'I'm beginning to think so. Let me have a think over the weekend, and I'll come up with some ideas. You need to have ideas first, before you commit to anything.'

'Right you are.' Theo beamed at her. 'I don't suppose you fancy a pizza, do you? There's a nice place, around the corner from here...'

Theo had been missing Hope fiercely, all weekend. Looking around his flat, seeing it through her eyes. Even dreaming of her, when sleep robbed him of the discipline to prevent himself from wondering what it might be like to be more than a friend to her. On Monday morning, after a full list of patients, he was catching up with his notes and wondering what to have for lunch when Hope walked into his consulting room, carrying a box. She laid it on his desk with something that looked like triumph in her green eyes and, caught unawares, he found himself melting in the heat of her gaze.

'What's this? A kitchen blender?' It was an effort to look away from her smile and focus on the box.

'No, that's just the box. It's something for Willow.'

That was nice of her. Theo got to his feet, peeling back the packing tape and taking out the bubble-wrapped package inside.

'This is lovely. Don't you want to keep it, Hope?' A blue and green dragonfly-design Tiffany-style lamp had emerged from the wrappings. The shade was fringed with iridescent beads, which caught the light, and the brass stand gleamed softly.

From her no-nonsense glare, he'd clearly said the wrong thing. 'I have a pair that I like much better in my sitting room. This one's been wrapped up in storage for years, and there's no point in it if it never sees the sun, is there?'

'I suppose not but—are you sure?' Theo couldn't help asking, even if his question clearly didn't conform to whatever plan Hope had.

'Positive. Some of the beads have come off, but they were saved.' She reached into the box and drew out an envelope. 'And there's an electrical place in the old town, which will test it for safety and change the fitting so that you can use it with an LED bulb.'

It was time to give in and accept the gift gracefully. 'Thank you. Willow will love it.'

Hope gave him a luminous smile. 'It's my pleasure. I hope it's a nice welcome for her.'

'It will be. I'll take it down to get it fixed and tested at the weekend, and leave the beads for her to reattach. She's good with her hands, she'll make a better job of it than me, and she likes making things.'

'It'll look as good as new, then.' Hope was looking at the lamp with obvious satisfaction.

'It'll be better than new. It's a lovely gift.' And the best gift of all was her smile. For some reason this meant something to her, something more than just the perfect decoration for a bland and uninspiring room. It meant more to Theo as well, because it was important to Hope.

'Can I buy you lunch?' Maybe Hope would give him a clue about why this gesture seemed of such consequence. 'Or dinner?'

'Absolutely, but I have to take a rain check for today, I'm really busy. I'm glad you think Willow will like it...' Hope turned on her heel, hurrying out of the room almost abruptly, leaving Theo to wonder what had just happened here.

He sat down, running his finger through the hanging beads that fringed the glass shade. Hope might appear enigmatic at times, but he'd learned that there was always a method, always some plan behind everything she did. If he waited, then perhaps she'd share it with him.

CHAPTER FOUR

PRIDE CAME BEFORE a fall...

Hope had done some serious thinking over the weekend. And Theo had given her the jolt she'd needed to go and investigate the contents of some of the crates that were stacked in the front bedroom. After several hours of searching she'd found the Tiffany-style lamp that almost matched the two in the sitting room, but not quite, and then there had been the added excitement of sorting through the stack of flattened cardboard boxes, to find one that was the right size.

'There you go, Dad. You said they'd come in handy at some point, didn't you?'

She'd murmured the words, hoping that no more justification was needed to put the treasure she'd found on the back seat of her car, ready to take into the medical centre on Monday morning.

And she *was* proud of herself. She'd found a home for something she'd never use, and, even if it made no discernible difference to the collection of things that filled the room, it was a first step in the right direction. And Theo had clearly liked her gift. She'd escaped back to her own consulting room before she'd been tempted to hug him.

They'd been busy that week, and lunch would have to wait. Theo had unexpectedly said that he'd go and see Amy and her family on Thursday evening, and Hope hadn't argued. He'd seemed confident about going alone, and she'd had another plan forming in her head.

Hope sat down for half an hour with her customary after-work cup of tea and then set to work. She changed into a pair of comfortable sweatpants and pulled the loft steps down from the ceiling. The loft was boarded out and well-lit and it was easy to find the three matching side tables that she had in mind. They were plain and simple, of good quality, and they'd do for both Willow's bedroom and the sitting room. She'd take one of them downstairs, clean it up and show Theo a photograph tomorrow. Hope manoeuvred the table carefully out of the loft and as she carried it downstairs, she wondered whether deliv-ering the tables might be a good excuse to go and see Theo at the weekend...

And then she came back down to earth with a bump.

Breathe for a moment, or at least try to. Take it slow. Don't panic. That was all good advice, but all Hope could hear were her own whimpering cries. The shock of falling halfway down the stairs had scattered her senses, and then the table had landed on top of her and sent agonising pain shooting up her left leg.

'Don't cry...' That was too late, she was already crying. 'ABC.' The protocol for dealing with an injured patient didn't help either. Hope knew her Airways were clear and that she was Breathing, and couldn't feel any signs of major blood loss that might compromise her Circulation. All she could feel was the pain in her leg.

'Get help.' That was easier said than done. She'd taken her phone with her when she'd gone up into the loft, but it must have slipped out of her pocket as she fell, because it wasn't there now.

First things first. Her head swam as she sat up, and just

removing the broken pieces of the table from her legs really hurt. Her left ankle was already swelling, and a little gentle probing with her fingers told her that although it was showing all the signs of being fractured, the fracture wasn't displaced. That was good news.

Only to a point. Hope was feeling a little light-headed, and just touching the cool quarry tiles beneath her made her feel queasy. The emotional shock of the fall was beginning to set in, and she had to call someone.

'Phone…' She looked around and saw her phone lying on the floor, within reach. By some miracle it was still working, and before she'd had a chance to think, she found herself texting Theo. He wouldn't be answering his phone if he was still with Amy and her family, but he was the only person she wanted to call. The only one she could call.

Please call me.

That sounded a little too urgent.

When you have a chance.

She sent the text and then reconsidered, wondering if that didn't sound urgent enough. She was typing a second text when her phone rang.

'Theo!' Tears of relief started to run down her face.

'What's up?' The tension in his voice told her that he already knew something was wrong.

'I fell.'

'I'm in the car now. Give me your address, Hope.'

The question didn't register. 'I think…my ankle may be broken…'

'Hope. Listen to me. Give me your postcode, for the satnav.' His tone was calm, suddenly, reassuring. Of course. The first thing he needed to know was where she was. Hope gave him her postcode and then her house number. That would be enough for him to find her.

'Wait a moment while I get the directions. Stay on the line, Hope.'

She heard the synthetic voice of the satnav repeating back her full address, and that prompted more tears. 'That's right…'

'Okay, I'll be ten minutes. What's the best way for me to get into the house?'

'Back door. Walk round to the back door.' Force of habit lent certainty to her words. He mustn't see…

'Got it. Back door. I want you to stay where you are. Wait for me to get there.'

No chance. Hope was beginning to feel a little better now, if she ignored the pain in her ankle. It was one thing for Theo to come to the house, and quite another to have him walking through the hallway, where he might find a reason to go upstairs.

'I'm okay, Theo. I don't need you to stay on the line. Just concentrate on the road and I'll see you in ten minutes.'

She heard him chuckle. Clearly the application of two slightly longer sentences had reassured him. 'Sure you don't want to answer a few easy questions?'

'No, Theo. I'm fully conscious, breathing without any difficulty, and responsive.' Somehow it was a little easier to remember basic medical checks, than it was to think about the complexities of this particular situation.

'Fair enough. Stay put and I'll be there soon.'

As soon as she'd ended the call, Hope ignored Theo's perfectly reasonable advice. Sliding across the quarry tiles in the hall was painful but easy enough, and she couldn't fall any further than this. The wooden floors of the seating space to one side of the kitchen were no problem either, and Hope could reach up and flip the latch on the door.

'Almost done...' She muttered the words, holding her left leg clear of the floor as she slid carefully towards the sofa. Then she could reach for one of the cushions, place it under her ankle, and relax.

Theo looked around as he opened the glazed back door. There was a large kitchen area to one side of the wide space, with a table and chairs in the middle. Further along, by a brick fireplace, two sofas. Then he saw Hope, sitting on the floor in front of one of the sofas, her leg propped on a cushion.

Leaving the door on the latch, in case he needed to go back out to his car, Theo applied a smile to his face. He could see no evidence of Hope having fallen in here, but decided to leave that particular question, in favour of a few more medically relevant ones.

'Heard you could do with a doctor.'

'A friend...' That answered one question, at least. 'Although I could do with a doctor, as well.'

Theo nodded, kneeling down beside her. 'May I take a look?'

Hope nodded, a trace of reluctance in her face. The leg of her sweatpants was pulled up, and he could see that her ankle was already red and swollen. She twisted her face as he gently probed it, deciding that Hope had self-diagnosed correctly and she was going to need an X-ray. But her pallor and the telltale shakiness that accompanied a bad fall were worrying him a little more at the moment.

'Looks like you took quite a tumble. Did you bang your head?'

'I don't think so.'

Theo took that as an invitation to check for any lumps or

contusions and found nothing. Then he clipped a pulse oximeter from his medical bag to her finger, and took her blood pressure, checking her breathing for good measure.

'Not bad.'

That prompted the response he wanted, and Theo saw a spark of outrage animate her face. 'Not bad? What do you mean, not bad?'

He grinned. 'Pretty good, actually, considering the circumstances. May I take a look at your other leg?'

Hope pressed her lips together, allowing him to roll the leg of her sweatpants up. She had a graze on her knee, and more red marks that would be turning into bruises over the next day or so. She'd fallen from a height.

'Okay. This didn't happen in here, did it?'

The look on her face told him that his suspicions were correct. 'I was carrying something down the stairs and I lost my balance...' A tear rolled down her cheek.

All he wanted to do was to comfort her, but Theo needed to know. He got to his feet, pushing the kitchen door open and looking down the hall. There was a mess of wood at the bottom of the stairs that looked like the remnants of a coffee table, and when he saw the patterned quarry tiles of the floor, and thought of her crashing down onto them, it was an almost physical shock.

He turned, closing the door behind him, and made his way quickly back to her. Hope was trying to wipe her face with the sleeve of her sweat top, and Theo did the one and only thing possible. He took her gently into his arms.

She flinched a little as she stretched up to hug him, but that didn't stop her from hanging on tight. Theo felt her heart racing, or maybe it was his.

'I've got you. It's going to be all right.'

'I'm so sorry, Theo. Bringing you all this way...'

'This is exactly where I want to be. Never doubt that, Hope.' Right now, he was no doctor. He was someone who wanted to dry her tears and comfort her. A man who wanted to hold her and keep her safe.

But this wasn't the practical help that Hope needed. He had to assess her injuries. He held her close for a few moments longer and then gently disengaged her arms from around his neck, resisting the temptation to leave just one fleeting kiss on her cheek.

'You're going to need an X-ray on your ankle, and someone should take a look at those bruises as well.'

She nodded, twisting her lips in an expression of regret that made his heart jump wildly. It *hadn't* been just a hug of reassurance, which could be left behind without a second thought. Theo ignored the feeling that something special had been found and then lost again, and pressed on.

'Before we go anywhere I have to check there's nothing more...' Hope knew exactly what he meant. It was unlikely that there was anything more than bruising to her ribs and hips, Hope had obviously contrived to get from the bottom of the stairs to here, but Theo had to make sure.

He unzipped her sweatshirt, pulling up the sleeves of the T-shirt underneath. She had an angry red blotch on one shoulder and he reckoned that there were probably bruises forming on her hip, as well.

Then the hard part. Theo applied all of his concentration to looking for signs of injury to her ribs and hips, his fingers checking for anything untoward, his gaze on her face for any signs of pain. Once that was accomplished, he turned to the less challenging task of applying a flexible splint to her ankle and bandaging it.

'Got any ice packs? We'll probably have to wait a while, in A & E.' He sat back on his heels, and Hope nodded.

'In the fridge. There are tea towels in the drawer next to the sink.'

'And they say doctors make the worst patients.' He chuckled as he opened the large fridge-freezer, and then reconsidered as he turned and saw Hope easing herself carefully up onto the sofa. 'Hey! What do you think you're doing?'

'Now you've splinted my ankle, I think I can make it around to the car...' Hope was gripping the arm of the sofa, clearly trying to struggle to her feet.

It wasn't so much a matter of losing his head, more a case of finding out what he was really here for. He strode to the sofa, sitting down next to her. 'Hold on to me, Hope. I've got this.'

Her eyes widened suddenly, and then she put her arm around his shoulders, clutching at his shirt. This *was* what he was here for, to be strong when she was hurt and vulnerable.

'Thank you...' She nestled against him as Theo lifted her up in his arms, and carefully carried her out to the car.

The A & E department of the local hospital wasn't too busy, and they were in and back out again within two hours. Theo had been as solid as a rock. Strong, steady and yet almost unbearably tender. He'd lifted her up effortlessly, and she'd clung to him as he'd carried her to the car, feeling his warmth and the swell of muscle beneath her fingertips.

This wasn't Hope's imagination and it wasn't the instinct to cling to someone who'd come to the rescue when you were hurt. It was something more, but Hope couldn't think about that. She'd let Theo inside her house because she'd had to, and managed to avoid allowing him to see upstairs. That could only last for so long. And his presence here in Hastings wasn't permanent either, it was probably only until Anna Singh returned from maternity leave. Even if he could accept her most embarrassing secrets, he'd be moving on.

It was dark by the time they got back, but the security lights flipped on as they walked back around the house to the kitchen door. Hope wasn't used to the two elbow crutches and the orthopaedic boot, which reached almost up to her knee, but Theo let her struggle a little, there to catch her if she fell but allowing her to find the best way of doing things on her own.

She breathed a sigh of relief as he closed the kitchen door behind them. 'Thank you so much, Theo. I don't know what I would have done without you.'

'I'm glad I was here.' He shot her a querying look. Maybe he saw the oddness of it all, the big, empty house, no one but him to call when she was in trouble. But he said nothing.

'You should be going. You have work tomorrow.'

'That's okay. It's too early to go to bed and I've nothing else to do. Why don't you sit down and I'll make you a drink?'

Hope hesitated. The doors were all locked upstairs, and she'd retracted the loft steps before bringing the table down. If he did stray up there, she could just tell him the same as she'd told her mother's carers—that the first floor of the house was closed up. She hadn't really needed to crawl in here, earlier, but she'd panicked at the thought of Theo coming to the house.

And she wanted him to stay. She could tell him not to make a fuss of her, but that was what she really wanted Theo to do. She could take a risk for the reward of having him close a little longer.

'I don't suppose... Would you mind just sticking around while I take a hot shower? The bathroom's right next door and I had grab rails and a shower seat installed for Mum.'

He nodded. 'I'll collect up that broken furniture from the bottom of the stairs, shall I?'

Hope swallowed hard. 'Thanks. But don't take it back up-stairs. Leave it outside, by the back door, and I'll have it taken away…' She supposed that was one way of decreasing the collection of furniture, but having to throw herself down the stairs made it a one-time-only solution.

'Sure.' He shot her another of those querying looks. 'Are you okay?'

Hope straightened herself, smiling. 'Yes, I'm fine. I'll be better when I've had a shower and changed out of these clothes.'

'All right. Call if you need me.'

She didn't need him, and she didn't call. Hope showered, and changed into her most sensible nightdress and dressing gown, finding that the hall had been cleared and swept when she emerged from the bathroom. Theo was in the kitchen, making hot chocolate.

'Better?' He turned, smiling.

'Much.' Hope was suddenly very tired, hiding a yawn behind her hand.

'You want to go and lie down? I'll bring your drink in to you.'

Lying on her bed was so far down on her list of embarrassments about her home that it didn't even feature. Hope made her way slowly into her bedroom, and Theo followed, propping pillows behind her back and under her legs and handing her a couple of painkillers with hot chocolate to wash them down.

'Ah… Thank you, Theo. That's so much more comfortable.' Hope was beginning to feel really drowsy now, but she wanted him to stay. 'How did things go with Amy this evening? Is she okay?'

He took the hint, sitting down in the armchair by the window. 'It was good. Amy's coming to terms with the idea that her parents need some support with this as well, and isn't giving Joanne such a hard time about going to a group herself.

We talked a bit about saying how you felt without making it sound like an accusation.'

Hope nodded. '*I feel this* instead of *You did that*.'

'Yeah. I had to help with a bit of rewording, for starters, but it turned into a really constructive conversation.'

'Is she sleeping any better?'

Theo shook his head. 'No, and that's not helping. I'm loth to prescribe medication though, and so I made a few suggestions about a more natural approach. Joanne said she'd try those out too, and Amy seemed to like the idea.'

'Sounds good. Even if it doesn't work, they'll be doing something together to care for each other. It sounds as if Amy's beginning to see that it's not her against the world.' Hope stifled a yawn, trying to keep her eyes open, and the next thing she knew Theo was gently removing the cup of hot chocolate from her grasp.

'I think we won't add scalds to bruising and a broken bone, if that's okay with you.'

'Anything you say, Theo...'

'Really?' She heard him laugh. 'You're starting to worry me, now.'

She chuckled drowsily. She was warm and comfortable, and no longer frightened and wondering how badly she'd hurt herself. Theo had made everything right.

Hope must have dozed off, because when she opened her eyes she could hear Theo moving around in the kitchen. She went to sit up, and groaned as pain shot through her shoulder and hip. Theo appeared in the doorway of the bedroom, a plate of toast in one hand and a mug in the other.

'You should be getting home. It must be late. Why are you making toast, Theo?'

'It's seven o'clock. You've been asleep for nearly nine hours.'

'Ah. That explains why I'm aching so badly.' Hope sat up gingerly. 'And feeling so awake.'

'Yeah, probably. Look, I need to get going in half an hour, to get home and changed before I start work. Is there anything you need?'

'Coffee...?' She looked at the mug he was carrying.

He put the mug down on the bedside table, and Hope caught the scent of a fresh brew. 'Anything else?'

'No. Thank you, Theo.' A thought occurred to her. 'You haven't been up all night, have you?'

'No, I crashed out on the sofa.' He grinned. 'Much more comfortable than that old sofa you used to have in your student digs.'

'That's not saying much. I'll be in a little late today—'

'No, you will not. You're not coming in to work at all.' He frowned at her.

'But it's Sara Jamieson's day off today. She's working this weekend. I'll be okay. I just need to take things slowly.'

'Yes, you do need to take things slowly, and no, you won't be okay coming into work. I'll get Rosie to organise some help from the practice nurse and the physician associate and between the three of us we'll manage.' Hope opened her mouth to argue and he silenced her with a glare. 'What happened to "Anything you say, Theo"? Have you forgotten about that?'

'I was half asleep. Clearly I was incoherent.'

He chuckled. 'Thought it was too good to be true. By the time you've got up, had a shower and iced your bruises it'll be lunchtime. I'll speak to you then.'

Maybe he was right. Maybe not. 'You don't happen to know where my painkillers are, do you?'

Theo clearly reckoned that was a tacit agreement. He grinned, disappearing for a moment and coming back with the box of tablets. 'See you later?'

'Thanks, Theo. Yes, I'll see you later.'

CHAPTER FIVE

THERE WAS A long list of patients for Theo to see this morning, but by one o'clock the pressure had eased. People seemed to be disappearing from his list, and Theo reckoned that Rosie must have set up an impromptu triage system, and was diverting patients who didn't need to see a doctor to Colette the nurse, or Amir, the physician associate. His phone rang, and Rosie instructed him that he now had half an hour for lunch. Theo decided not to enquire too closely into how she'd managed to engineer that, as half an hour was exactly what he needed right now.

He picked up his phone, dialling Hope's number. Her ringtone drifted through the open window and he frowned, getting to his feet and following the sound along the corridor. As he paused outside her consulting room, she answered.

'Hi, Theo.'

Her voice sounded bright and firm. Theo pushed open the door and saw her sitting behind her desk.

'How are you doing?' He walked into the room and sat down, trying not to frown. 'Resting up?'

She flushed guiltily and then shot him an annoyed look. 'All right. Clearly I was going to mention that I was here, at some point.'

'Of course. Because clearly I was going to notice.'

'Theo! Don't make a fuss about it. I was feeling okay and

starting to get bored, so I called a taxi to bring me here. And you can't tell me you didn't need the help. I've seen four patients in the last hour.'

'And I expect your ankle's hurting…' Perhaps he should sound a little less annoyed. Patients generally didn't like it when their doctors were unsympathetic to their pain. Although Hope was neither a patient nor a doctor at the moment, she was a friend who he cared about.

'Not really. Throbs a bit.' She jutted her chin in his direction.

'If it's throbbing then you should be elevating it, not sitting behind a desk. And by the way, what's with texting me yesterday evening, instead of calling?'

'I knew you were with Amy and I didn't want to interrupt.'

'So you fell down the stairs, broke your ankle, and thought that wasn't important enough to call me. That's just perverse. Whatever I was doing could have waited.' What really hurt was that Hope wouldn't acknowledge how much she meant to him. She'd been his first priority last night, and she was his first priority now.

'Remember what you were saying about Amy and her family last night, Theo? About accusatory language?'

'Oh, so you *were* listening to something I had to say.' That was unnecessary, as well as accusatory. Theo tried to reword, but his jumbled emotions wouldn't allow him to. 'I… It was a shock to find you here.'

Suddenly the angry fire in her eyes died. 'Look, I'm really busy at the moment, and so are you. Can't we talk about this later?'

Later. That was a very good suggestion. Theo nodded and got to his feet.

Hope had half expected him to slam the door behind him. At least that would have given her the opportunity to shout something about not coming back until he'd readjusted his attitude, in his wake. That would have let off a bit of steam, but in the long term it wouldn't have solved anything.

Theo was right to be angry with her. Coming in to work today had felt like a good idea, but she should have listened to him, because it wasn't. She'd leave him to cool down for a while and then go and apologise.

But he beat her to it. Fifteen minutes later, there was a tap on the door, and he entered, carrying a cup of coffee from the café across the street.

'I'm really sorry. I was upset that you were hurt, and angry with myself because I felt it was my fault. I shouldn't have blamed you for that.'

'You have nothing to apologise for, Theo. Why on earth would you think it was your fault?'

He shrugged. 'When I cleared up the mess at the bottom of the stairs, it was difficult not to notice that it was a broken coffee table. Would it be presumptuous to assume that it had something to do with my empty sitting room?'

She hadn't realised... Hope supposed she could tell Theo that it was nothing to do with him, and that she'd had a sudden urge to move furniture around. But in this, at least, he deserved a bit of honesty.

'It was for you—if you wanted it. It's presumptuous to assume that it was your fault that I fell. That's entirely down to me. I'm not inclined to accept an apology for that.'

He put the cardboard beaker down on her desk and took a seat. Clearly that wasn't all Theo had on his mind.

'What else, Theo?'

'I just... I heard the alert for your text while I was driving and I was going to call you when I got home. Then I got stuck in traffic at the lights...' He shook his head. 'I can't help thinking that I nearly left you lying at the bottom of the stairs while I got home and made myself a cup of tea.'

'That was my decision too, Theo. If it's any consolation, I was typing another text to say it was urgent, when you rang.'

He smiled suddenly. 'Yeah. I would have answered that, even if I'd been clinging to a cliff face, over a pool of crocodiles.'

Hope chuckled. 'Easy to say in Hastings. We don't have much of a crocodile problem here.'

'Hanging by one finger, watching a crack open up above me, at Beachy Head?' That toe-tingling grin of his was making her ankle throb.

'Yes, I guess you could have been doing that.' There were questions that Theo still wasn't asking. The answers were embarrassing but he deserved to hear them and suddenly Hope wanted to close the gap that existed between them.

'To be honest, Theo… You're the only friend I could call. I don't want to presume on you always being there.'

He shot her a look of honest disbelief. Hope supposed it wasn't the most obvious of things to say. She'd lived in Hastings almost all her life and was surrounded by people.

'You had loads of friends at university…' he murmured.

'Yes, but that was different. When you're a carer you tend to keep people at arm's length, because you know that if they suggest doing something you'll end up either saying no, or cancelling at the last minute. I *do* have friends, really good ones, mostly other carers that I've met. We've supported each other for years, and we understand that a message on an Internet group is generally the most we can do.'

'And you needed someone who could come.' Understanding sparked in his eyes.

'Yes. I still keep up with the group, but in the evenings, no one can leave the person they're caring for alone. You were the only real friend that I could call, and maybe you don't know quite how much that means to me...' Hope was feeling a little breathless now. She'd practically admitted that Theo was becoming the centre of her world.

'I didn't realise.' His brow creased. 'That's what you're doing here now. You wanted people around you.'

'Does that sound stupid?'

'No.' Theo shook his head. 'Everyone loses their confidence a bit after a fall like that. I'm glad you called me, last night. I wouldn't have wanted to be anywhere else.'

He meant it. She could see from the warmth in his eyes that he *really* meant it. They were both finding their way in a new world and maybe they both needed this friendship a lot more than either was willing to admit.

Hope focussed on the mug on her desk. 'I don't suppose the coffee's for me, is it?'

'Yes, of course it is.'

'That's really nice of you. Thank you.' She peeled open the lid and caught her breath. 'Theo! Whipped cream and chocolate curls.'

'Can't go wrong with chocolate curls.' He pursed his lips. 'Would it be too pushy of me to ask whether you're intending seeing any more patients this afternoon? Rosie caught me on my way back in with the coffee, and I can handle all of the appointments myself.'

'My leg is beginning to hurt a bit. I have a few patient reviews to catch up on.' Maybe she should compromise and offer to go home and do that.

'I'm sure there's nothing that wouldn't wait until Monday.' Theo shot her a grin. 'But since you're here, you may as well be comfortable.'

He pulled the curtains back from around the couch in the corner of the room, and released the lever to lower it. Then he raised the backrest. It *did* look far more inviting than her chair felt at the moment. Hope got to her feet, and Theo waited while she grabbed her crutches and walked slowly towards him.

'Good idea.' She smiled up at him, and Theo nodded.

She sat down on the couch, swinging her legs up onto it. Theo leaned over to adjust the backrest a little, and put a pillow beneath her injured leg, and then fetched her laptop from her desk. Then he took the plants off a small side table by the window, and placed it next to her, with her coffee within reach.

'That's much better. Thanks, Theo.' His help was a little different now. Theo wasn't just someone who would care for her when she was hurt, he was a man who claimed the right to do so. And Hope had to admit that managing on her own lost its lustre when he was around. She could still feel the brush of his fingers, still smell his clean, warm scent.

She couldn't help gazing at him as he walked back towards her desk, seeing only the coiled strength in his body. Hope swallowed down the lump in her throat as he picked her phone up, then turned, smiling as he handed it to her.

'Call me if there's anything you need.'

'I will. You have your car here, today?'

'In the car park.' The amused look in his eyes told her that he wasn't going to offer, she would have to ask. She was going to have to meet him halfway, because that was what friends did.

'Would you give me a lift home? I'm comfortable here, and there's plenty I can be getting on with until you're ready to leave.'

His smile somehow managed to combine a hint of triumph with its warmth. 'My pleasure...'

As apology experiences went, that had been a good one. Willow had taught him that chocolate was capable of some heavy lifting when he needed to express remorse, and Hope had confirmed the theory. She was perfectly capable of making herself a bit more comfortable, but she'd let him help her. And the *way* she'd allowed it, making it seem like something she wanted as much as he did, had quietened his raging heart.

He was tempted to rush through the patients that remained on his list for this afternoon, but he knew better than that. Hope was able to access the network from her laptop, and he had little doubt that she'd be checking his notes on a few of the people who she'd been scheduled to see for follow-ups. Anything less than his usual meticulous notes wouldn't do, and so he listened carefully to Mr Constable's update on the situation with his garden fence, knowing that stress management was an integral part of his physical ailments. It was six o'clock before he bade his final patient a cheery goodbye, but the look on Hope's face when he tapped on the door and walked into her consulting room told him that she'd been more than happy to wait.

'How did it go with Mrs Abeila?' Hope clearly wasn't going to allow him to prioritise her own injury.

'Much happier with her new medication. It doesn't upset her stomach as much. I suggested that she might try taking it in the afternoon or evening, to see whether that improved things even more.'

'Mr Constable…?'

'Apparently his new neighbour is much more reasonable than the old one, and they've sorted out the boundary dispute amicably. I wouldn't like to say that's entirely responsible for his blood-pressure reading, but I expect it helped. Didn't you read my notes?'

Hope flushed slightly, and Theo felt an inexplicable urge to press his lips against her cheek. 'Sorry. I'm not checking up on you.'

'That's okay, check all you want. Just remember to save and close when you've finished reading something, because we can't both update the same patient record and I got locked out a couple of times.' He grinned at her.

'Right. Will do.' Hope pressed a couple of keys on the laptop, clearly saving and closing something, and shot him an impish look. 'Are you ready to go?'

'Absolutely.'

Theo threw her empty coffee cup into the bin, and put everything back in place, while Hope threaded her bag across her body so she had both hands free for her crutches. They took the small lift down to the ground floor, and he let her walk on her own down the ramp that led to the car park. She juggled a little with the crutches when she reached the open passenger door of his car, and Theo gave in and offered her his arm.

The big, well-kept house was protected from view by a deep rhododendron hedge full of buds, which were about to burst into bloom. Theo parked next to Hope's car, in front of the house, and she turned in her seat, seeming a little nervous.

'Would you like to come in for some tea? Or do you have to rush off?'

Theo wondered *where* Hope might possibly think he was rushing off to. Friday evenings weren't quite as full as they had been eighteen years ago, when there was always somewhere to go to celebrate the end of a long week.

'Tea would be nice, thank you.' He ignored the sudden craving for her company, concentrating on the idea that winding down for the weekend wasn't entirely possible until he'd seen Hope settled safely at home.

'Um... Right, then.' She seemed suddenly at a loss over the practicalities of getting back out of the car, and Theo hurried around to the passenger door to help her. As soon as she was on her feet again, she started to make for the paved pathway that led around to the kitchen at the back.

It was quiet here, the well-tended garden at the back surrounded by an old wall, which lent privacy and charm. Maybe a little too quiet, a little too secluded for Hope's peace of mind at the moment. She opened the back door, leading him into the open-plan kitchen living room.

'Shall I make the tea?'

Finally Hope smiled. 'Thanks for the offer but…go and sit down.' She gestured towards the seating area. 'Let me manage for myself.'

He could do that. Even if sinking into an armchair wasn't entirely relaxing, because every muscle in his body tensed when she reached for something or fumbled with her crutches. As soon as the tea was made, he felt justified in getting to his feet and carrying the two cups, while Hope followed. She sank down onto the sofa, opposite where he'd been sitting, and slipped off her shoe, propping both feet up on the cushions next to her.

'Ahh! That's better.' She reached for her tea and took a sip. 'It'll only be a couple of weeks, at most, before I can put some weight on my leg, and one crutch will be a lot easier than two.'

Theo nodded. The more she rested now, the sooner that would be, but he didn't need to tell Hope that. Something was still bothering her, though. He'd noticed that her hand shook a little as she picked up her cup. If anything, she seemed more nervous, more defensive, now that she was home.

Eighteen years suddenly felt like a very long time, as all the things that could happen to a person crowded in on him. All of the sorrows that a place might hold, which he could only guess at, but seemed written into the tension on her face.

'You have a lovely home.' The kitchen was modern and well

equipped but welcoming as well. Everything that Theo wanted to create, in the family home that he so longed for.

'Thank you.' Hope pursed her lips thoughtfully, looking around her. 'I have a lot of good memories stored up in this house. Although I have to admit to feeling a little lonely here, since Mum died.'

He got that. Maybe it was time for him to stop thinking, and start saying. They'd never hesitated to tell each other what was on their minds before. 'Why would you have to admit to it, when that's perfectly normal? You've lost someone you love, and yesterday you fell and hurt yourself. If it was me, I'd be feeling very sorry for myself.'

Maybe he'd said too much, Hope stared at him, almost spilling her tea. But then she smiled. 'This is what I miss. Someone telling me what they really think. Mum always did that, even if it got very muddled towards the end of her life.'

Theo nodded. 'It's what I miss about Willow's teens, sometimes. She had no filters between what she thought and what she said. It prompted tears sometimes, not all of them hers, but...' He shrugged.

'Then she learnt tact?'

'Yeah. It's a lot less awkward, but thankfully she's not so good at it that it's a major problem.'

Hope was trembling again, and a tear appeared in the corner of one eye. She put down her mug, struggling to her feet, and Theo wondered whether he'd inadvertently been tactless.

'Are we going somewhere?' He was at a loss to know what to do next.

She nodded, and started to walk towards the door that led into the hallway. There was nothing else Theo could do but follow her.

Hope stopped at the bottom of the stairs, handing him one of her crutches and gripping the banister. The look on her face resembled that of a mountaineer, standing at the bottom of a precipice, trying to gauge what dangers the route ahead might hold.

'We'll do it this way.' He leant the crutch against the wall, moving behind her and slightly to the side, and coiling one arm around her waist. His other hand went to her shoulder, which felt suddenly anything but professional. Theo was about to loosen his grip and think of another way to get her up the stairs safely, when he felt Hope lean against him.

'That's good. Thank you, I feel a lot more stable.'

And he felt... Protective. Determined to keep her safe and so, so happy that she wasn't fighting him. 'Off you go, then. One at a time...'

CHAPTER SIX

THIS HADN'T BEEN as hard as Hope had thought it might be, but that didn't mean it was anything approaching easy. Feeling Theo close helped, though. Knowing that he'd catch her if she fell, and hoping that he might know what to do when she ripped the dustcovers off her biggest secret.

She wobbled a bit, halfway up the stairs, and felt his grip tighten around her waist. Breathtakingly strong and solid. 'Okay?'

Not really. She'd seen all kinds of human frailty in her time as a doctor, and she knew that Theo had too. The hoard was something he could treat with understanding, just as she'd understood when she'd realised a patient was in this situation. But could Theo understand why she'd kept it a secret for so long?

'I'm fine. Keep going.'

They made the top of the stairs, and he guided her towards the row of six storage boxes, stacked two high against the wall. Hope turned her face away from him, wondering if this was the moment she dreaded.

But instead of wanting to know what was in them, he leaned down pressing his hand on the top of one of them. 'These okay to sit on, while I fetch your other crutch?'

She let out a breath. 'Yes. They're not going to collapse.' They were full of old newspapers and would easily support her weight. Hope sat down, watching as he hurried down the stairs, and then back up again.

He handed her the second crutch, and then sat down on the two boxes next to hers. Hope took a breath.

'When I fell yesterday... I should have asked you to help me bring the table downstairs, but I couldn't. No one's allowed up here.'

Theo nodded slowly, obviously going through all of the options in his head. 'How long?'

'Since I was seven. Mum and Dad always used to organise a big birthday party for me, they'd put a tent up in the garden...' The memory of those sunshiny days hurt, and she brushed away a tear. 'They had the main bedroom and mine was the second biggest. The others had...things we didn't use, stored in boxes. Old furniture. One of my friends came up here, and when her Mum came to collect her she told her that she'd seen...'

He was beginning to understand. 'What happened?'

Hope shrugged. 'Mum looked really embarrassed and my friend's mother shushed her and told her to be quiet. I thought everyone had rooms like that in their house, and it was the first time I realised that ours was different and I had to keep it a secret. So I did, and whenever I had friends round after that, Mum used to lock the doors of the back bedrooms.'

'And...the rest of the house?' Theo enquired, gently.

'It was a little full. Quite cluttered, if I'm honest, but my dad loved all kinds of interesting things and I grew up surrounded by treasures. When Dad died, Mum didn't want to sleep upstairs any more, and so I helped her move her bedroom downstairs. I reorganised and boxed up a lot of things we didn't need and put them upstairs. She wouldn't think of letting me throw anything away, but I had to give her a safe, ordered environment. When we needed carers to come in for her, I locked all of the upstairs rooms and told them that I'd closed them up because the house was too big and Mum couldn't manage the stairs.'

'Hope, you did everything you could for your mum. You didn't force her to throw things away, and you provided her with a safe living space. It must have been hard for you.'

Theo had reacted just as she'd expected. He'd listened and he hadn't judged. But sooner or later he'd start to make the connections she dreaded. 'Remember Andrew Locke? How you said that the hardest thing was that no one knew he was using cocaine?'

'That's not the same thing, Hope. He was putting himself at risk—'

Theo stopped, shaking his head as Hope looked down at her orthopaedic boot. 'That's the wrong answer, isn't it? How about the answer I don't want to give, because I find it really hard? We all like to pretend that everything's under control. I did when Jonas died, but in fact I was sitting, staring at a blank wall every evening, not eating or sleeping. It took six months of therapy before I could even talk about it.'

'That's been your secret?' Suddenly everything shifted. Despite her aches and pains, and all of the fear she'd felt over bringing Theo up here, Hope felt strong again. She wanted to be strong, for Theo.

'Yeah. And this is yours. But we're both doing our best to move forward and remake our lives.'

Hope thought for a moment. 'Thank you for telling me, Theo. I knew your change in direction was important for you, but I didn't realise how important.'

'Because I didn't tell you. We should have told each other about these things, but we didn't and that's okay, because we're both human.' He reached down, tapping one of the boxes beneath them. 'So... What exactly am I sitting on?'

'Take a look.' Theo clearly couldn't talk any more about Jonas, but if Hope could be open with him about her own issues then that might help him to trust her with his.

Theo got to his feet, lifting off the hard plastic cover and reading the banner on the newspaper inside. '*The Hastings Weekly Digest.*'

'Yes, my dad used to get it every week. Even when he wasn't well, he'd go out to the newsagent for his copy.'

'And they're all in sequence?'

Hope nodded. She probably shouldn't care about that—she never looked at the newspapers. But her dad had always kept them carefully folded and in date order. Suddenly she didn't want Theo to disturb them.

'I'd love to see them some time. Not now, though, they're filed away so neatly.' He understood without having to ask.

'You can look in the bedrooms. The keys are in the lock box on the wall.' She pointed to the small key safe, reciting the combination.

Theo fetched the keys and then opened the doors of all four bedrooms in turn. Then he came back to sit down next to her, his brow creased in thought.

'There's…it's a lot of memories.'

At least he hadn't said *rubbish*. Hope nodded. 'That isn't all. The loft's been boarded out and there's a lot up there as well. It all feels…there's so much of it.'

'When someone dies, going through their things is really hard. Maybe this is a version of Willow's trunk and you have to keep these things until you're ready to let some of them go.'

'It's a bit bigger than Willow's trunk. Dad had extra beams put into the floors up here when I was little…'

'That's sensible.'

Theo's reaction made her smile. 'Nothing about this is sensible, Theo.'

'Not sensible maybe, but it makes sense.' He sat down next to her again. 'You'll work it out, Hope. And if you want me to help you with any of it, then you know where I am.'

'Thank you for not fainting with shock.' She smiled up at him.

'There's still time. You haven't got a basement, have you?'

Theo had always been able to make her laugh, and she appreciated that now more than she ever had. 'No. I do have a potting shed, full of garden equipment. Some of which is broken.'

'Since that's not actually *in* the house, would it be splitting hairs to ask how you feel about that?' He grinned.

'Theo! Yes, it would be splitting hairs. Although you have a point. I'm not sure I feel quite the same about three or four broken lawnmowers. Dad hated gardening, and after things got a bit out of control, he got someone in to keep the garden neat.'

'There you go, then. Perhaps that's the place to start.'

A start. The thought made her almost giddy with elation. Hope got to her feet, almost losing her balance as her crutch slipped out of her hand, rolling onto the floor. But Theo was there, steadying her.

Suddenly she was caught in his gaze. Lost in his smile. 'Careful...' The word seemed to form the shape of a kiss, and Hope shivered.

'Let's both be careful. We'll look after each other's dreams.' They both knew how important those dreams were, now, because Hope had shared her secret and Theo had shared his.

'That works for me. Thanks for listening, Hope.'

'I'd like to listen some more. Whenever you're ready.' Hope sensed that Theo wasn't ready yet, but she'd be there for him when he was. 'In the meantime, shall we start by taking it carefully down the stairs?'

Theo chuckled. 'Absolutely. Then I may insist you sit down, while I cook for you.'

'You cook?'

'Of course I do. How do you suppose I've eaten for all these years? I upped my game a little when Carrie left, Willow and I made a thing of going to markets together and learning to cook dishes from whichever country we were in. Mexico was a big success for us.'

'Can you make tacos?'

Theo chuckled. 'Can I make tacos? Our next-door neighbour taught us. One taste of her special seasoning and you'll never look at the tacos you get at the supermarket again.'

'You're full of surprises, Theo. But I don't have anything in the fridge, so we'll have to make do with a takeaway.'

'Sounds good. I'll bring some things over tomorrow and cook then, instead.'

'You're cooking me dinner tomorrow?' Hope smiled at him, forgetting all about the resolution she'd made to manage for herself. 'That's nice...'

Four terms. Eighteen years. Two weeks. How did they add up to what he and Hope had now?

Theo wasn't sure. The four terms that they'd spent together had been a blossoming. Their friendship had grown into an easy relationship where they could share anything. When he thought about it their one kiss hadn't been a mistake, but a natural progression of a relationship that could no longer be contained within the boundaries of friendship.

The eighteen years—life had intruded and they'd followed different paths. If asked, Theo would have answered that he'd made his mistakes, but on balance he would have made the same decisions. He guessed that Hope's answer would be the same.

And now, two precious, head-spinning weeks. Both older and wiser, and carrying a lot more baggage. The friendship—that instant connection—was still there, but their different lives had left them needing very different things.

But this wasn't the time for equations. Hope had to take some time to heal, and Theo would be there for her. Everything else could wait.

He was up early the following morning, and had shopped for two in the supermarket, stopping off to fill his own fridge before going on to Hope's place. He found her standing in the open doorway of the potting shed, regarding its contents. It was so full that it was going to be necessary to take some things out before it was possible for either of them to go inside.

'What do you think?' Her voice trembled slightly. This wasn't going to be as easy for her as she'd made out yesterday.

'I think it'll take a while to do this properly.'

She shot him a helpless look. 'Properly?'

This wasn't like Hope at all. She was one of the most capable people he knew, but somehow her parents' possessions seemed to strip her of all of her resourcefulness and leave her lost and vulnerable.

'I imagine there are some things there that you'll want to keep. I can see some gardening tools over there in the corner that look to be in good condition. There may be some chemicals that have been banned now, and so the best thing to do with them is find out how they can be disposed of safely. Then for the things you don't need, we can find out about recycling or reuse. I'd be surprised if too much has to be thrown away.'

She nodded. 'That sounds good. I'd like to put as much as possible to some use, even if it's just recycling. I can get started on that today, and do it bit by bit.'

'Would you like a hand? It'll go quicker with two.' And easier, probably. Hope knew exactly what she wanted, but she seemed to need someone to give her permission to go ahead and make it happen.

'Don't you have your own things to be getting on with?' Hope looked at him thoughtfully and Theo avoided her gaze.

'They'll keep. Since I'm here now, with all the ingredients for tacos, then the least we could do is work up a bit of an appetite...'

CHAPTER SEVEN

EVERYONE AT THE Arrow Lane medical centre had rallied round. He and Sara Jamieson were covering Hope's home visits. Terri, the receptionist, fetched and carried for her, usually before Hope had even asked for something, and Rosie swung into a fierce but smiling organisational mode, making sure that everything ran like clockwork. Rosie picked Hope up on her way to work in the mornings, and Theo claimed the right to take her home again, sometimes staying to cook, and sometimes leaving when Hope chased him away.

It wasn't permanent but it was a comfortable routine that supported Theo as much as it did Hope. He'd almost managed to forget that he'd spoken about Jonas and he'd pushed those feelings to the back of his mind, where they couldn't hurt him.

'Theo, we need you in Reception. It's an emergency.' Rosie's voice was level and calm, which told Theo that he should hurry.

Before he'd made it downstairs he heard a baby screaming. The reception area was empty, and Rosie was on the phone. A young woman lay on the carpeted floor, her feet propped up on a couple of cushions, and Hope was kneeling awkwardly beside her.

'Bee sting. She's in anaphylactic shock...' Hope's voice was calm as well, and the emergency rating in Theo's head ratcheted up a notch. An empty handbag was lying on the floor, along with a mess of contents, and Hope was holding an epinephrine auto-injector, the orange needle cover extended, indicating that it had just been used.

He took the auto-injector from her hand, and Hope nodded, picking up the second one that lay on the floor beside her and leaning over to catch the woman's attention.

'Tina… Tina, look at me. Gracie's all right, she's safe in her pram. She's just crying. Try to relax.'

To be fair, the baby didn't sound all right, and her cries were obviously agitating Tina. Theo knelt down beside her. 'The bee sting's out?'

Hope nodded. Tina was still very pale and struggling to breathe, and there was a bright red swelling on her left arm, obviously where she had been stung. She didn't seem to be responding to the first dose of epinephrine as well as they might have expected.

'We'll sit her up for a minute?' Theo suggested.

'Yes, that may help.' Hope shifted towards Tina's shoulders and together they helped her sit up. 'Is that helping you breathe, Tina?'

Tina shook her head, the wheezing in the back of her throat getting worse as she tried to reach for her baby. Everyone else was busy, Rosie was on the phone to the emergency services, and Terri was shepherding patients who were already in the building out, and making sure no one else entered.

'It's been more than five minutes. I may have to give her another shot of epinephrine.' Hope inclined her head towards the screaming baby in her pram and Theo nodded. Keeping her quiet couldn't do any harm and it might help her mother to relax and breathe.

He got to his feet, greeting the baby with a smile, and gently taking her from her pram. Theo started to sing quietly, and suddenly little Gracie stopped crying, looking up at him. He rocked her in time with the song and Gracie joined in with a few baby moves, waving her arms at him.

Out of the corner of his eye he saw Rosie grinning, the phone still pressed tightly to her ear. He turned to glance at Hope, who was smiling as well as she reassured Tina.

'There, see? I think Gracie's just made a new friend. I want you to try and relax if you can.'

The painful wheeze seemed to ease a bit and Hope helped Tina to lie back down again. But it wasn't enough. Hope was checking Tina's heart rate and breathing, and clearly wasn't happy with the situation. She administered a second shot of epinephrine and after a minute of silence, broken only by Hope's quiet reassurances, Tina's chest heaved as she sucked in a breath.

The relief was almost palpable. Gracie started to fret in his arms, and Theo quieted her, moving around to allow Tina to see her child. Feeling that tiny body move against him, breathing in the gorgeous baby scent, would make anyone relax and he couldn't help smiling. Hope grinned, telling Tina again that Gracie was fine and monitoring her recovery.

When the ambulance arrived, Tina was better still, but she still needed careful observation at the hospital to make sure her symptoms didn't return. Rosie handed over a printed set of patient notes, which included a written record of the treatment Tina had received this morning, and the paramedic turned to Theo.

'Wish all our calls went this smoothly. You're the father…?'

'Um… No.' He could see Rosie hiding a smile behind her hand and shot her a querying look. 'What's happening with Gracie?'

'I called Tina's partner and he's on his way to pick Gracie up. I said we were managing.'

'Thanks. We'll keep the baby here until then.' Maybe calling Gracie *the baby* would instil a note of professionalism into the situation, but when he looked back down at her Theo couldn't help falling in love all over again. 'I'll be upstairs.'

He stopped, to let Tina say goodbye to her daughter, and to reassure her that he'd take the best care of Gracie until her father arrived. Then Theo retreated to his consulting room, where he could sing his entire repertoire of Elvis Presley's greatest hits without interruption.

Hope had seen a new side of Theo. He was first and foremost a doctor, but he'd seen that she had the medical aspects in hand and done what was most needed to calm Tina down, and quietened Gracie. It was just a matter of practicality, wasn't it?

But there was nothing practical about the besotted smile he'd given Gracie. That was all Theo's rock-steady heart, which had been captured by a pair of blue eyes and shock of red-blonde hair. Seeing him with the baby had prompted two opposing reactions in Hope. She'd wanted to go and hug him, to be a part of that simple warmth. But at the same time, the knowledge that this was what he wanted for himself, and it was something she might not be able to give him, had clawed at her.

Gracie's father arrived, and Theo brought the baby downstairs, handing her over. She started to fret, obviously missing him already, and Hope thought she saw a quick flash of longing in his eyes. Theo was clearly missing Gracie already as well, although he made a point of telling her father that thanks weren't needed, and he should get on his way to see Tina.

Theo retreated to his consulting room, and Hope stayed in Reception while Rosie consulted the list of patients for the afternoon.

'We gave them the option but it seems no one wanted to wait. I'll call round and rebook the appointments.'

Hope nodded. 'Okay. I'll stay late if anyone wants to come back this evening. Have I got ten minutes?'

'Your next patient's not due until after lunch—you've got half an hour. I might take a break myself, to get over how good Dr Lewis is with kids. He can have my two for the weekend any time he likes.'

Hope chuckled. It was going to take her a good deal more than half an hour to get over the sight of Theo crooning to Gracie. 'You might have a fight on your hands, getting them back again.'

Rosie laughed. 'Does he have kids of his own?'

'A daughter. She's twenty.' And he'd missed being a dad when Willow was a baby. Hope knew what it was like to miss out, and maybe it was time to give him a nudge. 'Take a break, Rosie, and make sure that Terri does too. You've earned it this morning. You were both brilliant and we couldn't have done without you.'

Despite having an orthopaedic boot and two crutches, Hope managed to give the impression of breezing into his office. Theo wasn't sure how she did that. Maybe it was something to do with her summer dress and her smile, which made him think of sunshine and a gentle, scented breath of wind.

She sat down, grinning at him. Maybe he was supposed to go first, but he wasn't entirely sure what was on her mind.

'All right. Spit it out.'

'I'm just wondering how I could have been so wrong about you, Theo.'

He raised his eyebrows. Hope was being extra-ambiguous, which meant he was probably in for a telling-off about something. He'd better get it over with.

'Cut to the chase, Hope. Haven't we got a whole roomful of people downstairs that we need to see?'

'It seems they all decided to go home and come back later. I dare say we'll be working a bit late this evening. We don't often have emergencies here.'

'Is that it? You've decided we need a few more emergencies?'

'No, one was enough. I like the opportunity of getting to know my patients, and preventing things from happening to them.'

'Yeah. Me too. What was Tina doing here, anyway?'

'I'd only just seen her, to give Gracie a check-up. Apparently she went outside, and Terri heard her scream. A bee had flown into Gracie's pram and Tina was flapping it away from her and got stung. We all know that Tina carries an epinephrine auto-injector as a precaution—she was stung several times as a teenager.'

'This time was worse?' Theo asked. That was usually the case with this kind of allergy.

'Much worse. There was only localised swelling before and her consultant didn't think that immunotherapy was necessary. We'll see what the hospital says this time around, but I think they may offer it to her.'

Theo nodded. 'I imagine she's probably got used to just stepping away when she sees a bee. But she was trying to protect Gracie.'

'Yes. I think that's exactly what she was trying to do. Theo, I can handle Tina's ongoing care. What I came to say...' She stopped short as he chuckled. 'What?'

'Go on. Don't let me stop you now.'

Hope shot him an injured look. 'What I came to say is that I'm so grateful for all you've done in the last couple of weeks. You've been amazing. I'm just concerned and I'd really like you to spend some more time looking after yourself.'

'What brought this on?' Theo thought he knew. Gracie had

slid in under all of his defences and allowed him to think that he could have the life he wanted. Settled and fulfilled. Maybe even a family...

She shrugged. 'You've been through a lot, Theo. You told me that you were looking to settle, and build up a supportive framework, but you're not doing anything about it.'

Hope underestimated herself. She was insightful and unerring in her aim when she wanted to be. Theo wondered if she knew that he'd been imagining a baby that looked just like her in his arms, and decided that was beyond even her capabilities.

'It'll happen.'

'No, it won't. Not if you don't make it.'

Suddenly, in Hope's clear gaze, it all seemed so obvious. He *did* need a home, a place of strength from which he could reach out. 'I guess I could go and look at a few houses, just to get a feel for what I want. Scan the situations vacant columns.' None of that seemed terribly appealing.

'You want a hand with it? I don't have much experience with either of those things so you'd need to contribute all the opinions. I'll just listen and agree with whatever you say.'

Theo chuckled. Suddenly house-hunting and job-hunting didn't seem quite so bad. 'I'm definitely taking you up on that, Hope. I'm not passing up the chance to watch you agreeing with everything I say.'

'I might be asking a few pertinent questions, though.' She shot him a grin that made her green eyes dance with mischief. Suddenly everything he wanted seemed like a possibility.

'I wouldn't expect anything less.' He looked at his watch. 'We *will* come back to this, but you're probably as hungry as I am, and we've got a long afternoon ahead of us. What do you say I pop out and get sandwiches?'

'Good idea. You'll find me in my consulting room, laying plans for your future.'

Theo chuckled. As long as Hope intended to include herself in those plans, she'd get no arguments from him.

They were making a slightly different routine. Saturday mornings were devoted to finding him a permanent job and a place to live, and Hope's enthusiasm for the task had convinced Theo to at least consider several options. Then he cooked, using one of the recipes he and Willow had most enjoyed on their travels. They'd been to Mexico, Italy and then India, and by the time they got to Germany Hope was moving around more easily, putting weight on her injured ankle and using just one crutch.

Theo had been waiting for a good moment to broach the subject, and when they retired to the sitting room to finish off glasses of German beer with their coffee, now seemed as good a time as any.

'I've been thinking. About your collection…'

A flash of panic showed in her eyes. Hope had gradually got the message that the secret hoard above their heads was nothing to be ashamed of, but she was still protective of the memories that were stored upstairs. All of her old dresses and toys from when she was little. Stones from trips to the beach, all boxed up and labelled with the date. A whole wardrobe full of things saved from her parents' wedding.

She hesitated, but Theo knew that curiosity would win out in the end. 'Okay. What are you thinking?'

'I did some digging, and there's a project based in Eastbourne, which collects all kinds of documents and scans them. The plan is to make them accessible to everyone on the Internet, and they're sharing the scans with local records offices to make them as widely available as possible.'

Hope thought for a moment. 'What happens…afterwards?'

'After they're scanned? They'll give them back to you, I suppose.'

'What?' Her eyes widened. 'No, that's not going to work for me, Theo. I *told* you, when you asked whether I was regretting giving Willow the lamp, that if I can find a good home for something, I'm never going to allow it back in the house.'

Theo had reckoned that might be a step too far with her father's newspapers. 'They're in touch with several different physical archives, and they'll find a home for things.'

'Newspapers? Photographs?'

'Photographs?'

She puffed out a breath. 'There are a couple of boxes of old photographic plates that Dad got from a shop that was closing down. Views of old Hastings, that kind of thing.'

'I don't know. We could take a look at their website.'

Hope got up from her chair, and Theo resisted the impulse to help her. He always received the same impatient wave of her hand when he tried that, and had to admit that helping her was often a matter of his own pleasure in feeling her close. She fetched her tablet from its place under the TV, and tapped the screen, handing it to him before sitting down on the sofa next to him. Theo called up the website and felt Hope lean against his arm as she craned to see over his shoulder.

'It says…yeah, they can scan photographs and any negatives or photographic plates. Ah, and see here. They credit anyone who's given them anything.'

'Let me see…' Hope grabbed the tablet from him, navigating to the credits page. 'That's really nice. Do you think they'd put my dad's name on there?'

'I'd imagine they'll put any name you like. They have an open day at one of the libraries in Eastbourne every Sunday, where people can go and talk to someone about the project. You could ask them yourself.'

'Yes, that's a good idea. I'll go…' Hope frowned down at the boot on her leg. 'When I can drive over there.'

Too much time to think about things generally meant that Hope sank back into the despair of looking at the whole task and finding it too much to contemplate. Picking off one job at a time gave her a boost of success. 'We could go tomorrow. The estate agent I saw last week gave me a list of different local areas, and said I should rate them in order of preference. Since I don't know any of them it's difficult, so I thought I might have a tour round and see what they're like.'

'Sounds good. You obviously like this one a lot better than the last two you went to see.'

'Yeah, I do. She hasn't suggested any underhand ways of knocking the asking price down yet, which is a definite point in her favour. I might even marry her—that would knock two items off my to-do list.' Theo was joking, but he couldn't help liking the way Hope shot him a disapproving look when he mentioned marriage. Lately it had been her smile that had welcomed him home in the dream-like visions of the life he wanted.

'You're not taking this too seriously, are you, Theo?'

'I'm taking the job and somewhere to live seriously. Maybe I'm a little too set in my ways to consider dating as something that needs to be project-managed.'

'Have you been texting Willow again?' Hope grinned.

'Yeah. She sent me a questionnaire she found, and I only got four out of thirty. I'm clearly not great partner material.'

The way Hope looked him up and down made his finger-tips tingle. There was something about the coolly assessing look of an intelligent, beautiful woman that was a real turn-on.

'I don't know. You're good-looking. Great sense of humour. Kind.' A trace of mischief showed in her smile. '*Very* charming.'

'Thank you. You make me sound far nicer than I actually am.'

'No, you're far nicer than you think.'

Theo sighed. 'What about you, then? Any plans?'

Her lovely eyes focussed suddenly on his face. 'Tick-tock, Theo.'

He shook his head. 'What does that mean? You're thirty-nine. You still have time for a family, if that's what you want.'

'It's not that simple.' She turned her gaze onto him. 'You've had relationships in the last eighteen years?'

'You know I have. Not so much after Carrie left, but that was because I wanted to provide a stable home environment for Willow. Even if she did have other ideas, and developed a habit of playing matchmaker.' Then it hit him. Hope had always seemed so comfortable in her skin, so at home with being an attractive woman. She was capable of flirting mercilessly with him and he'd assumed…

'It's been different for me. I dated a bit while I was doing my foundation training, but even then I didn't have the time for relationships to get too serious, and when I moved in with Mum that was an end to that side of things.'

Theo swallowed hard. 'You mean…?'

'Theo!' She dug her fingers into his ribs and he jumped. 'I know what sex is, and I've been there and tried it. More than once. I just never had those years when I was free to explore how I wanted to live my life. I've got the opportunity to do that now, in lots of different ways. Maybe I'll take a year's sabbatical from work and go travelling. Maybe I won't, but I have the opportunity to make those decisions now.'

Theo frowned. He should have seen it, but he'd been too busy thinking about himself. How Hope was the woman he'd been looking for all of these years. He'd turned his back on the obvious truth—that she'd never been in any position to look.

'So you're planning on making a few mistakes, are you?' He *really* didn't like that idea. Theo didn't care if he made a fool of himself by betraying his feelings, he'd put up a fight to keep her from hurt.

'I've been in general practice and looking after my mum for most of the last eighteen years, and both of those things teach you a fair bit about human nature. So no, mistakes definitely aren't on my bucket list. But you've had the opportunity to explore and try things out. Can't you see that's what I need?'

He could see it. And maybe *he* needed to do a bit of growing up if he thought that their differences were just a matter of circumstance—Hope had the emotional maturity to know that it was more than that, and she understood that it might be too late for her to have a family before she got to the point of wanting to settle down.

'You're a very smart cookie.'

She chuckled. 'I'm just facing the facts.'

Putting his arm around her shoulders seemed suddenly like crossing a line that had just been drawn between them. Hope saw his hesitancy and bumped her shoulder against his, smiling. So Theo threw caution to the winds and did it anyway.

'Are we okay?' Hope's question reminded him that she must know there was a little more than 'just friends' to their relationship. Even if wanting more would never allow them to lead the lives they wanted.

'We're always okay, aren't we?'

Every step with Theo was a risk. Every secret, each admission. But Hope had to accept that he was the one who got away, and that they were too different now to be anything other than fond friends. That reward made her bold enough—or maybe foolish enough—to take any risk. And each time he'd come through for her. That was what friendship was all about, wasn't it?

'I have a plan forming.'

He chuckled. 'Go on, then. Give it some room to breathe.'

'The table that I brought down from the loft...would it have done for Willow's room, beside her bed?'

Theo thought for a moment. 'Yeah, it would have done very well. You want me to see if I can put it back together?'

She couldn't help rolling her eyes. 'Theo, I'm quite capable of noticing that something's broken, and that one's marked for recycling. But there are two more in the loft, along with some other bits and pieces. Picture frames, and so on...'

'No, Hope. You are *not* going back up into the loft. If I have to kidnap you and lock you in my flat until Monday morning, then I will.'

'Goes without saying. I was actually thinking that you might go up there. I'll just stand at the bottom of the ladder and shout a few helpful suggestions.'

He nodded. 'Okay. I can get behind that as a plan.'

Having him follow her up the stairs, there in case she lost her balance, gave her time to think. And waiting on the landing listening to him moving things around in the loft gave her even more time. Then he appeared in the opening at the top of the steps, and his smile told her that this new foray into her family's secrets hadn't been a mistake.

'Do people *really* collect this much furniture?'

'We did. Dad and Mum married a little late in life, and so they both had their own places already. This house used to belong to an old lady who'd died, and a load of furniture came with it. Then there were the things that they bought together.'

He nodded. 'That accounts for it. You have some nice things up here.'

'Dad always used to say that they'd come in handy some time. They just never did.' Hope frowned, feeling a tug of regret.

'He was right. I found the tables and one of them will be perfect for Willow's room. It just needs to be cleaned up a bit.'

That made her feel a great deal better. 'Now it's just a matter of finding somewhere for all the rest of it.'

'One thing at a time. You don't need to do everything at once, you just need to make a little progress in the direction you want to go.'

'Stop being so wise, Theo, and get on with it. There are some picture frames over to the left, above the front bedroom, I think.'

Theo brought the table down from the loft, along with a box of picture frames, which was a great deal larger than she remembered it. He took everything down to the kitchen to be cleaned up and while Hope was looking under the sink for a tin of wax polish, he found treasure.

'Hope. You *have* to keep these.'

'I thought the whole idea was *not* keeping things…' She turned and caught sight of the partially unwrapped frames. 'Oh! I think I remember them.'

'You do?'

'Yes, my grandad had something like this in his sitting room. I think he might have made them himself. He was a carpenter.'

Theo laid the frames carefully on the kitchen table, and left Hope to tear at the wrappings. Neither frame was damaged, and they looked like the ones she remembered. She studied them carefully and found what she was looking for.

'See, in the corner here. Those are his initials: *AA*.'

'And this one?' Theo indicated a pair of initials on the other frame. *MA*.

'That's my grandmother. Albert and Margaret. And look, what's this underneath?'

Theo went to the sink to fetch a damp cloth, and handed it to her. Hope carefully cleaned away the accumulation of debris under the initials. 'It says…looks like a nineteen…and then

"October 1932". Theo, I think that's when they got married. Do you think he made them for her, as a wedding present?'

'Can you check?' Theo's face reflected the same excitement of discovery that she felt.

'There's a photograph album in the sitting room. In the glass-fronted cabinet...'

'I'll go and fetch it. See if you can clean the frame up a bit more.'

It took half an hour to find the photograph and reveal the lettering on both frames. But when they had, everything became clear. The date on the back of her grandparents' wedding-day photograph matched the one carved onto the frame. And then Theo looked again at the photograph.

'Look, isn't that these frames on the wall behind them?'

Hope had looked at the photograph hundreds of times before, but that detail had been hiding in plain sight. 'Yes, I think it is. I'm so glad we've found these, Theo. It's not all about throwing things away, is it?'

He grinned. 'No, it's about taking ownership of the things that mean something to you. Thinking about it, that might be the next thing on my to-do list as well. Finding a place that means something to me and taking ownership of it...'

CHAPTER EIGHT

THE LAST COUPLE of weeks hadn't been easy. They'd both been on edge, unsure of the changes they were making, and that had caused a few arguments, when either Theo pushed a little too hard, or Hope did. But her ankle was feeling much stronger now, and she could walk around indoors without crutches, although she still needed one if she was on her feet too much. The black bruises on her back and side were fading, and she'd be able to drive her own car soon, instead of relying on lifts and taxis.

And Theo had stuck with her. After speaking to the woman in charge of the scanning project, in Eastbourne, Hope had decided that this was where she wanted her dad's newspapers to go. It had been a difficult process, but Theo had been patient, taking scans of all the articles she wanted to keep, before she folded each paper back into the box. And today, they'd be delivering the boxes. Hope wasn't entirely sure how she'd feel when it got to the moment of handing them over, but she knew for sure that it was what she wanted to do.

Theo tapped on the kitchen door at eight in the morning. The boxes of newspapers and photographic plates were still upstairs, waiting for him to carry them down to his car.

'Hey.' He sat down at the kitchen table with her. 'How do you feel? I could do with a coffee before we get started.'

That was nice of him. Hope could do with a moment, too. 'Toast?'

'Yes please, if you're making some.' He reached into his pocket as his phone rang, and Hope got up from the table to make the toast.

'Willow. Willow, stop for a moment and take a breath. Where are you now? Okay, that's good. Do you have someone with you? Let me speak to them.'

That didn't sound good. Hope turned, and the look in Theo's eyes told her that there was definitely something wrong.

'Hi, Phoebe. Thanks so much for looking after Willow. I'll be there in an hour. Would you be able to stay? Thank you. If she seems drowsy...'

Someone spoke at the other end of the line and Theo smiled suddenly. 'That's great, then you know what to look for. Call me if you're at all worried about her... Yes, thanks.'

The phone was obviously passed back to Willow, and Theo told his daughter that he loved her, and he'd be there soon. Then he looked up at Hope.

'I'm so sorry. It's Willow, it sounds as if someone spiked her drink last night. A couple of her friends went home with her, but she's pretty shaken up. One of the girls she lives with, Phoebe, is a medical student and she seems to have everything under control, but I have to go...'

'Yes, of course.' Hope wondered whether she was overstepping their boundaries, but at the moment she didn't much care. 'I'll come with you.'

Theo hesitated. 'I'd love you to, but I think this is going to take a while.'

'Does she need to be examined by a doctor? She needs you to be her father, right now.'

Theo stared at her. 'Do you think...?'

'I don't think anything at the moment. From what you say,

it sounds as if her friends were looking out for her and she hasn't been assaulted. But whatever's happened, Willow may want to talk to someone and I'm really sorry to have to say it, but that someone might not be you.'

He thought for a moment. 'You're right. I'd be so grateful, Hope. If someone has to examine her I'd rather it was you.'

'Don't stand around being grateful, go and get my doctor's bag. It's in the cupboard underneath the stairs. And bring one of my crutches—they're in the hall as well. You've got Phoebe's number?'

'Yes, she's texting it to me.' Theo was already on his way out of the kitchen, and Hope picked up his phone, copying the number on the text that had just arrived into her own phone.

She collected her bag, and Theo brought her jacket through from the hall. Hope was wondering whether she might need Theo to take a few breaths before he got into the car, but he was suddenly icy cool. She'd seen that before, Theo was taking a step back from his emotions, and concentrating on what needed to be done.

As they neared Brighton, Hope called Phoebe, introducing herself and asking for more details about what had happened. Theo turned into the car park for a small group of purpose-built houses, switched off the engine and leaned back in his seat.

'Okay. Before I go in with a thousand questions, what did Phoebe say?'

'Willow's okay.' She started with the news that Theo really needed to hear. 'Apparently she went out with a group of friends last night. They all live together?'

'Yeah, that's right. The university owns these houses and they rent them out to second- and third-year groups of students.'

'They went to a bar, down by the beach, and Phoebe found

Willow in the open-air area in front of the bar. She said she was feeling really tired and wanted to go home. Phoebe said she'd go with her, it was getting late and she was tired too, and they got a taxi back here with another girl. Willow just went to her room, and they thought she was okay.'

'She wasn't...' Theo waved his hand, unable to ask the question out loud.

'Her clothes weren't torn, and she didn't say anything about being attacked. They have trackers on their phones apparently and when Phoebe checked Willow's location history, she hadn't been off the premises. She says the open-air part of the bar is pretty crowded on a Friday evening. There are always plenty of people around.'

'Okay, thanks. So how did they know anything was up?'

'Willow banged on Phoebe's door, early this morning, saying she had a splitting headache and couldn't remember anything from last night. They knew that Willow hadn't been drunk—they'd been together for most of the evening and Willow was drinking orange juice and lemonade. So they calmed her down a bit and called you.'

'We'll need to have her seen by a doctor...' Theo shook his head. 'That's us, isn't it?'

'It's me, yes. But—one more thing—Phoebe's feeling really bad about this. She told me that she should have known that something had happened—'

'No. No, you can't always tell. Even if you *are* a third-year medical student.'

Hope nodded. 'Well, I think that message might sink in a little better if it came from you.'

'Got it. Can we go in now?'

Theo had left the car keys in the ignition and hurried ahead of Hope, leaving her behind. A young black woman answered the door, exchanging a few words with Theo before standing to one side to let him into the house and then waiting for Hope to catch up.

'Hi, I'm Phoebe. You're Hope?'

'Yes. Thanks for waiting for me. Theo seems to have forgotten all about my doctor's bag. I don't suppose you could help me with it, could you?'

Phoebe smiled. 'Give me the keys, I'll go and get it for you. What did you do?'

'It's a Weber A fracture.'

'Ah, yes. I know what that is. It must be great for Willow, having two parents who are doctors.'

Hope chuckled. 'I'm not Theo's partner, I'm just a colleague. Personally, I think one doctor's bad enough. He knows far too much about what could happen in any given situation.'

'He's much calmer than *my* dad would have been.'

'Trust me, he's nowhere near calm. If Willow wants to talk to me alone, then I'm relying on you…' Hope saw Phoebe's look of uncertainty and caught her arm.

'Listen, Phoebe, this is important. Theo knows that it's not always easy to spot when someone's drink has been spiked. And he's grateful that you all look after each other when you go out together. It sounds as if the situation that Willow was in last night had the potential for all kinds of harm to come to her, and it was your rules that kept her safe.'

Phoebe had been studying the ground between them, but when she looked up at Hope she was smiling. 'Thanks for that. Stay here, I'll go and fetch your things.'

'It's the nylon bag, in the boot. Next to the box of picture frames…'

The student houses had a kitchen and sitting room on the ground floor, with eight bedrooms on two floors above that.

Someone, Phoebe probably, had taken charge of the situation, and the group of young women huddled together at the kitchen table looked up at them as they passed but said nothing. At the top of the stairs another of the house residents, who appeared to be standing guard, scooted out of the way to let them past.

'Hey, Willow.' Phoebe's first words were for her adoptive patient, and Hope nodded her on. She was handling this in exactly the right way. 'Look who's here. It's Hope.'

Theo was sitting on the bed, a bundle of red corkscrew curls wrapped in a colourful quilt in his arms. A pale freckled face, streaked with tears, looked up at them, and Hope wondered fleetingly whether Willow would even know what she was doing here.

Willow managed a fragile smile. 'I've heard all about you.'

'I sent Willow some pictures of the lamp you gave her...' Theo added hastily, in an obvious attempt to give the impression that Willow hadn't heard *all* about her. 'I think she'd like to talk to you. Is that right, sweetheart?'

'Yes, Dad. That's what I want.' There was a hint of firmness in Willow's tone, and Hope smiled. Clearly the two of them had already worked that out between them.

'Okay, well...' Theo seemed disinclined to let Willow go, and Phoebe stepped in.

'I bet you could do with a cup of tea, Dr Lewis. Come and sit in my room. It's just next door.'

Theo still didn't move, and Hope pulled a chair from the desk on the other side of the room, sitting down opposite them. 'Theo...'

'Yeah. Right.' Theo shot her a smile and let go of his daughter. 'I'll be right here, Willow...'

'I know, Dad.'

Phoebe hustled Theo out of the room, closing the door behind them. Willow watched them go, pulling at the sleeve of her grey sweatshirt. 'He's a bit...'

Overprotective? Hope had been on the receiving end of that and it wasn't so bad. Terrified for his daughter? That just made Theo human. 'He just wants to be here, for you.'

'Yeah, I know. Dad's really good about things, on the whole.'

'I imagine so.'

That was the first question covered, and they could move on to the more difficult ones now. 'Look, Willow, you're in charge of everything that happens next. You can say whatever you want to me, and it won't go any further. That includes your dad. He knows I won't be telling him anything that you haven't specifically asked me to.'

Willow shook her head, miserably. 'That's the problem. I don't know what happened.'

'What do you remember?'

Willow's eyes filled with tears. 'Going out, being in the bar. I was feeling a bit hot and dizzy and then... I woke up, this morning. I didn't even know how I got here, until Phoebe told me. I don't know what happened to me.'

Hope reached forward, taking Willow's hand. 'Okay, honey. I imagine that's a really difficult thing to think about. If you want me to, I can find out how you are now.'

Willow nodded. 'Yes. I'm not sure I *want* to know, but I think I need to.'

'All right. There are a number of things we can do together. I can look at your clothes, and examine you for any bruises or injuries. I have a test kit in my bag and if you want we can do a urine test to find out a little bit more about any drugs that are still in your system...' Hope skimmed over the details, not wanting to make any assumptions.

'What about my blood?' Willow frowned. 'Do we have to report it to the police?'

'That's up to you, Willow. If you want to report this, then your dad and I will be with you all the way. If you don't then that's okay too. The thing is that any tests which I do are considered purely diagnostic, and not part of the chain of evidence, so they'd need to take their own blood sample.'

Willow nodded. 'I'm not sure… I don't even know if anything's happened for me to report.'

'That's fine. Why don't you think about it and tell me what you want later? But there's one thing that I do want you to know. We suspect that someone might have spiked your drink, yes?'

Willow nodded.

'Well, if they have, that's a crime—something that's been done to you without your consent. You couldn't have done anything about it, and it's not your fault.'

'I bet Dad's thinking that I could have been a bit more careful.' A tear rolled down Willow's cheek.

'No, he isn't. He knows the score on this, probably better than most people. I promise you, Willow, Theo's not going to blame you…'

Maybe that betrayed a little too much about Hope's relationship with Theo. But she believed it without question, and it was what Willow needed to know.

She nodded. 'I kind of knew that. Thanks for saying it.'

'Okay, so shall we get started? I'm not going to write anything down, but you can if you want.' Maybe that would give Willow a sense that she was in control of this.

'Yeah. I'd like to write it down.' She slid off the bed, a little more self-assured suddenly, and picked up a notepad and pen from her desk. Finding a blank page, she wrote her name at the top and two sentences underneath in capitals.

THIS HAPPENED TO ME. IT'S NOT MY FAULT.

Hope smiled. 'Good start. Shall we take a look at your clothes now?' She pointed to the jumbled pile on the floor at the end of the bed. 'Is this what you were wearing last night?'

It had been an hour and counting. Hope was obviously taking things at Willow's own pace and giving her a chance to talk, and that was just what Theo had wanted her to do. It was excruciating, though.

Phoebe had apologised for the mess in her room, which must be a reference to a couple of pencils that weren't quite straight on her desk, because Theo couldn't see anything else out of place. She'd fetched him a cup of tea, along with a sandwich that he'd been unable to even look at, and he'd remembered Hope's instruction and thanked Phoebe for looking after Willow, telling her that she'd done more than anyone could have asked.

That seemed to do the trick, and Phoebe gave him a smile. She told him about the arrangement that the girls had, if they went out together in the evening. They always came home in groups, leaving no one unaccounted for, and had alarms on their phones to alert their friends if they were in trouble.

'That's really useful.' Phoebe had showed him the tracking app on her phone. 'Do your partners mind that everyone else knows exactly where you are?'

Phoebe gave him a startled look, as if he wasn't supposed to know about overnight stays with boyfriends. 'Not if they're worth our time, they don't.'

Theo chuckled. 'Good answer.'

There was an awkward silence, when he contemplated the sandwich and decided again that he couldn't eat anything. Then Theo asked Phoebe how her course was going.

'I'm doing orthopaedics at the moment. How is Hope doing with her fracture?'

This he could handle. 'It's a Weber A fracture. She fell down the stairs. What will you be looking for on the X-rays, and what's your advice on managing the injury...?'

Finally, Hope had tapped on the door and Phoebe had ushered her in, leaving them alone to go and sit with Willow. Hope handed him a sheet of paper, and Theo recognised Willow's handwriting.

'She took notes. She's asked me to show them to you. I think it's a bit easier for her than telling you face to face.'

Theo couldn't help smiling. 'So you figured out Willow's way of making sense of things.'

'Not really. I mentioned she could if she wanted to, and she seemed to like the idea.'

Theo nodded. 'Thanks for telling her this.' He pointed to the words at the top.

'Read, Theo.'

He took a breath, and scanned through the closely written words. No tears or damage to her clothing, no bruises or contusions. No signs of assault. He got as far as the urine test and the words began to blur in front of him.

'She can't spell benzodiazepines.' His hand was shaking now, and his heart thumped with a cocktail of emotions he wasn't quite ready to name.

Hope let the comment go, taking it for what it was, a desperate attempt to normalise the situation. 'She's asked me to take a blood test and we can find out which one.'

'Did she say...?' Theo stopped himself just in time. He knew that Hope would have promised Willow confidentiality, and if he wanted to know anything he had to ask his daughter.

'She asked me to tell you that any drug that's in her system isn't self-administered. If that's what you're wondering.'

He nodded. 'Thanks.'

'And she wants to report this to the police. I told her that it was her decision and no one was going to pressure her either way, but she was quite insistent about wanting to help stop this from happening to anyone else. She's a very brave young woman, Theo. You have a lot to be proud of in her.'

'We need to call them?'

'I did that, and Willow spoke to them briefly. I insisted they send someone here. I don't want her having to go down to the station. It may be an hour or so, but Willow's okay with waiting.'

'Hope, I can't thank you enough for this.' He felt tears on his cheek and brushed them away, impatiently, getting to his feet. 'I'm sorry. I should go and see her...'

Hope was on her feet too, barring his way. 'She's trying really hard to be strong, Theo. You know your own daughter best, but can I suggest that you might need to be stronger and let her know how you feel about this?'

He nodded. Hope was right. He'd hidden his emotions from Willow when her mother had left, knowing how frightened she was. They'd worked it out, but it had taken a while and several temper tantrums from Willow before Theo had realised that what she'd most needed was for him to be honest with her.

And right now, *he* had one overwhelming need. Hope seemed to know that too, and she wound her arms around his waist. He hugged her tight, suddenly able to breathe again. It was love in its purest form, and needed no explanations or justification.

When he drew back, he could see it in her eyes. It quietened his raging heart, allowing him to think more clearly and do what he needed to do.

'There's one more thing, Theo. I imagine Willow might want to come back to Hastings with you for a few days, and I think that might be a good idea. If you both want, then you can stay with me.'

'No, it's really good of you to offer, but...' Hope didn't have people back to the house. She had her own issues in that respect.

'It's okay. You've helped me come to terms with the hoard, and if Willow can accept it then I can too. There's plenty of room downstairs. She can have the spare bedroom and you could take the sofa bed in the sitting room. It's only five minutes from the surgery so you can pop in to see her for lunch if you want, and there's the garden if she wants to sit outside. She can borrow my car if she likes. I haven't used it for four weeks now so it could do with a drive around...'

And there was the kitchen. Hope wouldn't know this, but one of Willow's coping strategies was to cook.

'If you're sure? You might find yourself presented with a three-course dinner every evening. Willow's a good cook.'

'In that case, I'm going to have to insist.'

Suddenly his brain stopped turning. Theo wanted to do something, and couldn't think what. Maybe falling at Hope's feet and telling her that he wasn't sure how he'd lived this long without her.

'Off with you.' Clearly that wasn't on Hope's mind as a possible next move. 'Go and give your daughter that hug she's waiting for...'

CHAPTER NINE

IT WAS A long day. The young woman police officer, who arrived within the hour, was sensitive and kind, but had to admit that it was unlikely that the person who'd spiked Willow's drink would ever be found.

'We'll be reviewing CCTV footage and what you've told me helps us to build up an overall picture,' the police officer told her. 'It gives us a start with identifying areas of danger and preventing this kind of thing from happening again.'

Then there was a visit to the local sexual assault referral centre. Their tests confirmed Hope's findings, and that too didn't completely set Willow's mind at rest.

'What if they...touched me?'

Hope hesitated, but Theo knew how to answer that question. 'What do we know, sweetheart? You can't always stop people from doing things to hurt you. But you can decide how you're going to deal with it.'

Perhaps he'd said that to her when her mother left. Willow smiled suddenly and nodded.

He was a rock. One that allowed itself to have a tender heart. Theo waited patiently while Willow packed some things, and then gave her some time with Phoebe and the other young women in the house. Willow was slowly beginning to emerge from the shadow of last night, taking a peek at the sunshine of today.

The spare bedroom, which had once been Hope's mother's room, was light and sunny, with a coat of new paint on the walls. Here, Hope had been able to let go of the old bedding and specialist equipment, because she'd never felt it was a part of either of their lives, just a practical necessity. She put Willow's clothes into the wardrobe and chest of drawers, and then stopped for a moment to take a breath. *This* was what all the stress of clearing the house was for. Having somewhere that might shape the future, instead of living always in the past.

Willow had seen the spices in the rack in the kitchen and smiled when Theo asked her what she fancied for dinner.

'Your special tacos, Dad.' She turned to Hope. 'You'll love them.'

Hope *had* loved them, but she wasn't going to deprive Willow of the pleasure of seeing her love them all over again. And the momentary exchanged glance with Theo sent shivers down her spine. That could be their little secret.

Willow started to yawn before they'd finished eating, and went to bed early. Theo sat with her for a while and Hope heard them talking quietly together, before he joined her in the sitting room.

'Asleep?'

Theo nodded. 'Yeah. One minute she was talking to me about this term's course project and the next she was out like a light.'

'You want a drink?' Hope had been on her feet for much of the day, and she waved her hand towards the cabinet that held glasses and bottles, a little too achy to move.

'I'll have the other half of your tonic water, if you're not going to drink it.' He indicated the open bottle next to Hope's glass.

'Help yourself. It'll only go flat if you don't.'

He nodded, fetching himself a glass, and filling it, then sitting down next to her. 'How's your leg?'

'Oh...you know.'

'Yes, I do. That's why I asked.'

'It hurts a bit. It'll be better in the morning.'

He nodded. They were filling the silence, because that contained all of Theo's hopes and fears for Willow.

'How are *you* doing?'

Theo grimaced. 'Coming to terms with the idea that I could actually tear someone limb from limb. Is that a red flag for you?'

Hope shook her head. 'Only if you actually do it. It's perfectly understandable to think it. Maybe imagine me beating them with one of my crutches?'

'Okay. There's a boundary to aim for.'

He was tapping his foot, turning his glass in his hand. Theo never hesitated when something needed doing, but when there was nothing he could do, it got to him.

'You could take those boxes over to Eastbourne tomorrow, if you need some lifting to work off your frustration. I'll stay here with Willow.'

'I might just do that. They'll be at the library?'

'Yes, they said they would when I called to say we weren't going to be turning up today. You can take them any time.'

'Tomorrow would be good, if that's okay. Thank you. For everything...' He reached for her hand, curling his fingers around hers. An echo of this morning, when intimacy had seemed so uncomplicated.

'My pleasure.' Hope readjusted the thought. 'Not really pleasure... I wouldn't have wanted to be anywhere else, though.'

He lifted her hand to his lips, planting a soft kiss on the back of her fingers. Shards of a more compelling emotion began to pierce her heart, and Hope knew that she had to let it go.

'So what's Willow's term project all about?' She gave Theo's hand a squeeze, before reluctantly drawing back.

'Something you might be interested in. It's all about art and design as a way of ordinary people telling their stories.'

'How does that work?'

'I'm not entirely sure which direction she's taking with it. But she showed me some pictures of embroidery done in the early years of last century and pointed out the centrepieces. Purple and green...'

'Suffragette colours.' Hope smiled.

'You're ahead of me. I didn't see it at first. Once you knew, though, the designs made complete sense. Like statements of intent, hiding in plain sight.'

'That *is* interesting. Like my picture frames.' Hope nodded towards the two frames that had been professionally cleaned and polished, and were hanging in pride of place on her wall.

'Yes, exactly. You should show them to her. She'd be interested. If you don't mind her taking a few photographs, and maybe including them in her written submission.'

'No, of course not. I'd rather like that.' Hope thought for a moment. 'What's with the quilt that she was hanging onto? It took me a while to get her to let it go, so that I could check her for injuries, and I see she's brought it with her.'

Theo chuckled. 'That's made from pieces of fabric she picked up when we were in Kenya. That was during her year out, before we came back to England, and I was doing my thing while Willow got involved with a scheme for digging wells in rural villages. She started coming home with fabrics she'd bought, telling me that it was her way of supporting local economies, but it was a lot more than that to her. Then she cut the lot up, and made quilts out of it, one for her and one for me.'

'You still have yours?'

'Of course. I may travel light, but I keep the things that really matter. That was the year that Willow started to branch out, and do things her own way.'

An idea started to form at the back of Hope's mind. She wasn't sure how it might work, or whether it was even something she wanted. Maybe a good night's sleep would dismiss it as impractical.

'Will you sleep?' She stifled a yawn, indicating the pile of bedding stacked on the sofa-bed on the opposite side of the room.

'I'll be out like a light. Maybe wake up once every hour, listening for her.' Theo shrugged. 'It's a while since I've done that.'

'They do say that you never stop being a dad.'

'I'm hoping not. It's one of the best things that's happened to me so far, however many ups and downs there are to it. Why don't you turn in?' He nudged her gently.

'I think I might. I'll just sort out the duvet for you…'

'I can do that. Go and get some sleep.'

That wasn't a bad idea. Before she gave in to the feeling that she was becoming a part of Theo's life, and curled up with him on the sofa bed, there to comfort him if he woke. That would definitely be stepping over the boundaries she'd set. She had to let Theo face tonight alone. Anything else would be selfish. Hope slid to the edge of the sofa, concentrating on not looking back as she made her way slowly towards the door.

Theo *had* woken during the night. He'd listened for Willow, and a couple of times stood quietly behind her open door, listening to the sound of her breathing. Somehow he'd managed to stop himself from moving towards the door of Hope's bedroom. If she'd left it open, then he wasn't sure whether he'd be able to resist the temptation to wake her, just to spend a few moments of a lonely night with her.

But Hope was at a crossroads in her life. She had a chance to tackle some of the regrets that haunted her and Theo's part in it all was to accept that at some point he'd have to stand his ground, smiling as he waved her off to the new adventures that she could only experience alone.

But he could make the most of a new day. By the time Hope appeared in the kitchen, up and dressed, and then Willow, still wearing her pyjamas, he had several breakfast choices ready and waiting. Hope tucked into eggs and bacon, with toast, and Theo tried not to notice whether Willow was making inroads into the muesli and yoghurt she was toying with.

Hope waited until they'd all reached their second cup of coffee, and then swung into organisation mode. 'I'd love to hear a bit more about this project that your dad's been telling me about, Willow. It's a nice day—we could go and sit in the garden?'

Willow grinned. Hope had unerringly identified the thing that was keeping her going at the moment, and Theo felt the muscles that had obstinately refused to relax overnight begin to loosen.

'I haven't decided what to call it yet. I'm thinking *Ordinary Histories*.'

'Sounds fascinating. Are you still up for taking my little piece of ordinary history over to Eastbourne, Theo?'

'What's that?' Willow asked.

'It's not something that people have made for themselves,' Hope explained. 'Old newspapers, for a local history archive.'

'Oh. Yeah, I'm more interested in more personal voices. Expressed by making things,' Willow agreed, and the prospect of having to sort through ten boxes of newspapers a second time receded. Theo was happy to miss out on that. The first time had been difficult enough for Hope.

'I could. Unless there's something I can do here?'

Hope's raised eyebrow and Willow's pained expression told him there wasn't. 'Dad, you know you're no good at sitting around when you could be doing something useful.'

The most useful thing that he could do at the moment was something that made his daughter feel better. But Hope had that covered for the next few hours at least, and Theo couldn't deny that inactivity wasn't going to make *him* feel any better.

'You're sure?'

'Stop fussing, Dad.'

'Yes. Stop fussing, Theo.'

He chuckled. Theo knew his limitations, and taking both Willow *and* Hope on when they'd both decided on something was obviously unwise. 'Okay. You want me to get something for dinner, on the way back?'

Hope nodded, and Willow shot her a querying look. 'Would you mind if I cooked?'

'Feel free to cook as much as you like. The kitchen's all yours whenever you want it.' Hope grinned at her.

'Thanks. I'll give you a call, Dad, and tell you what to get...'

The trip over to Eastbourne had taken a bit longer than expected because Theo had stayed to help catalogue everything, knowing that Hope would appreciate a copy of the list. Then Willow had called, with her shopping list, and he'd had to visit several shops to get everything. Clearly she had a Kenyan curry in mind for a late lunch, this afternoon.

He knew that Hope would look after Willow, but still his heart began to beat a little faster as he parked at the front of the house and made his way round to the kitchen door. There was a rug, spread out on the grass in the back garden, with no one sitting on it. And in the kitchen, some of Willow's books and coursework were on the table, but no one was there, either. He dumped the shopping bags, wondering if Hope and Willow had decided to pop out.

'Anyone here?' he called, and heard the thump of sudden activity above his head.

'Up here...' Hope's voice drifted down the stairs.

Hope never let anyone upstairs—at least, only him. Theo climbed the stairs, reminding himself that he didn't begrudge Willow this gesture of trust.

He found them in the front bedroom. A space had been cleared around an old-fashioned, heavy wardrobe, and the contents had been sorted into piles on the floor. Willow had clearly been doing the fetching and carrying, while Hope sat in one of the two single seats contained in the S-shaped frame of a Victorian conversation seat.

'Hi, Dad.' Maybe Willow had worked out that this was his and Hope's secret place, because the look on her face was identical to the one that had greeted him when she was a teenager and he'd discovered her doing something she shouldn't.

'We've been having a good time, while you've been gone. I asked Willow to come and have a look at some of my mother's old dresses. She says she can make something for me, from all this.' Hope's firm tone indicated that if there was any blame attached to the enterprise, then it lay firmly with her.

'I suppose as long as you think this is having a good time...' Theo teased, and Willow rolled her eyes at him.

'Dad!' She grinned in Hope's direction. 'He doesn't understand about clothes.'

Fair comment. These things meant something to Hope, and Willow loved old styles and fabrics as well. It was probably best to move on, and get the full story from Hope later.

'I got all the shopping you wanted. I'll help Hope clear up here if you want to get started.'

Willow flung her arms around his neck suddenly, kissing his cheek. 'Thanks, Dad. Can we talk, later?'

'I'd really like that.' He gave his daughter a hug.

They heard Willow reach the bottom of the stairs, and Hope looked up at him thoughtfully. 'She's putting a brave face on it all. I told her that you were doing the same, and suggested that maybe you should talk to each other about that.'

'You never did do anything by halves, Hope.'

'You want me to?'

He shook his head. If he'd thought that Hope would give Willow anything other than good advice, he'd never have left them alone together today. If it was confronting, then so be it.

He walked over to her, sitting down in the empty half of the conversation seat. Each facing different ways, but when he leaned back they were almost face to face. It felt gorgeously intimate.

'Are you sure about this… Willow making something for you?'

'Which one of us don't you trust?' Hope's gaze met his.

'That's not an answer, I trust both of you. But you do know that when Willow makes things it almost inevitably involves scissors.'

'Yes, I know.' She was almost whispering, as if the piles of clothes might hear her.

'And you're happy with that. Willow taking a pair of scissors to your mother's dresses.' He nodded towards one of the piles. '*Your* dresses, from when you were little.'

'It'll be really good for her to have a project. Something to think about…'

Theo leaned towards her, his forearm resting on the padded rail between them. 'I appreciate the sentiment, and you're right. But I want to know how *you* feel about it.'

Hope lay her hand in the crook of his elbow. Each sensitive

nerve screamed for more, although the architecture of the seat prevented it. Theo had never thought about furniture too much before but the magnification of each look, each gesture, was a triumph of desire over the manners of a bygone age.

'I knew all of this was here, my mum's wedding dress and my dad's suit. But I realise that I've never actually looked at any of it. Mum certainly didn't in the ten years I was living here. She knew that it was all stored up here and that seemed to be enough for her. When Willow took them out of the wardrobe, my dad's suit was full of moth holes, and all of the lace on my Mum's dress was gone as well.'

A tear formed in the corner of her eye and Hope blinked it away, smiling as he reached across to brush his fingers across the back of her hand.

'It's okay. It made me see that I can't preserve anything of my parents' lives together by locking it away and letting it slowly decay. It has to change to stay alive. So I'm going to let Willow make something of it all.'

'Willow's good with her hands, and she's got a talent for fabric. I'm not sure I could live with some of the things she comes up with, but they always have something about them.' But this was a bold step for Hope. 'As long as you're really sure.'

'Really sure is a bit much to ask, Theo. Don't you dare tell Willow that, because I've just spent half an hour convincing her that it's okay. But I want to do it, because I have to make these decisions if I'm ever going to be able to walk across any of these rooms without having to weave my way around boxes.'

'Okay. So when is she going to be starting this project?' Theo wondered if he might have a word with Willow and get her to take the dresses back to Brighton, for this mystery project, so that Hope didn't have to actually witness the first cut being made.

'That's another thing. She needs a bit of help with it, and

she has a couple of friends who she says are pretty good with a sewing machine. She reckons Phoebe will be up for helping as well. I imagine they'll need a bit of space so I suggested she ask them over here. Willow said she wanted it to be a surprise, so I said I'd go somewhere next weekend and leave them to get on with it.' The slight quirk of her lips told him that Hope wasn't a hundred per cent comfortable with the idea.

'You're…?' Theo shook his head. 'Can't they go to my place?'

'I suppose they could. But I've got more room, and… I was thinking I might go away for the weekend. Or if you wanted to stay here with them, perhaps I could stay at yours? Just for the Saturday night. If you didn't mind, that is…' She took her hand from his arm, breaking the connection between them. As if she had no right to depend on their friendship.

Theo sighed. 'How about this? Your ankle's not really strong enough to drive yet, and if you stay at mine you'll be at a loose end and sitting around wondering what's happening here. I'll pick you up on the Saturday and we'll drive in whatever direction the wind's blowing. Find a hotel for the night and come back on the Sunday evening.'

Had he just asked her to go away with him for the weekend? Theo hadn't meant to, but it did sound suspiciously like it. Hope had the grace not to look quite as shocked as he felt at the idea.

'I haven't been away for the weekend in years.'

Hope had spent far too long looking out to sea and dreaming. It was time for her to start exploring a little. And Theo couldn't deny wanting to be a part of this first foray into the unknown.

'That's one good reason to go, isn't it?'

She thought for a moment, and then smiled. 'It's a really good reason to go. Let's do it, Theo.'

CHAPTER TEN

HOPE HAD BEEN waiting for something to go wrong. But things had gone smoothly at the medical centre, and there were no sudden emergencies that demanded their presence over the weekend. Willow had been slowly coming to terms with what had happened to her, and had spent the week filling a notebook with sketches and shopping for supplies, neither of which Hope enquired too closely about. Theo's car hadn't broken down, and neither of them had been struck down by a sudden, mystery illness.

She was up early, choosing a pair of wide-legged trousers that would accommodate the support boot, in case the wind was blowing in the direction of any long walks. Her favourite, colourful top made her feel ready for anything the weekend might throw at her. Theo arrived at eight o'clock, looking even more mind-numbingly gorgeous than usual, in a pair of pale chinos and an open-necked shirt.

'We're going to do this?' She walked out to his car to meet him.

'Looks like it. Are you still on board with it all?'

'Willow's already asked me this morning. It's a *yes*.'

Phoebe and two other friends arrived at eight-thirty, crammed into a car with several large boxes and a selection of bags. Hope's weekend case was already in the boot of Theo's car, and she waited as he said goodbye to Willow, giving her a hug.

'Which way is the wind blowing today?'

He grinned, jerking his thumb in a westerly direction. 'That way?'

Theo clearly had something planned. That was okay because being a doctor, or a caring daughter, generally implied that Hope was the one who applied forethought and planning to any given situation. Today there was none, and it felt deliciously adventurous.

'Sounds good.'

The morning was clean and crisp, with clear skies promising a warm day ahead of them. Theo was keeping to minor roads, avoiding the main coastal towns, and winding his way westwards through farmland and villages. They stopped for coffee in a pretty high street, parked for a while at the top of an ancient beacon to admire the view, and marvelled at wall paintings in a tiny thirteenth-century church. Today was all about the journey. Their destination would wait until they were ready.

By the early afternoon they'd reached Dorset, and Theo turned onto the motorway, grinning when he saw Hope's look of disappointment. 'We're a little behind schedule. We'll be there in half an hour.'

'So there *is* a schedule? And a *there*? I thought we might just be driving until we ran out of road.'

'And then building a boat?' He teased her. 'We only have two days. Keeping going until you run out of road is going to take a bit longer than that.'

All the same, their meandering pace had disconnected Hope from a world where time was everything and stopping to investigate whatever the horizon presented them with felt like a good thing. They left the motorway, driving down towards the coast, and Theo parked in a small car park, behind a pebble beach with a jetty running out to sea.

'I thought you said you weren't planning on running out of road?' Hope got out of the car, feeling the warm wind tug at her hair and clothes.

'We haven't. Not quite, anyway.' Theo pointed towards a string of rocky outcrops, which curved away from the beach. The larger one, right at the end, boasted a small cluster of stone clad buildings nestling amongst the trees.

'We're spending the night there?'

'We can. If you want to.' He grinned. 'Actually, I have reservations, but that doesn't sound so much like an adventure.'

'It is for me. Thank you, Theo.'

'My pleasure.' He looked at his watch. 'We have half an hour to wait. They bring a boat over every hour on the hour. There's a café over there that they recommend.' Theo nodded towards a brightly painted building a little further up the beach.

'Or there's the beach.'

He nodded. 'You want to look for fossils?' This stretch of coastline was known as the Jurassic Coast, because the steadily eroding cliffs contained thousands of fossils of creatures that once swam in the Jurassic seas.

'Only if they're within an arm's length. I'd like to just sit and watch the world go by.'

Theo decided to go in search of a cup of tea, and Hope watched as he strode along the beach. That was almost becoming a hobby, not so much because the back view was any better than the front, but because she'd never be able to look at him like that when he was walking towards her. A little forbidden pleasure went a long way, and she felt a tingle of appreciation at his broad shoulders and well-knit frame. The way he seemed so free, here, the wind tugging at his shirt and ruffling his hair.

He returned with the tea, and they sat for a while, looking out to sea. They'd come so far together since Theo had walked unexpectedly into Hope's consulting room, but it had taken this journey for Hope to be able to focus on what really mattered to her.

'Don't forget me, Theo. We're both going to be moving on, but...' Now that she'd said it, the admission that he meant more to her than just a friend seemed all too clear in her words.

He turned towards her suddenly. 'I never forgot you, Hope.'

Maybe she should leave it there. It was what she wanted to hear, even if Theo had looked away now, and was spinning stones from the beach, down towards the water line. The movement of his arm was becoming more and more forceful, until one, long throw propelled a stone into the sea.

'Stop, Theo.' Hope lay her hand on his arm. 'What's bugging you?'

He heaved a sigh. 'Did your heart ever break, Hope? For the first time.'

She nodded. Hope didn't dare say his name...

'Mine broke when you left.' Theo whispered the words so quietly she could hardly hear them over the crash of the waves.

'Mine too. When I knew I couldn't come back to you.'

They stared at each other. This was all Hope needed to hear.

'Then we both know why we shouldn't do it again.' Theo's fingers brushed her cheek and she smiled at him.

'Yes, we do.' She picked up a stone, throwing it towards the water. An incoming wave meant that at least it got a little wet when it hit the ground.

'Not bad.' Theo was weighing another stone in his hand, clearly intending that it should go further, even if it was bigger than the one that Hope had just thrown.

'What have you got there, Theo?' Hope stopped him from throwing the piece of striated grey limestone just in time. He looked at it more closely, and she saw a small, ribbed section of rock sticking out on one side. 'Is that an ammonite?'

'I think you're right. Hold on...' Theo got to his feet, jogging to the car, and came back with a small bag that contained a hammer with a chisel head and two pairs of safety glasses.

'You always keep these handy when you travel?'

'I had the advantage of knowing where we were heading. And your collection upstairs proves that you have a history of sorting through stones on the beach.' He handed her one of the pairs of safety glasses, and balanced the stone on its side, tapping it carefully with the chisel end of the hammer head.

Nothing happened. Perhaps this stone didn't want to give up whatever treasure lay at its core, and they should leave it be. Hope was about to suggest as much, when Theo found a weak point in the striations and a sharp blow opened up a split in the stone. He grinned, handing it to Hope, and she carefully prised the two pieces apart, gasping at the intricate patterns inside.

'Look, Theo, there are three of them.' One ammonite was almost an inch in diameter, and there were two other smaller ones, all perfectly preserved. 'Aren't they beautiful?'

He nodded. 'You'll take that home, won't you? It's something special.'

'Not all of it.' She handed him one half of the stone, and he shook his head.

'These belong together.'

'Half each. So our hearts don't break again.'

He smiled suddenly, closing his fingers around his half of the stone. 'Yes.'

They'd seen the boat setting off from the island, and by the time it arrived, Theo had collected their bags from the car, and they were ready and waiting on the jetty. The boat moored several feet away, and a tanned, middle-aged man strode towards them.

'Hi, I'm Tim Rutherford. Dr Lewis...' Tim shook Theo's hand vigorously. 'And Mrs Lewis?'

'Dr Ashdown,' Theo murmured and Hope wondered whether taking a step away from him might have eased the confusion. She let go of Theo's arm, deciding to climb into the boat on her own.

'Dr Ashdown. Apologies... Let me help you with your bags.' Tim bent to pick up their luggage, and saw the folding walking stick that lay across the top of Hope's weekend bag. This time he jumped to the right conclusion, grinning at her and holding out his hand to help her safely into the boat.

It was only a few minutes before they reached the island and were shown along a wooded path that led to the hotel. The reception area was light and airy, and as warm and informal as their welcome had been. Tim tapped the keyboard of a computer on the reception desk, extracting two key cards from a drawer and pressing them against a card reader.

'These are your keys. My partner Denny and I run this place, and if there's anything you need then we're here to help. There isn't a great deal to do here apart from eat and relax, but I trust you'll find both of these activities a very special pleasure.'

'I'm sure we will. It's beautiful here.' Hope looked up at Theo and he nodded, clearly pleased with his choice of destination.

They were shown through to the back of the building, and Tim opened two adjoining rooms, glancing around each of them to make sure that everything was in order. Then he indicated a bell-press by the door, which would summon a member of staff, and left them alone.

The rooms had a calm, modern-traditional feel and were decorated in muted shades of blue and cream. There were large, luxurious beds, timber furniture, and in Hope's room a large bay window made the most of the spectacular view, while Theo's had French doors that opened onto a balcony.

'This is beautiful, Theo. How ever did you find this place?'

'It was recommended by a friend I used to work with. She and her husband come here every year and unwind for a week. If I'd known it was this nice, I might have saved it until we could stay a little longer than just one night.'

This night was perfect, because it was the first one that Hope had spent away from home in a very long time. She'd wanted to remember it, and it was becoming increasingly obvious that it would be impossible to forget.

Hope loved looking out to sea. Just standing on the beach, taking a few deep breaths, always seemed to separate her from her troubles and doubts, and crossing the water to an island made them feel very far away. She could concentrate on a leisurely walk with Theo, taking his arm when the ground was a little too uneven for her. Then showering and changing, to meet him in the restaurant downstairs. They ate a superb meal, the muted sounds from the kitchen and bar drowned out by the crash of the waves outside the floor-to-ceiling windows.

It seemed so natural to go back to Theo's room together for coffee, opening the French doors and sitting on the small patio outside. The hotel was small and built for privacy, and there was no one but Hope to see Theo's smile of relaxed pleasure as he stretched his long legs out in front of him.

Sunset was a time for talking. Hope spoke about her father, how he knew so much about so many different things and how he could make anything seem full of magic. How her parents had met a little late in life, but had been made for each other.

Theo responded with tales about the places that he and Willow had been, and the highs and lows that accompanied caring for a troubled teenager.

'It can't have been easy. But she's turned into an amazing young woman.'

Theo chuckled. 'Most of that is her doing, not mine. I just provided her with bed and board and watched her grow, and I wouldn't have missed that for the world. In case you hadn't noticed, I'm in the process of letting her go now.'

'Ah. Which is why you've practically been living at my place over the last week,' Hope teased him. 'Not that you weren't entirely welcome. And deeply needed.'

'That's different. She's an adult now, and she can make her own decisions. I get to listen and say what I think, without any expectation of her actually taking my well-thought-out advice.' He waved his hand, dismissing his own input. 'I still can't help wondering what she's doing now. If she's okay...'

Hope looked at her watch. She had the answer to that. 'Drinking and dancing, probably.'

'What?' Theo's head snapped around suddenly. 'Don't tell her I asked, but do you think she's really up to that right now?'

'It's okay, Theo, she's not making the rounds of the Hastings hotspots. I had a telephone conversation with Phoebe, and asked her to bring some music along with her, and she made a few suggestions about their favourite cocktail ingredients. I thought that they might like to party a little, just the four of them, but that Willow would need a safe space to do it in.'

The lines of worry in his face softened. 'That's really thoughtful of you. If they make any mess...'

'She's twenty years old, Theo. I assume she knows how to use a vacuum cleaner and get a few stains out of the carpet. They might be in the garden, anyway. There's nothing nicer than dancing in the dark on a night like this.'

'Yeah. Now you mention it...' His lips twitched into a smile. 'Would you mind holding that thought?'

'Happy to.'

Theo got to his feet, walking through the room and out into the corridor. Hope watched him go, then allowed herself a few moments to savour the thought of dancing in the dark. She heard the door open and close behind her and turned to see Theo, holding a bottle of champagne in an ice bucket.

'May I suggest a drink and a dance?'

'You may.' Hope walked into the room, where Theo had put the ice bucket onto the credenza and was bending to take two glasses from its shelves.

'And will you accept the offer?' He seemed keen to hear her say it.

'Yes. A drink and a dance would be very nice.'

He nodded, opening the champagne and pouring it. Everything else seemed to be slipping away, borne on the soft breeze that billowed in from the sea as Theo picked up the TV remote, switching to an easy-listening music station, which filled the room with the soft tempo of dance.

His gaze didn't leave her face as he handed her one of the glasses. His free arm wound around her waist and she felt the rhythm of his body against hers. Swaying together in the half-light, letting the exquisite feeling of having him close lead the way. Hope raised her glass, tipping it against his when he did the same.

'What should we drink to?' he asked.

The tenderness in his face, maybe. Or the way her body seemed to be melting against his, a perfect fit.

'Remember the last time we kissed, Theo?'

'Vividly.'

And then he'd broken her heart. And she'd broken his. The thought gave her courage to do things differently this time. 'I regret so many chances I've missed. The one I regret the most is the chance we missed together.'

They were locked in each other's arms. She could feel every line of his body, but it was impossible to tell what Theo was thinking.

'I'd love nothing more than to spend tonight with you, Hope. But we'd be foolish to promise each other anything more.'

'Then we won't. I still want this chance, Theo.'

He nodded. 'To tonight, then. And no regrets.'

'Tonight.' The clear tone of their glasses meeting sealed the promise. Hope took a sip of her champagne, moving against him in the slowest of slow dances.

He took her empty glass from her hand, putting it with his on the credenza, and suddenly he was all hers. Strong and steady, letting her dictate the pace. When she stood on her toes, reaching up to kiss him, he responded with an unhurried passion, which might just drive her mad with longing.

'I'm not going to break, Theo.' He'd always treated her as an equal, demanding just as much from her as he demanded from himself, but he obviously felt that now was the exception to that rule.

'I might.'

'Then take me with you when you do.' Hope kissed him again, allowing her lips to linger against his until she felt him tremble. She didn't have the experience he did, but she knew all she needed to know. Theo was an honest and caring man who was never afraid to challenge her, and that was what she wanted from him now.

She kissed him again and fire started to flicker between them. They'd always talked, and now, in the soft quiet of the night, their whispered words had a physical power that drove them both on. Turning in time to the music, savouring each moment.

He caught her hand, laying it on his chest, and Hope slowly unbuttoned his shirt, allowing her fingers to explore his skin. 'You've been taking care of yourself.'

He smiled. 'Just keep the reassurances coming, eh? You're even more perfect than the day we first met.'

'Nice to know. Even if it's not quite the case...' She gasped as his gentle fingers skimmed her dress, then cupped her breast. When he pulled her close again, she could feel how much that turned him on.

'Let me hear that again.' There was an edge of demand in his tone, which sent thrills down her spine.

'You have to work for what you want, Theo.'

He smiled. Theo never turned away from a challenge and he was giving this his undivided attention. Trailing soft kisses across her cheek, searching for the most sensitive skin. One hand slid down her back, pulling her in tight. The other moved against her breast, and a sudden, urgent feeling of desire rose from the pit of her stomach.

Watching and listening, exploring. Finding out the little things that aroused him and letting Theo discover ways to arouse her was the most exquisite delight.

They were both so close to losing control. He turned her around, backing her against the wall. One hand on the fabric that covered her breast, still, his fingers finding that sweet spot of sensation. The other travelling downwards, gathering the skirts of her dress, until she felt his hand skim her thigh.

'Theo...' She gasped out his name, giving in to a rush of pleasure and longing. That wasn't enough for him, and he didn't stop until she let out a trembling sigh.

Suddenly a knock sounded at the door.

They both froze for a moment and Hope felt a tear run down her cheek. No... *Please*... Had Theo remembered to hang the

Do Not Disturb sign on the door? Hope glanced towards it and saw it dangling from the handle on the inside of the room.

Theo laid one finger across her lips, and called out, his voice sounding strangely normal. 'Not now. Thank you.'

'Dr Lewis. Sorry to disturb, but we have an emergency...'

CHAPTER ELEVEN

IT SURPRISED THEO how quickly he could come down from a feeling of intense and overwhelming pleasure. He gestured to Hope to stay where she was, out of sight of the doorway, buttoning his shirt quickly before flipping the lock to open the door.

Tim was suitably contrite over disturbing them, but when he quickly explained that the cook had had an accident with a cooking knife and was unconscious and bleeding heavily, Theo dismissed his apologies.

'You were right to let me know. I'll come straight away.'

'I will too…' Hope called to him, and when Theo looked round, she'd flipped into professional mode as quickly as he had.

'Thanks, I really appreciate it.' Tim's face remained impassive, as if it were perfectly unremarkable to find Hope in Theo's room, and Theo sent a silent thank-you for his discretion.

'Do you need to collect your ankle support?' Hope's ankle was strong enough to bear the weight of normal activity, but Theo didn't want her to slip and fall, in what sounded like an emergency situation.

'That's not a bad idea. You go, and I'll be there in a minute.'

Tim was already on his way, and Theo had to jog to catch

up with him. When he followed him through the restaurant and into the kitchen, he saw the reason for the rush.

A man, dressed in a chef's white jacket, was lying on the floor, with another man leaning over him, applying pressure to a towel folded over his leg. At a quick estimate, there was probably half a litre of blood soaking the towel and on the floor.

'Have you called an ambulance?' Theo asked Tim.

'No, I thought it was best to come and get you first.'

'That's fine—call now. Tell them exactly what you told me, and that there's a doctor in attendance but we need someone here as soon as possible.'

'Right. Will do.' Tim got his phone from his pocket, and Theo turned quickly to the other man.

'You're Denny?'

'Yep. I was right here but I couldn't stop him from pulling the knife out, and then... There was so much blood...'

'What you're doing now is exactly right. That's the knife?' Theo glanced at the bloodstained kitchen knife on the floor and it looked undamaged, so hopefully there was nothing left in the wound.

'Yes.'

'Okay, that's good.' Theo quickly checked that Denny had managed to staunch the bleeding and gave him a reassuring nod. 'Can you keep up the pressure for a minute more while I check his breathing?'

Denny was pale with shock, but he nodded. Theo reached into the medical kit that was open on the floor and pulled on a pair of gloves. He bent down to check the man's breathing and heard the characteristic sound of Hope's boot on the tiled floor, behind him.

'Oh!' Hope's steps had quickened, and Theo felt the brush of her skirt on his arm as she came to a halt next to him. She didn't interrupt, but he knew she must be making her own assessment of the situation.

'His airways are unobstructed and he seems to be breathing without any difficulty. Will you keep an eye on that and I'll help Denny.'

'Yes.' She laid her hand on his shoulder, steadying herself as she sank to the floor. Hope hadn't needed to ask whether she could touch him a few moments ago, but now her murmured 'Excuse me...' confirmed what he already knew. Their delicious intimacy might not survive this interruption.

There was no time to think about that now. Theo fetched another clean towel, laying it over the top of the one Denny was holding. He leaned in, applying pressure, and on his word Denny pulled his hands away.

'What happened?'

'He put the knife he was working with into his pocket to go and wash his hands. He slipped on something and... He got up again, and I saw the knife sticking out of his leg. Before I could stop him, he'd pulled it out and it started to bleed. He took one look at the blood and fainted.' Denny shook his head. 'If I've told him once, I've told him a hundred times about carrying knives around in his pocket.'

Denny was beginning to disconnect from the trauma of the situation, and Theo needed to keep him on track for a while longer.

'You did all the right things, Denny. Can you tell me approximately where the knife was sticking out from his leg?'

'Right here.' Denny pointed to his own leg, indicating a spot where a wound might well damage the femoral artery.

'Okay, thanks. Go and wash your hands and take a couple of deep breaths. Then come back here. We may need your help.'

Denny returned his smile. 'Right. Gotcha.'

Theo kept up the pressure on the wound and heard Tim call

out behind him. 'They're asking if we can get him across to the mainland by boat.'

'Tell them no,' Hope replied. 'It looks as if the femoral artery is damaged and he needs to be transported carefully. Is there anywhere on the island for the air ambulance to land?'

'Yes.'

'Okay, that's what we need. If there are any problems, I'll speak to them.' She glanced across at Theo and he nodded. At least nothing had got in the way of their ability to second-guess each other in an emergency situation.

The man started to stir and Hope leaned over him. 'Welcome back. You're okay, but I need you to stay still.'

'It hurts… There was blood…'

'I know.' Hope laid her hand on the side of his face, blocking his view of the pool of blood that Theo was kneeling in. 'The doctor has to press hard to stop the bleeding. What's your name?'

'Sam.' Hope had neglected to mention that she was a doctor too, and maybe Sam had come to the conclusion that she must be an angel. Her approach was always pragmatic and Theo knew she'd go with whatever got him through this.

'Hello, Sam. Now, listen to me. I know this hurts, but we really do need you to stay still.' She waited until Sam nodded his assent. 'Did you bump your head when you fell?'

'I don't know…'

'Okay. Let me just feel the back of your head… That's fine. I'm going to look at your eyes now…' Hope reached for the medical bag and tugged a penlight from the elastic insert panel at the top. She carefully completed her examination and then beckoned Denny over.

'Keep talking to him, and let me know if he becomes drowsy or non-responsive,' she instructed quietly, then turned her smile onto Sam. 'Denny's going to look after you while we see to your wound. Okay?' She squeezed Sam's hand and somehow got a smile out of him before she scooted awkwardly around to Theo's side.

'We're going to need to dress this if we can.' Theo had been watching carefully and blood was now starting to show on the surface of the clean towel. 'Can you see if you can find the pressure point?'

Hope nodded, taking dressings and tape from the medical bag in readiness and then finding a pair of scissors to cut the waistband of Sam's trousers and then down as far as she could towards the wound, so they'd both be able to see what they were doing. She carefully positioned the heel of her hand over the spot where the femoral artery ran closest to the surface, at the top of Sam's leg, warned Denny that he'd need to keep Sam still now, and used her weight to push as hard as she could. Sam groaned in pain, and Hope ignored him, leaving Denny to grip his hand tightly.

'Have I got it?'

'Yeah, think so.' Theo cautiously decreased the pressure, only now feeling the sharp throb in his arms and shoulders from the effort of staunching the flow of blood from the cut. 'Can you keep it up? I'm going to try to dress the wound.'

'Yes.'

They both knew that would be hard work for Hope, particularly as she couldn't rely on as much body weight as Theo could. There was no need to discuss that right now. Theo carefully removed the towels and, as soon as he'd satisfied himself that the bleeding was temporarily stopped, began to work as fast as he could.

The wound was small, but very deep. Theo cleaned it quickly, and then packed it, binding each layer of dressings tightly. Then he bandaged the wound, holding a clean towel ready.

'Done.'

Hope nodded, releasing her pressure on the artery slowly. Theo watched for any signs of blood and saw none. 'I think we're good. I'll maintain compression, just in case.'

'Hear that, Sam?' After their concentrated effort, there was time to reassure Sam now, and she turned to him, smiling. 'Everything's fine, we just have to wait for the ambulance...' She turned to Tim, who had ended his call to the emergency services, giving him a querying look.

'The air ambulance should be here in five minutes. I'm just going to switch the lights on in the wildflower meadow.' Tim hurried away.

'You have a helipad disguised as a wildflower meadow?' She turned to Denny, the slight twitch of her mouth telling Theo just what she was imagining. An island with hidden mechanics below ground, which would roll the meadow back to reveal a fully equipped launch pad.

'It's a flat space with some landing lights. We had to provide access to the hotel for the emergency services, but it's never been used.' Denny didn't get the joke, but Hope flashed Theo an amused look. It was her way of dispelling the tension that hung over the small group, and he felt the muscles in his jaw begin to relax a little.

'Well, it'll be useful now. They'll be able to get you to hospital in double-quick time, Sam.'

'My wife... Will you call her?' Sam asked Hope.

'Yes, of course. Denny and Tim have her number?' Denny nodded. 'We'll her know that you're safe and on your way to the hospital.'

'Tell her... Tell her not to come.' Sam was pale and clearly weakened by shock and loss of blood, but he reached for Hope. This was important to him. 'Don't tell her I fainted.'

Hope smiled, taking his hand. 'No, we won't. Although

I don't blame you for fainting. I probably would have done the same.'

'She has to stay home and look after the baby. There'll be no one to take her at this time of night.'

'I see. You have a little girl? How old?'

'Three months.'

'Ah. They're so beautiful at that age. I'm sure you'll be well enough to see her very soon, Sam.'

This wasn't just idle conversation. Hope was calming Sam, getting him ready for the flight ahead of him. If he was relaxed, maybe thinking of his wife and daughter, then he'd be able to face whatever came next.

Theo heard the low beat of a helicopter, circling and then coming in to land. Then Tim ushered the air ambulance crew into the kitchen, calling over his shoulder that several of the guests were asking what was happening, and that he'd be in Reception if anyone needed him.

The two paramedics brought blood and plasma with them, and a transfusion was set up immediately. The dressing on Sam's leg seemed to have stopped the bleeding temporarily, and the specialised gauze in the bleed control kit wasn't needed, but Theo felt more confident now that it was available, if the wound did start to bleed again.

'Going in five minutes. We can take a passenger.' One of the paramedics looked up at Hope.

'I'll go with him, thanks.' She answered immediately, turning as Theo cleared his throat softly. 'What, Theo? You're covered in blood and so is Denny.'

When he looked down, it came almost as a surprise to find that his pale chinos were dark with blood now. And Denny's shirt wasn't much better. Somehow Hope had managed to carry out a demanding medical procedure and only get two inconspicuous smudges on her dress.

'But how are you going to get back here?'

'That's no problem,' Denny interjected. 'You have your phone with you?'

'Yes, it's in my bag.' Hope gestured to her handbag, which was lying on a worktop near the door. She must have thought to grab it when she went to her room to fetch the support boot. 'Theo has the number.'

'Okay, I'll call Sam's wife and then text you my number. Call me when you're ready to leave the hospital.' Denny reached into his pocket. 'Here's some cash for a taxi. I'll bring the boat over and be waiting for you in the car park.'

'Perfect. Text me the number for Sam's wife as well so I can call her with an update...' She looked round as Sam was lifted gently onto the basket stretcher, and prepared for the journey. The ambulance crew wouldn't wait, but she made the time to shoot Theo a brilliant smile. 'Got to go. See you later, partner.'

A shaft of pure longing embedded itself deep in his heart. They *were* still partners, working together with the same synchronicity they'd always had. He watched as Denny produced a jacket with the hotel's logo printed on it, and wrapped it around Hope's shoulders. Then she was gone.

Denny broke the silence. 'Will he be all right? He has a wife and baby...'

The question that everyone needed to ask, and which no doctor could answer with one hundred per cent certainty. 'They'll be doing scans when he gets to the hospital and Hope will be able to tell us more then. But from what I saw, he has a very good chance of being up and around soon.'

'Thanks. And thank you for all you did.' Denny's face was still troubled. 'I don't think Sam would have made it without your prompt intervention.'

The minutes that Denny had been here alone, trying to save Sam and waiting desperately for help, must have seemed like hours. Hope would have gone in for a hug at this point, but Theo's style generally involved a little gentle logic.

'It's frightening how fast someone can bleed out from a wound like that. If you hadn't acted quickly and applied pressure to stop the bleeding, Sam could have died before I even got to him. You saved his life, and all of the chances he has now are there because of what you and Tim did.'

Denny nodded. 'Thanks, I really appreciate your saying that. Why don't you go and take a shower, and I'll send someone up with whatever you want from the bar? Or some tea if you prefer?'

Sitting alone, waiting for Hope, didn't appeal right now. 'Or I could give you a hand clearing up here. We may as well do it now.' He indicated his bloodstained trousers.

'Absolutely not, Theo. You're done here. I'll deal with that.' Denny dismissed the suggestion.

'To be honest, I'd welcome something to do. I'll be waiting up for Hope anyway, and she'll be at least an hour or so.' Their moments together had gone now, and Theo suspected that they wouldn't be able to recreate them. The least he could do, though, was to be there when she returned, to reaffirm their friendship. That had been lost once, and Theo prided himself on learning from his mistakes.

Denny shook his head. 'I suppose…if you absolutely must…'

He'd helped clean the kitchen floor, then showered and changed his clothes. Theo had then wandered back to the reception area, in search of something else to do, and Tim had intercepted him and insisted on ordering tea and keeping him company.

After two hours, Denny appeared, saying that Hope had called to let him know she was on her way, and he would take the boat across to the jetty and wait for her. He returned fifteen minutes later, Hope leaning on his arm as they walked, and then Tim and Denny disappeared, leaving them alone.

'You waited up.' She smiled up at him.

'Nah. Just happened to bump into you, by chance.'

'Thank you for bumping into me, then.'

Theo offered her his arm, and she took it. 'Is your leg hurting you?'

'It aches, but the boot protected it really well. I'm really glad I went. The scans showed that there was just a small nick in Sam's femoral artery, and they took him straight into surgery to repair it. I spoke to the surgeon afterwards, then called his wife, and I think I was able to put her mind at rest. She'll be going to see him first thing tomorrow, and I expect he'll be awake and recovering by then.'

'That's a good end to the evening, then.' Not the one he'd wanted, but they both understood that sudden interruptions went with the territory. Theo stopped outside the door to his room, pressing the key card against the reader. If Hope wanted to say goodnight now, then he had to let her go, but that didn't mean he couldn't suggest an alternative.

'Would you like something to drink? I've been making good use of my time while you've been gone, and have permission to use the staff drinks cupboard for tonight.'

'Nice going. So I have a choice between instant coffee and a crumpled teabag?'

Theo chuckled. 'Tim and Denny do things a lot better than that. There are at least a dozen different strengths of coffee, various different teas including herbal. Cocoa, hot chocolate...' He let the idea of hot chocolate sink in a little.

'Do you think hot chocolate would be too much?'

'No. Sit down and I'll go and get it.'

'Take your phone and get pictures of the cupboard, as well.

I may have to accidentally leave them around on Rosie's desk,' Hope called after him.

When he returned with the hot chocolate, she'd taken off her boot and propped her leg up on a couple of cushions. Her ankle looked a little swollen but she was wiggling her toes with obvious pleasure as he set the mug down beside her.

She took a sip, smiling at him. 'You haven't lost your edge, Theo.'

'Neither have you.' Theo sat down opposite her. 'We were pretty good together once upon a time.'

'You make it sound like a hundred years ago. We still are.'

Theo turned his attention to his drink for a moment. Maybe that would give him time to think, but he suspected that no amount of thinking would change the conclusion he'd already come to. The one that all of Hope's body language was telegraphing.

Now was the time to just say it. To bring closure to what might have been, and save what they actually had. 'I think... The moment for champagne is gone.'

Hope twisted her mouth in a gratifying expression of remorse. 'Yes. This sounds really crazy but... It's one thing to allow the night to carry you away, and quite another to *decide* on it.'

'It's not crazy. I feel that way too.' If they spent the night together now, that would be a thought-out commitment. Something that could be broken. 'I don't regret knowing that you wanted to, though.'

Hope smiled suddenly. 'Me neither. We never understood that about each other before.'

But even that wasn't going to change their minds. There was nothing more to say now, but they could sit together, keeping each other company as the sound of the sea drifted in through the still-open French doors. Hope didn't seem disposed to move yet, and maybe she wanted the reassurance of his company, as much as he did hers.

'So what's next on your to-do list?' Late at night, with the moon rising clear in the sky, those kinds of questions came more naturally than in the heat of the day.

Hope thought for a moment. 'I reckon... A few more weekends away. Without the stabbing part, of course.'

'Naturally.' Theo decided not to ask whether that included him. Maybe Hope wanted to go alone.

'And a party. I'd like to have a party when the house is a bit clearer.'

'Sounds good.' A party was much more likely to involve him.

'What about yours?'

Theo considered all of the things he *might* want and then settled on one concrete object that he really did want. 'I'd like a table. A big, sturdy one, that's gathered a few bumps and scratches over the years. One that I can fill, for Sunday lunch.'

Hope chuckled. 'You haven't had a table before?'

'Yeah, loads of them. And Willow and I have filled them up on plenty of occasions. I never did have a table of my own, though.'

'I get that. I like the table I have in my kitchen. I probably have a couple more upstairs you could have, but that's not the point, is it? It's got to be bought especially for you.'

'Yeah. I'll be seeing whether you'd like to help me choose it, when I have a room large enough to put it in.'

Hope smiled. 'Yes, I'll definitely do that.' She suppressed a yawn. 'I think it's time I went to bed. I'll dream of weekends and parties, and you can dream of tables.'

That didn't seem much of a trade for having Hope by his side. Curling up together, and dreaming only of her. But none of this was about things, it was about giving each other the space to grow. He got to his feet, picking up their cups and putting them onto the credenza, next to the bottle of champagne. He could carry them back down to the kitchen later.

Hope was on her feet too, the cushions back in their place, and the support boot tucked under her arm.

'Goodnight.' She smiled up at him.

'Goodnight, sweetheart. Sleep well…'

CHAPTER TWELVE

HOPE HAD WANTED to wake early on Sunday morning. Make the most of the island and take a walk, maybe. Then have a leisurely breakfast with Theo, in the open-air seating area outside the restaurant.

But going to bed alone had allowed her thoughts to wander, to places they shouldn't. How would it have been if she and Theo had fallen into his bed, together? What if they'd changed all of their plans, and by some twist of fate it had all worked out?

She knew the answer to the first question. The echoes of what they *had* done were still thrumming through her, convincing her that what they might have done would have pushed all the boundaries of marvellous. The second question was more difficult and she lay awake for some time, trying to find an answer that didn't involve catastrophe.

The first light before dawn was filtering into the room before she finally got to sleep and Hope woke late. She showered and dressed quickly, finding Theo in the very same spot she'd reckoned on having breakfast with him. He was sitting alone, an empty coffee cup in front of him, reading the Sunday paper.

'Sorry…' She sat down opposite him. 'Why didn't you wake me?'

'I've only just got up myself. I reckoned on doing the crossword over a second cup of coffee before I gave you a wake-up call.'

Or he could have knocked on her door. After last night, maybe that was a step too far. 'That's okay, then. I feel a bit better about oversleeping. You want a hand with the cross-word?'

He smiled, handing over the paper. 'I'll take wild guesses and you can write down the right answers.' He looked up at the waitress, who'd seen Hope arrive and come to take their order. 'May we have another pot of coffee, please? And...?'

'Croissants for me,' Hope added.

'Croissants for two, then. And I don't suppose you have a spare pen, do you?'

The waitress nodded, taking a pen with the name of the hotel inscribed on it from the pocket of her apron and hand-ing it to Hope. 'I heard about Sam. Thank you for all you did. He's a good guy. Great cook as well.'

'It was our pleasure.' Theo smiled up at her. 'Have you heard how he is this morning?'

'Yes, Tim said that his wife called. I don't really know the details but he's going to be fine. That's what matters, eh?'

'Yeah. It is,' Theo agreed. 'We'll be shifting for ourselves at lunchtime, I guess?'

'No, Tim and Denny worked all of the menus out with Sam, and they're stepping in.' The young woman leaned forward conspiratorially. 'They'll be fine with entrées and the first course—they often help out if we're busy. Between you and me, I'm not so sure about the desserts.'

'Good to know. Thanks.' Hope smiled at the waitress and she turned away, leaving them to the crossword.

Everything between her and Theo was just as it had been. When they'd finished the crossword, he divided the paper in half, and they sat in the sun together, swapping pages as they read them. They took a walk down to the beach that Tim had recommended yesterday, to look for fossils, but this time they found nothing. Lunch was marvellous, and when Hope took a risk on the chocolate mousse, it tasted delicious.

But something was missing. The easy friendship, the jokes and the pleasure in each other's company—they were all still there. But the frisson of excitement, wondering what was behind the warmth in Theo's eyes—that was gone. They packed their bags and exchanged hugs and handshakes with Tim and Denny before one of the other staff took them back over to the mainland. As they got into Theo's car, it was clear that the wind had changed, and was blowing them back home.

'Look at this.' Tim had handed Theo a sealed envelope as they'd left, telling him to open it later, and he'd torn it open before starting to drive.

'Oh! Two vouchers for a weekend break at the hotel. That's so kind of them.'

'Yes, it is. Have you still got Denny's number in your phone?'

'Yes, I'll call him when we get onto the road and thank him. You keep them both safe.' Hope handed the vouchers back to Theo, wondering whether Willow might like a spot of fossil hunting. The hotel was wonderful, but she'd left memories of what might have been behind her there. She wasn't sure she wanted to go back again.

Their route home was less meandering than the one they'd taken yesterday, and Theo stayed on the motorway for most of the way. Then, unexpectedly, he drove straight past her house.

'What's going on?' Hope turned in her seat, wondering if Theo had caught sight of something she hadn't.

He turned the next corner and came to a halt. 'It's ten to six.'

'That's okay, isn't it? Willow said about six.'

Theo laughed dryly. 'Yeah. When Willow says about six, she means that she'll be racing around in a complete frenzy until exactly six o'clock. Being ready for something early just isn't in her repertoire.'

'Ah. We'll wait, then, I wouldn't want to cramp her style.' Hope folded her hands in her lap, staring ahead of her. She'd forgotten all about what Willow and her friends might be getting up to this weekend, but now they were home…

'Nervous?'

'Terrified.'

Theo nodded. 'Me too. It'll be okay, though. I have a lot of confidence in Willow. She won't let you down.'

'I have a lot of confidence in her too. It's *me* I'm worried about. Suppose I find that I've promised more than I can deal with, Theo? That she's done something wonderful and I can't bear to look at it?'

Theo reached out, brushing the back of her hand with his fingertips. One of those simple gestures that they'd thought nothing of before, but this was the first time he'd touched her since… Since every caress had provoked fire.

'I have *every* confidence in you, Hope. You've taken your time and thought about what you want to do. I think you've made some great decisions about how to repurpose things in a constructive way.'

'Thanks. You make me sound almost well adjusted at times…' She grinned at him, reaching out to take his hand. Theo flinched momentarily and then smiled back, winding his fingers around hers. He felt the awkwardness too.

But they were putting it behind them, and moving on. After a laughing countdown to six o'clock, Theo turned in the road and parked his car behind Phoebe's in Hope's driveway. He followed Hope around to the back of the house, and they saw

Willow rush to the kitchen door, flinging it open. 'Dad! I said six o'clock!'

Theo gave her an amiable smile, ignoring the sounds of frenzied activity coming from somewhere at the front of the house. 'It *is* six o'clock, sweetheart.'

'Well…couldn't you be fashionably late, for once?'

Probably not. Theo needed to have a good reason to be late for anything. Hope stepped in, giving Willow a hug. 'Did you have a good weekend?'

She felt Willow's exasperation melt away as she hugged her back. 'We had a great time, thank you so much. We danced on your lawn in the dark, like wood nymphs.'

'Sounds fabulous. We'll just go and sit in the garden, until you're ready, shall we?'

Theo nodded, and Willow jumped as Phoebe burst into the kitchen. 'Hi, Dr Lewis. Hope, thank you so much, we've had a wonderful weekend.'

Willow shot Phoebe a querying glance and Phoebe nodded. Willow ushered them inside, taking Hope's hand to lead her towards the sitting room. Phoebe followed, making polite conversation with Theo.

Their friends, Jo and Alice, were standing by the fireplace. Willow turned Hope around to face the sofa and she gasped.

'Do you like it?' Willow whispered, agitatedly.

'I…' She was speechless. But she had to say *something* because everyone seemed to be holding their breath. 'It's beautiful, Willow. Give me a minute to take it all in…' Hope fanned her face, looking at the quilt that covered the sofa.

There were two central panels, each with a different appliqué picture. A couple standing in front of a church, a family at the seaside… But they were personal, something just for her. The little girl wore a blue patterned dress made from the fabric of one that Hope had worn as a child. The couple at the church were fashioned from material from her father's suit, and her mother's wedding dress.

Around the pictures, there were entwined strips of fabric from clothes that had been worn and discarded, but were now brought back to life. And the deep borders of the quilt featured patchwork squares and diamonds, arranged by colour to give a shaded, rippling effect.

'I love it. I *really* love it. How did you do all this in just two days?'

Willow beamed at her. 'I had it all planned out and I did the templates for the appliqué during the week while you were at work. Then I cut and placed everything, while Jo and Alice sewed. And Phoebe made the book—did you see that?'

'Because I'm no good with a sewing machine.' Phoebe picked up an album, hidden under the quilt, and shyly gave it to Hope. Inside were photographs of each of the items of clothing that had been used, some on hangers, and some arranged carefully on the floor, with folds at the elbows and knees that made them seem almost alive. Phoebe had used different backdrops, tiled and wooden floors, along with the white walls of the spare bedroom and the exposed brickwork in the kitchen.

'You're brilliant with a camera. This looks like a fashion shoot. And it's a lovely memento of what it all looked like before it became a quilt.'

'It's documentation, really.' Phoebe was clearly pleased with Hope's reaction.

'Way to go, Phoebe.' Theo was craning over, looking at the pictures. 'A good doctor documents everything.'

Hope laughed. 'He hasn't mentioned that before by any chance, has he?'

'Of course I have,' Theo retorted, shooting Phoebe a conspiratorial look.

Alice brought out a cake and some sparkling orange juice from the kitchen, and Hope made sure to thank everyone individually.

'You're sure it's okay if we use pictures of the quilt in our end-of-term project?' Jo asked her.

'Of course. Willow asked me and I'd be really pleased if you did. You've all put a lot of thought and work into this. You'll take the rest of the fabric as well, I hope. Willow said that you could use it.'

'If that's okay... We had an idea that we might make a quilt about healing. You know, what happened to Willow and how making the quilt helped her.' Jo grinned. 'It's kind of circular. A quilt telling the story of a quilt.'

'That's really interesting. I'd love to see it...'

The room was alive with chatter, and Hope noticed that Theo was circulating too, making sure to speak with everyone. Finally he made his way back to her.

'What do you think?'

'I think this is...just more and better than I could ever have imagined. It doesn't feel like letting go of things, it's like regaining them. It's so impressive that they did all of this in such a short time.'

Theo nodded. 'They're smart young women. Unfortunately even their organisational flair isn't going to fit four people, two sewing machines and goodness only knows how many boxes of fabric into Phoebe's car.'

'Now you mention it...' Hope frowned. 'They could leave the fabric here if they wanted, I suppose. Collect it later.'

'And you're going to be able to resist sorting through it all again?'

Hope knew what she'd find, and she was okay with the idea that the clothes had been cut into pieces. That didn't mean she actually wanted to see them in that state. 'It's a bit like having an operation. You're really happy about the results but you don't necessarily want to see the blood and gore.'

He chuckled. 'Only you, Hope. Steady as a rock when it comes to blood and gore, but liable to faint clean away over some fabric. But since that's the case, I'll take Willow and the boxes back to Brighton, and Phoebe can take Jo and Alice, along with the rest of their things.'

'No, Theo! You've already driven a long way today. Leave it here. I'll put it upstairs, lock the door and you can hide the key.'

His eyes softened suddenly. 'How else am I going to say goodbye?'

She hadn't thought about that. Waving everyone off, and then finding herself alone with Theo. Feeling the warmth of a beautiful gift, and the excitement of his smile. They'd made their decision, and it was the right thing for both of them, but that didn't mean she couldn't be tempted.

'Theo, I don't regret one moment of this weekend. But you're probably right.'

He chuckled. 'Yeah, I think I probably am. I'll go and have a word with Willow, before she decides that she, Jo and Alice are going to have to take the train back to Brighton.'

When Hope had waved them all off and closed the front door behind her, the house seemed suddenly very still and quiet. Willow and her friends had left everything clean and tidy, and there was nothing to do, apart from soaking her dress in cold water to get the spots of blood out. Then she was alone amongst the memories.

She walked into the sitting room, moving the quilt aside a little to sit down on the sofa. Each piece of it held a fragment of the past. The texture of a dress with a shirred bodice that she'd had when she was little, secured with tiny stitches and preserved. Tiny seashells and stones on the beach, made from the sequins on one of her mother's old tops, which shimmered in the light. A piece of one of her father's shirts from the eighties. Crying a little seemed okay, because they were happy memories that were no longer locked away upstairs.

But Theo…? She was so desperate to keep his friendship, it had made her ruthless in cutting away things that might spoil it. It was a hard road, and both of them were fighting to allow the other to reach a place where they could find peace with the past.

Tomorrow would be another day. The memory of what they couldn't have would fade, and Hope would begin to focus on what *was* possible. She slipped off her sandals, curling up on the sofa, under the warm comfort of the quilt.

CHAPTER THIRTEEN

SOMETHING HAD BROKEN between them. Hope seemed just the same, and Theo imagined he did too, but he knew it wasn't his imagination. The jokes between them seemed more brittle, more needy of the other's smile. Touching her was no longer a careless warmth and coffee was something he drank alone.

It would mend. It *had* to mend, because nothing else could justify the decision they'd taken. Then, suddenly, it did. On Friday afternoon, Hope walked into his consulting room without bothering to knock, put a mug of coffee down in front of him and plumped herself down in the chair on the other side of his desk.

'Are you thirsty? Or just hiding out from someone, before afternoon surgery begins?' Theo smiled at his own joke, and didn't care that Hope wrinkled her nose in reply, because her green eyes were warm and alive.

'Neither. The coffee's to give me a kick-start for the afternoon, and I've been talking to Sara Jamieson about something that might interest you.'

He could identify with the need for a kick-start. Hope had been looking tired this week, and he'd had difficulty sleeping as well.

'Okay.' He picked up the mug, taking a sip of his drink. 'What on earth...?'

'Is that mine? I used the emergency rocket-fuel capsule,

and put some sugar in it.' She tasted hers and nodded. 'Yes, this one's yours.'

Theo didn't feel a trace of embarrassment about swapping cups. They were definitely back on track and all he needed to find out now was what had prompted the rocket-fuel coffee and Hope's change of heart.

'What's up? You could have given yourself heart palpitations in your own office.'

Hope smirked at him. 'It's really not that bad. It tastes pretty strong, so you just think it's waking you up. Sara Jamieson passed me a letter that I thought you might be interested in. It's from a drugs charity...' She slid the piece of paper she was holding across his desk.

'Yeah, I've heard of them. They do a lot of good work.' Theo started to scan the letter, but Hope clearly wasn't in a mood to wait while he read it.

'They're setting up a scheme for general practices, initially in the South-East, but if it's a success they want to go countrywide. They say that GPs are often the first line of support for drugs patients, and often we don't have the support or the knowledge to be able to give them what they need. I thought of you.'

So that was what had brought about this change. He and Hope had never had any hesitation in calling each other out on things, and that was what she was doing now.

'Sara mentioned something of the sort to me, although she didn't say that there had been a letter. I told her that I thought it would be better if someone else represented the practice.'

'Yes, she told me. What were you thinking, Theo?'

It was a fair question, even if Sara Jamieson had neglected to ask it. He was well qualified to help the practice out with this.

'I was thinking exactly what I said to Sara, that I'm only

here on a temporary basis and that liaison over a valuable, ongoing project such as this is much better done by one of the permanent staff. Such as you. And…' Theo shrugged. He didn't need to tell Hope what had happened to him.

'And that you burned out.' Her tone held all of the warmth and understanding that Theo knew Hope was capable of.

'Yes. Although I didn't mention it. I'm not going back, Hope.'

She pursed her lips. 'That's not what I'm asking you to do. I've already told Sara that I want to be involved, so you wouldn't be letting anyone down if you dropped out. But this might be an opportunity for you to revisit a medical field that was a big part of your life. Gain a little perspective, and perhaps some closure, which will allow you to go forward with more certainty.'

There was no disagreeing with Hope sometimes. She knew that he was proud of the difference he'd been able to make for Amy and her family, and that Theo had begun to wonder whether he'd thrown the good things about his previous job away with the bad. 'I'm not making any commitments, but if I *did* decide to get involved…?'

'Second page of the letter. Selected practices have been invited to a one-day informal meeting, to exchange ideas and identify areas of need. We could be a part of making this work, Theo…'

He held up his hand, and Hope fell silent. 'You know you can squeeze a *yes* out of me, but I need to think about this. If I do go then I want to give it a hundred per cent.'

She nodded. 'It didn't occur to me that you wouldn't. It's not an easy decision, and it's yours to make.'

'And the meeting is…' He flipped the letter over. 'Tomorrow week?'

'Yes, the letter took a week to get here, and then Sara had

it on her desk for a few days. I'm going to get back to them straight away and say that the practice would like to be a part of this, and that I'll be attending. They need final numbers by next Wednesday, so you'll have to let me know by then if you want to be involved.'

It had taken a difference of opinion to break the ice and carry them back to where they wanted to be. But then most of their disagreements were born out of concern for each other, not about pulling in different directions.

'Okay, thanks. I'll let you know as soon as I decide.'

'Great. Do you want another gulp of my coffee before you start your afternoon surgery?'

Theo chuckled. 'Are you trying to poison me?'

'Not right now, you probably have a full list of patients for this afternoon. Maybe later...'

Theo had turned the idea over in his head, and slept on it. Hope was right, this did feel like going forward, rather than going back. He picked up his phone, writing a text to let her know what he'd decided and then deleting it. Since when had he texted Hope, when it was possible to call?

She sounded as if she'd slept in this morning, but she woke up as soon as he told her that he'd be joining her next weekend.

'That's great. You can give me a lift up there.'

He smiled. Hope would always turn things around, pretend that he was doing her a favour by coming along, when she was the one who'd done him a favour by challenging his doubts.

'I'm going over to Brighton tomorrow, to see Willow for lunch. Jo and Alice are busy but Phoebe's probably going to join us. Want to come?'

There was a pause. Maybe he'd assumed a little too much.

'Yes, that would be nice. What time?'

* * *

The room was only half full. Looking around, Hope couldn't see anyone from the other general practices in Hastings, and the staff of the South London charity who'd welcomed them here were glancing nervously at their watches.

'Do you think everyone's turned up?' she murmured quietly to Theo.

'From the number of coffee cups and pastries over there, I'd say no.' He nodded towards the refreshments table. 'Perhaps there's a hold-up somewhere on the Tube and they'll all come flooding in a bit later.'

'Hope so. I was looking at the display boards and they've done a lot of work on this…' She turned as a man of around fifty, with close-cropped grey hair, hurried up to them.

'Theo! As I live and breathe. What are you doing here?' The two men shook hands warmly.

'I could say the same. Willow and I are both based on the south coast now. She's at university and I'm working as a GP.' Theo turned to Hope. 'This is my colleague, Dr Hope Ashdown. Hope, this is Dr Ted Magnusson. He's a psychiatrist specialising in the treatment of addiction. I've been trying not to bump into him for the last fifteen years now, and he turns up in the most surprising places.'

Ted shook Hope's hand. 'Nice to meet you, and don't listen to a word that Theo says about me. Which practice are you from?'

'Arrow Lane in Hastings.' She saw Ted suppress a smile. 'Probably the worst-named medical centre since 1066.'

Ted laughed, and Theo shook his head, chuckling. 'This is your project, Ted?'

'Not really, we're looking to recruit someone to lead it, and it's not been easy to find the right person. I've been the head of Community Outreach here for a couple of years and just taken a step up to CEO, so I'm babysitting today.'

Theo nodded. 'And how's Jenny?'

'Still running rings around me, without even breaking a sweat. Actually she is breaking a little bit of a sweat at the moment. We're about to become grandparents, and she's more nervous for Jess than she was when all three of ours were born.'

'Congratulations.' Theo shot Ted a delighted smile. 'When's the baby due?'

'Yesterday. I'm rather hoping I'm not going to get a call today...' He looked quickly around the room. 'We thought we'd have more people coming. Perhaps it wasn't such a good idea to have it on a Saturday.'

'The practice couldn't have spared both of us during the week,' Hope observed, and Ted nodded.

'That's exactly what we were thinking. But GPs are under a lot of pressure and I think that a project like this sounds like just one more thing to have to take on board. It's really not. It's intended to make their lives easier.'

'I'm all for that.' Hope smiled at him. 'I've got a few questions, for the Q & A, later.'

'Marvellous. The more the merrier. I think if we can start a discussion then people will start to see the potential of the project a bit more clearly. You know your own patients best, and you have a key part to play in co-ordinating services, but sometimes it's difficult to know where to start.'

'I can identify with that. Theo's been steering me in the right direction with one of my patients recently.'

'You had access to the best. We'll be more than happy if we can reach the giddy heights of second best.' Ted laughed as Theo shook his head. 'Look, I'd better go and circulate. Catch you later...'

Theo watched Ted go, and then turned to Hope. 'Don't listen to him. Ted was my team leader when I started out, and he taught me everything I needed to know, and then a bit more for good measure. What do you say we get the ball rolling with some hard questioning? He'll appreciate something to get his teeth into...'

When everyone had been ushered to the lines of seats, for a short presentation followed by questions and discussion, Theo made a beeline for the back row. Hope followed, realising that the strategy was intended to include everyone in the to and fro of questions and answers.

Ted's presentation was met with obvious interest, and a low hum of conversation between the other delegates. But when he asked for questions, silence settled on the room.

'Ladies first...' Theo nudged her to her feet and she saw heads swinging round to follow Ted's gaze.

'I'd like to ask—you talked about a knowledge base and person-to-person advice, which doctors can access. What form do you expect those resources to take, and how could I integrate them into a busy working day?'

'Thanks. That's the crucial question. How can we add to your effectiveness, rather than simply burdening you with another layer of administrative effort?' Several people in the audience nodded their heads. 'We're very open to your comments on this one, because you know what you need better than anyone. But we envisage it working like this...'

By the time Ted had finished answering, his audience was hanging on his every word. Theo waited a moment in case anyone else wanted to ask a question and then got to his feet.

'I have a foot in both camps. I worked for many years in drug-related fields, and I'm now working as a GP.' Hope had wondered whether he was going to come clean about that, and from everyone's reaction he'd done the right thing in making his position clear. 'How are you going to reconcile the different approaches of various different drugs agencies?'

Ted's smile broadened. 'I thought you might want to know about that.' His gaze swept the audience. 'Theo and I have worked together before, and he's touching on an issue that we've both faced. Let me explain...'

The question opened out into a wide-ranging discussion, which involved several other members of the audience. Theo was enjoying this. Hope had always known he'd have something positive to give to the day, but he seemed inspired, as if the young man who wanted to change the world had just resurfaced in him. She'd encouraged him to come here, and it suddenly felt as if it was a first step towards losing him.

The Q & A session ran for longer than expected, and by the time it was finished the room was buzzing with conversation. Ted held up his hands for silence.

'Thanks, everyone, for a great session. I've learned a lot. I'm going to hand you over to my colleague Ahmed, who'll be leading the afternoon session, where we'll be listening to what you want and need from an information service. But first, there's a buffet lunch waiting next door, and please do feel free to enjoy the sunshine in our roof garden, which is through the doors on the right.'

There was a burst of applause, and Ted hurried over to Theo and Hope. 'Guys, you really got things moving. I can't thank you enough. I'm really sorry but I have to go...'

'Jess?' Theo asked.

'Yep, Jenny texted me fifteen minutes ago and they were just leaving for the hospital.'

'What are you doing still here? Give them both my love, and if you get a moment, let me know how everything goes.'

'Of course, leave your number with Ahmed and I'll text you. Thanks, Theo. And you too, Hope, it was such a pleasure—'

'Go!' Hope laughingly commanded him. 'Before anyone catches up with you to ask any more questions...'

'Good day?' Hope took his arm as they strolled together in the evening sunshine, towards the car park.

'Yeah, really good day. You were right, when you persuaded me to come.'

'How right? One hundred per cent? Two hundred...' Hope bit her tongue. Why spoil this good day?

Theo shot her a querying look. 'What do you mean?'

Suddenly she wanted to be anywhere but here. Anything but right. 'You're not done with this kind of work, are you? It still excites you.' Her words sounded more like an accusation than anything.

He didn't answer straight away. That was answer enough. 'I find that I have something to give. But it was just one day.'

'You can't deny it, Theo, you have a lot to give. People who have fresh ideas and the ability to make them work don't grow on trees.'

'Making ideas work takes time, and I have other commitments at the moment. Today was great and seeing Ted again was a real pleasure. But it's not enough to throw over everything I've worked for in the last year.'

They'd reached Theo's car now, and his phone beeped. He leaned against the driver's door, taking his phone from his pocket, his movements sharp and cross. Then all of a sudden his face was wreathed in smiles. 'Look.'

He turned the phone around, and suddenly Hope had to smile, too. A newborn baby, its little face wrinkled in an expression of pure outrage.

'Ooh! Poor little mite.' Every instinct was commanding

Hope to hold the baby in her arms and comfort it. 'Don't worry, darling. There's a beautiful world out there, waiting for you.'

Theo chuckled, turning the screen back towards him to read the accompanying text. 'It's a girl, eight pounds two ounces, and mother and baby are both well. No name yet.' His phone beeped again. 'Ah, look. I think she heard you.'

The little girl had clearly come to terms with her situation, and seemed to be dozing peacefully. Then another photograph arrived, this time of the baby with a serious, wide-eyed look on her face.

'If I know Ted at all, she already has him wrapped around her little finger.' Theo started to type a return text.

'Are you sending love? Send some from me, too. She's beautiful.'

Theo nodded. Ted's little granddaughter had done one of her first good deeds in the world, and lifted the mood between them. Hope had so wanted Theo to find his place in the world, and didn't much like herself for allowing her own feelings of rejection to get in the way.

'You want to come round to mine for something to eat?' She held out an olive branch and Theo grinned, stretching out his hand. Hope took a step towards him and he enveloped her in a one-armed hug.

'I'd love to. But I told Willow I'd give Phoebe a call tonight. Willow says she's starting in Thingy-atrics next week and she's got a few questions. She won't be around tomorrow when I go over to Brighton.'

'I know a thing or two about Thingy-atrics. You could bring your laptop over and I'll shout a few well-chosen words, while I cook something.'

'Since you're the expert, you speak to Phoebe. I'll cook.'

'We'll both speak to her. Then we can both cook.' Hope didn't know how she was going to let go of Theo, but they'd made their decisions and it was inevitable he would be moving on at some point. This friendship was far too precious to spoil, and if she was going to let him go, then she had to do it well.

CHAPTER FOURTEEN

THEO WOULDN'T HAVE blamed Hope for reacting badly to Ted's latest email. He had his own reservations about giving up the chance to see Hope every day, even if he knew that it would be coming to an end soon. Each moment of it had become precious.

But they'd already decided which promises to make to each other. Their commitment was to be friends, rather than lovers, and he'd promised that he would find a way to move forward and build a settled life. It was time to put those promises into action.

He walked into her consulting room at lunchtime on Wednesday, and she smiled up at him as he put the cardboard beaker down in front of her.

'Is that what I think it is?' She stripped off the lid and took a sip. 'Ah. That's nice. You can stay.'

In Hope's ever-changing world of favourite cafés and beverages, it seemed that caramel cream cappuccino hadn't been knocked off the top of her list yet. Theo probably spent far too much time noticing the trends, but the information could be useful at times like this.

'I've received an email. From Ted.'

She looked up at the two pieces of paper in his hand. 'Two pages? Sounds interesting.'

'He wants to set up a meeting. This is not an offer, but he's wondering if I want to explore possibilities.' He handed the job description over, and Hope focussed on it.

'Hmm. Head of Community Outreach—that's Ted's old job, isn't it?'

'Yes, they've decided to promote Ahmed and have him lead the project we were talking about on Saturday. He's got a lot of potential but not much experience, so he'll need some extra guidance.'

'And you'd be heading that up.' Hope looked up at him. 'But you said you weren't interested in going back to work with addiction-related issues full time?'

That was fair enough, he'd shut that conversation down once. 'I've thought about it, and...it's still something I really care about. In my last job, the travelling didn't give me a chance to build up a solid support framework, which is what everyone needs when they're dealing with difficult caseloads. It's something I'd want to discuss in depth, but I think this job will be different.'

Hope nodded, and then went back to the letter. 'Limited travel in the UK, not more than two days a month... Based in their London office, but after an initial settling-in period there's the possibility of working from home one or two days a week...' She looked up at him. 'Is this basically a PR job?'

Theo smiled. 'That's another thing I'd want to discuss. I don't imagine so, because Ted knows I wouldn't be interested in something like that and wouldn't even bother offering it.'

Hope nodded, smiling as she finished reading the letter. 'That's nice. The last paragraph. Ted obviously thinks a lot of you.'

'I think a lot of him. If I didn't know him and feel that he'll give the charity strong and imaginative leadership, I'm not sure how much serious consideration I would have given this letter. But as it is...'

'You're considering it.' Hope had the grace not to even hint at an I-told-you-so.

'What do you think?' If Hope asked him to stay, even if it was just on the basis of seeing where that led them, he'd write back to Ted this afternoon and tell him that he was in no position to take him up on his offer. He could find another job in Hastings, after this one came to an end.

'I think that you should at least talk to Ted about it. That can't hurt, can it?'

Somehow it did, though. Theo took a sip of his drink to conceal his dismay.

'I guess not. Ted suggested in the covering email that I go over to his place on Sunday, to meet the chairman of the board of trustees and several of the other executive committee members. Jenny will do one of her famous buffet lunches, and Jess will be there with her husband and the baby. We'll retire to his study for coffee and talk business.'

'He wants you, doesn't he? Softening you up with lunch and a baby...' Hope flashed him an amused look.

'That's very much Ted's style. But yes. I've got to admit that the baby's his secret weapon. Only Sunday may be a problem...'

'Because that's your day for lunch with Willow.' Hope had a habit of seeing straight through him. 'Why don't I ask her over to mine? And Phoebe as well, or anyone else that Willow would like to bring. It'll be nice. Bit of girl-talk.'

'Am I ready for girl-talk between you and my daughter?'

'I'd say so. I know these Sunday lunches are your way of keeping an eye on her without crowding her, and I'd be disappointed in Willow if she doesn't know it too. This can be your weekend to back off a little, and receive a full report afterwards. In writing if you desire.' Her green eyes flashed with humour.

When Hope was in this mood, the one and only thing he desired was her. But he'd asked her what she thought, and she'd told him. Going back to question her again sounded as if he hadn't believed her the first time.

'Thank you. I'll give Ted a call now, and tell him I'm interested in talking some more about this.'

'Good.' She shot him an impish smile. 'Do I get a favour in return?'

'Anything you like.'

'Careful what you let yourself in for, Theo. Mrs Perkins is coming in this afternoon, and she's struggling with the exercises the physiotherapist has given her. I wouldn't mind a second opinion, and she could probably do with a bit of encouragement from two doctors, instead of just one.'

Theo grinned. 'You underestimate yourself. But I'll be happy to see her if you think I can add anything useful.' He picked up his coffee, getting to his feet. He should listen to the advice that he would almost certainly give Mrs Perkins, and accept that Hope was right about most things.

It had been a nice day. Willow and Phoebe had turned up with home-made tiramisu, which Willow had balanced on her lap in a cool bag all the way from Brighton. They'd cooked and eaten and then gone to sit in the sun-filled lounge, where the quilt still commanded pride of place on the sofa.

Willow had hugged Hope before they left. 'Thanks for a lovely afternoon. I hope Dad didn't make you feel that you had to take over from him, while he's away at this mysterious work thing up in London.'

'I was the one who elbowed him out. I wanted to see you.' Hope shot Willow a conspiratorial look. 'Are you telling me that you feel a bit crowded?'

'No, not at all. I love that he's always there for me. I was worried that I was crowding the two of *you*. He told me about the hotel vouchers you were given and it would be nice for you to go away for a break.'

Was Willow trying to play Cupid? Hope ignored the thought. 'Have you mentioned this to him? That you'll be okay if you don't see him every weekend?'

'Not in so many words. I told him that the counselling from the university service is helping a lot and that I feel better.' Willow grimaced. 'Not completely better, but better than I did…'

'Recovering,' Hope suggested.

'Yes, that's it.'

'Your dad knows that there are things you need to do on your own, and things that he can help with. Just tell him.'

Willow thought for a moment. 'Could you tell him? He listens to you.'

Hope ignored that, too. She'd tried to conceal her feelings about what was happening over this new job of Theo's because she was the one person he really didn't need to listen to.

'He has to hear it from you as well. We'll both tell him, eh?'

'You've got a deal.' Willow grinned at her. 'See you later, then.'

'Soon, I hope.'

'Yes. Soon…'

Hope was sitting in the garden when Theo arrived, trying not to look as if she was waiting for him. He was carrying an armful of bound documents, and she didn't need to ask whether the day had gone well. Before he even got close enough for her to see the excitement in his eyes, she could tell his mood from the way he moved.

'Interesting day?'

He nodded, sinking into the empty deck chair next to hers. 'Very. How was yours?'

'It was really nice. Willow has something to tell you.'

He narrowed his eyes. 'Is she going to bail out on me next Sunday?'

'I think she's ready to. Do you mind?'

'No, I'm glad to hear it. As long as she's happy with that.'

Hope nodded. 'She seems to be. She told me she was feeling better about things, although not completely better.'

'Recovering.' Theo echoed Hope's assessment of the situation and she smiled.

'That's it. She wanted me to mention it, and I said I would but only on condition she told you herself.'

'Thanks.' Theo sighed. 'I've talked with so many young people in crisis, and I've learned to know when it's time to back off. It's so much more difficult to gauge when it's your own child.'

'I imagine so. Is it just me, or does Willow never say goodbye to anyone? Always "See you later".'

Theo chuckled. 'It's partly you. Willow doesn't say goodbye to people who mean something to her. At first it was to do with her mother leaving, but I think it's just something she says now, as a way of telling people she values them.'

'That's nice. Listen to her, Theo. She knows you'll always be there when she needs you.'

He nodded, catching her gaze. Those silent gestures had always spoken more loudly than words, and Hope was going to miss them.

'So tell me all about *your* day. You want something to drink, I have plenty of juice in the kitchen. Cold chicken and homemade tiramisu leftovers.'

'Sounds nice. I've got a lot to think about...' He tapped his finger on the pile of bound documents that he'd dumped on the grass next to his chair.

'I'm not reading all that, Theo. I'll never get to work tomorrow. Give me the edited highlights.'

He chuckled as he followed her into the kitchen, putting the documents down on the table. Hope added the leftovers from lunch and two glasses, and sat down.

'So… I'm going to assume that no one's turned anyone down yet.'

Theo shook his head. 'We talked for quite a while, and they offered me the job. I have a week to think about it, and if I say yes they'd like me to start as soon as possible. They realise that I might not be able to.'

This was all going much faster than Hope had thought. She poured herself some juice, swallowing down the lump in her throat.

'And your thoughts?'

'My initial concern was whether I wanted to go back into working in the charity sector, dealing with substance abuse. I explained exactly why I left in the first place. I thought it was important to be up front about that. The emphasis of this job is different, though—my day-to-day dealings will be with other medical professionals, along with many different kinds of agencies and employers.'

'And the part about whether you'll be using your medical skills?'

'Absolutely. Ted's very clear about that. The charity was actually founded by a group of six doctors who wanted to take an evidence-based approach to addiction issues, and fund research, as well as running clinics. The last CEO was keen to move away from that, but in promoting Ted the trustees have made a decision to return to their original remit. He's encouraging qualified staff members to spend an afternoon a week at their London clinic and take on their own cases. Doctors don't just deal with a client's substance-abuse issues, they have a holistic approach and support them in all of their medical needs if necessary. I said that was something I'd be very interested in doing.'

Hope nodded. 'Okay, I'm getting the idea that this is something you feel you can commit yourself to. I imagine you'd have to move to London.'

He twisted his mouth in an expression of regret and she looked away. Seeing London as a problem would only eat away at Hope's resolve to think about what was best for Theo.

'One of their staff is going up to Scotland for a year, to help set up a network in Glasgow. He's renting out his house in South Norwood, and Ted suggested I speak to him if I wanted to move in closer to the office. This is going to be a demanding job, and coming down here at weekends would be easier than commuting up to London every day.'

Weekends. The thought made Hope tremble. Theo would clearly be coming to see Willow, but in a whole weekend he'd have time to see her as well. She swallowed down the idea, trying to think clearly.

'Then it all comes down to whether this is what you want. Is it?'

Theo rubbed his hand across his face, seeming suddenly at a loss. 'That's the question I don't know how to answer. What do you think?'

Hope thought the same as she always had: that she didn't want to lose Theo. 'It sounds like something that you *could* commit yourself to. Only you know whether it is.'

'But…' He reached across the table, taking her hands in his. 'I don't need to take this job. If you asked me to stay, I would.'

Suddenly, nothing else mattered. All that she could see

were the new possibilities that flooded her world, leaving no room for anything else.

'This isn't fair, Theo. It's your decision and I can't make it for you.' Maybe he had a plan that he wasn't telling her about. Had Theo found a way to confound the inevitable?

If you asked me to stay, I would.

The words were tearing at her heart as Theo raised her fingers to his lips. This intimacy, never far from the surface, was so easy to fall into. So natural. Fighting it was so hard.

'Hope, I'm not asking for promises. I know you have your own life, and I have mine, and that our plans are very different. But there's something between us that just feels so right. We have unfinished business, and if you'd like me to stay until we've worked it out, then I will.'

'You mean...you and me? Together?'

'I mean that I'll keep the flat on, so that we can see as much or as little of each other as we like. Give ourselves time to see where that leads, and wherever it *does* lead then at least we'll both know that it was our decision, and we didn't allow circumstances to part us.'

'It's not even a matter of wanting different things, Theo. We have different pathways to follow if we're ever going to be the people that we need to be. I won't be the one that stops you from finding the healing you need.'

He shook his head. 'I'd never stop you either, Hope. But how can we really know that things wouldn't work out if we don't give them a try? We've both spent our lives juggling different priorities—we know how to do that, don't we?'

Theo's dark eyes were so tender. And he believed what he was saying. That she could venture out into the world, and he could find a home. That he could give up a job opportunity like this, without the sacrifice eating away at him.

That she would be able to bear his disappointment if she

couldn't give him children. That loss and regret wouldn't sour their future together, and tear them apart. Some things could be changed and compromised on. Others couldn't.

'Theo, I'm sorry. I can't see how we can be together without hurting each other. I want you to go.' She didn't want him to go at all, but she wouldn't give him hope when there was none. She couldn't give herself hope.

A shadow fell over his face. Would this be the way she'd remember him? When all she really wanted right now was to see his eyes shining with warmth and humour.

He nodded. 'Then there's no more to be said. You've always spoken your mind, Hope, and I may not like it but I do appreciate it.'

He gathered up the bundle of bound documents. Hope watched as he walked to the kitchen door, willing him to look back and tell her she was wrong, but she knew he couldn't. He pulled the door closed behind him and she heard his footsteps on the path that led around the side of the house as he walked away.

Theo was gone. She hadn't even said goodbye because she couldn't bear the finality of it. And 'See you later' was far too big a lie.

CHAPTER FIFTEEN

TIME HAD SLIPPED through her fingers, spilling at her feet like a shattered dream. Hope had arrived at work early on Monday morning, because there was no point in staying in bed if she wasn't going to sleep. She'd got through the day, promising herself that tomorrow was time enough to figure out what she might say to Theo when the time came for him to leave. Something that was both regretful but conveyed her fond hopes for the future, maybe. Empty words that couldn't express her feeling of loss.

On Tuesday she felt a little more equal to the ordeal that loomed ahead of her. A constant stream of patients in the morning gave her no time for lunch, and in the afternoon she had home visits to make. She made it back to Arrow Lane at half past six, wondering if Theo would still be there, and she'd have the opportunity to speak with him.

Sara Jamieson intercepted her at the top of the stairs, beckoning her into her consulting room, and waving her towards the seat on the other side of her desk.

'Theo's made a list of outstanding issues. I'll be passing most of them over to Anna Singh in the morning, but there are a few that need your attention.'

Wait... Time finally stood still for a moment.

'He's gone already?'

Sara looked up at her in surprise. 'Didn't he tell you?'

'Um...yes, I knew that Theo had another job offer.'

'Yes, it all worked out very well. Couldn't have been better, in fact. I spoke to Anna just last week and she told me that she was seriously considering coming back to work early, because her husband's been made redundant. When Theo came to tell me about his new job on Monday, I called Anna and she said she was keen to come back right away. Her husband's been looking around, but things are very tight in his line of work so it makes sense for him to look after the baby for the next few months, while she works. And Theo's new employers wanted him to take up his new role as soon as possible. It sounds like a really exciting opportunity, doesn't it?'

'Yes. Yes, it is.' Hope was on autopilot now, numbed by shock. 'I didn't realise it would all happen so soon.'

'I expect he means to call you. Since you were out this afternoon, when he said his goodbyes.' Sara paused, looking at Hope intently.

'Of course. Or I'll call him. I dare say we'll have lunch before he leaves.' It was surprisingly easy to smile. When you could feel nothing, it was just a movement of the lips.

'I hope he keeps in touch. Although of course we're already involved with the project run by the organisation he's joining, so we'll be seeing him again, no doubt. Anna said she'd be interested in being copied in on what you're doing there.'

'I'll go through it all with her when she's settled back in. She's welcome to attend the next session in a couple of months' time. It would be good if she's involved too.' A glimmer of feeling was tugging away at her heart, and Hope needed to cut this conversation short before it started to grow and overwhelm her. 'What's on Theo's list?'

'Ah, yes.' Sara handed over a typed sheet. 'He's up to date on everything, but there are a few outstanding test results, and he's listed those out in case they fall through any cracks.

And, of course, Amy Wheeler. I see from Theo's notes she's doing very well.'

'Yes, she seems to be. She's attending all of her therapy sessions and she and her parents are keeping up a dialogue. It's early days yet, but the last time I spoke with Theo about her, he was very optimistic.'

'Ah, good. Theo's jotted down a few things you might want to look at in the future and…well, I suppose we can always refer back to him with any concerns.'

Or maybe Anna would, if Hope could persuade her. She stood, before Sara could think of anything else she wanted to say. 'I have a few things to do before I go, so if that's everything…'

'Yes, I'd better get on myself. I have evening appointments to attend to. Thanks, Hope.' Sara smiled, pressing the intercom to summon her next patient.

Her legs felt like lead, and even walking was an effort. Hope reached the safety of her consulting room and dumped her bag down next to her desk. Tomorrow would be soon enough to take her laptop out and transfer the patient notes she'd made onto the system. Right now she had to get home before she fell to pieces.

She counted the steps, down the stairs and out to the car park. Took a couple of deep breaths, before she started her car and drove home. The back door was too far to walk and as soon as the front door closed behind her, Hope sank to the floor and finally gave way to tears.

Theo couldn't shake the guilt. The one thing he'd thought about on the drive back from Ted's home was that this job offer was going to change everything. And he couldn't take it up without asking Hope, one last time, if this was what she really wanted.

And he'd lied. To himself and then to her. He'd pretended that there was a chance they could reconcile all the different things they wanted from life. Theo had tried to clip her wings, when he should have allowed her to fly away.

But he'd asked his question and she'd given him her answer. And when everything had happened with unexpected speed, he'd left without a word. Because there was nothing he could say to Hope that would make things any better.

He'd moved from Hastings to London on the Wednesday and Thursday, then gone into the office to meet Ted for an orientation day on Friday. The weekend had been spent reading up on policy and procedures, and Theo had started work on the following Monday. For the last month he'd done little but work, eat and sometimes sleep. Trying to forget Hope and knowing that he never would.

'Two days.' Ted walked into his office, sitting down on the sofa in the corner. That was an obvious invitation for Theo to leave his desk and join him.

'Is that a challenge, or an observation?'

'Bit of both.'

Theo leaned back in his seat, smiling. Ted had a habit of opening a conversation in broad terms and allowing someone's reply to shape the direction it took.

'Don't let me stop you from getting to the point, Ted.'

'Since you're not going to talk about it, I suppose I'll have to. You've been working twelve-hour days, and had two days off in the last month. And you only took those two Sundays to see Willow.'

'I'm getting to grips with a new job, Ted. That all takes time.'

'Don't.' Ted frowned at him. 'You know what I think about that—this work is demanding and a work/life balance is everything if you're going to stay the course. You used to understand this. You've always worked hard but you made time for other things as well.'

Theo sighed. There wasn't any point in denying it, because Ted was far too canny for that. 'Yeah. You're right.'

Ted waited, and Theo resisted the impulse to explain.

'I'm right? Is that all you're going to say? Tell me something I didn't know already.'

'I'm not one of your patients, Ted.'

'No, you're not. My responsibility is much broader than that because you're my friend and you also happen to be an employee of the organisation that I head.' Ted grinned. 'For my sins.'

Theo held up his hands. 'Okay. As a friend, will you answer me one question?'

'Sure. Fire away.'

'You've been married for thirty years, and I know that Jenny has her own career and aspirations. That she doesn't always make the same life choices as you.'

'Thirty-two, actually. And yes, of course that's the case. I think that's why we've made it this far, and why we're planning on making it for another thirty-two years.'

Theo smiled. 'What do you do if things are leading you in one direction and her in another?'

Ted thought for a moment. He'd never give a glib answer when there was a more helpful one to be had.

'This is about you and Hope.'

'Is it that obvious?'

'Afraid so. I've known you for a while now, and it didn't take much expertise in body language to come to that conclusion.'

Good to know. It was actually *very* good to know that he wasn't the only person who thought that he and Hope were made for each other and that Ted had seen what Theo had considered the one, ultimate truth. The one he'd been hiding from for the last month.

'I'll rephrase, then. If Hope has one set of aspirations, and

I have another, conflicting set, how do we even think about making a relationship? It's nothing to do with my having taken this job. It runs a lot deeper than that.'

'It's a tough one. I'm not sure that there's one definitive answer but… When Jenny and I found ourselves in that situation, we both sat down and thought about what was important to us personally. Just one thing. Whatever it was we couldn't do without.'

'And that worked?'

'It did for us. Made things a great deal simpler, and we each knew what the other couldn't compromise on. Does that help?'

Maybe. Theo would have to think about it. 'Yeah. It's something to consider.'

'Anything else?'

'No. Thanks, Ted.'

Ted rolled his eyes. 'You win. Only…since I'm the boss around here I get to win sometimes as well. Not quite as often as you might think, but this is important. You're going to slow down a bit. At least take your weekends off, and going home at a reasonable time would be good too.'

'I hear you.'

'Are you going to do anything about it?' Ted clearly wasn't going to let go of this without some kind of assurance.

'Yeah. Actually, I am.'

Hope was just wondering where Willow and Phoebe had got to when she saw them walking towards the kitchen door, talking to each other intently. She opened the door, and Willow bounded forward, flinging her arms around her.

'I'm so glad to see you! You didn't mind me calling, did you?'

'Of course not.' Hope had already decided that there would be no embarrassed elephants lurking in the corner of the room.

'Your dad moving away doesn't mean we can't keep in touch, does it?'

'No, it doesn't.' Phoebe shot Willow an I-told-you-so look. 'Break-ups are always difficult when there's a child involved.'

Willow's eyebrows shot up. 'What child? You don't mean *me*, do you?'

Hope decided that shooing the elephants away was going to be more difficult than she'd thought. 'Sit down, both of you. I've made a cake.' Hope went to fetch the carrot cake she'd made, which was the latest in a series of experiments, and put it down onto the table next to the knife and plates.

Willow examined the cake carefully. 'Looks nice. You've been baking?'

Yes, actually. In the four weeks since she'd seen Theo, Hope had cried a great deal and baked. She had to admit that there was something to be said for baking, but it hadn't yet mended a broken heart.

'Cut a piece, and see what it's like on the inside. You'll have coffee?'

'Tea for me, please,' Phoebe asked, watching as Willow carefully cut a slice of cake. 'The cake looks fine in the middle.'

Willow broke off a piece. 'Tastes good, as well.'

'Help yourselves, then.' Hope brought the coffee and Phoebe's tea over to the table and sat down. 'And tell me what you've both been up to.'

'I've finished in Paediatrics, and I'm in A & E now. It's really hard, but I love it.'

Hope nodded. 'It's been a long time since I worked in A & E, but if I can help with anything give me a call. Have you decided on what you want to specialise in yet?'

'If I do well on this rotation, maybe Emergency Medicine.'

'Well, good for you. Motivation always helps. I'm sure you

will do well.' Hope's heart began to thump in her chest. Those days when she'd thought she could do anything. The ones spent with Theo. 'How about you, Willow?'

'I've just bought a car. I've been saving for a while and Dad topped it up so I could afford an electric one. This is the first time I've taken it for more than a few miles. It's outside.'

'I'd be interested to hear what you think of it. I'm considering changing mine.'

Willow nodded. 'It's great, better for the environment. And it'll be handy for going up to see Dad...' She frowned. 'Sorry.'

'What for? You are allowed to mention him, you know.' Hope could bear it. She *had* to bear it.

'I just thought... Dad didn't say anything, but frankly he's pretty transparent most of the time and we know you were dating. We didn't come to pry. We just wanted to know that you're all right. Didn't we, Phoebs?' Phoebe nodded, the two of them looking so downcast that Hope felt suddenly guilty about not telling them the truth.

'It's complicated.'

'Yes, we got that. It often is.' Phoebe summed the situation up neatly.

Hope puffed out a breath, feeling a tear roll down her cheek. That was the one thing she'd promised herself not to do, and now that it had happened almost anything seemed possible.

'Theo and I were good friends. Really good friends. Nothing happened between us...' Maybe Willow should hear that.

'Shame. Perhaps it should've. He might not look quite so lost now.' Willow grimaced.

Too much information. Or...not enough. 'Is he all right?'

'He's good. Likes the new job, although he's working really hard. He gets that break-up look in his eyes every now and then.'

Hope supposed that Willow would recognise that, since she'd seen Theo's break-up with her mother. 'Has he said anything?'

Willow shook her head. 'No, Dad and I don't go into a lot of detail about our relationships. He gets embarrassed...'

Hope suspected that it wasn't a case of embarrassment on Theo's part. 'Or maybe he trusts you?'

Phoebe nodded. 'That's a thought. If you want to see embarrassment then try talking to *my* dad about boyfriends.'

'Well, that's all there is, really. Things didn't work out and I miss him. It'll mend, for both of us.' Hope knew that it wouldn't ever mend for her, but she couldn't think of anything else to say. If life was a series of what-ifs and broken dreams, then she'd keep that to herself.

'Hmm. Platonic affair.' Hope hadn't heard the term before, but Phoebe nodded in agreement with Willow's assessment.

'You think so?'

'I had one last year. It was just like having an affair, only without the...you know.'

'Sex, Willow. You can say it.'

Willow grinned. 'Well, we thought we'd better get around to the *sex*, and... It was a bit of a disaster, really. We kissed a bit but we just weren't feeling the feels, and we ended up going to the pictures, instead.'

Right, then. Nothing like her and Theo. 'At least you had the gumption to do what you really wanted.'

'Yeah, Dad gave me that talk. It's excruciating. He gets so embarrassed. You're not like that.'

Hope had been feeling very old. As if life had passed her by, and she'd never get any of it back again. But she still had some things in common with these young women. She could still feel the feels, and still dance in the dark.

'Good to hear.' She got to her feet. It was time to move on

now, from Theo. She'd have plenty of time to think about him later. 'I've saved a few things for you. I don't know whether you can use them for your quilts or not.'

She fetched the cardboard box from the top of the fridge, putting it onto the table and laying her hand on the flaps at the top to stop Willow and Phoebe from looking inside.

'Here's the thing. If you can use any of this, then please take whatever you want. If you can't, I'm not interested in just passing my junk over to you so you have to deal with it. I can take it down to the charity shop.'

Phoebe nodded. 'Gotcha.'

Willow opened the box, tipping its contents out onto the table. 'What? Don't you want these? They're lovely.'

'It's old costume jewellery, and I don't have a clue where it came from. I'm never going to use any of it, and it doesn't have any sentimental value. Like I said, if you want it, take it, but don't feel you have to.'

Willow nodded, sorting through the collection of old brooches, rings and pendants. 'Look at this one, Phoebs. Very retro.' She held up an enamel pendant that looked as if it came from the nineteen sixties. 'Oh, and look at this. It would be great with your green top. I can use any of this for quilts. I'm getting into adding all kinds of things...'

Examining everything took a while, and by the time they'd finished there was a large pile that Willow wanted to take, and two much smaller piles, one for Phoebe and one for the charity shop. Hope had felt she needed Theo to help her move on, and she had, but this was fun as well.

'I don't suppose... You could stay for dinner if you wanted. If you're not doing anything.'

Willow and Phoebe looked at each other. 'Well...if you don't mind. You still have to try out my car, to see whether you like it.'

Suddenly Hope had everything in common with these young women. 'Stay. I insist. You want some music while we cook?'

Phoebe took out her phone. 'I've got a sixties mix. I can connect with your speakers...'

'Yes, connect away.' Phoebe would have to show her how to do that some time. It didn't look too difficult. Less than a minute later, Phoebe was dancing across to the fridge to inspect its contents.

'You know...' Willow was still sitting with Hope at the kitchen table and clearly had something on her mind. 'Did Dad ever tell you when he adopted me?'

'It was after he married your mother, wasn't it?'

'Yeah, that's when I agreed to it, and they started all the paperwork. It takes a while.'

'Okay.' Hope waited, wondering what on earth Willow wanted to say.

'When Mum left, she left all the papers behind. She'd signed her part and had it witnessed, but Dad hadn't yet. He showed me, and I thought he was going to tear it all up and send me home. But he just wanted to ask me if it was okay for him to sign them.' Willow shrugged. 'The next day we went to the solicitor and that was it. He'd adopted me.'

Tears were never too far away these days, and Hope felt them running down her cheeks. 'Theo didn't want to miss his chance.'

Willow shrugged. 'I don't know about that. I wasn't exactly the perfect child at the time. But the thing is...my dad's the most faithful person I know. He's always stuck by me.'

Hope hugged her. 'That was his privilege, Willow. I wouldn't have expected anything else from him, but thank you for telling me.'

It was something for Hope to remember, if she ever plucked

up the courage to see Theo again. Whatever happened, however that worked out, she already knew that she could rely on him to be faithful to his word.

CHAPTER SIXTEEN

THEO WAS AS nervous as a kitten. A very small kitten that had been separated from its mother. It wasn't an emotion that he was all that familiar with, and that unnerved him even more.

He was back in Hastings to finish clearing out the flat before the lease was up and…

Strike that. He was back in Hastings to see Hope. If he couldn't admit to it anyone else, and maybe not even to her, then he had to admit it to himself. Over the last week, he'd mentally prepared for every possible outcome of their meeting so it would be foolish to try to convince himself that this wasn't his purpose.

He parked in the road, outside her house, feeling that he'd probably lost driveway privileges. Kitchen door privileges as well, so he knocked at the front door. Her car was here, but there was no answer.

He was here now. He had nothing to lose, and probably nothing to gain, but he had to see her. Ask one final question—one that wasn't totally impractical this time—and hear her answer. He took the path around the house, stopping suddenly in his tracks as he saw her sitting on the patio, outside the kitchen door.

'Theo!' She almost jumped out of her skin, and he took a step back. She looked so beautiful, her worn jeans and T-shirt covered in grime, and her hair tied up in a colourful scarf. Just exquisite.

'I...um... I was in Hastings anyway...' That wouldn't do. 'I came to see you, Hope. There's something I want to say to you.'

She looked at him thoughtfully. And then suddenly she smiled. 'Then come and sit down. I won't bite you, Theo.'

Maybe she was considering poisoning him, instead. He walked over to her, sitting down opposite her at the small table. Hope was always dazzling, but after five weeks of darkness, it was almost impossible to look at her.

'What do you want to say?' She seemed composed, but her question was almost a whisper. Hope was feeling something, but keeping it to herself. Theo couldn't blame her for that.

'Before that... I want to apologise.'

Genuine surprise flashed in her eyes. 'What for?'

'For leaving. Without saying goodbye.'

'I let you go, without saying goodbye. Doesn't that make us even?'

'Not really. I asked you an impossible question. I see that now.'

She didn't answer, raising the cup of tea beside her to her lips. Theo saw her hand shake, almost spilling it before she took a sip. Hope was holding out on him, and he realised that there *was* something far more hurtful than anger or weeping. Then suddenly, a tear rolled down her cheek.

'Theo, I saw Willow last weekend.'

'You did?' He swallowed hard. 'I mean...good. I'm glad you didn't feel that you shouldn't.'

Hope took a breath. She was holding some emotion in, but Theo couldn't tell what it was. 'We're not as clever as we thought we were. She'd worked out that there was something going on between us. She came to see if I was still talking to her, and I made it quite clear to her that I was. I didn't tell her any of the details and she didn't ask.'

'Thank you. I'd hoped that Willow wouldn't be caught up in this but… I should have known you'd be kind to her.'

'Well, she was kind to me. She told me that you'd finalised her adoption after her mother left—' Theo opened his mouth to ask what else he would have done and Hope held up her hand to silence him. 'She said that you're the most faithful person she knows. I knew that already, but I just needed to be reminded of it. So tell me what you've come to say, Theo. Whatever it is, I'm listening.'

Sudden warmth filled his veins. It was as if his heart had stuttered and then restarted, and he could almost feel his mind clearing itself of all the hurt and pain. Tears started to course down Hope's cheeks, and they came almost as a relief to him. He was prepared for this, and reached into his pocket for a handkerchief.

She wiped her eyes, leaving a smear of dirt on her cheek. Theo took a breath…

'I've been talking too. In broad terms…' He didn't want to give the impression that he'd gone into detail, either. 'Ted.'

She smiled tearily. 'I expect broad terms with Ted is worth about an hour's worth of detail in anyone else's currency. Go on.'

'We want different things, Hope. All kinds of different things. But sometimes you have to look at the one, most important thing that you want. The thing you'd sacrifice everything else for. And my one, important, all-encompassing thing is you.'

She flushed, bright red. 'But…?'

'I have no doubts, and there'll be no regrets. I love you, Hope, and I want to be with you.'

She started to cry again. Anything would be better than this…

'I love you too, Theo. You're my one important thing, and

being with you would be the only adventure I ever needed. Can't you see that's why I asked you to go?'

That made no sense. And then suddenly, in a blinding flash of light, it made perfect sense. He wanted only the best for Hope, for her to fulfil her dreams. And she wanted the best for him.

'Because you thought that a job was more important to me than you are?'

She shook her head. 'We could have worked that out. But you still have the opportunity to start another family, Theo. I don't know if I can give you that.'

He could tell her that didn't matter to him. But now was the time for complete honesty, even if it might not be what Hope wanted to hear. 'I can't say that it wouldn't be a disappointment to close that door but… A family isn't just children, it's a loving partnership. You're the one, true love of my life and if it doesn't happen for you then it doesn't happen for me.'

She stared at him. 'You're sure, Theo.'

'I've never been so sure of anything. If the one thing that we both want is to be together, then everything else falls into place.'

'That sounds…' She reached for him, and his whole being trembled in anticipation of her touch. Then suddenly she pulled her hand back, as if she'd realised something. 'I'm all dirty.'

He took her in his arms, kissing her. 'So am I, now.'

They'd spent a long time, kissing out here on the patio. Each time was better than the last, more tender and more exciting. Theo really did know how to kiss a girl.

They both knew that they could wait. Hope was sure of him, and she knew that Theo was sure of her. No more rushing to grab at moments that might not come again. He laugh-ingly enquired exactly why she was so grubby, and Hope took him upstairs.

'Wow! This is an amazing room.' Theo looked around the empty front bedroom. 'You've cleared all of this? Not just put it somewhere else?'

'All of it. I decided that finishing one room would spur me on to do the others. I worked pretty hard at it.' Theo had dark rings under his eyes, and Hope realised that he'd been work-ing much too hard, as well.

'We can take a rest now.' He put his arm around her, bend-ing to kiss her. 'Both of us.'

'I've taken some holiday next week. I was going to clean up in here and give it a coat of paint. Open the shutters and let the light in. I wish it were all done now.' This would be a beautiful room to spend their first night together in.

He smiled down at her. 'I have Monday and Tuesday off work. Ted put me on notice that if I didn't take some of the days owing me, he'd suspend me.'

Hope laughed. 'He wouldn't...would he?'

'He might. I decided not to put up a fight.'

'So, that's four whole days, Theo.'

He nodded. 'I wonder...shall we see which way the wind's blowing? Since the fates seem to be on our side today?'

That would be wonderful. Too much to hope for, maybe. 'You could try. But we might be disappointed.'

There was a light in his eyes as he took his phone from his pocket and dialled. A quick conversation, mostly 'yes' and 'no' and then a 'thank you' didn't tell Hope all that much, and she waited impatiently for him to end the call.

'Well?'

'Shame...' He shot her a solemn look. 'They're booked up

this weekend, and all that Denny and Tim can offer us is one room. And a bottle of champagne.'

'Theo!' She launched herself at him in delight, flinging her arms around his neck to kiss him, and he took a step back against the wall. Now the back of his shirt was probably covered in plaster dust.

'We can stay for an extra couple of days if we want, and when we get back we'll set to work on this room. Make each other happy.'

'And if we make a baby, at the same time?' Hope asked him.

He smiled. 'Do we need any other plans? We could just take one day at a time and see what happens.'

'Yes. We'll do that.'

'Only… There's one thing I don't want to leave to chance.' He fell to one knee. That was his trouser leg all dusty now. Then Hope forgot all about that, because he'd taken something from his pocket.

'Will you marry me, Hope? It would be the honour and delight of my life if you said yes.'

It was perfect. Theo always had liked to do everything the right way, and he couldn't have made this moment any better.

'Yes, Theo. I want to marry you more than anything.'

He slipped the ring on her finger. Three diamonds glistened in the light, and she kissed him, tears in her eyes. 'It's so beautiful, Theo. And I love you so much.'

He smiled down at her. 'So you'll run away with me now?'

'I'll follow you anywhere. Only won't you need some clean clothes? I'm all for running away in comfort.'

'I have some at my old flat. The lease isn't up until next week and I only took what I needed when I first moved up to London.'

'Go. I'll be ready by the time you get back.' Hope wondered

whether her eagerness might be construed as a little unromantic. 'Am I rushing too much?'

He hushed her, kissing the finger that bore his ring. 'We have a future now, Hope. It means more than anything to me that you can't wait to get started on it.'

Waking up in the room by the sea was nice. Waking up in Theo's arms was the best thing in the world.

'Awake?' His fingers moved against her skin, and she shivered.

'You haven't been watching me sleep again, have you?' She moved against him, feeling their bodies easing together in that sweet synchronicity that seemed to govern every part of their lives.

'No, you made your views on that very clear last night. I was listening to you sleep.'

'That's worse, Theo.' She snuggled against his chest, and he kissed the top of her head.

'Did I make you happy?'

'Very happy. Several times. Did I make you happy?'

He chuckled. 'You need to ask?'

No. Hope didn't need to ask. She'd known that Theo would be an amazing lover and he was a generous one too, sharing everything with her. 'I'm going to hold you to all of those promises you made.'

'I'm counting on you to do just that.'

They both jumped as a knock sounded on the door. Then Theo chuckled. 'I'm pretty sure no one's stabbed themselves. It's half past ten, so that'll be breakfast.' He got out of bed, grinning at her as she unashamedly watched him walk across the room, to fetch his dressing gown.

He opened the door, looking outside, and Tim's voice floated into the room. 'Sorry to disturb, lovebirds.'

'Thanks, Tim,' Theo called back along the corridor, then wheeled the breakfast trolley into the room, closing the door.

He slung the dressing gown onto a chair, coming back to the bed. Hope loved the way that Theo was so comfortable in his skin, so unaware of his gorgeous nakedness. She was becoming less self-conscious of hers, because he never failed to tell her how beautiful she was.

'So what's on the agenda for today?' she asked, pouring the coffee as he slid back beneath the bed covers.

'Umm. Some romantic fossil hunting? Romantic walks around the island…' Hope's phone beeped as Theo elaborated on the list.

'Ah. First we'll have to do some romantic texting.' She scrolled through the text that Willow had just sent. 'Apparently Willow tried both our mobiles, yesterday evening, and then tried us both at home. Then she called your parents this morning, to see if you'd gone over there to see them, and your mother told her that you'd mentioned you were taking this weekend off because you were going down to Hastings…' Hope scrolled a little further. 'Where are we? What are we doing?'

'Ah. Is she all right?'

'Yes, she says she's texting me because you might fly into a panic and wonder whether she's all right. You're not panicking, are you?'

Theo shook his head. 'I'm just enquiring. Are you going to text her back?'

'What do I say? In Dorset. Having sex.'

Theo snorted with laughter. 'Not quite how I'd put it. I'd go for Romantic engagement weekend. That way she can decide for herself what we're doing.'

'She knows what we're doing, Theo. How's this for a compromise?' Hope started to type.

Having romantic engagement sex…

'She's going to call…' Theo chuckled, sipping his coffee.
'No, she isn't.' Hope sent the text, reaching for one of the warm croissants. Her phone beeped again, and Theo picked it up. 'What does she say?'

Delighted scream. Catch you both later.

Theo nodded. 'That works for me.'
'Me too. Did I just lie to your daughter? We're actually having breakfast.'
'No.' Theo put his coffee to one side, and took Hope's croissant from her hand. 'Romantic engagement sex sounds like a fine way to start the day…'

EPILOGUE

Three years later

'HOME.' THEO GOT out of the car, taking their two-year-old son, Jack, from his car seat. Next to Jack was the carrycot with their newborn baby girl, just two days old and sleeping peacefully.

'Home, Daddy!' Jack took his father's hand, craning to see his little sister as Theo walked him slowly to the front door, the carrycot in his other hand. One more view of Theo's back that Hope couldn't resist.

Willow's car drew up behind them, and she jumped from the driver's seat, sprinting across to Hope to help her out of the car.

'Thanks, I can manage.' Hope grinned at her. 'You might want to go and help your dad out.'

Willow whirled round. 'Dad! Freeze!' she called after Theo, just as he executed a deft manoeuvre that allowed him to keep hold of Jack and his little sister and open the front door, all at the same time.

'Managing,' Theo called back. 'Why don't you give Hope a hand?'

Willow rolled her eyes. 'Make up your minds, people!'

'Sorry, sweetheart.' Hope shot her an apologetic look. 'If you could bring my bag in, that would be a real help...'

The house really *was* a home, now. The first floor was full of light, instead of boxes, and housed their own bedroom along with a room each for Jack and the baby, a guest room and a good-sized office for the two days a week that Theo worked from home. Downstairs the two bedrooms had gone back to their original purpose, a dining room and a TV room. It was a place they both loved, and would always come back to, full of memories and hopes for the future.

Theo had planted several trees in the back garden, which would be tall enough for them to sit beneath in twenty years' time. And the large oak table that Theo's parents had bought them, as a wedding present, had developed a few small scuffs courtesy of their son and would no doubt gather up a few more when their daughter got a little older.

Coming back home was always special, because Theo had made sure they went away to special places too. They'd been to Japan for their honeymoon, and to Venice for Jack's first birthday. Last Christmas had been spent in Canada and they'd travelled the length and breadth of the British Isles, sometimes going with Theo for work trips, and sometimes for short holidays.

Hope had decided to give up work when Jack was born, wanting to spend as much time as she could with him until he started school. That had opened up new horizons, too, and her work with several different local organisations had led to her becoming a trustee of a medical charity for children. Speaking on their behalf had been nerve-racking at first, but Theo had supported her all the way and Hope had derived a deep satisfaction from her role in heightening awareness and raising funds. He'd encouraged Hope to write a children's storybook too, which Willow was illustrating. Theo had been right. They'd both taken the one thing that they really wanted, and everything else had followed.

Hope was chivvied upstairs and ordered to rest, and Theo

carried the baby up and put her into the crib next to the bed. Willow took charge of Jack, and Theo brought Hope a cup of tea.

'What are they doing down there?'

Theo sank down onto the bed next to her. 'They're in the garden. Willow's dancing and Jack's running.'

'Good. Next time just freeze when she tells you, eh?'

Theo leaned back onto the pillows, his hands behind his head and a besotted grin on his face. 'I had it all worked out. Jack and I practised with his stuffed giraffe.'

'You used a stuffed giraffe to stand in for our daughter?' Hope nudged her elbow into his ribs in mock horror.

'Jack insisted. Who am I to argue?'

'You're such a softie, Theo.' Hope leaned over to kiss him. 'That's why I love you so much. Have you thought any more about a name?'

'What do you think of Clara?'

'Mum's middle name?' Hope leaned over towards the crib, calling the name softly, and the baby's eyes opened suddenly.

'You're not humouring me at all. She didn't just react to the sound of your voice.' Theo chuckled.

'Clara's a lovely choice of name. I think she's definitely a Clara. Thank you for thinking of it.'

Theo propped himself on his elbow, looking at little Clara. 'Are we going to stop now? We have so much more than we ever dreamed we would.'

'Yes. I think so.' Hope's second pregnancy had been a little harder than the first, and she knew that Theo had been worried at times. 'There are lots more adventures waiting for us.'

'Yeah. I was thinking that, too.'

Hope fed Clara, and then Theo rocked her back to sleep. Then Willow appeared in the doorway, holding Jack's hand. 'He wants to come and say hello.'

Theo nodded, beckoning to Jack and lifting him up onto his lap. Willow gave a wrapped package to Hope.

'Is this what I think it is?' Hope opened the parcel, holding up the quilt that was inside. 'That's beautiful, Willow, thank you so much. We've decided on a name for her. It's Clara—what do you think?'

'I like it.' Willow grinned. 'Can I have a picture? Of you all.' She took her phone from her pocket.

'Don't you mean of *us* all? Come here.'

Clara was wrapped in her quilt and put into Hope's arms. Theo shifted so that Willow could sit in between them, and Jack slid over onto her lap. Theo held the phone out, his other arm around Willow's shoulders. Their family. Brought together by chance and held together by love.

* * * * *

If you enjoyed this story,
check out these other great reads from
Annie Claydon

Neurosurgeon's IVF Mix-Up Miracle
Winning Over the Off-Limits Doctor
Country Fling with the City Surgeon
Healed by Her Rival Doc

All available now!

A KISS WITH THE IRISH SURGEON

KRISTINE LYNN

MILLS & BOON

To Patrick and George.

Your time together was never going to be long enough.

This book is my way of saying thank you
for the love you've given Iz and I.

CHAPTER ONE

PATRICK QUINN STARED at the suitcase. It wasn't even half full, and yet he couldn't imagine a single other item he wanted to pack. A glance at his mostly empty closet confirmed the unease growing in his chest, then spread from limb to limb like a phantom illness.

Rachel's things were gone by now, donated to a women's shelter where they'd be loved and appreciated. But even his side of the walk-in closet haunted him.

The shirts were his, technically, but she'd bought them, citing his horrible fashion sense. So, they'd stay. He could buy new shirts in the States.

The scarf in County Kerry's colors she'd bought him as an anniversary present still smelled like her. Yeah, that was going to the shelter next.

And the stethoscope? Something he used every day at work as the head oncology surgeon at St. Michael's Hospital? He should pack it—the tool was still in great condition and buying another was a pointless expense. But an image of his late wife wearing it—and nothing else, a present to him the day he'd become a surgical general practitioner—was one more ghost chasing him out of the life they'd built together.

No. This move was a fresh start from every angle. Everything must go.

Because it wasn't an invisible plague haunting him day and night until he'd had no choice but to take the job in Boston in the hopes of quieting it. The memory of his wife was a very real thing, and it was everywhere. While that had been a good thing at first—comforting, even—now it held him hostage, refusing to let him move on.

And he was ready to move on. The irony that it was Rachel's last request before nurses had moved into their home wasn't lost on him. He ran a hand along the only item of hers he was taking with them across the Atlantic as she'd requested—her ashes in a simple silver urn she'd picked out on their last weekend together.

It should have been, if not a happy weekend, at least a peaceful one with lunch at their favorite pub. But that day three years ago, they'd walked by a funeral home and Rachel, clad in a headscarf to hide her chemo-ravaged hair, had insisted they go in.

There, in front of a dozen choices of receptacles they were supposed to choose from to put her remains in, she'd held his hand and issued words no husband should have to hear.

"I want you and Aoife to be happy, Patrick. And that means letting me go."

"I can't," he'd sobbed into her frail arms. The morbid urns and caskets and smell of death had almost suffocated him. Even now, he could still smell that room where it'd finally hit him—his wife would die and he'd be left behind to raise their infant daughter alone. "I promised to love you forever."

"No." She'd smiled, her lips cracked and dry from the chemo, "you promised you'd love me all my life, and that's over now. It's not going to do you any good to mourn me like Miss Havisham, love. Make a life for you and our daughter and bring me home to my parents."

"You *are* home," he'd whispered into her paper-thin skin that smelled of chemicals.

"She needs to meet them, Patrick. No matter what my parents said about you, about me, about us, they deserve to know their grandchild and say goodbye to me."

He'd choked on a half sob, half grunt of disapproval.

"I mean it. Aoife's only got you and her precious innocence to help her grieve. Give my parents the chance to help." He'd nodded, but she must have seen through it. She'd poked his chest. "So help me, if you sit around Dublin moping, I'll haunt you."

Patrick put the urn in his backpack and sighed. It was strange to think that soon, he wouldn't have it anymore.

"Oh, darling, you haunt me still," he whispered into the room he'd say goodbye to for the next nine months, if not forever. Maybe when he got home after the interim chief of surgery contract in Boston was up, Rachel's ghost would be gone. Or maybe he'd sell this place so he'd feel less guilty for moving on when she still seemed to be everywhere. But his American bride had been right about one thing—it was better for him and Aoife both to move forward with their lives.

He'd loved and lost, but that happened to people every day—he saw it in the hospital waiting room more often than he dared to admit.

What mattered most was caring for Aoife, who he loved as much as life itself. This temporary move would be good for them both.

"Da!" a small but mighty voice called out. He smiled. His little love was awake, finally. They had to head to the airport in less than two hours. *"Da!"*

"I'm coming, love," he called out.

He strode down the hallway and turned the corner into what he could only describe as chaos, plain and simple. "What's going on here, *mo grá*?" he asked, pointing to the pile of dresses and shoes at the foot of his daughter's bed.

"My clothes for the trip," Aoife said, putting a piece of paper on the top.

"I packed for you, love. Your suitcase is already in my room. Now clean this up before Mamó comes to pick us up. We don't have much time and you still need to eat."

"Da," Aoife said, her hands on her hips as if she commanded all of the European Union and not only his attention. "You packed my trousers and sweaters and nothin' pretty."

He saved a chuckle from escaping his throat. He'd run surgical programs, trained field medics, lived on two continents and still his daughter eluded him.

"I'm sorry. An oversight, I assure you."

"Okay. But I still need these. Put them in the case?" she asked. "Puhleease?" His daughter's smile was one more reminder of Rachel he was taking overseas. This one, he'd pack happily.

"I'll toss them in," he said, picking up a few. The slip of paper fell and he caught it midair.

"What's this?" he asked, reading it over. He marveled at the words that were actually legible, if he read them phonetically. Mamó, his mom, studied with Aoife on the days she didn't have preschool and was working wonders on Aoife's reading and writing. That, and her uncanny way of making him forget she was barely four every time she spoke, would serve her well in America.

"A list for the fairies," she replied, tossing her crimson ringlets over her shoulder. "I asked them for things I really, *really* want since it's almost St. Patrick's Day, but then I got to thinking…"

She pointed at the dresses in Patrick's arms, a frown on her pouty little lips. "What if they don't know where I'm going?"

He tried to keep up. Fairies had been Rachel and Aoife's thing, hers and Mamó's after that. He preferred the grounded world of medicine where every ailment had a cure, each injury a treatment plan.

"I'm sure they've got a network of fairy friends who will

track you as we travel," he said. That obviously wasn't the right answer given the way her brows pulled in at the center.

"They're not *Santa*, Da. They don't have elves. I know the fairies here, and I want them to remember what I asked for in case they can't fly over the ocean." God, she was growing like a primrose in spring. Her sass and intelligence were growing faster.

Patrick glanced over the list.

P-u-p-y was written on the top. "You want a dog?" he asked.

She nodded. "Like Susan and Clara down the hill. They don't let me pet their wee thing anymore so I want my own."

His chest ached under the weight of all he couldn't give his daughter. Hopefully what he could—love, financial security, a life of stability—would be enough.

"We'll talk about it when we're back. Dogs don't travel well in the belly of a plane."

The pout grew. Fascinating that women learned the skill at such a young age. He chuckled until his gaze fell to the item at the bottom of the list, a star by it, indicating its importance.

"A new ma?" he asked. His chest now felt like an anvil was sitting on it. Cardiac arrest wasn't common in men in their late thirties, but it wasn't impossible, either. He rubbed at the area absently as he thought through how to answer.

"That's a tough one for the fairies to tackle, Aoife," he started. Hopefully she wouldn't notice the catch in his throat. "A ma is something that isn't just dropped from the heavens into our laps."

Strictly speaking, that wasn't entirely true. Rachel had, in fact, fallen into his lap at O'Shanahan's Irish pub in South Boston when a billiards player had knocked into her. She'd always claimed it was fairies that had led her to him just as he finished his residency and was moving home to Dublin to start at St. Michael's.

He cleared his throat. "I had to work hard to find the one

that brought you into this world, and it would take a lot more work to find another." That part was true.

"Well, I'm leavin' it on there!" Aoife exclaimed. She picked up a pretty dress. "You hafta go, Da. I need to change. Mamó says real princesses don't wear tights to fly."

Her small body corralled him toward the door before she shut him on the other side of it.

He sighed, still holding the list in his hand, which shook. Not a good look for a doctor taking on a chief of surgery position.

A new ma.

The words rubbed like sandpaper down his heart, agitating it.

It wasn't like he hadn't thought about starting to date, or inviting someone else into his and Aoife's lives. He had, and the idea sent a whisper of a thrill coursing through his blood. But then it would meet with the almost crippling guilt blocking the entrance to his heart, and he would abandon the idea. He had to care for Aoife; that was the most important thing.

But now... Well, he couldn't be sure her list wasn't a prescription for how to do just that.

Too bad they were bound for Boston, the one place he'd sworn he'd never return to. Too much damage over too long a time to think of it as anything other than a means to an end. He'd bring Rachel's ashes home to America, then be done. Which meant, even if Aoife's list made sense, nothing permanent could happen there—not a puppy, and certainly not a woman in their lives. But when they got back to Ireland, he'd make an effort to put some thought into what was best for him and Aoife moving forward. Even dating.

Will you be ready by then?

Thankfully, the interim chief job was for a full nine months—enough time to figure that out. And to help an old friend who'd mentored him in medical school cover a position while the actual chief took her maternity leave, introduce Aoife to her grandparents and say a final goodbye to Rachel, who wouldn't be making the trip back to Dublin with them.

How could she, when her mother and father desperately wanted their girl back home, the girl they claimed he'd stolen from them? He owed them that, at least. It'd been impossible for him to come with her when Rachel visited each year—until she'd gotten sick. Not just because he'd never been welcome—which he hadn't. But because he'd been dedicated to his career for too many years. He'd thought he'd have plenty of time with Rachel after he'd gotten ahead at work, but time was the one thing life hadn't given them.

Now, he needed to make things right and honor his late wife's wishes by bringing her ashes home. He might have failed Rachel in a thousand other ways, but this one thing—giving her back to her parents—he could do. If only it didn't mean going back to Boston, where it'd all begun. In that way, nine months was an eternity.

But then he and his daughter could start their lives over, this trip finally behind them. It was enough to make a widower feel a little hope blossoming in places where light rarely shone.

"Boston, I hope you're ready for us," he whispered. He pulled up the airline tickets and patted the pocket on his backpack, making sure the passports were there.

He'd feel a whole lot better if this trip wasn't happening on St. Patty's Day, the day he'd met his future wife a decade earlier.

"Aoife," he called back. "Let's get going. If you can hurry, *mo grá*, I'll stop at Liam's for a cranberry scone."

She squealed and shouted, "I'm coming, Da, but my clothes—"

"Leave 'em," he shouted back, slinging his backpack over his shoulder and grabbing the cases in his free hands. In the kitchen, he left a note for the housekeeper to start with Aoife's room once they'd left. It felt odd, leaving the place where Aoife was born, where she'd taken her first steps, where her mother took her final breath.

But the sooner they left, the sooner they could say a final goodbye to Rachel, then hurry back to their side of the pond and leave America—with its own brand of tragic memories—behind for good.

CHAPTER TWO

SORCHA KELLY STARED into the glass of Jameson whiskey, wishing it had the power to reflect something other than her solitary image back at her. The raucous music blaring from the speakers was in direct opposition to her mood. Give her a maudlin ballad instead.

Even today. *Especially* today.

The crowd grew in size and noise, their celebratory cries of *"Sláinte!"* reaching a crescendo as soon as the fire marshal popped in to say they'd reached capacity.

Sorcha smiled and took the shot in a single swallow. The more things changed, the more they stayed the same. She waved at Kellan, the fire marshal who'd pulled the short straw that year. No one wanted cops and fire personnel in uniform, not on St. Patty's Day. They'd drink for free in plain clothes, but in uniform? They were the enemy of fun.

He waved back, an improvement from last year when he'd flipped her off.

It wasn't her fault. She'd turned him down kindly enough. She just didn't have the time or heart for a guy in her life, not that she expected him to understand. To her, a family meant inevitable loss and heartache, a lesson hammered into her during her own childhood. Her parents had never gotten over the loss of Sorcha's sister, which begged the question of why she'd willingly invite that kind of pain into her life. Especially when she could work at a hospital and save other families from experiencing that loss instead.

It really wasn't a question—she never wanted to put her heart ahead of her work, no matter how nice guys like Kellan O'Connor were, or how much her parents tried to convince her to put work aside and honor her Irish Catholic ways.

Right. The Irish Catholic ways.

Marry, breed, fight, drink, and then start the whole process over again. She'd been told by more than one of her fellow first-generation Irish American friends that going against the grain was like turning your back on the sea—highly dangerous and bound to take you under eventually.

So far, she'd escaped the trappings of a tethered life, but she worried she'd have to turn around and face the storm sooner or later.

She tapped the bar.

"You having another? Aren't you usually out as soon as Kellan or one of his comrades comes around?" Sam, the bartender, asked. He was the only Scottish man allowed behind the bar of the Irish pub run by three generations of O'Shanahans, thanks to his luck at falling in love with an O'Shanahan daughter. He also knew what drew Sorcha out each St. Patty's Day, and how drastically her mission to get obliterated once a year differed from everyone else in the bar's.

Rachel. Sorcha shook her head so the ghost of her dead best friend would leave her alone. She didn't normally drink—no time for it when her sole focus was getting her clinical trial up and running. But St. Patty's Day was different. St. Patty's Day was hers and Rachel's, and Sorcha didn't see a need to find a new way of coping with Rachel's loss, or her best friend's betrayal ten years earlier that made the loss even more acute.

Whiskey did the trick just fine.

"Yup. One more and I'm out. Big day tomorrow."

"Bigger day than today? Isn't this ten years since—"

"It is." Sorcha waved him off, her head a little light from the booze and the proximity of so many screaming banshees dancing behind her on O'Shanahan's small linoleum dance floor. Their joy was palpable. Annoyingly so. "But it doesn't matter. Mick's giving his speech tomorrow at the hospital. It's finally happening."

"Congrats," Sam said. He grabbed a glass, poured himself a shot of whiskey and topped hers off. "To your trial finally getting funded."

They clinked glasses and both tossed back the amber liquid at the same time.

Sorcha hissed. Whiskey was a fine way to forget, but she didn't do it often enough to make it burn less.

"Sláinte," she said, putting her empty glass on the bar with far less enthusiasm than the giggling women next to her. An image of her and Rachel in those same seats, similar smiles on their faces, almost suffocated her. "So, what's the craic, Sam?"

"Not much. Kiera's up walking and said her first word."

"Lemme guess—*da*?"

"Nope. *Ma*. I lost that bet." They laughed and it felt good to do that again, on St. Patty's Day no less. "Speaking of the guy," Sam said, pointing to a table behind her and she squinted.

The crowd was thinner by the tables—no one wanted to sit when dancing and drinking was the name of the game. But the combination of self-pity and alcohol had caught up to her, and everything farther than her hand was blurry.

"Speaking of who?" she asked Sam.

"Mick. Isn't that him?"

"Mick?" she asked. Surprise twisted her lips. But yeah, there he was—her boss, Dr. Michael O'Shea, who ran Boston General's medical program, in South Boston at a dive bar, alone.

"Dr. Kelly?" her boss replied. The formality of his address

didn't sound right with the steady hum of joviality in the background. "I didn't know you lived in South Boston."

He looked less surprised and more...*guilty*?

Someone started a round of "Drunken Sailor" and the rest of the bar—everyone but her and her boss, locked in a staring stalemate—joined in.

She shook her head, and a wave of dizziness crashed over her. The chorus of voices thrummed against her chest and she recalled another reason she didn't drink—she didn't like bars, didn't like the way they dulled her senses. As a surgeon, and a research surgeon at that, she couldn't afford to dull anything.

"I don't," she shouted over the music. "I come here every year for a friend." Her throat was raw from the whiskey. She'd feel this tomorrow. Oh, well, all she had to do was give the speech to her new staff, a speech she could repeat on no sleep or food, half-drowned in whiskey. She'd been rehearsing it since Dr. Collins had announced her maternity leave.

Boston General Hospital would need an interim chief of surgery for nine months, and Sorcha needed a way to get her trial in front of the hospital's board of directors without waiting in line behind the other ambitious doctors with billion-dollar medical innovations to pitch. Only a certain amount of funding was reserved for trials, and she wanted in. *Needed* in.

They'd *have* to listen to the interim chief's proposal, and so she'd aimed to get the chief gig no matter what. She was indispensable to Mick now, and, according to Mick's assistant who liked the Irish scones Sorcha had been baking her for years, the job was all but hers.

She just needed to formally accept it tomorrow.

"Must be some friend," Mick said, fiddling with the paper sticker on his beer bottle.

"She was," Sorcha whispered. "The best. But we had a falling out."

"Over a guy?"

Sorcha smiled, but it felt as weak as the rest of her. "Sort of. She was supposed to meet me to move into my apartment at CUNY School of Medicine, but called to tell me she was moving to Dublin with a man she'd just met. Here at this bar, actually. It was the only St. Patty's Day I couldn't make our annual date. She...she didn't even say goodbye."

The memory of her best friend's face over video chat three months later, when she'd finally called Sorcha to apologize, a ring on her finger, was etched on Sorcha's mind. Rachel had been happy, and in return, Sorcha had been cruel and unforgiving. Rachel was the only one who knew what med school meant to Sorcha, how hard it was to do it without family support. And still, her best friend had done what mattered to her, and forgotten all about Sorcha.

They'd seen each other with their other girlfriends each St. Patty's Day Rachel had flown home to visit, but it was never the same as it'd been before, when the two women had been inseparable.

The thing was, it wasn't just Rachel's fault. Ten years of maturity and therapy, and Sorcha knew she wasn't responsible for Rachel's choices, just as Rachel wasn't responsible for Sorcha's. Still...

The guilt over all the things Sorcha should have said that night Rachel had called to say she was leaving for Dublin replayed on a tortuous reel.

Come home.

Do you even know who this man is?

I miss you.

I'm sorry.

Each year on St. Patrick's Day, she gave in to the spiraling thoughts and guilt for one night. She'd wallow, then suck it up, put her head down and work through it the rest of the year.

"I'm sorry to hear that. I hope you two have mended things," Mick said. He kept glancing at the door. She followed his gaze, somehow surprised at how she could feel such despair while the rest of the patrons with slung arms around one another seemed…happy. Or at least carefree in a way Sorcha had never been.

"She died before we could."

The rest of Sorcha's pain was a result of never making the flight to Ireland, not even when Rachel got sick. At first, Sorcha had blamed this guy—Patrick, who she'd never met—for taking her best friend away, but the truth was, it was Rachel's wild temperament that led her to Dublin, to saying no to treatment when she got pregnant. And it was Sorcha's own Irish stubbornness that kept her feet firmly planted in Boston instead of putting that all aside when her friend needed her.

Because of that, she'd still never met her best friend's daughter. She couldn't only fault her friend's widowed husband for that. But she *could* despise him for not forcing Rachel to get treatment.

If he was the doctor he was supposed to be, shouldn't he have saved his own *wife*?

She shook her head. No use dragging that all back into the present again. Rachel was gone and that was that.

"Anyway, what are you doing here, sir?"

Without your wife, she wanted to add, but thankfully, the whiskey's effects on her hadn't included sassing her boss.

He bit his bottom lip and she frowned. Mick was nervous.

"I'm…meeting a friend."

Sorcha's brows went up. She liked Mick, respected him. But she liked Mick's wife, Aisling, even more. The woman was one part doting wife and mother, two parts Irish smart-ass.

"Mick—"

He put up a hand, stopping her from blurting out the accusation swelling on her tongue.

"There he is now."

"He?" Sorcha asked.

Her head whipped around to follow Mick's gaze, and the effects made her dizzier. Backlit by the spotlights on the dance floor, she couldn't make out any features, save the broad shoulders and strong silhouette of the guy heading toward them, parting the throngs of laughing people as if he were one of the ancient Irish gods.

Mick wasn't at the bar to meet another woman at least.

So, why the shroud of secrecy?

A few paces away, the dim lights over the tables took over, illuminating the stranger's face. His jaw was set, strong, and his lips unsmiling. She got the impression that he was as unenthusiastic about being out on St. Patty's Day as her. But that's where the similarities between them ended.

He was tall where she was short, impeccably dressed in a tailored button-down and slacks that hugged thick ropey muscles while she wore tights, trainers and a baggy Celtics hoodie.

His emerald green eyes were hard, as if life had dealt him a rough hand. She'd had a tough time of it, too, but still found joy where she could. She, at least, knew how to smile.

And speaking of his lips…they were flat, pressed tight, but full. Her throat was suddenly too dry. She swallowed as the stranger's stony gaze landed on her.

There was one more similarity, something that nagged at her, tugged at a memory deeply buried in her subconscious. He was Irish—she'd bet on it.

But it was something else, too.

"Dr. Quinn," Mick said, standing and ignoring the stranger's outstretched hand and opting for a tight embrace instead. "Glad you made it safely."

Then she saw it. The eyes, lips and name coming together in one real-life package. She'd seen photos of this man—photos she'd tried to forget—but the in-person version was far more damning.

They clearly hadn't done enough justice to the power in his gaze.

"Quinn?" Sorcha asked. Three shots of alcohol in less than an hour had slowed her cognitive responses, but her mind finally caught up. "Like Dr. *Patrick* Quinn?"

Her pulse raced as the man's gaze took her in, from her sneakers to her long red—and unwashed—hair pulled back into a messy ponytail.

"Yes. And you are?"

The Irish brogue meant he wasn't just Irish by heritage, but flown-in-from-Dublin Irish. Sorcha rolled her shoulders back, attempting to look strong despite her disheveled appearance. She wavered on her feet, but steadied herself as she squared off with the interloper.

"I'm Sorcha Kelly. I'm sure you've heard the name before."

A shadow passed over Patrick's face, but otherwise his lack of reaction said it all; she'd been as unimportant to her best friend's husband as she'd been to her best friend in the end.

"Rachel's best friend," Patrick said, nodding. His accent was like home, the way he said *Ray-chel* warming her from the inside out like a cup of tea with soda bread by the hearth. She shook the familiar feeling off.

Especially since the man represented everything about the home that had been stolen from her.

"I didn't know you two knew each other," Mick said. "Well," he laughed, "that'll save me an introduction."

"Mick," Sorcha said, keeping her eyes on the stranger in front of her. "Can I get a moment with your *friend*?"

Mick's aversion to confrontation won out over his obvious confusion at the situation unfolding in front of him. "I'll see about getting some food while you two catch up."

He walked away and the veil of pleasantries dropped. A dancer bumped into her, laughing and uncaring—a minor inconvenience compared to *Patrick. Here.*

Anger rose up like bile in Sorcha's throat.

Why was he here, now, talking to *her* boss in *her* bar on *her* continent?

"Yes," she said, finally addressing Patrick. "I was Rachel's best friend. Though after you stole her from me ten years ago, there wasn't much of a friendship left."

"I'm sorry," he said. Two words she'd waited a lifetime to hear, now fell flat. His emerald green eyes appeared to be lit from within and their gaze bore into Sorcha's chest, carving out the place she'd buried her grief. "I told her to come back more often, that she didn't need to worry about the money—we could afford it."

Sorcha grumbled dismissively.

"You don't get to be sorry. Not now. You should have been sorry enough to bring her home yourself, to have a wedding here where she could have had her family involved. Or sorry enough to make her fight for her life when she got sick." Sorcha was breathing heavily, the anger and grief mixing with the cheery background noise and the impossibility of seeing this man here, now.

Her head was woozy. She really should have had dinner, but she'd come straight from the hospital, a breakthrough in the lab more important than a sandwich. Now, regret came swift. She held the table for support.

"You're right," was all Patrick said, his strong—and frankly, attractive as all get out—shoulders stiff. "Everything you said is spot-on and I live with the regret every day."

Sorcha rocked back on her heels, surprised at his admission, at the realization that this man—who she'd imagined being tough and unfeeling like her Irish father—was a man grieving, too. It didn't fix how Sorcha felt, though. Didn't erase the past decade of needing her best friend since Sorcha's family couldn't champion her career in medicine, not when they'd worked their whole lives to keep their girls out of hospitals—or at least the daughter they'd cared for most.

Cara.

"What the hell are you doing here?" she finally asked. Exhaustion replaced the anger. It didn't matter that Patrick was here, only that he skipped back to his side of the pond as soon as possible.

That used to be your side of the pond, too.

She ignored her sober conscience.

She held up her hand as he opened his mouth to answer.

"You know what? It doesn't matter. I've got a big day tomorrow where I'll finally get a chance to do what Rachel and I used to dream about, and I don't need you distracting me from what really matters."

"And what is that?" Patrick asked. He leaned in, curious. As if the rest of the partygoers were turned to mute, she only saw the man in front of her. Everything, and everyone faded into the background, as if it was the middle of the day in her lab, not the heart of St. Patty's Day revelry.

Maybe it was the barrel of whiskey floating in her bloodstream, maybe it was having someone ask about her work after doing everything on her own for so long, maybe it was the scent of Irish tweed and coconut oil that had her answering against her better judgment.

"I'm going to be interim chief of surgery at the hospital I work at, and then I'll get to make my sister's death count for something." She held her breath as he leaned closer, his furrowed brows and parted lips a heady combination for a woman whose work drew limited interest from people. She continued, "I spent my childhood watching my parents say goodbye to one child and neglecting the one they still had, all while I watched my sister waste away from a brain tumor. Rachel was my best friend and supported me going to med school then surgical residency so I could find a way to save other kids with my sister's kind of tumor."

Why was she telling him all this?

Because he's safe. He doesn't know you, doesn't live here, can't judge you. And he deserves to know what he took from you when he stole Rachel away.

"And you have? Found a way to do that?"

Sorcha nodded, the realization that she was so close to her dream coming true hitting her with more force than the whiskey.

"I just need to get the clinical trial off the ground." Patrick smiled, and it broke whatever hold he'd had over her. At the same time, the party picked up in noise, a reminder of where she was and *why*. It might be a celebration to everyone else, but to Sorcha, tonight was a wake. "Anyway, I don't know why you're here and frankly, I don't give a damn. You stopped mattering to me the minute you let Rachel die."

"Dr. Kelly!" Sorcha whipped her head around, and her lips twisted in embarrassment. She hadn't seen Mick return with drinks. "That's no way to talk to Dr. Quinn. He's going to be your—"

"Colleague," Patrick interrupted, as he accepted a pint of beer from Mick. The men clinked glasses, the sound shrill to Sorcha's ears. "At Boston General. I start tomorrow, actually." He turned to Mick while Sorcha stared, wondering if she'd heard him right. Praying she hadn't.

Sorcha's mouth fell open. "No. You—you can't."

She was so close to getting everything she'd worked for and he—he'd distract her from that. She wasn't sure how, but the swirl of emotions she'd kept under lock and key all this time said enough; he was a part of her past she wanted to keep buried.

Mick frowned. "He can and he is. He and his daughter are welcome here, and we'll all make sure they feel that way.

Dr. Kelly, I suggest you go home and sober up before we announce it tomorrow."

His daughter...

Rachel's daughter was there, in Boston. A sob built in Sorcha's chest.

"I—I can't do this. I'm sorry."

With that, her fortitude finally gave in. She turned her back on the man she hated more than anyone else on the planet and ran out of O'Shanahan's, long overdue tears finally falling and chilling her skin in the cold, March air.

She didn't care what Mick thought of her outburst, whether Patrick Quinn felt welcome or not. Only erasing these feelings—guilt, loss, and fear—mattered.

So much for the magic of St. Patty's Day. Tonight, it only felt like a curse.

CHAPTER THREE

SORCHA WINCED. There wasn't much sun this time of year in Boston, but what there was shone like a spotlight onto where she was sprawled out on top of her comforter.

Her head pulsed, partly from the aftereffects of her overindulgence, partly because she was recalling the previous night's events.

Her boss had witnessed her in a sweatshirt and totally drunk the night before she was supposed to accept a promotion from him.

Then... *Oh, then*. Patrick Quinn in the flesh. On her continent. In *her* dive bar, in the middle of *her* annual pity session. And who was slated to start working at *her* hospital that morning. At least she'd be his boss and could schedule him as far from her as possible.

Then maybe she could forget his worst offense, the one that Sorcha had thought about day and night the past few years. Patrick Quinn, renowned surgical oncologist, had let his wife die of cancer without doing everything in his power to convince her to consider treatment.

He may have lost a spouse, his daughter a mother, but Sorcha had lost a sister, a best friend, her *person*. And right when she'd needed Rachel most.

Is that why you berated him in front of the whole bar, including your boss?

Her memories slowed down as she sat up in bed. She hissed

at the headache that sprouted behind her eyes and rubbed them to no avail. Gods above, please let the renowned Irish recovery that her father swore by kick in.

She'd never tested the limits of her drinking until the previous night. And it wasn't just the hangover that haunted her.

Oh, God. She had embarrassed herself, hadn't she?

Yep. She owed Mick an apology.

Not Patrick?

Her upbringing said yes, she should make things right with him, too. But her injured heart argued he'd had it coming for a decade and it wasn't her fault he'd waited so long to come back to Boston, on St. Patty's Day no less.

And to think she used to celebrate the holiday.

"Damn," she muttered, padding to the kitchen to remedy the part of her headache that could be fixed with a strong espresso. "Focus on your speech and let the rest work itself out."

She showered and dressed quickly, styling her hair and adding makeup subtle enough that she didn't look as if she was trying too hard, but enough to cover the bags under her eyes. She walked out to the light rail station a block away, tucking her chin against the biting wind that whipped around Faneuil Hall like a wild banshee.

"It's with great pleasure and full understanding of the responsibility that comes with this position that I accept the role of interim chief of surgery," Sorcha said, practicing her acceptance speech.

Thankfully the haze of last night had faded with her last cup of coffee. Perhaps her father was right—the real luck of the Irish was having a banger of a night and being able to bounce back the next day.

For good or bad.

When her sister had gone into the hospital for the very last time, Sorcha's dad had drunk enough each night to float the *Titanic* back to the surface. He'd come in, cursing God in Irish, and Sorcha would wish he'd hurt enough the next day that he'd never want to go back to the bar again.

He had another daughter at home, someone who still needed him.

But he'd wake up almost as if the previous night hadn't happened, leave without a word for the hospital to sit by her sister's side, and then, after a hospital cafeteria dinner, he'd head back to the pub.

It was a cycle of self-pity Sorcha would never repeat. Why not make real change instead?

The light rail arrived and she hopped on, grateful for the lack of people on board. That was usually the case the morning after what was arguably the biggest holiday in Boston.

"I'd like to use this opportunity to keep Dr. Collins's work on track as well as explore clinical trials that can catapult Boston General into the future of surgical interventions."

She didn't need her note cards anymore, but she paused, her mind blank all of a sudden. What came next? Why, suddenly, after weeks of knowing this speech by heart, were the words replaced by an image of Patrick's face, his stony green eyes assessing her, top to toe? His full lips, the bottom one pulled between straight, white teeth while she spilled her dreams at his feet—a distraction already, and she hadn't even started her first day with him.

Sorcha frowned. The city rushed by her at a breakneck speed. In the distance, Fenway Park immortalized the bleeding heart of Boston's sports enthusiasts, bookended by TD Garden, where the Celtics played. The Irish name and colors of the team had always made her feel at home.

"*Ray-chel*'s best friend," Patrick had said. Oh, that *accent*. *That* was home for her and yet, until she'd heard the rich lilt of his vowels, the way he concentrated on the *r*, she'd almost forgotten where she really came from.

"Trials…" She stumbled on the word. Why was Patrick

coming to work at Boston Gen? From what Rachel had said, he couldn't wait to get back to the white sand shores of Bray. "Trials," she whispered. *Oh, yeah!* "Starting with a groundbreaking new surgical technique that will make pediatric neuroblastomas a thing of the past."

The trial that would honor her late sister and make sure no families went through that kind of loss ever again. What she'd worked her whole life to obtain.

The hospital came into view next, and the lit sign above her announced her stop. She pulled the hood over her head and walked to the entrance of Boston General, as much a home to her as the small apartment she kept.

When the doors hissed open, her future felt like it was doing the same thing. Chairs were set up in the lobby, a stage and podium erected for the announcement of Dr. Collins's temporary replacement, as well as some other important news like the new oncology floor being built in the surgical wing.

Excitement, dormant in her chest cavity since Rachel's death, fluttered to life as if it'd been hit with three hundred volts from an AED.

Until her gaze landed stage right.

Patrick and Mick were shoulder to shoulder, chatting up the president of the board.

Alarms rang in Sorcha's mind.

No, no, no, no, no.

She strode up to the stage and stared at Mick until he finally met her gaze. Guilt lined his eyes.

"Dr. Kelly," he said. She raised her brows in response. "Why don't we talk over here?" He hopped off the stage and led her to the small alcove off the nurses' station.

"Tell me you didn't bring Patrick Quinn here for *my* job, the one I've been working for since I got here, Mick."

He bristled at the use of his nickname. The man was a stickler for the rules—including titles—but had a soft spot for Sorcha. Not soft enough, judging by the way his chin fell to his chest as if in defeat.

"You have to understand, Dr. Kelly. Until last night, I wasn't sure he'd come."

"Yes, but why is he here *at all*?" To her credit, her voice didn't shake near as much as her hands, which she shoved into her blazer pockets. She glanced over and Patrick met her gaze. His expression was neutral, no sense of gloating. Only a mild curiosity.

"I brought him here to help with the new oncology floor."

"In what capacity, Mick?" Forget titles and standing on ceremony. She knew what he was getting at, but wanted to hear him say it.

"He's taking the interim chief position."

"The job you all but promised to me?" she asked. Her voice held only a fraction of the waver she felt. "The one I've worked for, tirelessly day in and day out without so much as a complaint? The one I'm *made* for?"

More like she'd made herself *into* the job trying to get her trial off the ground, but that didn't mean she wasn't a perfect fit.

"Dr. Kelly, we can find something else—"

"I don't want a pity position, Mick. I want the job I earned. No one's worked harder than me, you know that."

He sighed and pinched the bridge of his nose. Bags under his eyes said he wasn't getting a good night's sleep, either.

"Maybe that should change, Sorcha." She rocked back as if hit by shock paddles. He'd always called her Dr. Kelly. "You do work harder than anyone here, but I have to ask myself why."

She stared at him, willing her chin to stop quivering. "You know why, Mick. You're one of the few people who know."

He put a hand on her shoulder, meant to be comforting most likely. But her skin only itched under the pity and scrutiny.

"What happens if the trial gets rejected? Or better yet,

picked up by the Board of Surgeons and taken out of your hands? Then what?"

"Then I get back to surgery," she answered abruptly. But doubt crept in. Rachel had asked her the same thing, what felt like a million years ago. As an impulsive, spontaneous woman, Rachel couldn't ever understand what it was like to work toward one singular goal for any length of time.

This—the trial based on a surgical procedure that would have saved her sister's life twenty years ago if it'd existed—was all Sorcha had.

"Listen. I'm not saying this as your boss. But I'd like to think we're friends after all this time."

"Friends don't sabotage their friends' careers without telling them first," she snapped.

"Fair enough. But I need you to hear this, Sorcha. All I want is your happiness."

"I *am* happy, Mick," she said. But the words sounded flat.

"Find other things to add to your life, Sorcha. Prove to me you're more than this job."

"What's wrong with being dedicated to my career?" she asked. "It's going to save thousands of lives when I get this procedure approved."

"It will. But who will you save next? And when will the tally be enough to give you peace?"

Sorcha rarely cried, not in public or in the privacy of her home. When things were tough, she threw her shoulders back and got to work. Sadness had swallowed her mother whole after Cara died, leaving Sorcha to question why having children was ever worth it. Either way, she'd vowed never to succumb to grief, not more than she could wash away with a night of liquor once a year.

Still, her eyes were damp no matter how hard she willed them to knock it off. One rogue tear fell from her lashes, traitorously landing on her cheek.

Not here, not with him *watching.*

Patrick stood over them on the stage and had likely heard their whole exchange, even though he pretended to fiddle with the sheet of paper in his hands. Fire rose up in her chest, burning away all she'd dedicated her life to. Or rather, handing it over to the man who'd been the cause of so much personal grief in her life already.

"Patrick is here as a favor to me. He's going to use his connections to help the oncology floor go in and we need that now. We'll look into funding your trial when the time comes, okay? But until then, make me this promise, Sorcha. Find joy outside these walls, or trust me—you'll never find peace inside them."

She nodded. What was her other option? To beg for what was rightfully hers in front of the board? In front of the man who'd now robbed her of *everything*?

The doors behind her hissed open again, which didn't grab her attention as much as the way Patrick's eyes lit up, the smile that blossomed on his lips. Objectively speaking, he was as fine a human specimen as she could conjure up in her science-based imagination. Strong, tall, talented. But that smile...

After his terse interaction with Sorcha last night, who knew he was capable of it?

As a woman, she couldn't help but wonder what made him grin like that. She followed his gaze and gasped.

There, in tiny human form with a bushel of red curls and pink frills, was an exact replica of Rachel.

All she had was a name written in the last letter Rachel ever sent her.

"Aoife," she whispered at the same time Patrick shouted to the girl over the crowd. Pronounced like most other Irish words so different from its Irish spelling. *Ee-ffa.* Sorcha had shared with Rachel the name she'd choose for a daughter if she ever had kids, which, given her aversion to familial ties, wasn't likely. So Rachel had "borrowed" the name and asked only for forgiveness.

Sorcha thought she'd prepared for this moment. But she'd miscalculated.

Because nothing could have prepared her for the sweet smile of her best friend's daughter beaming just feet from her as an older woman deposited her in Patrick's arms. Or Patrick laughing with her as he spun her around.

Nothing would be the same after seeing Aoife's wide, happy eyes staring at the hospital with the same awe Sorcha had when she was Aoife's age, right around when Rachel and Sorcha had met, actually.

The walls crumbled, and despite the risk to her heart, Sorcha found herself following her feet toward the girl and her father. The speakers came to life and a man from the board urged folks to take their seats so the meeting could begin. Sorcha ignored him.

Patrick smiled as she approached, welcoming her in.

"Can I meet her?" she asked Patrick.

He nodded. "Rachel wouldn't have had it any other way."

More tears fell, but this time, Sorcha let them. "Hi, Aoife," she said, kneeling on the cold tile floor and offering her best smile, a smile she'd been saving for this moment if it ever came. "I'm Sorcha, your mom's friend from America."

Aoife curled her brow like she was a curious teenager and not the young sprite she was.

"If you're from America, why do you sound like us? 'Cause everyone else sounds funny here. They call me *Oh-iffa* instead of *Ee-ffa* like they're s'posed to."

"Aoife—" Patrick said in a stern tone, but Sorcha waved him off, laughing.

"I know what you mean. For the first few years of school here, people called me 'Scorcher.'"

"You went to school here?" Aoife asked. Her eyes were wide and curious. "I'm going to school soon, to St. Brigid's."

Sorcha nodded, keeping her hands clasped tightly in her lap so she could resist the urge to tuck the girl's wild curls behind her ears.

"It's a good school. And Ireland's only female patron saint."

Aoife nodded. "And she's the one who sends the fairies."

Sorcha's chest constricted. She and Rachel used to ask the fairies for things each night—to watch over friends and family when they were younger, then to turn a boy's head when they became teens, and even now, from time to time, Sorcha would send up a quick ask that the next step of her trial be successful so she could make her impact on the medical world.

"You know, I still ask the fairies for things I need," she admitted. Patrick stiffened next to her.

"You do?" Aoife asked. "I asked my fairies for things before I left, but I'm afraid they won't find me here."

"Oh, they will. They follow the beat of your heart however far it takes you."

Aoife pumped her fists in the air. "I knew it!"

Sorcha giggled again. "What did you ask them for?"

"I made a list." Aoife tugged on Patrick's sleeve. "Show her my list, Da."

"We should sit," Patrick said, giving Sorcha a glance she couldn't read. It wasn't unfriendly, just…quizzical, as if he couldn't figure her out and wanted to. "They're about to start."

She swallowed hard. "Fine. Aoife, it was nice to meet you. I'm sure I'll see you around."

Especially since your dad is about to be my boss.

"Can we sit by her?" Sorcha heard Aoife ask.

"No, *mo grá*. We shouldn't."

Not *can't*, or *aren't allowed*. But *shouldn't*. What did that mean?

She still cared deeply about the loss from earlier, but she

also couldn't stop watching Patrick and Aoife together. They were different than Sorcha imagined. *He* was different. Less… awful, even if he had stolen yet one more thing she cared about.

Oh, Rachel, she thought. *What have you done?*

CHAPTER FOUR

PATRICK MADE IT THROUGH the ceremony announcing not only his new role, but also the hospital's expansion—an expansion he'd oversee. It was work that had the power to change lives.

But he'd barely heard much of the praise accompanying Dr. O'Shea's introduction. His eyes flitted back and forth between his daughter and Sorcha, the former who would wave at him, then Sorcha. The thing was, Sorcha waved back to her, even tossing his daughter a few silly faces.

It was adorable. Or would be, if the woman interacting with Aoife wasn't a complete enigma—and the one variable he hadn't considered when he'd accepted the interim position. And there'd been a lot to consider.

Boston was rife with memories of his life *before*—before Rachel, before his rise to the top of his surgical field, before Aoife. But not many of them were *bad* memories.

He'd seen the Red Sox beat the Yankees after a flyball turned out to be a triple-hitter.

He'd walked the Irish Heritage Trail and marveled at how strong his people were.

He'd stood onstage at graduation as Harvard University's first Irish valedictorian.

He'd met Rachel at an Irish pub just as his residency at Boston Gen came to an end.

However, the secondhand memories that followed, souvenirs of Rachel's fraught trips to visit "home," weren't anywhere near as pleasant. Her parents had taken the news of their elopement about as well as he and Rachel had expected, the weight of her previous spontaneous decisions catching up to her.

Each trip home, their relationship grew worse until, when she got sick, her parents chose not to come to see her. Here she was again, they'd said, following a knee-jerk impulse to carry a baby to term instead of receiving lifesaving medical help.

Patrick sighed. That'd been her last decision, as fate would have it, and the heaviest one for him to carry. He knew what people whispered.

Why couldn't the world-class oncological surgeon save his wife from cancer?

It was a decision he'd replayed at least once a night after Rachel's death—should he have tried harder to push her into treatment? Until he realized something vital, it didn't matter.

He had Aoife, a little ball of love as a gift of Rachel's selflessness. Whether it damned him or not, he didn't think he could make a decision that meant his daughter didn't exist, even if he had the chance.

Look at her, flashing a wink and peace sign at Sorcha.

Ah, Sorcha Kelly.

Rachel's best friend, at least until she'd joined the camp that thought Rachel was making a mistake not getting chemo. What kind of a friend must she be, he'd wondered, if she didn't support her friend's decision and understand how difficult it must've been for her to make?

But... Sorcha wasn't at all how he'd imagined. Rachel had described her as cold and serious and yeah, maybe the night before at the pub he'd seen some of that, but it was understandable, given the circumstances.

The woman currently sticking her tongue out at Aoife didn't seem chilly in the slightest.

Not that he had a clue what to do with that observation. His heart thumped against his rib cage as he observed something else, something far more troubling.

Sorcha was *stunning*, which he hadn't noticed last night, between the sweatpants and fiery words flung in his direction. With her long hair draped across her shoulders, she looked every bit the Irish lass from his homeland, but with curves and strength he'd only dreamed about. To make matters worse, from what he'd gathered late last night as he'd pored over her test protocols on neuroblastomas in youth, she was brilliant to boot.

Too bad, his subconscious argued. *She's so off-limits she might as well be the next in line to the British throne.*

"Thank you all again for coming," the president of the board said, raucous applause making it hard to hear the soft-spoken man. "Now, let's get to work making Boston General the premier hospital on the east coast."

More applause and then the crowd dissipated.

To his shock, Aoife didn't rush to the stage, even though the nanny he'd hired was on her phone and not watching the girl. He made a mental note to find a replacement as soon as he could. St. Brigid's didn't start for a few weeks yet, and he needed someone he could trust *now*.

His daughter ran to Sorcha's side, hugging her leg. His heart thumped louder than the speakers' whine as the staff disconnected the mic.

Ignore it. You just haven't been with a woman in years.

That had to be why his pulse stayed elevated as if he'd just completed hours of CPR on a patient, not watched his daughter hug a beautiful woman.

He and Aoife were in America for nine months and even if that wasn't the case—if they somehow decided to stay in Boston for longer—his conscience was right. His wife's best friend was off-limits.

She's also your employee.

Aye, she was.

"So, *mo grá*, are you ready to head back with Penny?"

"Do I hafta?"

She stuck out her bottom lip and Patrick almost caved. He should take some time to show Aoife around, but at the same time, Mick needed him to meet with contractors that afternoon to discuss equipment for the oncology floor.

"You do. I'll come home as early as I can, okay?"

She appeared to give that some thought, twisting her lips. Finally she nodded.

"Okay. Only if Sorcha comes to supper," Aoife said. "I want to ask her more about fairies."

Patrick coughed, rocked back on his heels. He threw a glance at Sorcha.

"Um," he said, the words stuck to the back of his throat. "I'm not sure that's a good idea." Not because he didn't want to invite *her* specifically, or that eating with someone other than his daughter was unwelcome. But he and Aoife hadn't had anyone to their home since Rachel passed. He needed...time.

Sorcha's eyes grew wide and her cheeks flushed with color. Ah, Irish skin. It was one of their curses, every emotion flashing across translucent skin like paint-by-numbers art.

"What I mean to say is that we just got here and haven't even unpacked. Let's get settled before we invite houseguests."

Aoife crossed her arms and glared at her father with pouty lips and all.

"Fine. Sorry, Sorcha. My da said no."

Sorcha smiled, and the room brightened. Patrick liked the way her eyes crinkled around the corners.

"Thank you for the offer, Aoife. It was so nice finally meeting you. Your mom was special to me and I like thinking she's watching us now, making sure we get to know each other. Come talk to me anytime you want to hear about her." She glanced up at Patrick. "If that's okay with you?"

Patrick cleared his throat. "Of course. I'll give her to Penny and then get to work."

Sorcha nodded, her mouth open as if she wanted to say something.

"What is it?" he asked as Penny came to take Aoife.

Sorcha worried on her bottom lip.

"I only meant to say welcome to Boston General," she finally said. "You'll be good for the oncological department, and I'm grateful you let me meet Aoife. I meant what I said—Rachel was important to me."

Patrick nodded. "Thanks. And I'm glad you met, too." He'd never seen his daughter take to a stranger like she had to Sorcha. Hell, he'd never been drawn to a stranger like he was to her, either.

"But…" she added, a glint in her green eyes that made her look like her own brand of Irish fairy, albeit one up to no good.

"You know everything you say before 'but' doesn't count, right?"

She only smirked and shrugged.

"But you made me look like a fool last night," she said.

"That was never my intention." He didn't look at the crowd that dissipated into their workstations around the campus, a campus he hadn't even seen yet. "I'm sorry."

"Thank you, but lack of intent doesn't mean lack of impact. You took my best friend, which I'll forgive since that was as much her fault as yours. And now you've taken this job. Dr. Quinn, forgive me, but it's hard to imagine this isn't personal."

"Believe me, Sorcha. Mick never mentioned someone else was vying for the position. Especially not you." Even if he had, would it have changed Patrick's mind? He'd needed the change as much as Mick claimed to need him. It was the only thing that would have inspired him to finally bring Rachel home.

"I wasn't vying for it. I *earned* it after years of dedication to this institution, to the medical advances here. And then you show up and steal it out from under me. Not to mention, Patrick…"

"Yes?"

"You didn't save her when you could have, which I'll never get over."

He stared into her eyes, the passion in them evident.

"Me neither. It's something I'll carry with me to the grave, but if given the chance, I'd never do anything to not have that little girl on this earth, and Rachel felt the same."

Sorcha looked at the doors and Patrick followed her gaze, wondering what she was thinking. This had to be a lot for her to process.

"Anyway, I only mean to say that from now on you owe me honesty."

"I've been honest—"

She held up a hand as if she were, in fact, his chief of surgery. "You didn't tell me why you were here and if we're going to work together, which is impossible to avoid since we're two of the four full-time oncological surgeons. You have to tell me what I need to know to do my job. You owe me that much."

He nodded. How this woman wasn't the boss of everyone he couldn't figure out. He wasn't sure how anyone denied her anything. She was so similar to his daughter. "Deal. If you do one thing for me."

She looked sideways at him. "It depends."

"Tomorrow, I'd like you to show me around where I'll be working. So much has changed since I was here last." Her nod felt like a badge he'd earned. "And start with your research lab. I want to see the medicine you're working on."

CHAPTER FIVE

SORCHA HAD MADE IT THROUGH the rest of the day without seeing Patrick, which meant she could keep her racing heart at least semicalm. He'd asked to see her research, which, given his new title, was his, too. He wielded power over her future, and she didn't like it. Not one bit.

Especially because, the next morning as they walked down the long, narrow hallway, his coconut oil and Irish clover aroma washed over her, bathing her in the scent of her homeland. Wrapped up in a sharp suit that accentuated his masculine physicality, to boot.

She pointed out places of interest to him—the surgical suites, the imaging center, the recovery rooms—explaining that much of it would change as the surgery wing expanded.

It made sense that he'd been asked to head that up. In Rachel's visits, she'd described Patrick's meteoric rise to success in the oncological department at St. Michael's. Cancer treatment needed a certain kind of doctor, one with a precise mind, caring heart, and forward-looking vision.

Was that Patrick?

"What's wrong?" he asked her.

Caught staring up at him, she felt the blood pool in her cheeks.

"Nothing. Sorry. I'm just thinking about the job, honestly. About your vision for the hospital."

His speech at the meeting earlier had laid out his plan to

continue patient care without interruption during the build, and how he'd like to grow the department according to Dr. Collins's wishes.

"Do you have an issue with it?"

She shook her head. "No," she admitted. "I'm still processing it. I could have, *would* have loved bringing the patients through the construction myself."

"It would have pulled your focus from the trial at a crucial stage," he said.

"Maybe," she conceded. She couldn't give him the win, even though...he was right. Mick had, in a way, done her a favor giving the job to Patrick. "Except now—"

They'd stopped in front of the opaque glass door with her name across the center.

"Now you wonder how, without the job, you'll get funding for your trial."

She nodded. Turning the corner, they bumped into one another and their hands brushed.

Something sparked where their skin touched, but biologically, she knew that was impossible. It was far more likely that her lack of dating and interaction with handsome men meant her hormones and pheromones were fully aware of Patrick's... *attractiveness.* Clinically speaking, he was a perfect human specimen.

That's a classy way of putting it. Admit it—you'd jump him if given half the chance.

Maybe that would be true if he wasn't who he was. If she had an itch, she'd be scratching it somewhere else.

"Um, this is my lab," she said, opening the door. She was in the lab every minute she wasn't in surgery, but no one ever came back here to check in on her research. Perhaps that's why Patrick seemed to fill the space and suck the air from it.

"This is incredible. We didn't have anything like this when

I was here," he said. He ran a finger along the edge of her stainless-steel table, his eyes glued to her robotic arm setup.

"You wouldn't have. I built it. Been building it, actually."

He wheeled around, his eyes wide. "You designed this? Alone?"

"You don't have to seem so surprised," she snapped. A sigh followed. "Sorry; this is awkward, having you here, having to explain myself instead of focusing on my new position."

The word "my" hung between them.

"I understand."

No "sorry," or, "I'll make it up to you." Just that he understood.

"Anyway, yes, I did. It's the protocol I told you about when I—"

When I drank too much and spilled my personal secrets to you last night.

"When I met you."

"Can I see the data?"

Sorcha took a thick binder from next to three others and handed it to him. "This is the set of results from the most recent test, but the preliminary studies are all documented in chronological order in those folders over there."

He gazed behind her and she was struck by the magnitude of the work she'd accomplished when his eyes widened. His fingers tapped the hard plastic of the binder as he scanned page after page. She held her breath in anticipation.

"And you do all this on your own time?"

She bristled, throwing her shoulders back. "I don't waste hospital resources. This comes out of the research budget I received a grant for, a grant that is partially helping to fund the new oncology floor. But the time I spend on it is mine. I still practice and take cases."

Patrick shook his head. *Ugh.* It was the same old story—

no one cared about the groundbreaking research if she wasn't actively cutting.

"Listen," she started. "I know you're the boss, but before you got here—"

"Talk me through it," he said. "I want to make sure you have the time you need to pursue this."

Her lips parted and a small gasp escaped her throat. Since he'd been announced as the new interim chief, she'd expected to have to fight against him to gain even a little ground. Yet, here he was, on day two, offering to support her?

"You don't want me to shut it down?"

He chuckled. "That would be shooting myself, and this program, in the foot. But if you already received a grant, why won't that cover the remaining clinical trial?"

She exhaled. "It was money set aside for prelim studies. Next, the results get reassessed by the board and chief of surgery before being allowed to continue. The board earmarks some donor money for expanded trials, and I want this year's allocation. The results speak for themselves."

Patrick's pager buzzed in the sterile silence of the lab. He placed the binder down and checked it, frowning.

"They need us both in pre-op." He strode to the door, then hesitated just before he walked out. "Rachel told me about you, you know. About why this is so important to you."

"The story I told you last night?" Sorcha's skin crawled with awareness. The not-so-gentle reminder this man was inextricably tied to her past was needed.

He nodded, not quite making eye contact with her. "But she told me about your parents, too. I just wanted to say I'm sorry, and I know what this study means to you."

Sorcha willed her pulse to slow.

"It means a lot to hundreds of families who don't know it yet." She didn't know this man near well enough—not even through secondhand stories—to trust him with her truth just yet.

He met her gaze. His was softer than before and the pity—or perhaps kindness?—made her squirm. She'd expected stoicism from the brooding doctor, and that was all she was capable of meeting. Anything more and she'd break.

"We should go," she said, her voice just above a whisper. "If they called us both, it must be necessary."

Patrick nodded and she followed him.

There was pandemonium in the ER. Two sets of EMTs ran in with stretchers heavy with mangled bodies strapped down, each looking worse than the last. Two other pairs of medical transport teams jogged in, blood covering the front of their jackets. The Boston Gen staff called out where to put the patients, while others rushed in and out of rooms. The energy was frenetic and almost feral. Machines and voices blended into a cacophony of sound, jarring after the almost eerie quiet of Sorcha's lab.

"What happened?" she wondered aloud.

He ran a hand through his hair. "Let's find out."

Boston General saw a number of multiple-victim cases a year, either gun violence related, or vehicle crashes. But this seemed different. Sorcha hadn't seen such disfigured bodies before, not outside medical school. Judging by the way the other rooms in the emergency department were being emptied, there must be more victims on the way, too.

Mick waved them over. "Building collapse," he explained. "Six victims in-house, three obvious head injuries, but they'll all need to be seen for secondary injuries."

"Six more headed here and eighteen being spread out between municipal and county hospitals," Tina, the nurse behind them, shouted as she ran past, IV bag in hand.

"Any news on casualties?" Patrick asked.

"Five so far, probably more by the time the day's done."

"Damn," Patrick muttered. Sorcha nodded her agreement. This was awful—so many lives lost or irrevocably altered from one moment in time. It was the crux of her career, mitigating that where she could, assisting in the healing when she was able. But so much of life was out of her control no matter how well trained she was. "Where do you want me?"

Mick lifted his palms up as if to say, "take your pick."

Tina shouted that she needed doctors and Patrick ran over, Sorcha close behind. Mick came along as well.

"I need two," Tina ordered.

Mick stepped back to let the surgeons in. "Sorry for the short welcome," Mick said. "But thanks for pitching in."

Patrick was already gloved up, assessing the two patients lying side by side. "That's why I'm here."

He took the male patient, who looked like he'd been pulled from the rubble. Gashes across his torso and face were largely superficial, but the thready breath sounds indicated at least one collapsed lung, probably some fractured ribs and other internal damage. But the victims' heads were the real concern. The facial lacerations more than likely meant head trauma.

Sorcha threw on gloves and attended to the patient closest to the door. She pulled out a penlight and assessed brain function. The pupils weren't blown, but there was a sluggishness Sorcha didn't like.

"Call ahead to hold two surgical suites," Sorcha told Tina. She winced. As the interim chief, that was Patrick's call to make. She glanced at him and he nodded his agreement.

"Go ahead, Tina," he echoed. The nurse was new to Boston Gen, but her experience as a trauma nurse in downtown LA meant she came with experience they sorely needed.

Tina hung up the phone. "There's a wait."

"Thanks. We'll have to do what we can down here until something opens." To Patrick, Sorcha called out, "How is your patient looking?" She almost added, "boss," but stopped herself short. It might be true on paper, but he'd have to earn it as far as she was concerned.

"Not great. I'm more worried about the lungs than the head, though. Who do we have that I can call in?"

"Peters is cardiothoracic."

Tina shook her head. "He's not in today. Dr. O'Shea called him, but he'll be half an hour at least."

Patrick had his stethoscope on the man's chest, a frown on his face. "I don't like it."

"I can assist until Peters comes in. My patient is stable."

"Thanks. We're going to need to perform a thoracostomy and drain some of this fluid if he's going to make it to surgery. Have you done one?"

Sorcha nodded. "I have. What side?"

"Yours. It's clear over here, but the left side is thready."

"Okay," Sorcha said. "Scalpel."

Tina handed her the scalpel and, before she'd even cut, Patrick had the drain tube at the ready. He acted like he'd been on Boston's surgical service for years, not minutes.

She sliced and held out her hand. The tube was there without her needing to say a word. She inserted it, and Patrick had an ear to the patient's chest just as his body convulsed. They turned him on his side, and Patrick kept the stethoscope pressed above the patient's lungs. When his seizure passed, Patrick removed it.

"His breath sounds have improved, but we need to wheel him up *now*. Is your patient stable enough to wait?"

"She'll have to be. That looked like a grand mal."

"I agree. Likely due to the stress his body endured. We've got to find him a room."

Sorcha nodded, placing the tube and hearing immediate improvement. They'd need to perform a back-to-back operation on this patient's heart and lungs if they wanted to save him. But operating rooms had filled up since the accident.

The phone in the ER room rang and Tina answered it. "Surgery one is open," she said.

"Let's go." Patrick hit the button, opening the door, and swung the gurney out. Sorcha followed. If she'd ever believed in the luck of the Irish, she did now.

"We need someone on the female's service," she called to Mick. He nodded and sent another nurse into the room they'd just left. As he'd anticipated, there were three more ambulance teams wheeling victims in. "God, this is horrific. I wonder what building it was."

A nurse ran by with a gauze kit in her hands. "The boutique hotel on seventh. The corner of it is decimated. The news won't stop showing the carnage."

Patrick halted and Sorcha crashed into the gurney. He whipped around to face her, horror on his face.

"Aoife. That's our hotel."

"Go," Sorcha said, her stomach dropping out. "I've got this." He gave her a nod of thanks and sprinted away toward the hospital exit.

Please, please, please.

Sorcha wheeled the gurney to the elevators as she sent up the same plea she'd asked of the fairies from her childhood.

They may not have listened to her then, but they had to now.

Please let her be okay.

CHAPTER SIX

PATRICK DIDN'T RECALL running the three blocks to the hotel or pushing past the police barricade. He vaguely recalled thanking Penny, then releasing her to her boyfriend who'd driven over to check on her.

The first thing to register was Aoife, still clad in her dress from that morning running into his arms. He held her tight to his heaving chest, choking down sobs as he inhaled her blueberry-scented shampoo.

"Oh, *mo grá*, you gave me a scare there."

"I'm sorry, Da," Aoife said. Her voice was muffled so he released the tight grip he had on her. "It sounded like thunder in the movies. But it's sunny out. Then there were all these sirens."

"Yeah, there was a right bad accident. I'm actually helping some people that were hurt at the hospital."

She pulled back and frowned up at him. "Then why are you here? Don't they need you?"

Patrick's chest ached from the emotion of the last few days—years, even. She'd called him out on his greatest weakness. He'd always choose her. Even at the risk of losing his job, his other family.

His wife.

"I had to make sure you were okay."

His sassy four-year-old put her hands on her hips. "Da, you could have just called, you know."

He laughed then, and tousled her hair, which earned a deep groan of angst.

"I getcha, love. I'm going to have to bring you back with me, okay?"

Aoife smiled, all nods now. "Yes! Does that mean I get to see Sorcha again?"

Sorcha. Damn. He'd left her alone with their patient, who would need two extensive back-to-back surgeries.

"Maybe, but we've got to go quick. Can I carry you?"

"On your shoulders?" She clapped.

"Of course, *mo grá*."

He was torn square between two worlds—one where he ran off with this child and didn't miss a moment away from her, and another where he got back to work doing what he needed to do to erase the gnawing guilt for letting his wife die under his watch. He might be ready to move on in so many ways, but that didn't mean he'd been absolved of his crimes.

He made his way back to Boston General, his heart rate slowing now that he had the most important thing in his world tight in his arms. The first thing he did was stop at the hospital's day care and ask if they had space.

They didn't, but would accommodate Patrick that week because of the unusual circumstances. He'd have to find an alternative solution between now and Aoife starting at St. Brigid's. They hadn't even moved out of the hotel, though that was changing tonight.

"I love ya, my little gremlin," Patrick said, repeating the phrase he used to say good night to his daughter each evening. "I'll be back soon to check on you, but I've got to see if I can help Sorcha."

"Then go already," she said, shoving him out the door. What was it about Sorcha that had his little girl so intrigued?

Probably the same thing that has you so curious.

He couldn't lie about that. Rachel had had her grievances

with her best friend, which he'd understood at the time. But even the limited few interactions with Sorcha had left him feeling like he shared more in common with her than he'd realized.

Before he knew it, he was inside the scrub room, hands sanitized and gloved and being fitted with a surgical mask.

"Where can I help?" he asked as the doors hissed open to the surgical suite.

Sorcha, a trained professional, didn't turn around, but her head tilted up.

"Is Aoife okay?" she asked. "She wasn't hurt?"

Patrick took the assisting surgeon spot across from Sorcha and for a brief moment, she met his gaze over their masks.

"She's okay." He grabbed a pad of gauze and handed it to her.

She patted the bleeder, from what Patrick could see was a small nick in a vein from the internal damage causing trauma around the patient's good lung.

"Thank goodness. What happened?"

"I didn't stay long enough to find out. But the building collapsed on the opposite side from our room. It's horrific, Sorcha. Debris and mayhem. They won't find all the bodies for days."

"My God." She reached up, and he handed her the number ten scalpel. "Thank you. Wait—you didn't leave her there, did you?"

Patrick shook his head and held the retractor back so Sorcha could fix another bleeder.

"She's here, in day care. For now, anyway."

"You brought her to the *hospital*?" Sorcha asked.

"Where else should I have brought her? We just moved here, and our apartment isn't available until tomorrow."

"Sorry. I didn't mean to talk to you like that. I know you're my boss—"

"I may be your boss, but you can speak freely to me."

She seemed to consider him, passing a brief glance his way. If he didn't know better, he'd say shock widened her eyes.

"It's just a bad time to be here with all the hotel patients… Can you pass me the—"

Patrick already had the suture kit threaded and ready to go. The patient was doing well, all things considered. And thank goodness, too, since they still needed to relieve the pressure in his skull.

"Thank you again." She paused, just before applying the first surgical knot to close the patient's chest. "How do you keep anticipating what I need?"

He shrugged, having wondered that himself. "You're following the same procedure I would."

The steady beeping of the monitor was all that filled the space while Sorcha worked in silence. He assisted where he was needed, the quiet not at all uncomfortable. If he was being honest, he hadn't worked this well with anyone since medical school.

He thought about what she'd said, about him being her boss, and wondered why it didn't feel that way to him. Maybe it was jet lag, or that he was still getting his bearings, but he felt more like they were equal colleagues.

"You said Aoife's in day care *for now*? What did you mean?" she asked, breaking the gentle tension as they both re-gloved and moved to the top of the patient's head. "Take the lead?"

Patrick nodded, and they switched sides without another word. This time it was her anticipating his needs and she handed over a twelve blade.

"Thanks. I need to find something till preschool starts in a few weeks. The nanny I hired from a service is about as observant as a wrong-way driver on a highway. Aoife'll have outsmarted her by the end of the week."

"So," Sorcha said, handing over the bone drill, "what's your plan?"

Patrick waited until the loud whir and crunch of the procedure was over and traded the drill for the gauze Sorcha handed him. Immediately, the pressure in the patient's head dropped. The only thing to do now was to wait overnight before closing him up to see if he was out of the woods and had any deficits.

That, and do the same for the dozen or so other victims in the triage rooms. Patrick sighed as he placed the dressing that would prevent infection, but allow the pressure to continue to drain. It was a simple enough procedure, but any number of complications could occur between now and the next day when they reassessed.

It was going to be a long night.

"I don't have one, to be honest. I'm flying by the seat of my trousers with Aoife. Rachel was…well, she was always the one mothering came easy to. My ma helped out a bunch as well. I love Aoife something fierce, but it's hard to know what to do."

"I don't want to overstep, but would your mom come out to Boston to help?"

Patrick shrugged. "You're not overstepping. I'm… I'm glad we can talk." He was, too. Sorcha's relationship with Rachel was a liability, but also a blessing, it seemed. She understood.

"I don't want to ask her. Coming here was supposed to be for us to say goodbye to Rachel, to fully move on, which we have to do alone. But I'm scared to the marrow of my bones I'm messing it up, you know? That Aoife deserves more than I could ever give her. That it should've been me instead of Rachel."

The gaping silence that followed was heavy and thick. He tried to take a deep breath as he cleaned up, but he couldn't find it. Those last words had lived on his heart for months, years, even, but he'd never let them take flight. Now that he had, he couldn't take them back.

"Sorry. I've never shared that. I apologize if it was too much—"

Sorcha started to walk out. He followed her as the nurses

moved the patient into long-term care so they could attend to the next hotel victim. At the scrub sink, she pulled down her mask and met Patrick's gaze head-on.

"When my sister got sick, my dad gave up. On life, sure, but on me, before anything. He wouldn't look at me, didn't do more than drop a plate of takeout in front of me before getting lost in grief. He certainly didn't ever hug me. My mom checked out on everyone for a while, but eventually came back." Sorcha chuckled dryly. "Still, she was so different, so much slower to love and show affection. I know why—that kind of loss sticks to your bones and lungs and makes it hard to function. But I always wished they could be a fraction of the parents you are to Aoife. I can tell how much she loves you and her energy—well, it's because you've made it safe for her to be who she is. That's no small thing."

The deep breath Patrick had been waiting for came in a wave, almost toppling him with the heat that followed. He'd only sobbed openly once before, at Rachel's bedside after she'd given birth to Aoife. As selfish as it was, as much as he'd loved his wife, the moment he'd laid eyes on their little girl, he'd known Rachel had made the right decision to bring Aoife into the world.

Now, he tried to keep the emotion at bay. It wasn't the time, certainly not the place.

"Thank you for saying that," he said, though even he could hear the gruff thickness in his voice.

"And I think I might have a plan to help. Temporarily, at least."

"Wha—" he started, but the rest of the word stuck in his throat. It'd been a whirlwind couple of days. "I mean, why would you help me when I've taken your job and best friend and who knows what else?"

Sorcha smiled up at him. It illuminated the dim, sterile room and broke through the wall erected between them when

Patrick had been given Sorcha's position. Maybe there was a way they could get through this without all the awkwardness weighing them down.

"Well, when you put it that way," she teased, before growing serious. "You and Aoife lost so much, too. I don't know you, and I'm not entirely sure I like you just yet, but she deserves to be cared for."

"Okay," Patrick said, his hands on his hips. Curiosity beat out the emotional exhaustion nipping at his heels. "What's *your* plan?"

CHAPTER SEVEN

SORCHA AND PATRICK were a week into her "plan," and all she'd felt since they instituted it was a sharp stab of regret.

Well, that wasn't true. She'd felt *pride* at being able to tweak her research times to care for Aoife while Patrick was still at work on days the hospital day care wasn't able to, until a spot in a preschool opened up. She'd felt *happiness* each time Aoife had run into her arms when Sorcha picked her up from day care, the effusiveness of the child's joy the most contagious thing in the hospital.

The only problem were mental red flags reminding Sorcha that her feelings—joy and self-worth—were fine, acceptable within the range of human emotion, but could spiral out of control into...*love* if she wasn't careful. And love was problematic for so many reasons.

Love led to dependency, which could only lead to loss. She'd seen what it did to her parents when her sister had passed, had felt it in her own way with Rachel's illness, then death.

No, thank you.

Loss was a variable she couldn't control, but love sure was.

Which was where the regret came in. Doting on the four-year-old was fun, especially the parts where Sorcha got to take her out for ice cream, or to the park on a sunny but chilly afternoon. But when Aoife held her hand and squeezed it— half of her wanted to not let go. The other half wanted to run for the hills.

And that was nothing compared to when Patrick met her at the apartment he'd rented for himself and Aoife. What Sorcha felt when he approached her was *much* more dangerous.

He'd been clinical at first, the paragon of professional. The third day, though, he'd smiled at her. The grin had penetrated Sorcha's armor and punched her right in the gut. A gut that was conspicuously warm and squishy every time Patrick was within eyesight. Day six and seven were worse; he'd offered to take them for ice cream, which was fine until he'd paid for Sorcha's and they'd each walked back to the apartment holding one of Aoife's hands.

It was entirely too close to being a family, at least on the outside. Sorcha didn't want another of those, but how could she stop giving that little girl everything she asked for?

How was she supposed to turn off the feelings brewing in her fickle heart for Aoife's father?

It was a mess. Especially since Patrick had asked if he could observe one or two of her patient meetings and surgeries over the next couple weeks—meetings with patients who would be afforded a chance to participate in the blind trial if it was funded.

What was his interest? He either didn't trust her ability to do her job or he wanted to be around her more, and neither was okay. The only thing keeping her tethered to the ground was managing to avoid him at work.

And now he wanted to *purposely* meet? Her heart fluttered. *Knock it off*, she admonished it.

"Good morning, Dr. Kelly," Patrick greeted her outside the patient's room. The formality was expected, but it stung a little to lose the "Sorcha" rolling off his Irish tongue in the way her name was meant to be pronounced. Even if it did speed up her pulse each time he said it.

"Good morning, Dr. Quinn."

He smiled, and dammit if it didn't have the same effect on

her as her name uttered from his lips. Her stomach flipped and thankfully, she wasn't hooked up to a heart rate monitor.

"Aoife wrote you a letter this morning," he said, his voice lower. He'd also somehow moved closer to her. A problem since she'd had her patient's chart ready to recite and the medical statistics were replaced with the scent of his cologne. Just a hint—nothing overpowering enough to bother a patient. "I'm sorry to say I can't report on its contents since she hid it under her pillow and then tucked it into her jacket pocket this morning."

"She wrote me a letter?"

Patrick shrugged, drawing attention to his broad shoulders draped in a lab coat. He looked both professional, and very much like a movie star playing a doctor on television. Cue her traitorous heart that thumped faster.

He's your boss. He's your boss. He's your—

"Said something about the fairies and how they listened to her ideas."

He brushed it off, but Sorcha's alarm bells went off. Aoife had already confided that she was pretty sure Sorcha had been brought to her by the American fairies. To what design Aoife hadn't said, and Sorcha was in no hurry to unearth that secret. Not if she wanted to keep her distance. "Anyway, it's my tiny terrorist's way of demanding sweets when you're with her. Feel free to tell the girl she can't subsist on ice cream—God knows I've tried and failed on that account."

Sorcha gave a half-hearted laugh and pulled up the patient's chart on her tablet.

"Sorry, Dr. Quinn, but I think we should get this going."

"Sure. Sorry." Why was he apologizing? He was her boss.

About time you *remembered that...*

Sorcha needed to focus on anything other than the doctor who made her feel less like a physician and more like a woman in want of something other than a career. She opened her mouth to rattle off the patient's name, age, diagnosis and prognosis, but stopped.

"Is this observation something you're doing for all the surgeons, or is there something you don't trust about my ability to do my job?"

If that was the case, it meant the feelings she was having—the inappropriate ones—were one-sided. She wasn't sure which way she wanted him to answer.

"No."

Damn. So, he wanted to spend time with her?

He raked his hands down his cheeks and she felt a twitch in her own palms, wondering what the trimmed beard he'd grown out would feel like. In the fluorescent lights of the hallway, it looked dirty blond, but in the daylight, she'd caught hints of red that gleamed.

"I'm sorry if I've been vague. It has nothing to do with your work, Sorcha. Boston General is lucky to have you on its team. I have no reservations about anything you do, honestly. Actually, my interest is in your research, and your patients are a huge part of that."

She opened and shut her mouth twice, unsure of what to say. He hadn't mentioned her research since the day she'd given him a tour of the hospital. A pair of nurses walked by them and giggled to each other after stealing glances at Patrick. He didn't seem to notice them at all, despite their lack of subtlety. Frustration prickled her skin.

"Why?" she finally asked.

"If you're going to apply for the next stage in your clinicals, you'll need a handful of observations and letters documenting how the patients would have benefited from being part of the trial. I'm just getting a head start on that process so when the time comes, you'll be ready. It'll also help the new oncology floor in the surgical wing become established as a specialized cancer center, to have the whole team behind the trial and its implementation."

The initial disappointment that his observation did, indeed, have to do with work gave way to excitement.

"A cancer center?" Her research was so specific, she wasn't sure it was eligible.

"Yes, the American Cancer Society won't list a surgery center on their register that hasn't been through the screening process for at least three clinical trials related to childhood cancers, and yours has three potential different trials that could put it to the front of the line and maybe increase funding possibilities."

"You really did read my research." No one else had ever taken the time, not even Mick. And here Patrick was, a week into the job, not only having read it, but planning her next steps and envisioning broader implications than she'd dared to dream of.

Patrick's brows furrowed and his lips twisted. "Of course I did. It's brilliant, Sorcha. It has a lot of potential, but if I'm being honest, your plan to move forward the application for funding without this kind of scaffolding worries me. It wouldn't have done ya any favors." The slip of a thicker brogue in his speech flicked at her heart, waking it up. "You're onto something but you've got to be patient."

The air around them stilled, charged with a tension now, at least on Sorcha's end.

"Patient?" she echoed. That one word slashed through the recognition of her work, all the kindness he'd bestowed on her. Her racing heart. "I've *been* patient." He swiftly moved them out of the hallway and tucked them into an alcove with patient room supplies. Her limbs tingled with pent-up rage.

"You want me to be patient, do you?" She poked a finger into his chest, but it met with a solid wall of masculine flesh. She winced at the pain shooting up her arm. She felt even more aggravation that *of course* this man was as strong as he was handsome. "That's *all* I've been since I was five years old. Wait for my parents to notice they still had a daughter. Wait to be old enough to go to medical school. Wait for a resident to check off my research. Wait to be allowed to continue what I've worked my whole life on. Wait to get the job that will help me finish this phase of the plan so I can finally start saving children's lives and get back to living my own."

She finished, breathless and hot behind the eyes.

He placed both hands on her upper arms, rubbing them with his thumbs. She hated that it calmed her down.

"You done?" he asked. She nodded, vaguely aware that she'd poked and screamed at her *boss*. Fire flamed her cheeks. "I didn't mean any harm by saying it, but I won't take it back, either. Your last month of data was rushed, and your funding letter was half-baked at best. If you want to do this, it has to be airtight. You've come too far to let it slip through your fingers because you raced to the finish line without triple-checking each step."

She breathed deeply, filling her lungs with the stale hospital air.

"You're right," she whispered. "I want this. More than anything else in my life, and it was so close to coming to fruition with the interim position. And then maybe, I'd—"

She cut herself off. This man had a way of drawing truths from her as if he was a skilled nurse drawing blood. She barely felt it while it was happening, but this one she caught just in time.

"Maybe you'd what, Sorcha?" Patrick had moved closer, and in the confined space, she felt trapped by his gaze, his scent, his accent. And she wanted all three with the deepest part of her, the part she kept tucked away and out of sight.

Human connection might be a liability, especially when it was combined with intimacy, but in her weakest moments, she craved it on a biological level. Around Patrick, all she seemed to be having were weak moments.

"Nothing. We're running late to see our patient."

"You can trust me, you know. Not because I'm your boss, or Rachel's husband, but because I want what you want."

Sorcha was thankful for the dim lighting in the small storage space. Maybe Patrick couldn't see the way the heat from her cheeks spread down her neck and shoulders. Because there wasn't any way he wanted what she was too ashamed to admit she desired—him, pressed against her. Hell, she wasn't sure it was actually what she wanted, just that in the moment, it was all she could think about. Guilt at lusting after her best friend's husband threatened to override her senses as much as desire did. Both warred with one another, neither winning out.

Could he sense that, too?

"The study to be funded?" she asked.

He paused, then nodded, stepping back. He put his hands in his pockets and gazed down at her.

"Yes. Of course. The study."

The end of Sorcha's tongue felt tingly as she chewed on Patrick's words. "I... I don't know what to say. Thank you, I guess."

She had been thorough, patient, and focused, which her mom called *tunnel-visioned*, with the data at least. At the risk of having anything resembling a social life. Maybe that's why she was fantasizing about a man who wasn't only her boss, but her dead best friend's husband. There wasn't any other excuse for her inappropriate feelings. She bit her bottom lip as guilt finally won out.

Patrick nodded, his gaze dipping to her mouth. One hand rubbed his chin thoughtfully. "So, we should get back to the patient, yeah?"

"We should. But thank you for taking an interest." He stopped and his lips parted. She shook her head. She'd never openly desired anyone before—and leave it to her to pick the least okay person as the one her body seemed to want. "In the research, I mean."

"Yes. Yeah. I mean, of course." He walked out of the storage room and through the doorway to her first patient of the day. "So, who are we meeting this morning?" he asked.

Sorcha put on a smile she reserved for her tiny tot patients and followed him into the room, grateful for work that would hopefully distract her from the man just inches to her left. If she couldn't focus and ignore his pull on her, this was going to be an excruciatingly long nine months working with Patrick Quinn.

For her sanity, her research, her future, it was imperative she do just that. Because she'd worked too hard to let her pesky feelings get in the way of her one goal. Except it seemed like it would take an eternity to forget the way her stomach flipped every time she shared a space with Patrick, the way her heart beat as if she'd been jolted by AED paddles when he smiled at her, the way desire for him flooded her nervous system when she let her imagination run wild.

And as he'd just pointed out—she wasn't exactly a patient person.

CHAPTER EIGHT

PATRICK LEFT THE hospital in a daze. The day had been long, with two follow-up surgeries on patients trapped in the hotel. One of them had pulled through and, save some wicked scars, would be able to resume life as usual in a few months. The other victim would never walk again, despite Patrick and his team working a cervical spine miracle to help him keep his legs.

He rubbed his eyes, but they burned with exhaustion. He needed a drink and a twelve-hour nap, but, like the previous five nights since Sorcha's little tirade in the storage room, he was certain sleep would elude him yet again.

It wasn't the work, even though the building renovation coupled with surgeries was mentally and physically draining. In fact, he'd been glad of that so he could go home, make dinner for him and Aoife, then crash when she did.

But that hadn't happened, not once.

Patrick lifted the collar of his coat against the April wind and walked to the elevated train station.

Every time he closed his eyes, he pictured Sorcha's cheeks as they warmed with heat, her bottom lip pulled between her teeth, the way her chest—her exquisite chest—rose and fell with each breath. He'd studied the wrong thing in med school, it seemed. Had he known there was an entire woman to dissect, to pull apart each action and word she spoke, he might have focused on a very specific aspect of human anatomy and damn the rest.

But then he'd never have met Rachel... That line of thinking sent the guilt and confusion spiraling from there. His brain went into overdrive the minute his head hit the pillow.

Was a second chance at romance possible after he'd been given a gift as precious as Rachel the first time around, only to squander it?

What would happen if he took Sorcha's hand while they walked down Newbury Street the way his daughter was able to without batting an eyelash? Would her hand be soft and pliable in his?

What would that bottom lip of Sorcha's taste like? God knew that one had kept him up more hours than the rest. Which led to other questions.

He'd loved his wife, but did his new feelings for Sorcha negate that? *Possibly.*

Did he feel lecherous lusting after a surgeon under his care? *Absolutely.*

Were Sorcha's own feelings about Rachel too complex to even consider blending them with his own? *Likely so.*

Was he capable of letting all of this go and getting to sleep so he could function at the top of his game? *Definitely not.*

The train came and Patrick stepped inside, the warm air like a balm to his heart. Unfortunately, it also made his eyelids that much heavier.

The whole thing was a mess, especially since he still had to find the courage to reach out to Rachel's parents, to introduce them to their granddaughter and say a final goodbye to his wife. It was getting harder and harder to do that, the longer he spent with Sorcha. What if they saw right through him for even considering another woman while his wife's ashes were still in his possession?

He walked up the stairs to his building and sighed.

That's not what's happening. I'm allowed to move on at some point. I have to, for Aoife's sake. I still love Rachel. I always will.

Not that it mattered. It wasn't like Sorcha had ever shown him anything other than mild professional courtesy; any actual kindness was aimed toward his daughter.

So, why couldn't he stop thinking about her as *more*—so much more—than just a colleague?

He took a deep breath and put his keys in the lock, opening the door to his and Aoife's apartment. Just thinking about his wife and Sorcha in the same breath sent waves of guilt crashing against his chest, where memories of life with Rachel lived.

A shriek greeted him, followed by another, louder, high-pitched squeal. They acted like a jolt of caffeine jabbed straight in his heart. He tore off to the back room where the sound came from, and stopped short when he turned the corner.

Oh, thank the gods.

He sighed with relief at the sight of Aoife doubled over laughing. He leaned an elbow against the door frame and took deep, calming breaths. She was okay, so he was, too. Until he glanced over at Sorcha on the floor, her red hair spread out like a crown of fire. Her shirt was inched up just above the waist of her jeans, giving him a peek at her taut stomach.

Oh, no. That small swathe of perfect, creamy skin was sure to take a starring role in his nocturnal imagination that night.

She giggled, her cheeks a different sort of red than they'd been around him. Her eyes were brighter, too. Till they landed on him. She sat up and ran her fingers through her hair, making his own fingers twitch with jealousy. Her light green eyes grew into jade stones.

"Patrick," she whispered, standing up and tugging down her shirt. She held his gaze and a fire grew in his chest. *This.* This was what confused things—the appearance of what a family might look like with Sorcha as part of it. Each time he had that thought, his memories of Rachel faded ever so slightly.

"Da!" Aoife yelled, and catapulted into his arms. He hugged her tightly, but his eyes didn't leave Sorcha. She'd pulled that infernal bottom lip between her teeth again. Couldn't she see it unraveled his good sense each time she did that?

"Looks like you've been having fun," he said to his daughter. He put her down on the floor in front of him and realized from her luminous smile how true the statement was.

"Oh, the absolute best! Sorcha and I were writing notes to the fairies and letting them know I still need a puppy—"

"Which I explained can't happen since Irish fairies can't risk the puppy falling into the Atlantic Ocean on their trip over. She'll just have to wait until she's home to have one," Sorcha added.

He mouthed, *thank you*, over Aoife's head. Sorcha nodded. But his heart thumped a little harder when she said "home." For the first time since he'd left for American medical school, he didn't picture "home" as his flat in Dublin. Hell, the image of Ireland didn't crop up at all.

Unfortunately, what did was a lot like this, Sorcha included. He swallowed hard.

"I know…" Aoife crooned. "But I had to put something in this letter. 'Specially since the fairies already brought me you, Sorcha."

The red painted on Sorcha's cheeks deepened, and he wondered if there was heat behind the color as well.

"Aw, that's sweet. What was it you asked the fairies for?"

Aoife nodded, running to her wardrobe. She retrieved the crinkled piece of paper Patrick recognized, and he froze as Aoife pointed out the bottom item on her list. His throat constricted and he held his breath, waiting to see Sorcha's response instead of intervening to change the subject.

Her chest hitched and her eyes welled with moisture. Was

that the quirk of a smile playing on her lips, or was he imagining what he wanted to be true?

No, you don't want her to want you that way. She was Rachel's best friend, and you stole her job. Those feelings are bound to confuse things.

He ignored his overbearing conscience.

You still have Rachel's ashes on your mantel.

He accepted that particular admonition, but still, his heart saw things a little differently. How could it not, when this woman was so magnificent with his daughter?

That's not entirely true, either. His conscience jumped in again. *You respect her for how she treats Aoife, but you like her for other reasons.*

That was closer to the truth, wasn't it?

Sorcha was good craic, and knew how to have a laugh.

She was brilliant at her job.

She cared for people more than they'd ever know...

Was *he* one of those people?

"You asked the fairies for a new mother?" Sorcha asked. She glanced up at him, her eyes searching his.

"I did. My da said the only thing less likely was a puppy, so do you think, now that I've found you, I could get one of those spotted dogs like the one in the park yesterday?"

"Oh, darling, that's a Harlequin Great Dane. They're more horse than puppy. Let's think through some other options that wouldn't give your *da* a heart attack. Now, why don't we clean up this mess so the fairies are more inclined to grant you two days of ice cream in a row."

Sorcha smiled and patted Aoife on the head, changing the subject for him. What did she think about Aoife's proclamation, though? She'd made it pretty clear she'd had a rough upbringing but did she want a family of her own? Maybe he'd ask her that evening—just out of curiosity, of course.

Hopefully her answer would provide some needed clarity to his other questions.

He looked up images of the Great Dane they must've seen. Sorcha was right—they were half equine to be sure. But they were beautiful. Graceful despite their size. And the black-and-white-spotted puppies… They were hilarious, floppy things. He chuckled, then stopped himself when the ladies looked his way. Something about the way Sorcha smiled at him loosened the knots in his throat.

He clicked out of the search. Who would watch the puppy while he was in surgery? Would they bring the small pony back to Ireland? No, obviously not.

Clearly he wasn't in the right state of mind to think through major decisions when he was this exhausted and hungry. Best let everything percolate and then dive in when his head was clearer.

"Where are we eating tonight, girls? I don't think I can do another lobster roll."

"Now you hush before the food gods smite you where you stand. Lobster rolls are heaven," Sorcha said. She scooched past him to put some books on the shelf, and he caught a whiff of spun sugar with some kind of floral undertones. Lilac, maybe?

He inhaled it into his lungs. Hell, the woman had infected him skin, mind, and heart, and she didn't have a clue. What would she think if she could read his sordid mind, the thoughts he had of kissing her and seeing if she tasted as good as she smelled?

She'd smack him back across the Atlantic was what she'd do.

"I like them, too, Da," Aoife said, hands on her hips and bottom lip pouted just so.

He sighed. Was there anything he'd deny her? His gaze flitted to Sorcha. Aoife thought she wanted another mother, but what would happen if Patrick entertained that? Would she grow up and feel betrayed that he'd moved on so quickly?

"Okay, then which food truck? MacMillan's or Finn's?" he asked. Anything to give his mind and heart some rest from the relentless pelting of questions he had no answers to.

They cheered and he had a startling thought.

He didn't know much, but he'd eat lobster every meal for the rest of his days if he could keep those smiles on their faces.

The alarm echoed off the vaulted ceiling in the bedroom. Patrick yawned and rubbed the lingering sleep from his eyes before stretching. Man, was he tired, all the way to his bones and the marrow inside them.

He'd gotten a better night's sleep than he'd had in over a week, but his dreams were strange and filled with scenes that left him wary and unsure where he was when he awoke.

For starters, when the alarm had first startled him awake, his hand had reached over and patted the still-made side of his bed. What had he been looking for?

He sat up and frowned.

Oh, yes. In his dream, Sorcha had been tangled in the sheets with him, her lips on—well, on places that made him half-hard just imagining it for a fraction of a second. He let the rest of the dream evaporate, but its aftereffects lingered while he dressed, dropped Aoife off at the hospital day care and walked to his office.

He might've gotten more sleep, but he sure as hell wasn't more rested.

On the way, he checked his email.

"Holy hell," he whispered when he saw one from the board, copied to Mick.

The subject line simply said: Re: Kelly Neuroblastoma Clinical Trial—APPROVED.

"She did it."

He didn't have time to process the good news, however. Mick caught up to him, two paper cups of what had better be straight espresso.

"Hey, there, Chief. How's it going?" Mick asked, handing Patrick a coffee.

"Pretty damn good, actually."

"Really? You look exhausted."

"Thanks," Patrick said, throwing back the scorching coffee and dumping the empty cup in the trash. He didn't even care that his taste buds were torched. The pain woke him up more than the caffeine would. "You get the email?"

"I did. Good news for Sorcha."

"For the hospital, too. That why you're following me to my office?"

"No, actually."

"Well, then, to what do I owe the honor?"

"I can't just want to talk to my good friend and find out how he's warming to being back in Boston?"

Patrick glanced at Mick whose eyes were downcast. "I've got some news I can't wait to share with someone much cuter than you. I've no time to chat," he teased.

Mick sighed. "I want to check on Sorcha. I haven't been able to connect with her lately, and I'm concerned about how she's taking things."

"What do you mean?"

Mick shrugged. "She's not in her lab when I swing by, and she's *always* in her lab. Hell, I had to lecture her about taking a break now and then. I'm worried she's depressed or something. Have you seen her?"

Patrick swallowed hard, his mind trailing back to the end of his dream that morning.

Not the way certain parts of my anatomy would like to.

"She's fine, far as I can tell. Been helping me out with Aoife."

Mick's mouth fell open. "She's *babysitting* for you?"

"I wouldn't call it that," Patrick said, annoyance creeping into his voice. Technically, Mick wasn't wrong, but it felt different somehow. Like they were a family of sorts. An unconventional family, but a caring, functional one nonetheless.

"Call it what you want—she's spending time with your daughter instead of working on her research? Does she know the trial has been approved?"

"No. I haven't seen her yet. But I'll let her know as soon as I do. Don't worry—she's up to the task of taking it on. Aoife and I won't get in the way." Why had Patrick added himself to the mix?

"Did you bribe her? Perhaps blackmail her with some sordid secret from her past?" Mick asked, still incredulous. Patrick frowned and crossed his arms. Mick threw up a hand. "Fine, fine. I'm not concerned about her work ethic, don't worry. I've just never seen the woman take more than a day off from the lab, and that was for a conference on pediatric neuroblastomas. I'm surprised, is all."

"It was her idea. Now, anything else I can help you with or can I get back to work making your hospital fabulous?"

Mick had the audacity to grin, hinting at a joke Patrick wasn't in on. "Sorry to bug you. Carry on and keep…doing exactly what you're doing."

Patrick's frown deepened, as did his confusion. "I will." He shook his head as Mick sauntered off, looking awfully pleased with himself.

Jeez. I need an IV of coffee and five minutes with my thoughts so I can plan out the trial's announcement to the public without Sorcha's scent infecting my rational thought and my boss being cryptic. And I have to find her to share the good news. Maybe then she'll forgive me for taking her job.

Patrick rounded the corner and stopped. Okay, maybe he'd get two of those accomplished right away. Never mind that they were out of order.

Sorcha was there, pacing outside his office. His heart palpitated in his chest.

"You're here early!" he proclaimed as he walked up. He smiled, unable to stop that little tic whenever he saw her. She didn't return more than a furrowed brow.

"I got called in by a nurse at the request of a family."

"They couldn't wait until you got in at seven? I'll talk to them—"

She put a hand on his arm and shook her head.

"What's wrong?"

"I know the family. Their little girl has been in twice before and this time...this time it's bad. I need your help," Sorcha said. He nodded, already willing to give her whatever it was she wanted.

"Anything."

"I can't quite figure out an approach for this patient." The frustration showed on her face and in her voice. He'd bet she wasn't stumped all too often.

"Show me the X-rays?"

She nodded. "They're up in the lab."

Seconds later, he stood in front of X-rays that were bleak at best. Sorcha had undersold the twisted neuroblastoma that greedily took up a large portion of the patient's films.

"Oh, no," he whispered, reaching for the chart on the desk in front of the images.

"She's seven, this is her second tumor," she said as he read the same information. He closed his eyes. A parent's worst nightmare. No wonder the hospital had called Sorcha in. Her bedside manner and surgical brilliance made her a favorite among the surgical staff. "The first one we resected, but this time, it's twisted around her spine."

Patrick pinched the bridge of his nose. "She'd be a candidate, wouldn't she?" he asked.

"If the trial was fully funded and ready to go, she would."

Which it wasn't. He was itching to tell her the good news, but it wouldn't help this patient, so he kept the celebration close to his chest. Best to keep her focused so Sorcha could save this little girl now. So they *both* could—this surgery would take two accomplished surgeons, and even then he wasn't sure they could pull it off.

"What do you want to do?" he asked.

Sorcha leaned in toward the X-rays and ran a finger along the border of the white strand of the tumor.

"I want you to help me find a way to save her."

Patrick inhaled and let the air calm his tachycardic heart. He didn't know if it was possible, especially since the trial wasn't going to be up and running soon enough. They weren't even meeting about the trial until the beginning of next month, and this patient didn't have that long. Bureaucracy would kill more patients than tumors.

Damn if he wasn't going to do everything he could, though—for the patient, sure. But also for the woman standing next to him.

After they saved the young patient's life, he'd tell her the news that would change both their lives and the lives of thousands of patients.

He smiled, despite the tension in the imaging room.

"Okay, let's make a treatment plan. And then, I'd like to grab a coffee and talk."

CHAPTER NINE

SORCHA WORRIED ON her bottom lip while Patrick scribbled on a tablet. She had her own open to the latest literature on neuroblastomas and spinal implications, but it didn't matter. This was the third time she'd read it that morning.

"We could go in through the front," she offered.

He nodded, but his frown said that wasn't the best approach.

"Or we could start with a posterior attack, get what we can, and then use chemo and radiation to shrink the rest."

"Maybe." Patrick opened his mouth to say something else, then frowned and closed it again. When he repeated the action twice more, Sorcha clicked off her tablet.

"Is it really hopeless?" she asked. The "without my clinical trial being funded five weeks ago" was implied.

"No. But you're not going to like what I'm thinking."

He turned the tablet toward her. The patient's scans were marked up with yellow and red highlighter, making the tumor look like part of a video game racecourse instead of a death sentence for a child not even old enough to play video games.

"You're right. I don't like it. Not one damn bit."

He scribbled something illegible in the corner. It wasn't the time to notice, but Patrick was adorable when his lips were twisted in concentration. What would it take for him to soften them, to relax?

"We can—"

She held up her hand. "I don't like it, but we don't have a choice. I agree with you that this is the best course."

"Are you sure?" he asked.

She nodded, and this close, his scent—that damned coconut oil and Irish pine—snuck around her throat, choking it like an invisible tumor that was less deadly, but still its own brand of dangerous.

"Okay. Let's get prepped, but I'd like to use your posterior approach if we get in there and it looks different than the scans show. This tumor's a beast, and I wouldn't put it past the thing to have grown since we took the images."

"I wish the trial was able to help her," she said quietly.

Patrick's face twisted. "I'd like to talk to you about that, but let's help your patient first," he said.

"It's your plan, so she's your patient. I'm just assisting on this one." Even though that was true, Sorcha mentally added Elsie to the growing list of patients that needed her trial. Even if it were approved today, it wouldn't be far enough along to change the need for this surgery, but the other patients like Elsie out there waiting...

Patrick was right; she had to go step by step or risk losing it—and every patient it could help. The thing was, it'd been easier of late to be more patient, to concentrate on something other than just her research.

Spending time with Aoife was hardly an imposition. In fact, it was nice to appreciate human interaction, and feel joy, again.

And then there was Aoife's father. Sorcha didn't mind the days and evenings in Patrick's presence as much as she had in the beginning. This man was so much more than a person who'd stolen her job, abandoned her best friend. She wasn't sure he'd actually done either. He was a man who'd woken her up to all she'd forsaken in the name of research, but how could she let those feelings take root when her other feelings—about caring for Rachel's husband and daughter—were the actual complication? Even if she looked forward to Patrick coming home at the end of the day, what could she really do about that?

Home.

It was *his* home, not hers; good grief, she had to stop imagining that he felt the same deep desire she did. But the sight of his smile when he walked in the door, his pronouncement that he'd be taking them to dinner before walking Sorcha home— she'd be lying if she thought her good sense had stuck around past meeting Patrick that first day.

Oh, Rachel. I'm so sorry.

Sorcha wasn't entirely sure what the apology was for, but she felt it reverberate in her bones.

She sighed and focused on the scans in front of her. This was what mattered most, or at least it should. Yet, somehow, against all reason, Sorcha found herself wanting more. Was that possible? She didn't know, but now wasn't the time for her to try to figure out her personal life. She had work to do.

They had work to do.

She didn't want to think about a young life cut short. If she did, she'd be forced to reckon with her own story that was marred by the same loss.

"Let's give this little girl her life back," she said.

Six hours later, the room erupted into applause as Sorcha put her tools back on the surgical tray. She grinned like a kid at Christmas behind her mask. They'd traded off midway, her approach the better one after all.

As a team, they'd done it; they'd saved Elsie.

"Congratulations," Patrick said, his eyes gleaming behind the protective glasses they wore. "You were incredible."

"We all were. Thanks, team." She turned to Patrick as she handed over the patient to the nurse to bandage.

She and Patrick stripped off their gloves and pushed through the heavy doors to the sterile washroom adjacent to the operating room. She pulled down her mask and inhaled deeply.

Only now did she let the nerves from before seep through. Her fingers were still steady—years of practice ensured that—but her bottom lip quivered.

"Thank you for trusting me with a plan B instead of scrapping the surgery."

Not many surgeons she knew would have relinquished control and admitted her plan was better.

"Of course. Pivoting is vital if it means we can save the patient." Patrick washed his hands and watched her closely. "How are you?"

"Good," she lied. "I mean, it was an interesting case." She glanced through the window, at the small figure on the operating table.

"How old was your sister when she was diagnosed?" Patrick asked. How he understood so much without her saying anything astounded her. She'd known him for such a small length of time.

"Three. But she passed at seven."

Heat built behind her eyes, but she forced it back. This was neither the time nor place to stroll down that particular memory lane. Most of the time, the loss sat squarely against her heart, quiet and ever present, but her muscle was growing around it. It was mostly a driving force now, propelling Sorcha toward her singular goal—fund the trial and let it save countless children who would be luckier than her sister.

Which, if the board agreed, she'd get the opportunity to do.

"All we've done is buy her time. She'll need more than what we did for her today if she wants to go to her first school dance, to fall in love, or to find a fulfilling career. She needs—"

"To be part of your clinical trial," he said.

Sorcha nodded.

Patrick's eyes were trained on the young girl on the operating table, and Sorcha wondered if he was picturing Aoife there. It was a parent's worst nightmare, seeing your child go through something like that and being powerless to help.

Except he could. They both could.

When he turned around and faced her square on, she almost reeled at the intensity of his gaze. His eyes were emerald molten lava, liquid and emanating heat. He put a hand on her arm and his skin branded hers.

"Sorcha, you got it."

"Got what?" she asked. His smile was so out of place and yet familiar.

"The funding and approval from the board." He *couldn't* mean the trial funding because she hadn't submitted her paperwork yet... His smile deepened. "For your trial."

He squeezed her arm affectionately and maybe it was the human contact, or the fact that she finally understood what he was saying, but a few rogue tears escaped.

"But...*how*?" She wiped at her cheeks, which were damp. "When you got the interim position, I—" She choked out a sob when she realized what she'd done; she'd all but abandoned her work, partly out of grief, and partly out of appreciation for something new in her life.

A connection with two people who were growing to mean something to Sorcha, despite her adamant fear about letting anyone in.

"I never sent the final paperwork to the board."

He leaned in and whispered, "I did. After your final tweaks, it was ready to go and just needed chief approval."

"Okay. I mean, wow." Her trial was approved, *funded*, and she would finally be able to save lives. But...

"You didn't tell me you did that."

"I know, but I wanted to make right what I took from you."

It was a sweet gesture, but the circumstances... It was too reminiscent of her childhood where every decision was made for her, where she'd had no agency, no voice.

"Thank you. But can you promise me something? Include me in anything that concerns me next time, please."

He frowned, as if he hadn't even considered how his gesture could have rubbed her the wrong way. "Of course. Sorry."

"It's fine," she said. "I just deserve to know where we're at with something I've worked my whole career on." Still, excitement fluttered in her chest.

"Agreed. And I'm sorry. Set a meeting with me next week. We'll make a plan for what the trial will do to your caseload. But I have one stipulation."

"What's that?" There was always something. At this point, she'd all but sold her soul, her family, and her future for this, so what was one more concession?

"Let me work on it with you. You'll need other surgeons willing to help you on this project. I want in, Sorcha."

He took a step toward her, his gaze intense and unflinching. Between the musical quality of his accent and the way his green eyes resembled the hills of southern Ireland in the sunlight, she felt her own brand of powerlessness around Patrick. She all but forgot about her frustration with him.

Sorcha's heart rate increased.

"Why are you doing this?" she whispered. "If it's pity—"

He shook his head, cutting her off.

"I assure you it's not. Your study is what's funding my ability to be here with Aoife, to say goodbye to Rachel." Sorcha winced at the mention of her best friend. Would they ever be able to talk about her without guilt and shame tainting the conversation? "I don't take that lightly. Besides, I've seen the science. What you're proposing works, and I'd like to be part of bringing it to life."

Sorcha couldn't stop the rest of the tears from falling to her cheeks.

"Thank you, Patrick." She put a hand on his, no longer able

to ignore the pulse of energy that sang along her skin where they touched. He leaned in, dipping his chin.

Is he going to kiss me?

God, she wanted him to, wanted to know what he tasted like, and what his hands felt like tangled in her hair. She was surprised by the pulsing need thrumming beneath her rib cage.

But—

She forced herself to picture Rachel's smile, the one in the picture she'd sent Sorcha after her elopement to Patrick. When that didn't work, Sorcha reminded herself about her no-strings-no-hurt mantra.

But what if...what if we just spent the night together? Would that really be so bad? Is he a man you can spend one night with and call it good? What about his daughter? The fact he was once Rachel's husband? Could you ignore all those things?

As he leaned closer, only the scent of hospital soap and something so wonderfully masculine separating their bodies, she thought she might like to find out.

She didn't get the chance. The door opened and the nurse walked in, thankfully chatting with the anesthesiologist behind her so she didn't seem to notice the tension filling the small space.

Patrick cleared his throat and stepped back.

"Congratulations, Dr. Kelly. I'll see you first thing next week in my office."

With that, he walked out of the room, leaving her with the rest of the surgical team. His absence left a vacuum of desire in its wake but also the ability to think without being overwhelmed with the presence of a man who was changing her biology, making her want the unattainable.

But the same man had just delivered the dream she'd spent her whole life chasing.

"Woot!" Sorcha exclaimed the minute the doors shut behind him. The nurse and anesthesiologist startled. "Sorry, just excited."

"It was a good surgery. Congratulations, Dr. Kelly."

It was a damn fine surgery, but with her clinical trial approved, risky surgeries like the one she and Patrick had just performed were going to become increasingly rare. As long as Patrick kept his word, the trial was a go.

She did a little dance, her hips swaying in her scrubs, the mask around her neck joining the party. She almost forgot the way Patrick's eyes had glittered when he was mere inches from her, the way her stomach flipped with recognition at the way he looked at her, the suspicion he wanted her the same way she did him.

Ignoring his pull on her, she concentrated on the pervasive thought she'd been waiting to voice her whole life.

"We did it, Cara," she whispered victoriously. "We finally freaking did it."

CHAPTER TEN

PATRICK SLAMMED OPEN the door to his office. The hinges creaked under the force and the lab door next to him opened. A timid head peeked out.

"Sorry. Door just caught the wind."

The brunette with pink tips frowned and shut her door again.

Patrick sighed and pinched the bridge of his nose once his own door was shut carefully—and quietly—behind him.

What were you thinking? he chastised himself. *You almost kissed her in the middle of the scrub room.*

His fingertips still tingled where they'd grazed her arm. He ran them through his hair instead.

Honestly, what *had* he been thinking? That Sorcha would be so moved by his ability to do his job that she'd want to find the nearest supply closet and leap on him? What a fool he was.

The damned thing of it was, though, he got the overwhelming sense she was meeting him halfway.

It didn't matter if she'd jumped in his lap and said, "Do me, Doctor." Sorcha Kelly was hands-off, thoughts-off—forbidden in every sense of the word.

To start with, he couldn't think of her without thinking of Rachel—hardly a recipe for moving on. And what about Aoife? Sure, Sorcha and his daughter got along, but Aoife was too young to know how this might affect her future.

There was also the fact that he and Aoife were only in Boston for several more months. It'd seemed an eternity on the flight over; if he'd believed in fairies like Aoife, he'd have asked them to help him blink and it all be over, back in his own bed with his goodbyes to Rachel behind them.

But now…

Now he wanted someone else—a colleague, no less—and with each day that passed, he wanted less and less for the time to pass quickly. What a curse it all was—to desire something so far out of one's reach and want it more than anything else.

One last, insurmountable thing stood in his way. Though it was a small physical object taking up no more room than a flower vase on his mantle, it loomed large, blocking his view of anything beyond it.

It was time to say goodbye to Rachel—not her memory, which would always linger, but to his past. Maybe then he'd have an idea what to do with his future.

Patrick dialed a number he'd memorized but never used. It rang twice before a man's gruff voice answered.

"Hello?"

"Good evening, Mr. Walker." Patrick ran damp hands down his slacks. It was stifling in his office. He waited, silence the only thing greeting him on the other end. "It's Patrick Quinn."

"I know who you are. Figured I'd get this call a couple months ago when you first got here."

Patrick squeezed his eyes shut. If he wasn't a coward, he would have. He'd feared that looking into Rachel's father's eyes, seeing the grief he blamed on Patrick, might undo all the work Patrick had done to try and move on.

"I'm sorry it took so long. But I brought Rachel home to ya. And our daughter, Aoife." *There.* He'd said it, he'd opened the gates.

A deep sigh reverberated through the line, laced with years of disappointment.

"You'd better give me time to break the news to Joanna. You

can come by tomorrow afternoon, both of you. I can't promise much, but we'll be there to greet you. I'll text you the address."

Patrick agreed and hung up the phone. His hands trembled, not a brilliant thing for a surgeon.

He strode out of his office, his brain temporarily on hiatus after almost kissing his coworker and calling his former in-laws. He wasn't sure where he was heading, just that his body needed to move.

Aside from the impossible—saving Rachel's life through some magical, nonmedical means—he wouldn't have done anything differently. Aoife was a light in all his dark places, dark places that had existed while Rachel was alive. Any circumstance that led to Aoife not existing wasn't one he'd consider rewriting.

That had once led to crippling guilt, but it had lessened with time, until the only remorse remaining was his lack of guilt altogether.

Now, faced with a date and time to face Rachel's parents, it crept back.

Patrick passed by the surgical suites, noting the progress with the build. It was a slow process, but Patrick's meetings had been fruitful, and it looked like the board had approved funding for the upgrades to the equipment he'd suggested. There wasn't any use in having a new lifesaving space with out-of-date tools.

Speaking of lifesaving… Patrick realized he'd stopped in front of Sorcha's lab.

He ran a hand along the name placard on the door.

Dr. Sorcha Kelly

How many times had he heard that name, wondered about Rachel's serious supposed best friend who'd never made it to the Irish shores where Rachel lived? His wife had spoken about Sorcha first with awe, then with her own grief attached. In the last weeks of her life, she'd opened up about how her impulsivity had ruined nearly every relationship she'd ever had, including those with her parents and Sorcha.

Whenever he and Sorcha talked about Rachel, the hurt was mirrored in her bejeweled eyes. Once this meeting with Rachel's parents was over, maybe he and Sorcha could talk about Rachel, too. Not with judgment, but a sense of shared history.

The door swung open and a shocked Sorcha stood there, staring up at him. Her gaze dipped briefly to his lips, then a flash of pink painted her cheeks.

It undid a knot in his stomach, which had the simultaneous effect of sending blood to a part of his anatomy that wasn't invited to this conversation.

"Patrick." She shook her head. "Sorry, I mean Dr. Quinn. What are you doing here? Is Elsie okay?"

He cleared his throat. "She's fine. I'm just…walking around. Checking on the build. And you?"

Could she see the lie written on his face? Because what had actually happened was him following a magnetic urge to her door.

She licked her bottom lip and he swallowed a groan. What was it about her that had him reacting like a horny teenager instead of a medical professional who could separate a hormonal response to a beautiful woman from a bad decision?

"I'm headed to the cafeteria to eat a quick dinner before I dive into this next set of research. How is it coming along? The build, I mean."

He shrugged, more interested in her research—and also how her lips stayed that perfect shade of pink without lipstick.

"Good, I think. Do you mind if I join you? I'm starving."

She shut the door behind her and her lab coat got stuck. Frustrated, she opened the door again, freeing herself. Patrick swallowed a chuckle. Sorcha wasn't at all what he'd pictured. Yes, she was easily frustrated, but behind that was an intellect that was inspiring. Instead of the hard, overly focused woman

Rachel imagined her friend to be, Patrick saw a flexible, dedicated doctor and friend.

Friend?

For now...

He'd stopped denying he wanted more and focused on figuring out why and how she'd broken through his iron-clad gates.

"Sure." She stalked down the hall at her usual breakneck speed, but his long strides easily kept pace. It was adorable that the woman seemed to go everywhere with purpose. "What about Aoife? Don't you need to get home to her?"

"I do, and I will. But I hired one of the hospital day care employees as a sitter so I could get some work done tonight. I've got a couple hours left."

"Why do you only *think* things are going well with the build?" she asked, slowing halfway down the hallway to gaze up at him. He nudged her right at the fork instead of left to the cafeteria. "Wait, where are we going?"

"A secret dinner spot I discovered. Is that okay?" She nodded and he tucked her crooked smile into his memory for later, along with the catalog of her other idiosyncrasies.

They got to a side door of the hospital and he pushed it open, fighting against the wind. Sorcha tightened her coat around her core, shivering. Patrick took off his overcoat and wrapped it around her shoulders. The look she gave him with bright eyes that reflected the clouds above was a mix of appreciation and curiosity.

"Thank you," she whispered.

"No bother. Anyway, to answer your question, some shifts need to be made if we're going to make real progress in opening up access to the new floor. It's why I'm so glad your trial was approved."

"What do you mean?" Sorcha tripped, not exactly out of character, but it warmed him to his core that he was there to catch her. He left his hand on the small of her back, which all but made the chilly Boston air impermeable. He could have heated the whole city.

"Your trial doesn't care about employer insurance or premiums. It's just…good medicine." The way she beamed up at him, like he'd discovered vaccines himself, made him want to be a better man, better father, better doctor. He coughed. "So, where in Ireland is your family from?"

"Dingle," she replied.

"A west coaster, eh?" He tucked her tighter into him, and he marveled at how compactly she fit into the nook of his shoulder and side, as if he was made to support her. "I thought I detected a hint of a Kerry accent."

She playfully jabbed him with her elbow.

"Ow!" he teased. "You must've learned that from your countrymen, watching them play their lousy excuse for Gaelic football."

Patrick steered them inside a small, family-owned Irish restaurant, which was tucked away on the bottom floor of the apartment building that neighbored the hospital.

Sorcha made a mock gesture of her hand over her heart in exasperation. "If it weren't for corrupt managers and referees, we'd have had the All-Ireland this year."

He wagged a finger at her. "Tsk, tsk. David Clifford would have had the All-Ireland. Kerry still would have been buggered."

Sorcha opened her mouth as if to reply, but then they were inside the restaurant. She stared up at him, a wide smile on her face.

"What is this place?"

"It's Tammy and Aiodhán Sullivan's. They're friends of my family back home and used to have a food cart. They moved here about five years ago."

"How didn't I know this existed?"

"They're a well-kept secret and still usually sell out by the end of lunchtime. It's just local expats who know about it, I think. To be honest, this place is part of the reason this hospital means so much to me. It—" He swallowed the small stone of concern that opening up to Sorcha wasn't the right call. "It's nice having a piece of home nearby."

"You miss it?"

Patrick considered that. He was Irish, through and through, and Dublin had been his home, Aoife's home. And yet...

"I'm not sure," he answered honestly. "Parts of it for sure."

She nodded, then looked at the sparse menu, inhaling deeply with a smile on her face. Patrick shoved his hands in his trouser pockets to avoid running the heel of his palm down her cheek.

"What should I get?" she asked. When she drew in her bottom lip, her eyes were so uncharacteristically bright he couldn't help but smile, too. Bringing her here was a good move.

"You'd be a right eejit if you didn't have the stew and soda bread, but the pasties are pretty damn fine, as well."

A shadow passed over her face but she recovered her grin.

"Are you okay?" he asked.

She nodded, but her smile fell just enough that he noticed. "My mom used to make stew for us when my sister was sick. She stopped cooking altogether after—" Sorcha nibbled on the corner of her mouth and her eyes watered.

Damn it all, I can't watch her cry and not do anything about it.

Patrick rubbed her back. Was he imagining it, or did she lean into his touch?

"I'm sorry," he said. "We can go—"

"No," she protested. "I'll risk being an eejit for today since I have to get back and line up patients to invite to the trial anyway. A pastie sounds great. Thank you, Patrick, for bringing me here."

"Of course." He'd like to help with whatever trauma was buried beneath her beautiful exterior, what haunted her... But he had things to do before getting even closer to a woman inextricably tied to the past he was trying to move on from.

And you're leaving in seven months.

He wasn't so self-important that he believed it would hurt her if they started something and he flew back to Dublin, but it would crush him to leave her behind. Hell, he already couldn't imagine it, and they'd just broached the beginnings of friendship.

They placed their orders with the couple at the counter, and Sorcha shocked him further when she thanked them in Gaelic.

"Go raibh míle maith agat," she said to Tammy, who came across the counter and took Sorcha's hands in hers. "This place is amazing. I'll be back for sure," she added in English.

"Níl aon tinteán mar do thinteán féin," Tammy replied, her hands clasped over Sorcha's.

"No, there isn't." Sorcha's jaw hardened, but she sent Tammy a sweet smile.

Patrick stared at her until she turned to meet his gaze. Her eyes were lined with grief. It didn't take a medical professional to see the sadness wafting off her in waves.

"I agree there's no place like home," he said. He just didn't know where "home" was right now. "I didn't know you spoke Irish."

"My parents insisted that Cara and I learn. When she passed, I took up the charge. I'd have done anything they asked if it would bring them back to me."

"Did it?"

Sorcha shook her head. "No. We've met up for rare holidays, but it's hard forming a relationship with people who wished you weren't around most of your life."

Patrick's chest constricted like he was seconds away from a myocardial infarction. He put a hand on hers and when she didn't pull away, his heart fluttered. Okay, maybe he was closer to an arrhythmia than anything else.

"I'm sorry that happened to you. You deserved better."

Sorcha met his gaze and something passed between them. He couldn't name it, only felt it. It was as if a brick on the path behind him, the one headed back to Ireland's shores, just crumbled. He felt...unsteady.

"So, have you brought Aoife here?" she asked, finally pulling her hand away. Patrick let her have the topic change. They didn't need to dive into personal waters; he just wanted to spend time with her. Time that was whittling away at a faster clip than he was comfortable with. He could always ask Mick to extend his contract, but how long could he keep Aoife from her homeland? His family?

"I haven't. She actually hates Irish food, the sassy little *cailin*. Boston has ruined her even more with lobster rolls and sushi."

Tammy delivered their food and gave Sorcha a side hug.

Sorcha took a bite of her pastie. "This is delicious," she declared, her gaze trained on Patrick's stew.

"Want to try a bite?" he asked. Her smile brightened the room enough it didn't seem like gloomy Boston awaited them just outside the glass. Then there was the lip bite as she nodded. This woman was going to be the death of him.

"Yes, please."

He scooped a heaping bite onto his spoon and fed her across the table. You wouldn't know he was a world-renowned surgeon the way his hand trembled.

"Er-mer-gerd," she muttered, her mouth full. She swallowed and laughed, wiping at the drip of broth on her lips. Damn if he didn't want to do that for her. With his tongue. Jeez, why couldn't he keep thoughts like that at bay? "That was fabulous."

"Better than your mum's?" he asked.

Her smile didn't falter this time. "Close. Someday, you'll

have to taste hers." She dropped her voice to a conspiratorial whisper. "I think even Aoife would like it."

He leaned in, catching a hint of her floral soap. "Well, then, you'll just have to make that happen. I don't think I can head back to Ireland with an Irish lass who won't eat anything but American food."

If he weren't as close to Sorcha's face, he'd have missed the sharp intake of breath, the dilation of her pupils.

"I almost forgot your job is temporary," she whispered. The words shot straight to Patrick's heart, jolting it like three hundred volts of defibrillator right to the chest. The tips of her fingers met his on the table, barely grazing them. It was a tender enough touch it could have been an accident, but the heat in her eyes, the way the irises turned to liquid jade, said there was more to it. When her feet met his under the table, another zap of electricity shot through his core. She shook her head and straightened. "Well, we'll have to work on reforming her straightaway."

"We will." Patrick opened his mouth to reply but his pager went off, then hers. He frowned. "We need to go. Mick's paging both of us, it seems."

The words he'd been about to say—that if she wanted him to stay, to be there for the trial, for *her*, that he would consider it—were swallowed along with the stew he inhaled.

How was it that this woman, this frustratingly beautiful, serious woman he'd never even kissed, was making him forget not only his past, but his plans to return home?

Seven hells, she was making him forget the *definition* of the word *home*. Suddenly, it sounded a lot like a stormy night in the city, the paper wrapping from lobster rolls in the trash, the three of them cuddled up on the couch watching American TV shows.

The first order after dinner was figuring out why Mick had ruined a perfectly tender, vulnerable moment with a string of

after-hours pages. It damn well better be an emergency awaiting them. Nothing less was a good enough excuse for pulling Patrick out of Sorcha's orbit. Not even the work piling up
on his desk.

"Okay," she said, eating the last of her pie, "I'll follow you."

As Patrick used the pad of his thumb to wipe a crumb from
her lip, he wondered, *How far?*

CHAPTER ELEVEN

SORCHA GLARED AT her phone as she placed her empty plate in the bus bin of the small restaurant. The three notifications were from Mick: the first congratulated her, the second wondered where she was and the third wanted to meet—immediately, if possible.

She shot back a reply.

At dinner.

When her phone buzzed twice more, she sighed.

We're almost there. Had to finish eating before we came back to work.

Which is after-hours as it is, she wanted to add.

Sorcha strode through the door, holding it open for Patrick. Trial numbers ran through her head on the off chance Mick quizzed her. Anything to avoid wondering why the electricity buzzing between her and Patrick was strong enough to send a three-hundred-pound man into cardiac arrest.

Twenty-four patients to start. Three subsets of eight. First eight get the trial treatment and medication. Second eight get the treatment sans meds, and the last eight get the placebo.

Her gut churned at that last set of numbers. Placebos were a mandated part of every trial as a control group, but it didn't make it any easier to think about the children, the families, who wouldn't get the lifesaving treatment Sorcha's trial promised. The families knew what they were getting into when they signed up for the trial, but still… At least, at the end of it all, when her plan was approved, she'd never have to turn patients away again.

"Can I ask you something?" Patrick queried, slowing to a stop outside the maternity ward. Sorcha gazed at the babies in incubators, little pieces of joy and hope living outside their parents' bodies. Love tethered them to their families, but Sorcha knew the darker underbelly to that cord.

Fear.

She rubbed her chest. The proximity to the tiny swaddled bundles of Sorcha's worst anxieties made her skin itch as if she'd developed an allergy to connection, to love.

In a way, she had. It was sort of like a chocoholic finding out they couldn't have sugar anymore, though. She *desperately* wanted a family, cords tying her to others who could rely on her, who she could rely on.

Patrick had shown her that truth. Which meant she didn't want just anyone; for better or worse, she wanted him and Aoife—the family she'd inadvertently made over the past couple months.

But how was that possible? What she saw every day—the loss, the pain, the crevasse of grief that swallowed families whole? If she let that in, yes, she'd get the best parts of family—connection, support, and love. But the rest came with it, and she still hadn't figured out how to cope with that.

Her job was the only thing she could rely on; it was all she had.

Was it?

She turned her back to the nursery window and faced Patrick.

"Sure," she replied.

Patrick took her hand in his. "I'm not asking you this as

your boss, or the guy who promised you funding. I'm asking as a—" He glanced down at his feet. Was Patrick Quinn nervous? "A friend. Would you show Aoife and me around? It's been a bit since I've been here, and I'm woefully unprepared for having a kid in Boston. I keep taking her to the same three places."

As a friend.

She wasn't allowed to feel the tightening in her abdomen, or the flutter in her chest when she looked at him. She definitely wasn't allowed to dream about his crooked smile, or those lips on hers. All that was too close to "longing," which was on her "do not take" medication list.

But being friends was okay. Sorcha smiled. At least she had him in her life in some small way. It had to be enough.

"I'd like that." She pulled back her hand when she realized the heat between their palms wasn't very "friendly."

"I did promise Aoife I'd take her somewhere."

Patrick smiled, his eyes glittering with mischief.

"And where did my darling daughter demand you take her?"

Sorcha bit her lip. "In her words, she wants to see the leprechauns who throw the ball in the basket. The ones with the four-leaf clovers on their hats."

Patrick coughed.

"My daughter wants to go to a Celtics game?" Sorcha nodded. "Does she know what it is?"

"I tried to tell her, but she wouldn't listen. She said fairies and leprechauns talk and since she hadn't heard from her fairies since she'd arrived, it was important we go so she could chat with the leprechauns. Something about that list she showed us the other night?"

The color left Patrick's cheeks.

"Jeez. I didn't know she was hearing things now. Should I get her checked out?"

It was Sorcha's turn to laugh. "She's fine. She's just being four."

"What's her age got to do with it?"

"There isn't a child I work with who didn't bring an imaginary friend or two with them to surgery. And I don't think Aoife talks to them as much as wishes on them. I'll admit I did the same when I was young."

"To save your sister?" he asked.

She nodded, glad he understood. "And then to bring me another sister when the first request didn't work out." Sorcha tucked her hands into her lab coat pockets. It didn't hurt so much as ache in the place Cara lived in her heart. "The very next week Rachel sat next to me on the bus on the way to school. The first question she asked was if I believed in guardian angels. I taught her about Irish fairies and, well, the rest is history. I got the sister I asked for in the end."

Another ache, another loss. One Patrick confronted her with every time he smiled at her. Which was another reason all she could be was his friend—no matter how he made her feel.

"Rachel never told me that. But I see where Aoife gets it now. It's in the family all the way back to you."

Sorcha pushed through the steel doors of the surgical wing, ignoring the casual mention of her being part of Patrick and Aoife's family. Thankfully it was loud enough in the hallway he probably couldn't hear the way her heart slammed hard against her rib cage.

"Anyway," she said, desperate for a subject change, "how do you feel about basketball?"

Patrick's lips parted as Sorcha walked through the vacuum of space between the old part of the wing and where the new floor was being built. Whatever he'd been about to say was interrupted by loud shouting behind them. A high-pitched whistle rang against the steel door and she startled, losing her balance. Time slowed and the air seemed to still as she fell backward. Bracing herself, she waited for the crack of her head on the door. But it never came.

Instead, she found herself hitting a wall—of hard, sculpted flesh, anyway. Patrick's arms wrapped around her body, steadying her. Her pulse and blood pressure skyrocketed, wildly out of control, especially when his hands rested on her hips, righting her after her near fall.

Sorcha's breath hitched in her chest. Was Patrick's thumb caressing her hip bone, or did she imagine it? Either way, the perception of it, coupled with her imagination that ran rogue picturing what his hands might feel like on other parts of her— *all* of her—made her stomach dip.

"Um…thanks," she said. His breath was warm on her skin but still served to give her goose bumps. "I thought I was a goner."

"I'd never let anything happen to you, Sorcha," he said. His voice was thick and gravelly, as if he had something stuck in his throat. The thing was, she believed him. He'd been saving her left and right since they'd met.

Friends. We can only be friends.

The mantra felt shallow and without the same weight as before.

"Patrick, I—"

"Congratulations, Sorcha!" voices called out. She lifted her head and the blood rushed to her skin, while the whole surgery department stared at them.

She wriggled free and noticed the "Congratulations!" banner above the small crowd of nurses and surgeons. Even a few board members were there.

"What's this?" she asked. Although, as she recovered from the initial shock, she got it.

Patrick had taken her out to distract her.

The banner. The crowd…

She was at her first surprise party.

"We're celebrating your trial being approved," Mick called out. His eyes darted between her and Patrick, trying to work out what he'd just witnessed. "It was darn near impossible to pull off this surprise with you holed up in your office this afternoon, I'll tell ya that much. I thought we had it in the bag when you started spending nights and weekends—" he glanced at Patrick "—away."

Sorcha put on the most crowd-friendly smile she could muster. How much did Mick know about her free time spent with Aoife and Patrick? It wasn't like she'd done anything untoward, but Patrick was still her boss.

"Thanks, Mick. This is, er, great. What a surprise."

He grinned and pulled her into a bear hug. "You deserve it. I've never seen anyone work as hard as you. Until this guy came along," he joked, slapping Patrick on the shoulder with his free hand. "And it's a big win for the hospital. Some red tape to jump through with the board's allocation of funding, but this approval was an important step."

"Is the red tape anything to worry about?" Sorcha asked.

"Shouldn't be. But leave that to me. Right now, you two enjoy yourselves."

"Sorcha, congratulations. Unfortunately, I've got some work to do. But Mick's right. You deserve this." Patrick turned to leave.

"Nonsense, Dr. Quinn," Mick said. "You're not on call. Get yourself a piece of cake and some champagne. I insist. Sorcha, come with me and I'll introduce you to some of the board."

"Actually, can I chat with you real quick, Dr. Quinn?" Sorcha asked. When Mick sighed like he was testing his lungs with a spirometer, she glared at him. "I'll be there in a sec."

Mick nodded and joined the other surgeons around what looked like a makeshift bar.

Patrick turned to Sorcha. "Is everything okay?" he asked

her. The concern in his voice was clear. She had her own to sift through, though.

"I don't know," she answered honestly. "Were you—were you part of this?" she asked. Her skin itched, imagining that the only reason she'd been asked to share an intimate dinner with Patrick was to keep her occupied so the surprise could be pulled off. That, coupled with him submitting her trial paperwork on her behalf, made her feel...

As if her life were being lived *for* her, rather than her living it.

His eyes deepened in color, turning a deep sea-green like the Atlantic after a winter storm.

"No, *bean álainn*, I wasn't. I only wanted to go to dinner with you. Apparently we were both tricked."

The blush deepened enough she could feel the heat emanating from her skin.

"Oh." She swallowed hard. "You really didn't know about the party?"

Patrick's frown answered. "No. And I'm not sure why I wasn't invited. Mick knows we've been spending time with each other."

Sorcha's mouth fell open. "He does?"

"Of course. I wanted to be honest with him in case—" He shook his head and then met her gaze as if he was willing her to finish his sentence for him. She didn't dare in case her answer was off base enough to drive their new friendship away. "Anyway. No, I wasn't involved in the surprise."

His mind seemed to be whirring, his body torn between fleeing the scene and taking part in the festivities. His eyes darkened into jade stones before he grabbed her hand. All the blood that had pooled in her cheeks dropped to her stomach. People could *see*.

"Let's make the most of it, then," he said. "Starting with a drink. What do you say?"

What *could* she say? The man might have a hold of her hand, leading her through the crowd to the bar, but she would have followed him anyway. That secret she kept close to her heart, but it still felt like all the world could see it as easily as she wore a blush.

"Okay," she said. "Let's celebrate then. I'm buying," she teased.

CHAPTER TWELVE

AT SOME POINT, Patrick glanced up and realized the party was winding down.

"We're real party animals, aren't we?" Sorcha asked.

Patrick smiled and tucked a red curl behind her ear. Her skin matched the color of her hair, and he longed to feel the heat from her cheeks in the palm of his hand.

Sorcha hiccupped. "'Scuse me," she murmured.

A thrill whispered against Patrick's heart. And it wasn't just the champagne talking, either. He genuinely *liked* the woman, try as he had to avoid that more than minor complication.

"I must've had one too many wines."

Patrick grinned. "You've only had two. But we should probably get you home," he said.

"Thank you, Patrick. You know," she said, "you're kinda cute when you're not being an Irish know-it-all."

He swallowed a laugh since she seemed rather serious.

"Is that a fact?" She nodded. The woman was definitely scuttered. It was a relief to see her with her hair down, metaphorically speaking. "What is the difference between an Irish and American know-it-all?"

She scrunched up her lips into what could have passed as thoughtful if she weren't leaning to the left. A finger jabbed him in the chest.

"An American know-it-all doesn't actually know anything. And they don't have a sexy accent."

A single nod acted as punctuation. So, Sorcha found him both cute and sexy? *Hmm.* The information shouldn't make any difference to him, but somehow...he couldn't stop wondering what else she thought of him. They'd come a long way since he'd stolen her job, but was it too much to ask that she be as interested in him outside of work as he was in her?

But even if she was...what was he prepared to do about it? Memories of Rachel lingered just underneath his growing feelings for Sorcha, clouding them.

When Sorcha leaned on his shoulder, those feelings pushed the rest away. Patrick made a mental note that two tall glasses of champagne were the sweet spot to get Sorcha Kelly chatting. He nodded to Mick.

"I'm taking this one home. To her home, I mean. Then I'm going back to my place."

He cringed.

"Have a good night, Dr. Quinn," Mick said with a wink.

Patrick had texted the sitter he'd be late and she'd shot back to take his time; Aoife was asleep. Thank goodness for public transport since he'd had two glasses of wine as well. Holding Sorcha's hand, he meandered out of the hospital and into the cool spring night toward the train station.

When they got off a couple of stops later, the winds had died down and there was a hint of something floral hanging in the air. In a few weeks, the eastern redbud and cherry trees would be in full bloom. Spring was here, meaning there were only two more seasons for him in Boston. At the end of the year, he and Aoife would head back to Ireland, leaving their past behind them for good.

The wind wasn't the only thing that had calmed. This late on a weeknight, there weren't horns blaring, or shop owners yelling. Only the gentle hum of the city that had nurtured, helping him become the physician and surgeon that he was.

Even Sorcha had stilled, taking deep breaths that seemed

to sober her. Watching the corners of her mouth turn up as she faced the city she called home, he couldn't help but wonder—when he left, would he be leaving more than just his past behind?

"Have I told you how much I hated Boston when I was a kid?" she asked. He shook his head. "For years I thought it was a punishment for wishing my sister would get better so we could go back to Castlemaine. But now…it's grown on me." She inhaled with relish. "It smells like the inside of a flower shop," Sorcha said. "God, spring in this city is fantastic. Everything feels alive."

Patrick squeezed her hand. "It is grand, isn't it? Dublin's nice and all, but spring doesn't come till late June and by then, we're all just anxiously awaiting the one week a year we're able to hide away our slickers."

"Ah, I see where you've been tucking away your Irish slang, Dr. Quinn. Does it just take a couple of glasses of wine to bring it out?"

"Now that you mention it, I didn't really notice how much I hide my true self here. Rachel didn't understand half the things I said when we first moved to Dublin, so I think over time I carved 'em out to make room for her."

Sorcha slid up beside him again, her eyes glittering under the streetlights. "My friend was one of the best women in the world, but yer girl didn't much appreciate feelin' like an outsider."

"Not so much."

She grinned—the kind of smile he'd seen on her face in the lab when she got a result she'd been hoping for. Seeing it aimed at him sent flashes of heat from his core to his chest. And south.

Only a small pang of guilt accompanied the sensation. Talking about Rachel with a woman he'd imagined taking up her side of the bed was something he didn't think he'd get used to.

It was made all the worse by knowing Sorcha and the woman had been best friends.

Even though he'd thought about dating when he got back to Dublin, starting that off with a woman who had her own complicated feelings about his late wife felt like a betrayal.

But not enough of one to ignore the pull of his heart when she took his hand again.

"I think she had it all wrong." His stomach tightened. Could she feel the electricity buzzing against the polarities of their palms? Or was he imagining it?

He swallowed hard, tried like hell to remember why he'd felt guilty about something that felt this *good*.

"How's that?"

Patrick held his breath when Sorcha leaned in. "I think you're a right eejit for hiding who you are or where you come from, even for a second. Just be yourself, Patrick. There are those of us who'll love you for it all the same."

Love? Did she mean her? Forget his stomach tightening; it was in pure knots now.

"Um…thanks. And I'll try."

In the midst of the suddenly serious conversation, he hadn't realized they'd arrived home. Not Sorcha's, as he'd promised, but *his*. Sorcha had led him there and he'd let her. That was the only explanation for the fact that she was walking up his stairs, his hand still in hers. And he was following her without so much as an argument.

Any guilt he'd felt earlier must've floated away on the breeze. It was freeing, but he'd be lying if he didn't feel a hint of danger where the trepidation had once been.

"What're you doing?" he asked. He barely recognized his own voice it was so thick.

"Taking you home," she answered. He eked out a nod.

"Dropping me off?" he countered.

She shook her head, biting her bottom lip. Her thumb caressed the pad of his palm and goose bumps shot up his arm.

When her gaze dipped to his mouth, he didn't have any questions about what she wanted. And hell—he wanted it, too. Like chest-pounding, shout-from-the-rooftop wanted it. Wanted *her*. But...

"We've had a couple of drinks tonight, Sorch."

"I know what I'm doing." And with that, she closed the gap between them. She still wore her white lab coat, her name inscribed above the pocket—*Dr. Sorcha Kelly*, a name he'd known as long as he'd known Rachel. But the way *he* knew it wasn't tied at all to his late wife. It was his own, private knowledge.

For a split second, he imagined her jacket read *Dr. Sorcha Quinn*, and before his head got the message, his heart decided he liked that as much as he liked her palm pressed against his, as much as he appreciated her laugh, rare as it was. As much as he adored watching Sorcha and Aoife chat about fairies.

And that was all he needed to dip his chin and meet her lips.

When their mouths met, his hands—and the rest of his body—seemed to know precisely what to do. So he let them. He didn't overthink the way his fingers tangled in her crimson curls, or how soft they were. He didn't worry about how his hips pressed into hers, desperate to be as close to her as possible.

He especially didn't concern himself with the flame blossoming where their lips touched and spreading out from there like wildfire. Let him burn to ash if it felt this good, this satisfying, this—

Perfect. It's never felt this right before.

When guilt didn't follow at that admission, his lips parted and his tongue explored the curve of her lips, the shape of her mouth. She tasted like sugar and champagne, and it was enough to bring back his buzz, or at least the lightheaded giddiness he'd felt earlier.

Sorcha deepened the kiss, wrapping her arms tighter around his neck and pulling him close. Her tongue met his and he wasn't sure who moaned—maybe both of them at the same time—but he wanted her right then and there.

He slid his other hand down her back, around to her hip. Now it was definitely Sorcha who groaned with pleasure as his thumb slid between the fabric of her shirt and skin. He gripped her hip and ground into her.

"Patrick," she whispered into his mouth. His name on her lips was the second sexiest thing about her.

A dog barked somewhere behind them and whatever spell he'd been under broke. He was making out with a woman on his doorstep? The reality of their situation left him aware of just how close he'd been to damaging more than his memories of Rachel. He risked his reputation at the hospital, and so much more.

His heart, and Aoife's for one.

Patrick pulled back, breathless. This was wrong...wasn't it?

Why didn't it seem that way, despite every reason it should be?

He needed distance. Space to think.

As if anything but running back to Ireland would be enough to forget that kiss.

"Holy—" he started, extracting the hand from her mess of curls and running it through his own hair. "We, uh, *wow.*"

"For a man who's fluent in two languages and has an advanced degree, that's...one way to describe what we were doing."

She bit the corner of her bottom lip and every time she'd been stubborn, or frustrated seemed impossible now in the face of her smiling up at him like *that.*

"Yeah, I guess so. I'm just not sure what to say."

"Say you'll take me upstairs and finish what we started."

"Sorcha, I—"

Her eyes narrowed and her smile faltered.

"It's fine," she said, shrugging. For a self-assured woman at work, he was well aware of her insecurities in her personal life. *Damn.* He'd only been considering how he felt about kissing her, not what it would mean for her to give him that kind of trust. He'd really stepped in it, hadn't he? "You're right. We have a busy week ahead of us. Thanks for dinner, Patrick."

She leaned up and pecked him on the cheek before turning away and walking down the stairs.

"Wait," he called out, jumping down to the sidewalk in one leap. For the second time that night, he shut his mind off and let his body lead the way.

"Yes?" she asked. The hope in her voice was answer enough.

"I only hesitated because I want to make sure you really want this," he said. It was partly true. His body cashed in on the rest of the lie. She was in his arms again before he could reason his way out of them.

"I do," she whispered. "More than you know."

"If we do this," he began, his last attempt at sanity before he let this blaze consume him, "we can't let it get in the way of work."

"My thoughts exactly. Or your parenting. Aoife is what matters most. Even if I'm saying that through a lustful haze, I mean it."

Patrick stared at Sorcha. He believed her, that wasn't the problem. The issue was, he'd never been so turned on in his life. Sorcha hadn't just said Aoife mattered, she'd been *proving* it day after day as she helped him with his lack of childcare and then went above and beyond caring for his daughter in a way she'd been missing nearly her whole life.

And damn if that wasn't one of the sexiest things about Sorcha.

Leaving his arm around her waist, he escorted her up the stairs again. "Then, Dr. Kelly, will you come up to my place?"

"I'd like that," she whispered, leaning up and planting a kiss on his cheek. "Take me to bed, Dr. Quinn."

And that's the only thing Patrick thought about on the longest elevator ride he'd ever endured, through paying the babysitter and kissing his sleeping daughter good night.

When he came out to the living room of the apartment, Sorcha had shed her coat. Her hair was mussed, the curls and heat evidence of their earlier make out session on the stoop.

Her bottom lip was drawn between her teeth and the way she gazed up at him, eyes wide and bright, well…it was safe to say he'd never been as attracted to anyone. Ever. He let the full weight of what that meant fall to his feet.

It didn't change the love he'd felt for his wife—nothing could. But it did irrevocably alter the shame and guilt around that love and loss.

"You're beautiful," he said, taking her hand in his. Heat spread down her neck, a map of desire he wanted to follow as it meandered south.

"Shh. I don't know if you heard me out there, Patrick, but I'm a sure thing."

"That doesn't mean I can't tell you how I feel, now does it?"

She shook her head. More than likely, she wasn't the subject of much flattery locked away in her lab each day.

He threaded his fingers through her hair, cupping the base of her head. Drawing her in for a kiss, he whispered, "And you're sexy." She shivered in his grasp. He kissed her again. "You're also the most brilliant woman I've ever met." A moan this time, from deep in her chest. He kissed her a third time. "And you're the hottest doctor on the planet. Including those actors on *Grey's Anatomy*."

Sorcha giggled, but when he dipped down a fourth time, his lips brushing hers and his hands sliding down her back, her breath hitched in her chest.

Patrick cupped her butt, drawing her closer. She gasped.

"Tell me what you want. I want to give you everything you desire, Sorcha."

To prove it, he traced his lips and teeth along her neck. The sigh of pleasure that escaped her lips said he was off to a good start.

"That. Keep doing that."

Pulling down the fabric of her blouse, he traced her collarbone with his tongue.

"I—I haven't done this…" she breathed out. "I haven't done this in a while. I need you to take the lead. Please," she added.

"As you wish," he said. Cradling her in his arms, he didn't stop kissing her as he made his way to his bedroom. He set her on the bed and knelt in front of her. "Lift your arms for me," he instructed.

She obliged, and he pulled her blouse over her head. Her arms fell around his neck, but her eyes did, too.

"Look at me, Sorcha." Patrick tipped up her chin until her gaze met his. "I need to see you."

She held his gaze and he reached around, unclasping her bra. Her full breasts fell into his eager hands and damn if it wasn't all he could do not to come right then and there.

"Lie back," he told her. Sorcha nodded and lay on the mattress. He spread her legs and slid his hands and gaze down her curvy frame, marveling at her perfection. She arched her back when he teased her nipples between his thumb and finger.

"Lift your hips," Patrick growled. When she did, he unbuttoned her slacks and slid them off. His lips continued down her taut stomach and she gasped when his tongue traced her panty line.

God… His chest was tight with want, and his own pants were snug along the zipper. There was no way one woman could hold so much passion for others, such physical beauty, and such intelligence. It shouldn't be possible, but as he pulled her underwear down and his mouth pressed between her legs, he realized it was.

Sorcha Kelly was everything he'd ever wanted. At the absolute worst time for him to realize it. But that was neither here nor there. Not when *this* moment was in front of him.

"You're beautiful," he whispered, his chin resting on her thigh. She tried to shake her head, but he wasn't having any of that. He dipped his lips and thrust his tongue inside her folds, desperate to show her just how much he wanted her, how wonderful she was.

"Oh, Patrick," she moaned.

He sucked and pulled at her center until her breathing quickened.

"I—" she started. He flicked her tight core with his tongue. "Oh! Oh, God."

That was more like it. Sorcha did everything for everyone else. This was something he could give back. Something just for her pleasure. Patrick cupped Sorcha's butt and brought her hips to the edge of the bed. He swirled his tongue inside her, tasting and appreciating the brine that reminded him of the salt on his lips after a swim in the Irish Sea. He picked up his pace until her hips bucked and her knees tightened around his head.

"Yes," she called out. "I'm coming. So…close."

Patrick squeezed her backside and redoubled his efforts until her thighs spasmed and she released a cry of such exquisite pleasure all he could do was grin, his lips still pressed to her.

"Oh, Patrick," she whispered, her body still quivering. "I want—"

"Yes?" he asked. He'd give her just about anything, a realization that only mildly surprised him.

"I want *you*. Make love to me, Patrick."

"It's about damn time," he laughed. "I was hoping you'd come to yer senses and boss me around for a change."

She laughed, and as he stood in front of her, disrobing and sheathing himself with a condom, he wasn't sure he'd ever been happier. Or that he'd want to leave that happiness behind for a half life in Dublin.

And that *did* surprise him.

CHAPTER THIRTEEN

PATRICK'S EYES OPENED just enough to find the source of the pale light. *Aha.* He'd forgotten to shut the windows last night. The hint of dawn approached, and with it, a reminder of why he'd been so distracted the evening before.

Sorcha. In his home. His bed. *Finally.*

He stretched his arm out to bring her closer, only to find that side of the bed cool and empty. What the—

He sat up. Sorcha was climbing into her slacks, her blouse still thankfully missing. Memories of those perfect, full breasts in his hands, his mouth...

"Come back to bed," he growled, his body strung tight with lust again, as if they hadn't made love most of the night.

She squeaked with surprise, startling and almost falling as well. "I've got to go before Aoife wakes up. We didn't talk about...*after.*"

He patted the space beside him. "I'd like to, if you're okay pausing your stealthy exit for a minute."

She glowered at him in much the same way as when he'd been announced as the interim chief. Only this time, the corners of her lips quirked with the hint of a smile. "Fine. But only for a minute. She gets up early on nonschool days so she can have more time to play."

Was that true? He guessed it was, but in sharing parenting time with Sorcha, he'd overlooked some of the details of his daughter's life. It was nice, knowing she was cared for, but he didn't want to get complacent, either.

Sorcha sat beside him, and he wrapped an arm around her bare waist. It took all his self-control not to pull her on top of him and ravage her while he could. For some reason it felt like if she left, whatever magic had occurred the night before would evaporate.

Maybe it was high time he started asking the fairies for things of his own.

"Thank you for spending so much time with Aoife. You've been a blessing I never expected, Sorcha."

"Of course. She's amazing, Patrick. You've done a great job with her."

"I appreciate you saying so. She's a feisty one—her mother's daughter to be sure."

"It breaks my heart Rachel never got to see her grow up."

Patrick nodded, but the heat that used to build in his chest whenever he thought about that never came. He'd grieved the choice she'd made to refuse treatment, grieved her, grieved the future they were supposed to have together.

Now it was time for him to *live* again. What that life would look like, he couldn't say with certainty, only that last night's events confirmed he wanted it to include Sorcha.

One question remained, though.

"Where do you sit with Rachel?" he asked. Her eyes went wide, and she covered her chest protectively. "I think we're past pretending I haven't seen or tasted those perfect breasts," he teased. She smiled and he used the levity to pull her down onto his chest. "I want us to be able to talk about her, but I understand if that's difficult," he added. Sorcha's head fit perfectly in the nook between his shoulder and chest. Her finger rubbed lazy circles on his chest.

"It's okay. It's just—" She lifted her head to look at him.

"I hated you for so long for thinking you kept her from me, from her family."

That wasn't what he'd expected. There didn't seem to be guilt about sleeping with him, just hurt feelings about their complicated friendship.

"I know. You're not alone, you know. Her parents still want me dead." He grimaced.

"I believe it. Still, I'm sorry. I should have reached out to both of you. Life's too short for holding grudges."

Patrick kissed the top of Sorcha's head, inhaling her scent and committing it to memory. As if he'd forget even one minute of this...

"I get why you hated me, but why did you and Rachel fall out?" he asked.

"My parents and I were estranged at that point. They didn't approve of my choice of career—not when they'd 'done everything' to keep Cara and me out of hospitals."

Sorcha sniffled against his chest, and he felt the dampness where tears must be falling. He ran his fingers through her hair.

"When I got into medical school—my top choice—Rachel was supposed to help me move since my folks weren't answering my calls. Just like she was supposed to come with me to see my favorite rock band, The Frames, when we were in college. Like she was supposed to be my roommate in college."

The sun peeked over the edge of the horizon through the open windows. They were talking on borrowed time. Aoife would be up any minute. He could only pursue Sorcha with Aoife's full understanding and approval since her life would be irrevocably altered if this new thing with Sorcha went anywhere, but he wanted—needed—to take it slow where his daughter was concerned. And selfishly, he wanted Sorcha to himself as he got to know her in this way.

"Instead, she moved to Ireland with me that weekend, didn't

she?" Sorcha nodded. "I'm so sorry. I never knew. She told me that you didn't understand her, but that you'd come around."

"I didn't understand her, that much is true." She paused. "Do you mind hearing this? She was your wife, and I know you loved her."

Patrick considered that. At one point, he'd have defended Rachel to the last of his days. But Sorcha knew her as well as he did—maybe better in some respects. That they shared her should have made things more complicated, but really, it only brought him closer to Sorcha.

"She was and I did. Deeply. But she was your best friend, too."

"Thank you. Anyway, Rachel had a family who loved and supported her, passion enough to pursue anything, and yet it felt like she was always..."

"Running away?" Patrick suggested. Sorcha nodded again. "I know. It was one of our constant fights, the way she gave up immediately if things didn't go her way. Rachel was a lot of things, but persistent wasn't one of them."

Until the end.

"She was my only real family and she left me. I was so hurt, Patrick, but I still should have tried to fix things between us. Friendship should be reciprocal, but maybe expecting her to reciprocate in the same way I did wasn't entirely fair. It wasn't who Rachel was. God love her, but she danced to her own jig."

"She did, didn't she?" It was a perfect way to describe his late wife. The desire to tell Sorcha he could reciprocate, wanted to give her back all she'd given him, almost choked him. But something blocked the words from leaving his mouth.

Just when he'd thought he'd fully opened up to her.

The guilt Patrick had felt about pursuing Sorcha, his wife's estranged friend, released its hold on his heart now that her complex feelings about Rachel were out in the open, but the words still didn't come. He tipped Sorcha's head up and kissed her with everything he couldn't say. Deeply, passionately, and with all the understanding that their time with Rachel was left unfulfilled.

So why couldn't he find the words to tell Sorcha how amazing she was, or what he wanted?

A thought smashed against the back of his skull, almost breaking their kiss.

Because, when you invite another person into your life, how can you trust they'll involve you in theirs when things get tough? Is that why you turned in her trial paperwork? So there wouldn't be anything "tough" to go through with her?

Damn. He hadn't thought of it that way. Maybe.

But Sorcha wasn't Rachel, obviously; they could talk about the tough stuff.

Well, she could. He'd get there, too, in time.

Patrick kissed her again, this time softly, tenderly letting her know he was there, he heard her, and cared for her. When she shifted off him and wiped away a stray tear, his heart clenched.

"So, um, want to go grab breakfast?" she said. "I could pretend to come back over. We could take Aoife to a movie or something after."

His eyes widened. "Oh, I…"

"Sorry. I didn't mean to assume."

"No. That's not why I hesitated. I want to spend as much time with you as I can. There's just something I have to do first."

The truth hit him square in the chest. He'd come to Boston with two goals—to say a final goodbye to Rachel, and to introduce Aoife to her grandparents. And he hadn't done either. But somehow, he'd let himself develop feelings for another woman. No wonder he couldn't tell Sorcha how he felt; he was still tethered to his past.

Just a little while longer…

"That works. I'm sorry if you think I'm rushing things. I'm

just a little out of practice with—" she waved a hand between her half-naked self and his fully nude one "—this."

He leaned in again and kissed her.

"Me, too. But I like what we're doing."

"So do I." She got up and finished dressing, and he kissed her one last time at the door before she left. God, it was hard to watch her walk away, to leave his sight. That had to count for something, didn't it?

Patrick shook his head and went to Aoife's room. She was just stretching in bed, her hair a tangled mess of curls.

"Hello, *mo grá*," he said, giving her a hug. "How did you sleep?"

"Mmm… Good. I had dreams about the fairies again." Her smile was still sleepy, her eyes half-shut. "I think they finally got my letters."

"Oh, yeah?" Aoife nodded. "Why's that?"

She shrugged. "I heard Sorcha's voice. She's the one, Da. For you and me."

Patrick's heart pounded in his chest. "What about Ma?" Aoife had mentioned a new mother for herself before, but never a person for *him*. That she might understand the distinction, even a little, gave him hope. It also unlocked a new challenge— walking the line between the past and future with his young daughter. He wanted to show her where she came from but also where they could go. It was a tall order.

"I loved Ma, didn't I?" she said.

"Of course you did."

"And I love Sorcha, too. Can't I love two people at the same time?"

Patrick's throat threatened to close altogether. "Um, yeah, you can." Which meant…he could, too. Something cracked in his chest, letting in light. "I want to talk more about this, but can you do me a favor and get dressed pretty quick? I want to take you to meet some people."

"Mommy's people?"

Patrick smiled. "How did you know?"

She shrugged. "You told me we would when we got here."

He laughed and ruffled her hair. "You're too smart for your own good, love."

Aoife hopped out of bed, dragging the stuffed bunny rabbit Sorcha had bought behind her.

"Please let this go okay," Patrick whispered into the ether. Whether his words were meant for some higher power or Aoife's fairies, he didn't know. Only that he meant them with every cell in his body. His future depended on it.

Two hours later, Patrick and Aoife were both sitting uncomfortably in overstuffed chairs in the Walkers' living room.

And no, it was not going well.

Rachel's parents had agreed to meet them at their home, but hadn't said they were excited to see him and Aoife.

When they'd arrived, he'd seen why.

Joanna was a mess. She'd headed right for them, arms outstretched, and Aoife's face had lit up like she was under OR lights. But Joanna had bypassed Aoife and held her hands out for Patrick to put Rachel's urn in them.

Aoife had gazed up at him with hurt and surprise, and if he were a smart man, he'd have left. But these people had lost a daughter, and he knew grief did some pretty heinous stuff normal pathology couldn't explain.

But so far, all Patrick had accomplished was repeatedly answering Joanna's pleas to share Rachel's last words with her. David had demanded Patrick walk him through Rachel's diagnosis and treatment, wondered out loud why Patrick hadn't brought her "home to the States," and then had the audacity to openly blame Patrick for not being the surgeon to operate on Rachel's tumor.

"That's not how it works," Patrick had responded. "It's a massive conflict of interest to operate on family."

"Sure it is. Or it's a crime not to take your loved one's care into your own hands. You see it your way, we see it ours."

Patrick raked his hands down his cheeks.

"Aoife drew you a picture," he said. "Go ahead and show them, *mo grá*." Aoife, glad to be mentioned, held it up.

David accepted the paper, a crayon rendering of their family, with Rachel as an angel bearing wings, and the addition of a puppy and fairy to round off the image. It was so absolutely his daughter that Patrick smiled despite the atmosphere in the room.

"How old are you?" David asked Aoife without meeting her gaze. Patrick's shoulders tensed. Was this man finally realizing he had a flesh and blood granddaughter right in front of him?

"I'm four. But I can read already." She sat tall, poised, her shoulders back and smile proud.

Patrick wanted to wrap her in a hug and add that she wasn't just a reader, she was wicked intelligent, fun-loving, and the most caring girl he knew and should be as proud of herself as he was to be her da.

"Four," David whispered, glancing back at his wife, who hadn't said much of anything other than short whispers to the urn in her lap. "I can't believe she's been gone nearly that long."

Patrick's lips pressed flat. David and Joanna might be grieving, but they were also selfish, unfeeling, and blind if they couldn't see the darling girl yearning for their attention.

"Is this my mum?" Aoife asked. She reached for the photo on the table next to her chair.

David reached out and slapped her hand away. "Don't touch that," he growled.

Aoife pulled her hand back, and though the contact had

been swift and not terribly strong, her eyes brimmed with tears. Patrick had never laid a hand on her, and never would.

"Come here, *mo grá*." He pulled her into his lap. "Why don't you go play with Misty outside?" he suggested.

She nodded and skipped toward the family dog in the backyard as if nothing was amiss. God love his daughter with her innocent trust so easily repaired. When she was safely out of earshot, he wheeled on David. "Because you lost a daughter, I'll forgive you for laying a hand on mine. But don't *ever* think you'll get away with that again."

There was fire in David's eyes, but also pain. Patrick had released his own agony in order to care for and love Aoife the way she deserved, but reckoned if he hadn't, he'd look the same.

"She looks just like her, doesn't she?" David asked. His shoulders were slumped, and Patrick felt a wave of sorrow for the lost and broken man.

"She does. She's got Rachel's strength, too. If it weren't for her hair and eyes, I wouldn't be sure she was mine at all," Patrick replied.

Silence spanned the gap between the two men, punctuated by soft sobs from Joanna in the corner as she clung to the remains of her daughter. It wasn't as if Patrick didn't empathize; if anything ever happened to Aoife, he didn't know how he'd survive it. But David and Joanna had each other, and a grandchild, too, yet couldn't see beyond their grief to welcome those gifts.

Patrick's thoughts went to Sorcha, to the photo of her and Rachel on her desk at work. Even back then, in tattered jeans and fire-red hair wild in the breeze, she'd looked serious, like the world wasn't what she'd thought it was. She'd grown up with parents so wrapped up in their own guilt and grief they'd forgotten to raise her. And yet, in spite of them, she'd grown into a selfless, driven, beautiful woman. Serious, yes, but he'd seen her relax into childlike wonder at fairies, collapse into a fit of giggles with his daughter, too.

He had a new appreciation for Sorcha. For what she offered his daughter—despite not being a blood relation, she was taking the place of Aoife's family. For what she offered *him* just by making him feel emotions he'd thought were extinct.

Hell, if he were being honest, he'd never felt as safe and inspired by a woman in his life. Not even Rachel. It didn't mean he hadn't loved her whole-heartedly, just that it'd been different because *he'd* been different. Younger, less inclined to notice what sustained a relationship—trust, communication, and passion in equal measures. They hadn't had the time to learn about true connection and love before it was too late.

A flash of guilt splashed him. He hated that feeling, that he might have let his wife down by not loving her as deeply as he was able. But at the same time, he let it wash over him; he'd done the best he could at the time. If he was lucky enough to get a second chance at love, he'd learn from his mistakes.

"Son, I appreciate you bringing her here—both of 'em. But it's…" David's voice broke. "It's too damn hard. You need to go."

Patrick's jaw tightened. "You've barely spent twenty minutes with her."

"You have to understand." Joanna spoke up. "We lost the most important person in our lives and I heard what you said, that she wouldn't give up the pregnancy. I believe it. Our daughter was headstrong and impulsive from the day she forced her way into this world and almost took me out of it."

A soft sob escaped Joanna's throat. David put his hand on his wife's shoulder and squeezed, and Patrick felt the gesture like a vice grip on his own heart.

"But you were her husband and that little girl out there is just a painful reminder of what we've lost. We don't know her at all." She held up a hand. "Part of that is our fault, I'll accept that blame and carry it with me the rest of my days. But there's blame to be placed at your feet, too. We didn't visit, but we weren't the only ones."

Patrick felt *that* blow as if a three-hundred-pound man was doing CPR on him.

"I know. And I'm sorry. But we're here now."

Joanna turned to stare out the window, the conversation over.

Fine.

Patrick called for Aoife, who came running from out back, the dog at her heels.

"She likes me, Da!" Aoife exclaimed. She didn't need these people in her life if they didn't want to be a part of it. She had folks in her corner and would live a full life in spite of Rachel's parents. At least in Dublin, Aoife had grandparents who adored her.

"And I cleaned up her poop and put it in the rubbish bin. See? I'm ready for a dog, I think."

"You just might be." He had another idea, then. Patrick couldn't force Rachel's parents to love Aoife, but he could give her a life filled with love nonetheless.

"We're grateful you brought our girl home," David said stiffly.

"Of course. Aoife, say goodbye to David and Joanna." He wouldn't call them grandparents if they didn't want the job.

"Bye and thank you. Take good care of my mommy, okay?"

Patrick walked him and Aoife out, stopping just before David slammed the door in his face.

"We'll go, but know this—I won't bring her here again until I hear from you. So think long and hard about what you're giving up. You didn't have a choice with Rachel—she made that decision for all of us, God rest her soul. But you've got a choice now and you're making the wrong one, dammit. You're making the wrong one."

Patrick choked back a ball of heat that had built behind his throat as David shut the door. His eyes watered.

"Are they mad at me?" Aoife asked when they got in the car.

Patrick smiled down at her. He might not have a clue what he was doing raising a sassy little Irish lass, but he'd never let her feel unloved, unappreciated, or like she was an annoyance to be swatted away.

"Nah. How could anyone be mad at you, *mo grá*?"

Aoife scowled. "You were mad at me the other day," she pronounced. When his brows furrowed in confusion, she added, "When I took your lunch and fed it to the ducks."

He chuckled. "Yeah, I was, wasn't I? But that was more hunger, see? A man gets awful like a bear when he's hungry." He threw his head back and roared, then tickled Aoife, who giggled and begged him to stop. "But, Aoife, hear me loud and clear. Those people in there might share your blood, but that doesn't make them family."

"Because family shows up?" she asked, quoting him.

"Yep. Family shows up."

"Does that make Sorcha our family?"

Patrick rubbed his chest where a pressure had begun to build.

"Yeah. I guess it does."

To what degree? A partner? A *spouse*? That he couldn't answer. But he knew one thing for certain.

"Are you okay with me inviting Sorcha to spend the rest of the day with us?" It was a crumb dropped, to see if Aoife picked it up.

Aoife put her hands on her hips, leaned dramatically to one side and said, "Duh."

Oh, boy. He made a silent plea to the fairies to let Aoife's teenage years be easy on him.

Patrick pulled out his phone and dialed. Sorcha picked up on the first ring. "Patrick, hi. I was just thinking about you."

He smiled. "You were?"

"Yes. I'm going through the paperwork and seeing what needs to be tweaked before our board meeting at the end of the week."

"Oh, the trial. Well, I'll let you get back to it." He knew better. She was working, something he both admired and resented in that moment. The lilt in her voice, the way her Irish accent crept in when she was excited...

He wanted to be the cause of that.

"I was thinking of you in other ways, too, you know," she added. His smile returned. God, was he a goner. "So, what's up?"

"Nothing that can't wait," he replied.

"Is that Sorcha? Hi, Sorcha!" Aoife called. Patrick winced.

"Hi, Aoife. Wait, are you not here at the hospital, Patrick?" she asked. "I thought you had a surgery when I left, uh—I'm not on speakerphone, am I?"

"No. You're not."

"Do you need help with her, because I can—"

"I—we—actually came to see David and Joanna."

So we could put that part of our life fully behind us and start our future. With you, I hope.

"Oh."

"Yeah. It went about as well as you can imagine."

"I'm so sorry, Patrick. Aoife probably has so many questions." So did he. "What can I do?"

He closed his eyes, praying she wasn't asking just because of Aoife. He wanted her to ask because *he* mattered to her.

"Actually, I need a favor. Can you meet us at 1222 South Graves?"

The laugh he heard on the other end said she'd figured it out.

"Are you sure about this?" she asked.

"I am. You in?"

"Oh, I wouldn't miss this for the world. Her face will

be priceless." Patrick's smile deepened, but thankfully, she couldn't see that, either. "See you there, Quinn."

She hung up and Patrick, eejit that he was, couldn't wipe away the smile that grew each mile he got closer to their destination. Excitement at seeing her and exploring these new blossoming feelings overrode any frustration from earlier.

Despite the inauspicious start to the afternoon, it was sure shaping up to be a good one.

CHAPTER FOURTEEN

SORCHA TOOK ANOTHER PHOTO. It was hard to stop, when Aoife and the new Great Dane puppy were rolling around on the ground, the former laugh-crying with an abundance of joy while the bumbling ball of loose fur and floppy ears lapped up her tears, causing squeals.

"I love him, Da. I love him so much!"

The scene was positively adorable. A rogue wave of emotion crashed against Sorcha's chest when Aoife said, "Thank you, Da, thank you, Sorcha. Thank you, fairies, for making my family complete."

The wave didn't knock her over, though. It merely hit, a splash of water that woke her up and felt...warm. Good. *Nice.*

Which was an understatement compared to what Aoife's father made Sorcha feel. Delicious. Hopeful. *Loved.*

She shivered as his hand brushed against hers. Maybe—

No. It was impossible to expect her worldview to change overnight simply because these two had made her aware of what she'd been putting aside her whole life in order to protect her heart. She cared deeply for Aoife, for Patrick, but they were leaving at the end of the year. And then where would Sorcha be?

Alone, again. Always.

Still... When Patrick grabbed her hand and squeezed, then snapped a selfie with all of them in the frame, she couldn't help but think of her father's saying every time life took a turn he hadn't expected.

Is ait an mac an saol. Life is strange.

It certainly was. Either way, before she and Patrick slipped too cozily between one another's sheets, she should find out when exactly he and Aoife were going back to Dublin. It would be easier if she had a date in mind, and could protect her heart with a plan.

"What's his name?" Patrick asked.

"*I* get to pick?" Aoife asked. Immediately, the tears were gone and excitement took their place. "*Oh, my gosh!* I have so many ideas. But…" She frowned.

"But what?" Sorcha asked.

"But I don't want to make the wrong one. The fairies have been listening to me, which is why I have you for me and my da, and a dog for when you and my da are busy. What if I pick the wrong name and the dog doesn't like me?"

There was the wave again, stronger this time. Sorcha stumbled a bit.

"You won't get it wrong. Let the name come to you, love," Patrick suggested, saving Sorcha from having to respond through trembling lips. "Dogs and people come with a personality, and names that fit. You were always an Aoife. Strong, beautiful, and filled with joy."

"I was?" Patrick nodded and the wave of water rose up Sorcha's chest, with nowhere to go. It was getting hard to breathe.

"You were. Still are. So, what's this little ball of energy called?"

The puppy, as if he was suddenly aware of all eyes on him, put on a show of sniffing around their feet. He was such a curious dog, so filled with joy. He reminded Sorcha of the cartoon and kids' books she'd introduced Aoife to.

"I think his name is George," Aoife announced confidently.

Sorcha couldn't help but laugh. "I just thought the exact same thing."

Aoife's face lit up. "You did?"

"I sure did. Look at him acting like a detective, eager to find out everything he can about us. He's just like—"

"Curious George!" Aoife squealed. She clapped and the noise got the puppy's attention. He bounded over, jumped in her lap, and began kissing her face.

Both Sorcha and Aoife giggled.

Patrick's brows arched. "So, that's it? George?"

"George Floppy McFlopperson Quinn," Aoife announced, erupting into yet another fit of giggles.

"That's quite the birth certificate," Sorcha said. The little girl's happiness was contagious. All Sorcha's misgivings about what had happened the night before evaporated. "You might want to keep it to George when you call his name, though."

"Okay," Aoife agreed. "Maybe I'll call him Georgie sometimes, though?"

"Of course. Nicknames are required for dogs."

"I'd have thought a fairy name would be appropriate," Patrick said, scratching his chin as if he was trying to understand the scene he'd just witnessed.

"Fairy names are for *fairies*, Da." Aoife rolled her eyes and Sorcha bit her bottom lip.

"Well, I like George. It's a strong name, one I don't mind calling out in the park when he runs away." The full weight of his grin had a dizzying effect on her. She reminded herself she was a prominent surgeon who'd just had a prestigious clinical trial funded—and not a teenage girl with a crush.

"True." She smiled.

"How'd you both think of the same name?" he asked as they watched Aoife run off with the puppy. "It's like you two were speaking your own language."

When he wrapped an arm around her shoulders, she marveled at his strength, which seemed to biologically transfer to her when they touched. What might it have been like to face her challenges with the steadfast support Patrick seemed to offer? How much sooner might she have reached her goals? What new ones might have cropped up along the way?

It was a dangerous line of thinking, especially with how tenuous their future was. But it didn't stop her wondering. That was the power Patrick had over her—he allowed her to dream out loud for the first time in her life.

"It's from the kids' book *Curious George*. Did you ever read it?"

"I can't believe I missed that connection. Well, it fits. Thanks for this. It's nice to see her so happy."

"I'm curious about what happened with David and Joanna," Sorcha said.

Patrick sighed, the fires turning to dull embers. For the first time, she noticed the pain etched in the lines around his eyes. He'd been through so much, too.

"It was awful. They're still so wrapped up in their grief they ignored Aoife. Worse, they asked us to leave before they'd even asked Aoife one question about herself."

A shudder rolled through him, and it didn't take a physician to see how badly he was hurting.

"Give them some time," she said. "Let them grieve and—hopefully, with what I know of them, anyway—they'll come around."

Patrick's muscles tensed. "No. Absolutely not. They blew it. Like hell I'll give them another chance to hurt her."

Sorcha placed both hands on his shoulders.

"I know you don't want her to know any pain," she began. "But you can't protect her from every discomfort, either. That's the balance of being a parent. Rachel's folks never understood that, not really."

"Like your parents?" he asked. God, he saw right through her armor, straight to her bleeding heart, didn't he?

"No, they didn't understand, either. Maybe that's why Rachel and I bonded as quickly and deeply as we did."

"So how could I willingly throw Aoife to the wolves again?" Patrick's voice cracked and so did Sorcha's heart. She leaned her forehead against his.

"You don't. You give them time and space to grieve, then you open the lines of communication again."

"And if they don't respond? What then?"

"Then you give them more time and space. There isn't a statute of limitations on love. All I'm saying is, don't give up yet."

"Thank you," he whispered. His breath was warm and inviting on her skin. All she needed to do was lift her chin and she'd be able to claim his mouth with hers. The desire rocked through her like an electric pulse.

"Always."

She wasn't sure who moved first, but his lips met hers, lighter than the night before. He teased them open and traced them with his tongue, more tender than exploratory. She tasted salt as a tear met their mouths, but also a delicious sweetness. If she could survive on that taste alone, she would. Her fingers slid around the base of his head, fisted in his hair.

She wanted this man something fierce. He was uncertainty and disruption but also…*calm*. Sorcha eased into the kiss, deepening it.

Aoife screeched at the same time the large puppy collided with the couch. "Ew! Why are your mouths like that?" The chaos forced Sorcha and Patrick apart as if an explosion had erupted between them.

"Um…" he said, running his hands through the hair Sorcha had just had tangled between her fingers. "We were kissing," he explained. His gaze met Sorcha's and her cheeks warmed with mortification. They'd been caught red-handed doing something that was somewhere between actual kissing and something much...*more*.

"You don't kiss me like that."

Patrick cleared his throat, and Sorcha covered her laugh with a cough.

"No, I don't. When an adult likes another adult as more than a friend, as something special, they sometimes kiss like that."

Sorcha was divided between watching Aoife's grin widen and replaying his words over and over.

Likes another adult as more than a friend... Something special...

Sorcha had never wanted a family, had staved off dating to avoid the complication of caring for another person who had the power to distract her from her one goal—to help children like Cara.

Now she was playing with AED paddles—one wrong move and she'd kill the life she had mapped out for herself.

Her pager went off, breaking the mood and, thankfully, the tension.

Oh, no.

"What is it?" Patrick asked.

"It's Elsie."

He patted Aoife's head and sent her to get dressed.

"I'll get George settled and let the day care know Aoife is on her way. Meet you there?"

Sorcha nodded. Not needing to explain the urgency to Patrick was such an unexpected gift.

"I'll call ahead to the hospital and let them know we're coming." She ran out the door, her heart racing.

Patrick's scent and taste were still infused in Sorcha's skin, her lips, her hair, but her thoughts were laser-focused on the small patient they'd had on the operating table just days earlier.

She dialed the hospital on the way in, her hands gripping the phone like a lifeline.

The nurse's brief was laced with urgency. Elsie was in a medically induced coma to allow her residual swelling to subside, but when they'd attempted to reverse the effects of the anesthesia, her vitals had plummeted. It had to be an infection, but where?

Another surgery to figure out what was causing the infection was the only option. And it wasn't a good one.

"Please let her be okay," Sorcha whispered as she tore through the ER doors and sprinted back to the surgical wing.

And let the red tape get cleared on my trial as fast as possible.

That was the only sure way to save children with neuroblastomas. The crippling realization it wouldn't help Elsie, though, seized her chest like a STEMI heart attack. Sorcha barely made it through the scrub in, her vision narrow. Sounds reached her ear canal as if they'd had to travel through the whole Atlantic Ocean first. Her pulse was erratic. She knew the signs. A panic attack. She hadn't had one since she was a child, since the night her sister had passed and her parents had gone to sit vigil at the mortuary, leaving Sorcha alone with neighbors and her grief in her small room. They'd never come back to her. Not emotionally, anyway.

Would Elsie's siblings feel that same sense of loss if their sister died and took their parents' love with her?

Sorcha *had* to fix things. Had to forget about Patrick and keep her focus on what really mattered—saving lives.

But as her breathing became more and more shallow, as her vision clouded black along the edges, she wondered who was going to save *her*?

CHAPTER FIFTEEN

PATRICK PRESSED A HAND to Sorcha's forehead, another on the small of her back.

"I'm okay," she said. "It was a panic attack, I think, but I breathed through it."

"Okay. I'm still here." Her breathing slowed, her shoulders rolled back. When she gazed up at him, he was struck by two things—first, her beauty. He'd known gorgeous women in his time, his wife included. But Sorcha was magnetic, confident, and alluring in a manner that drew him to her in ways he was still figuring out. Even now, sweat dampening her forehead, her eyes wide with terror and pupils dilated, she was the most stunning woman he'd ever laid eyes on.

Which led him to the second thing he'd noted. He brushed her damp hair off her forehead and sat by her side.

I want to take care of her.

Not that she needed him to—which only added to the desire; she didn't rely on anyone, couldn't count on her family or anyone else, so he wanted to be there for her on the days she could do with someone to lean on.

Days like today, when all the independence in the world couldn't keep the worry at bay.

"She'll be okay. We know what we need to do and we got here in time."

Sorcha nodded and took a deep breath. "Thank you. I just—

I need this trial to go through. I can't lose any more children or see any more families have to—"

"I know. And it will. Mick is on it."

"I want to believe that, but he mentioned something about red tape and then we got this call about Elsie—"

Patrick squeezed her hands. "It's terrifying, I get it. But it's out of our hands. Right now, the trial isn't as important as helping this patient. Okay?"

"Yes." Sorcha shook her head. "Of course." He held out his hand and she took it. The immediate heat between their hands couldn't be ignored. This woman was his catalyst—whatever the chemical reaction was, he didn't care as much as the way she ignited him. "I'm sorry for breaking down."

"No apologies. But we should get in there sooner rather than later."

Risking a quick glance around, he planted a kiss on her cheek. Not for her, so much as him. But the smile that replaced her earlier frown was a nice ancillary benefit.

Patrick grabbed a tablet from the nurses' station in the ICU and pulled up Elsie's chart.

Sorcha sighed and he let out a low whistle.

"A cerebral edema," Sorcha declared. He nodded his agreement. "A bad one, too. I thought it was an infection."

Patrick pointed to a spot on Elsie's scan. "Me, too. This looks vasogenic, but I can't see where the swelling is coming from."

"Right here," Sorcha said, pointing to an almost invisible gray spot on the image. "The swelling is causing pressure to build up along her ocular nerve. If we don't get in there and relieve it, she'll lose her sight."

"Damn. Did I miss something in her last surgery?" Patrick wondered aloud.

"Not at all. This is a side effect of a traumatic surgery for a juvenile patient. It's why—"

"It's why we need a less invasive option like the trial," he said. She nodded and met his gaze. He understood now, in a way he hadn't until that moment. This singular focus Sorcha had wasn't without purpose. From a medical and scientific standpoint, he'd always known that, but the human component had eluded him. "This is what happened to your sister?"

She nodded again. "She died of complications from the surgery, yes. But the disease would have killed her either way. We simply didn't have the medical advancements we have now."

"Okay, you're on lead with this. Tell me what you need as your second so we can save this little girl."

The situation was fraught with tension, pressure, and risk. But she smiled. And he knew it would be okay.

Eight hours later, it was, but not without cost. Elsie's surgery was hard on the poor girl's body, and recovery would be a long road for her and family. But, sans an unforeseen complication, she'd get to walk the road not many children with neuroblastomas did. It'd never been more clear why trials like Sorcha's were necessary. All the modern, expensive surgical equipment he'd ordered wasn't going to be half as effective as fixing the problem from within, with a minimally invasive procedure.

Patrick leaned against the sterile walls and let himself slide down to the floor. He pulled down his mask and wiped the sweat from the top of his lip and forehead.

"You did amazing," he said, glancing up at Sorcha, who didn't look as half as fazed as he felt. "I'm going to tell Mick we need to get that red tape shredded, though. I can't keep having marathon sex sessions all night followed by eight-hour surgeries."

Sorcha's cheeks turned an adorable shade of crimson. She glanced around and he laughed.

"It's just us, Sorch. But does that blush mean you're embarrassed about sleeping with me?"

"No," she said, her smile crooked and oh-so-tempting. "But we're at work."

"Duly noted. You should be proud of what you did in there, by the way."

The blush deepened. "Thanks. You, too."

"Can we celebrate tonight?"

She opened her mouth to reply when Patrick's pager went off. He used the sink basin to help him off the floor. *Jeez.* Had he ever been so exhausted?

You didn't exactly get any sleep last night.

And he'd endure it again to have the time with Sorcha, vulnerable and freer than he'd ever seen her. Getting to appreciate that with his hands, his mouth…

"You'd think he had a listening device planted on me so he can reach me just before I'm about to crash."

"Mick?" she asked.

He nodded. "And the board. Must be about the contractor's bid. Mind if I take off and see what they need?"

"Of course not. But, Patrick?"

He turned around.

"I'd love to celebrate with you."

He smiled, the grin reaching all the way past the fear and trepidation, warming his heart.

"Great. I'll see you tonight. I can't wait." And that was the truest thing he'd ever said. He already hated the idea of walking away from her, but duty called.

Mick met him at his office door and gestured him inside, his eyes bright.

"Why do you look like you're up to something?"

"Because I am." Mick winked and Patrick's stomach swished with concern. Mick's plans—stemming back to when the two had known one another in med school—were usually half-hatched…yet too tempting to pass up.

"Tell me why I'm here," Patrick said. "Eight hours on my feet is only fun if it's at a U2 concert."

"Your patient is doing well?"

Patrick shrugged. "She'll live. Let's just say I'm happy about Sorcha's trial that will make invasive procedures like what Elsie went through no longer necessary."

He watched Mick's face, concerned with the half smile his friend gave him.

"Yeah. Anything we can do to help more patients."

Vague and dismissive.

"Is everything okay?" Patrick asked.

The words *Is the trial still on?* were on his lips, but it wasn't his question to ask.

His worry evaporated when Mick's smile broadened.

"Things are fab, friend. As long as you agree to be my permanent CMO."

Patrick exhaled shock. That wasn't what he'd expected.

"What happened to Dr. Collins?"

Mick waved the name off. "Staying home with her infant. She'll be back on the surgical staff next year, but she's decided the chief position is too much to take back on."

Patrick leaned against Mick's desk, his thoughts running wild. It would be a drastic shift for him and Aoife to move their lives to America. Not just for them, but for those who cared about Patrick and his daughter.

His folks would lose access to their granddaughter—at least on a consistent basis.

But... They could always fly out and visit.

"So?" Mick asked, leaning forward, expectant. "What do you say? Want to stay here and work with Dr. Kelly and me?"

Patrick perked up. He would get to work with Sorcha's brilliance each day.

And at night...

He cleared his throat. He'd be an ass if he made this decision so he could continue to sleep with Sorcha Kelly. At the same time, to pretend she wouldn't weigh into the decision would be lying to himself.

It wasn't the sleeping with her he wanted, but starting there and seeing what else was possible. A week ago, would he have thought it was a bad idea? Yeah. At the same time, *everything* had changed in a short amount of time. He hadn't set out to develop feelings for Sorcha; in fact, he considered it a small miracle anything real and substantive had taken root.

But it had. He liked her—a lot.

"I need to talk to Aoife and my folks," he said.

And Sorcha, too.

"See what they think. Aoife's life is in Ireland, and this would be a huge move for her."

Mick raised his hands. "Sure, sure. Of course you do. Get back to me by the weekend?"

"Got it." Patrick tried to keep his voice even. By the end of the weekend? That was three days away; how was he supposed to make such a life-changing decision so quickly?

"But, Patrick? Make no mistake. I want you for this job. You're the best man for it."

Patrick nodded, but his brain winced. He could use some real-life fairies right about now.

The text telling him that Aoife was fed, read to, and in bed warmed his heart at the same time it caused his stomach to drop out. As he made his way to his apartment, he knew that's all he wanted—a family for Aoife, a partner he could share long days and dreams with. Even challenge one another when they needed it. And okay, some spectacular lovemaking wouldn't hurt anything.

But was it too soon to make a major life-changing decision based on a couple great weeks and one sultry night together? It'd been good with Sorcha, really good. But to move here with the hopes that…

That what? She'd want to move in with him and Aoife and continue the happy family routine indefinitely? That they wouldn't get sick of one another, making work and their living situation untenable?

Um...yeah.

He frowned at the sheer audacity of his subconscious. But... It wasn't wrong; that's exactly what he was hoping for.

He got to the front door of his apartment and gazed up at the lit window above. Sorcha was reading in the chair closest to the window, her knees pulled up to her chest. Even from two floors down he could see her bottom lip tucked between her teeth. He knew that look—the book must be at an intense scene to warrant her most focused attention.

And that was it. One word settled in his chest, took root and blossomed all at once.

Home. He was home, much more so than in Dublin. He wanted to know more about the woman upstairs. He wanted to build a life with her, raise Aoife together and make her smile every damn day.

He took the stairs two at a time, desperate to get Sorcha's opinion on it all. Worry at what she would think nipped at his heels with each step.

She must have sensed his roiling emotions when he walked in the door. Frowning, she got up from her chair, the baggy cowl neck sweater falling to midthigh over tights and fuzzy socks. She was adorable, but also...sexy as hell.

"What's wrong? What did Mick say?"

He swallowed hard. The words were simple—*He wants me to stay on.* But the implications were vast and filled with risk, the kind Patrick had avoided since Rachel's death.

"Dr. Collins is leaving her position to stay home with her baby. She'll remain on the surgical staff, but the chief medical officer position is too much with a new family."

What a coward he was—he couldn't even say the most important part. Maybe that meant he wasn't allowed to want it—the family, the full life in America.

The woman.

Sorcha's face was neutral, no doubt waiting for him to continue.

"Mick wants me to take it."

There. That wasn't so hard, was it?

The smile on her face said maybe he'd spent too much time on worrying.

"Wow. That's an incredible honor," she said. He tried on a smile, but it didn't reach his eyes. "Isn't it?"

"It's a lot," he admitted. "An honor, yes, but at the same time it means giving up the life we had in Dublin."

Sorcha gestured to a doll and the pile of American Girl doll accessories. "She'll survive living her best life in America. She'll think the fairies made it possible."

"That's true."

Patrick watched Sorcha's face, not wanting to put any pressure on her, but desperate for a break in the armor to gauge her feelings about him, not the little girl sleeping in her room.

"We get to stay in America?" a small voice squealed from the shadows. Clapping emanated from the same spot.

Okay, so not sleeping as much as spying.

Sorcha shot Patrick a grimace. "Sorry. I checked on her just before you got home and she was fast asleep. The puppy is in your room, though. No way Aoife would go to bed with that little cutie taking the bait each time she dangled her arm over the bed."

He laughed and waved it off, then called Aoife over.

The little girl came out, hands trailing a blanket behind her. "I just wanted water, but then I heard you talking about staying here. Can we?"

Patrick didn't even try to mask his surprise. He'd known

his daughter loved it here, but thought he'd need to weigh both sides with her.

"You would really be okay living here forever? Or at least a good while?"

"Yes. I already asked the fairies to think about it, but that was just this morning! I *definitely* think they know I'm here now."

He sat and she crawled up in his lap, wrapping her small arms around his neck. "Will you miss Nan and Pop?"

His parents would miss *them*, that was for certain. But they were retired and he had the discretionary income to pay for them to trade off visits with him and Aoife.

And maybe Sorcha?

His chest swelled with hope. This time, he let it. He'd said goodbye to Rachel, talked to Aoife about the potential for moving, and been offered a job in Boston. With no other barriers in sight, it was as if the universe—aka the fairies—had nudged him in the direction of his heart.

"They can visit," she said. Patrick chuckled at the simplicity of her answer.

He kissed her head and put her on the ground, standing up.

"Fair play. I'll let Mick know in the morning that the Quinns will be sticking around for the foreseeable future. Only if a certain young lady gets to bed before I change my mind." Aoife tore off toward her room, eliciting laughter from the adults. When they were alone, Patrick asked the question that had been plaguing him.

"I want to keep seeing you if we stay. But I don't want to put pressure on you, either. Would it be okay to take what happened last night and expand on it?"

Sorcha nodded, her eyes damp.

"What's wrong, *mo grá*?" He cupped her cheek, desperate to kiss away the hurt that seemed etched around her eyes.

"Nothing. I'm just... I've never had anyone ask my opinions before, not about something this big. It's...nice."

Tangling both hands in her curls, he pulled her toward him and pressed his lips to hers.

"Then it looks like I'm meeting with a Realtor tomorrow to talk about selling my place in Dublin."

"And you're *sure* you're happy about that?" she asked.

"Oh, very. Accept that I'm here to do more of this." He kissed her shoulder. "And this." His lips grazed the nape of her neck. "And much more of this." He tipped her chin up and kissed her. His teeth playfully bit down on her bottom lip, sending a surge of longing straight to her core.

When he pulled back, her lips were swollen.

"I guess I could get used to that."

So could Patrick. For the first time in years, he saw a future that wasn't solely based on survival. He saw happiness, fulfillment, and passion, and Sorcha in the middle of it all. Maybe it was too soon—after all, they'd only slept together the one night—but he didn't care. He was going to do everything in his power to help her see a bright future of her own, and maybe, with a little fairy magic, she'd see Patrick as part of it.

With one more kiss, he laughed and picked Sorcha up over his shoulder, carrying her to his bedroom. Who'd have thought that the combination of an intoxicating woman, a sassy four-year-old, and a rambunctious puppy would have him so optimistic he'd put his stock in Irish folklore instead of science?

Only one thing was scientifically proven about Patrick's situation—he was smitten and it would take a cataclysmic event to change that.

CHAPTER SIXTEEN

SORCHA UNDID HER PONYTAIL and shook out the tension that had built at the back of her skull. Pressing her fingers to the bridge of her nose, she inhaled deeply. The faint scent of antiseptic singed the inside of her nose, but it was such a familiar smell, it didn't rile her the way it used to.

A glance at her schedule brought back the tension.

All surgeries. No meetings about the trial, the funding, or even a whisper of when she could move the research out of the lab and into the world. She set down the beaker she'd been using, and it cracked along the bottom.

She winced. Under the split glass was the name of her co-surgeon on most of the patient cases.

Patrick Quinn.

Her boss, colleague, and…and what? She hadn't figured out a title to give him. Boyfriend seemed too cheesy, but anything else scared the willies out of her.

Because…

He's staying in Boston.

She tossed the beaker in the glass recycling and went to retrieve a new one. The news that Patrick was staying was nearly two weeks old at this point, the contract signed, sealed, and delivered, but she still hadn't digested it. Maybe couldn't was closer to the truth. If she did, she'd be forced to reckon with two nagging questions.

Is he staying for me?

He'd denied as much, but if they broke up, would he resent her for giving up his house, his career in Dublin, his daughter's life back home?

Her second question was worse, somehow.

Am I willing to do the same for him?

It was not as if she'd been unclear; he knew how important the trial was to her. It was *everything*.

The guilt ate at her, but not solely because of Patrick's decision to stay.

Sorcha usually went home after him, but the gap between their departure times was shrinking week by week. She reasoned that it was because all she needed to do for her trial was wait for the red tape to clear, but the truth was...more complicated.

I want to be at home with him. I want to cook, laugh, and build a life with him.

More than complete her trial? She wasn't sure, nor was she certain it mattered. She could want two things at the same time, couldn't she?

Maybe it would be easier to figure out her feelings if the trial was going anywhere.

A knock on the lab door startled her.

She walked to the door, tentatively opening it.

As it always did when she saw Patrick, her breath stalled in her chest. Today, he wore a button-down fern-green shirt that brought out the flecks of gold in his emerald eyes. The shirt was fitted, rolled up along his strong forearms, with the top two buttons undone, showing a hint of his muscled chest.

Sorcha swallowed. "Hey, you," she said. "I thought we were meeting for lunch?"

"It's nearly two."

She grimaced. "I was in my head, I guess."

His smile disarmed her.

"I figured as much. That's why I come bearing treats," he said, holding up a paper bag. "I brought you a soft pretzel."

"You're a god," she said, her hand itching to tear the bag out of his grasp. Luckily, she didn't have to; he surrendered it with a peck on her cheek. If this was what a relationship was, she could handle it.

"A god, hmm?" He leaned in, nuzzling her neck, and her stomach roared with desire, hungry for something other than the pretzel in her hand. When he nibbled her earlobe, a flash of heat flooded the sensitive area just south of her abdomen. "Well, why don't we close the door and I'll show you just how godlike I can be."

She might've moaned, but then she shook her head. "Not here. Mick might swing by with news about the trial." Or so she could hope.

Her desire for both—work and time with Patrick—was a push and pull between her head and heart.

"Fair enough. Mind if I hang with you while you eat? I've got some time to kill before I pick Aoife up from day care."

Sorcha tore into the pretzel, ravenous all of a sudden. "Of course. Sorry I didn't come down to meet you. My alarm rang, but I thought it was for the sample."

Patrick waved her off. "How'd the sample perform?"

"The same. Perfect. I just feel like I'm wasting time now. Have you heard anything?"

Patrick shook his head and ripped off a small section of pretzel. She threw him a "you only get one of those" glance and he laughed. "Nothing from Mick, though I'd imagine you'll hear before me."

She nodded, cleaning up her station as she finished off her lunch. It had barely made a dent in her hunger.

"Wait," she said, realizing that Patrick picking Aoife up meant he was done for the day. "Why are you off so early?" she asked.

"I'm taking Aoife to see the Celtics play. Remember? You set it up for us last week."

"Oh, my gosh. And I told you I'd come—"

"Shh. You have work. It's fine. I can manage this little excursion."

"But... You hate basketball."

"How am I supposed to like something with half the excitement of Gaelic football and athletes that are paid more than I'll see in a lifetime? Though *she* thinks—"

"The fairies talk to the leprechauns," Sorcha said. He nodded, a grin as wide as the River Shannon making her heart thump a little louder.

How strange that this man made her long for her home country at the same time he made her feel like his apartment downtown was home.

"You know, we parlayed your tickets into a skybox thanks to some donor from the board who Aoife accosted after she saw his Celtics hat." He kissed her, his unasked question between their lips.

Would she consider joining them?

Sorcha looked at the lab. Her space was cleaned up, not that anyone else would care. There was no word on her trial, the surgical schedule was empty the rest of the afternoon, and besides, Mick could call if he needed her.

What did she have to lose?

You've never left in the middle of the day. Ever.

Well, maybe it was time she did.

Her brain quieted while her heart rejoiced.

"I'd love to. If you're sure Aoife wouldn't mind me hijacking her daughter-daddy date."

Patrick leaned in and kissed her square on the mouth.

"Not at all. I would have reminded you about it sooner, but I didn't want you to feel pressured to leave work early."

That's the thing, though. She didn't feel pressure from him.

Just care, comfort, and passion. It made the choice easier than it should've been.

"To be honest, it'll help distract me until I hear something from Mick. I'm going crazy."

That half-truth was better than what her heart whispered: *I like you and will go anywhere you ask.*

Patrick took her satchel and slung it over his shoulder. "I'll distract you any time you need it, *mo grá.*"

He held out an arm for her to take and she did, marveling at how biologically responsive her body was to his. As a scientist, she was so curious about the bond she shared with a man she'd sworn to hate for eternity. As a woman, she was curious about very...*different* things.

She was curious about the feel of his strength wrapped around her at night and how much stronger it made her. About the way his lips on hers ignited a fire in her chest, but still sent goose bumps across her skin. About what the indentation of their bodies on his pillowtop mattress said about how her dreams were changing.

"For now, a basketball game sounds nice."

Disregarding the sun high in the sky and the sound of her office door shutting while people still scurried around them, she decided to simply enjoy the day rather than worry about what she *should* be doing, or what was the point of leaving in the first place?

Two hours later, she, Patrick, and Aoife were on their feet, screaming at the top of their lungs at something Sorcha had no clue about. Only that the rest of people in the box were up in arms, waving at the refs as if they could be heard over the rest of the stadium's din.

"C'mon, ref!" Patrick shouted, his accent strong as ever. "That wasn't a foul. Je—"

"Da-a-a!" Aoife said, a frown on her face. "You're not al-

lowed to say that. No bad words, remember?" She crossed her arms over her chest, and Sorcha stifled a giggle.

"I do," Patrick said. Aoife went back to the game and he grimaced. "*Cailín*'s got me wrapped around her finger, doesn't she?" he asked Sorcha.

"That's an understatement. Hey, I'm going to grab a diet soda. Can I bring you something back?"

"The same. Thanks, hon."

Sorcha nodded and walked toward the bar before Patrick noticed the red on her cheeks. They'd slept together, woken up naked beside one another, but somehow hearing the pet name in public reeked of intimacy. Not that she minded…

She waited in line, caught up in a small fight under the Celtics' basket that had broken out.

"Quite a game, isn't it?"

Sorcha pulled her gaze from the court. "Um, yes." She smiled at the gentleman from their box in front of her, shaking her head. "Whew. That was only the first half and it was so exciting. I don't know how you do this every week and don't all succumb to massive heart episodes."

The man laughed. "My wife wonders the same thing. She says board meetings aren't this stressful."

"She's not kidding. I'm Sorcha, by the way."

"Harold. My wife is on the hospital board."

"Nice to meet you."

"Your daughter seemed to be having a great time," he commented. Sorcha glanced at Aoife, who was smiling and animatedly talking to Patrick and a woman—Harold's wife, she realized. Sorcha caught something about Aoife's whole list being granted thanks to her dad and his special friend. She grinned, pride blossoming in her chest until—

"Oh," she said, her cheeks burning. Harold might not have realized it, but Sorcha had fully let herself live in the fantasy that Patrick and Aoife *were* her family. "She's not my daughter. I'm just…friends with her dad."

What else could she say?

"Is he the doc that might move over here from Ireland?"

Might? Sorcha let the word roll off her back. Maybe Harold wasn't privy to the inner workings of the hospital board.

"Sure is. He's brilliant and we're lucky to have him."

Harold nibbled on the inside of his cheek as if he was thinking. "That must make you the surgeon who presented the neuroblastoma trial, then."

Surprised, Sorcha nodded. "I am. Your wife told you about it?"

"She did, but, uh, only in passing, of course." Harold's smile faltered. "Anyway, nice to meet you," he added.

Patrick met Sorcha's gaze and frowned.

Everything okay? he mouthed from across the skybox.

She shrugged, finally given her turn at the bar. She got the sodas but took her time walking back to Patrick. Sorcha didn't have much interaction with others in social settings, but the way Harold had walked away after mention of her clinical trial didn't sit right.

A beeping in the room got her attention. She followed the sound to Patrick.

"It's an emergency. Bus accident with Boston University's track team. They need a trauma-trained surgeon and I'm all they've got that's close. Dammit."

"Da," Aoife warned. He patted her on the head.

"Do you mind?" he asked, nodding down at his daughter.

Sorcha took Aoife's hand. "Not at all. Do you need me to come in with you, though?"

Patrick shook his head. "Mick didn't say as much, but keep your phone on you."

"Will do."

"Thanks, Sorch. You're the best." His mouth stayed open,

like he wanted to add something, but then he just kissed her instead.

Patrick left after kissing Aoife too, and Sorcha felt the overwhelming urge to text and ask him to check in with Mick about her trial after the emergency passed. There was something going on, and she needed to find out what. But putting her boyfriend on the case? Yeah, that was messier than when he'd just been her boss.

Had she made a mistake mixing pleasure with work? God, she hoped not.

But in that moment, Aoife's hand in hers, she knew—she'd crossed a line somehow and couldn't go back.

CHAPTER SEVENTEEN

PATRICK SLID HIS MASK down around his neck. "Wow!" he exclaimed, wiping his brow. "That was a brutal surgery."

The operating lights in the surgical suite were dimmed while the cleaning staff came in. The crimson splashes of blood on the floor were a pattern of near loss that, even when it was mopped up, left an indelible mark. And it was a pattern that could be avoided with non-invasive procedures.

The world needed more Sorchas, more doctors willing to put ingenuity and research above personal glory, more doctors willing to research instead of only cut.

Mick whistled. "It was a close one. But it brought back memories, didn't it? We were the surgical studs of medical school."

Patrick chuckled and threw his paper towel at Mick.

"Surgical studs? I don't know about that."

"Don't forget the fun we used to have just because you paired off with Rachel the minute you landed back stateside. We'd pull off surgeries twice as long and then hit the bar like we just woke up. Those were the good ole days."

"I don't know," Patrick said, watching the blood and antiseptic cleaner funnel down the drain, wiping the slate clean for the next surgery. Would it be needed, or something that an innovative doctor like Sorcha could have fixed with a little time spent researching other methods? "I'm starting to wonder if Sorcha is onto something."

"What do you mean?" Mick asked.

"Her trial for neuroblastomas has me thinking about small cell carcinomas and TBIs. Maybe I'll build off her research and see if I can get the trial extended to other similar traumas. It would do a helluva lot of good, wouldn't it? To save kids like that—" he pointed to the ICU room where the patient had been moved "—without the trauma to their bodies... It would change lives."

Mick sighed, ripping his mask off and tossing it. "Patrick, we need to talk."

The unease that settled low in his chest made him anxious. "What's up, Mick?"

His old mentor wouldn't meet his eyes, instead making a big show about gathering his lab coat, his wallet, and his keys from his personal locker. "Let's go grab a cuppa at the café across the street," he said.

"Mick," Patrick said through gritted teeth, "you've got three seconds to tell me what's going on before I go back to my girlfriend and daughter."

Mick at least had the grace to look at Patrick when he sighed, resignation in his eyes. "There's a problem with the hospital's funding. We need to make cuts."

Patrick's world slowed to a stop. He could hear his pulse keeping time—*thump, thump, thump*—the way he'd been able to in medical school when extreme focus was warranted, when his scalpel was paused above a malignant mass. He'd already put his house on the market, despite a warning from his parents to wait, to make sure his contract went through before he pulled a massive trigger like that.

Never in a million years did he think he'd have to call them a mere couple weeks later and tell them they were right, that his offer had been pulled.

"Explain in detail, Mick, and don't leave a damned thing out."

"Fine," Mick said. "But remember I'm just the messenger."

Patrick didn't say a word. His arms crossed over his chest, frustration and worry brewing below the surface of his skin.

"You know we've been struggling to finance the rest of the new oncology floor," Mick started. "That equipment you chose—"

"That you approved," Patrick added, though his pulse kicked up a notch.

Mick nodded. "Well, it tipped the scales and we're in trouble."

"So…"

"The board came up with three solutions and voted Monday night."

"I'm just hearing about this now?" Patrick asked incredulously. "Well, what did they decide?"

"They're using the funding the hospital set aside for the neuroblastoma trial." Any relief Patrick felt that his job was safe was short-lived.

Sorcha's trial. Her life's work.

"It's just temporary—a two- or three-year hold on all trials until we're back on track financially," Mick added hastily.

"Find it somewhere else. You can't cancel Sorcha's trial, Mick."

"That isn't the only place we're restructuring. We've had to make some hard, deep cuts to make things right."

His frustration from earlier blended with horror, resulting in anger. Deep, rolling anger. This was Patrick's fault. "Are you saying if I'd chosen different, cheaper equipment for the oncology floor—"

"We'd still be in trouble. Just not as bad."

"You can't do this," Patrick growled. "She's worked too damn hard and for far too long to have it taken from her now."

Mick's chin dropped to his chest. "This surgical wing is the part of the hospital we need the most. It covers us financially when other departments fall short—I mean, elective surgeries alone will account for—"

"Elective surgeries?" Patrick hissed. "You're cutting a

proven lifesaving new treatment plan, a protocol that will save hundreds of children's lives, for nips and tucks on people who have more money than sense?" He stood, shaking with rage at the unfairness of it all.

"Jeez, man. Don't act like you haven't had to make hard calls like this in the past."

"I haven't. I *wouldn't.*" And his hospital in Dublin never would have made him.

"Look, this isn't ideal—" Patrick shot Mick a warning glance that hopefully conveyed how much more than "not ideal" this was. He seemed to get the message. "But it isn't that we're canceling the trial altogether. We're just moving it back until we can refill the coffers."

"You said *years*?"

Mick had the audacity to *shrug.* Like this was just a minor inconvenience for him. "I don't know, to be honest. No one is scrambling to donate to big, corporate hospitals anymore."

"I wonder why," Patrick mumbled. He raked his hands through his hair and across his jaw. Was it just hours ago he was with Sorcha and Aoife, laughing and cheering on a sports team? And now the world as she'd created it was about to crumble around her. "She's gonna be crushed. I hate that I have to ruin her night with this."

Mick's eyes went wide and he stood straighter. "You can't tell her, Patrick. I'm sharing this with you in confidence as the CMO. But it's the board's responsibility for legal reasons to outline the shift in dates and approval. We're scheduling a meeting to let her know at the end of the week."

Everything became crystal clear, as if time had stilled, offering a slo-mo play-by-play of the past few weeks. Mick's distance. His appointment of Patrick as CMO. The odd look he'd seen on Sorcha's face as she'd talked to that board member's husband at the game.

"How long have you known?" he growled. Patrick's tone was even, but even he heard the threat coating the words.

"We've been in danger for a couple weeks, which you knew, to a degree." Patrick's brows shot up. He opened his mouth to annihilate his supposed best friend, but Mick kept talking. "But it was just Monday that we—they—voted."

"That's why you brought me on full time, isn't it?"

Mick shook his head. "I brought you on because you're the best man for the job—and I thought you could be objective about this. I'm sorry, Patrick, I really am."

"So, what? I'm supposed to go home and lie to her? She's practically living with me."

"No," Mick said. "You just go on and keep your work life separate from your personal one. I know you can do that."

The warning in Patrick's eyes turned molten.

"Don't you dare bring Rachel into this."

"I'm not. But this is messy with no easy way to fix it. We've both been there before is all I'm saying."

Patrick paced the small, sterile room.

"Why can't we close up the half of the floor that isn't finished yet and—"

"There's no way the inspectors will allow us to function in a half-finished space. It presents all kinds of health hazards."

"I'm well aware. I'm not suggesting we hang a tarp and call it good. I'm just saying there's got to be a way to fix this that doesn't lead to us terminating the most promising project this hospital's ever had." Mick's brows rose. Patrick pointed a finger at him. "And this *is* me being objective. That trial is brilliant and you know it."

"I do," Mick said. He pushed open the doors to the sanitizing room and looked back. "I'm upset about it, and if there was anything I could do to save it, I would. But unless you can magically find ten million dollars, it's over. The best you can do is help see this construction project through and then, down the line, help Dr. Kelly get the trial back on track."

Mick walked out, leaving Patrick alone in the still, quiet darkness. Normally, with a daughter, puppy, and girlfriend he cared about deeply all waiting for him at home, he'd follow after Mick and sprint till they were all safe and happy in his arms.

That was before he'd been told he'd have to wreck at least one—but perhaps both—of their worlds. He dialed his folks to see if they'd contact his Realtor in a couple hours when the Irish business world opened.

"Hey, Ma," he said when her voice came on the line. "How're you and the old man?"

"Patrick! Oh, darlin', it's good to hear your voice. We're doing well. Your father is like a new man now that he's retired. Says his goal is to be good craic and make a naughty name for himself in the village."

Patrick chuckled, but his heart was heavy. It was being pulled between three places, stretched too thin to imagine he was getting out of this unscathed.

"That sounds like Da."

"You'll like to hear the idea he had the other day."

"Oh, yeah?" Patrick threw the phone on speaker and set it down so he could press the heels of his palms against his eyes. Pressure and heat built up and he knew an eruption was close.

"He wants to come over to see ya. Not for a couple weeks, mind you, but maybe get a small cottage outside the city so we can live half the year with you and Aoife. What do you think about that? I didn't even have to hint at it."

"Aw, Ma. That sounds perfect." And it did. The tears still fell, though, hot and heavy.

"*Mo grá*, what're you hiding from me? Somethin's wrong, isn't it?"

His mother's voice reached across time and distance and acted like a balm on his bleeding heart. She knew him too well.

"It is." He filled her in and at the end of it, only silence met him on the other end.

"Oh, my. That's a tough one."

A cough. His mam must have put him on speaker at some point. "Hey, Da."

"Real poxy jam you're in, son."

"Yeah." What else could he say? It sucked. He wanted to tell Sorcha what was happening, but how could he without making things worse at the hospital? "Sure is. And I don't have a clue what to do, either."

Because what did he care about the hospital or his role as the CMO when Sorcha was about to lose everything?

"There's no way to get the money from somewhere else?" his mam asked. "Some other hospital?"

"Jeezus, Mary Kate. Doncha think Patrick would've thought of that already?"

"Well, jeez, maybe he—"

"No," Patrick said.

But...

Unless you can magically find ten million dollars, Mick had said.

"You're a genius, Ma."

"See, Tom? Patrick says I'm a genius. And he's a doctor, so he knows a thing or two about that."

"I'll call you guys soon, but could you please ask the agency to hold off on any more showings? I'd rather not deal with the nonsense until I get things figured out on this end."

"Don't worry, son. We've got you covered."

"Thanks," Patrick said. "I mean it. If I was there, I'd kiss ya both." His mam giggled and even his dad let loose a chuckle. "And thanks for thinking about moving out here. It means more than ya know."

"Of course," they said in unison. He hung up and got to work calling everyone he knew.

Lucky for him—Irish lucky—he had a few tricks up his sleeve yet.

CHAPTER EIGHTEEN

SORCHA TURNED ON the water, her hands rolling over her skin as she shed the baggy T-shirt—Patrick's T-shirt—she'd worn between bed and the shower.

She wished she had more of her own clothes at Patrick's place, but it was too soon for that. Even if she did look forward to coming home to Patrick and Aoife. George, too. The latter two would bound up to her, matching energy and noise volumes, stories to tell about their days together. It was safe to say Aoife and the rapidly growing puppy were in love with one another.

Speaking of love—or something close enough to it that it scared Sorcha senseless—Patrick met her each day with a deep kiss, a glass of wine or tea depending on some algorithm he'd designed around her mood. Wildly enough, he hadn't gotten it wrong yet. They all ate dinner as a family, Patrick's hand on her thigh, then she got Aoife ready for bed while he cleaned up. Each evening, they read Aoife a story together, save the couple nights one of them would be called in for an emergency surgery. Once Aoife was tucked in snug-as-a-bug-in-a-rug—a holdover from Sorcha's childhood she'd recalled and implemented—Patrick would whisk Sorcha away for a bout of lovemaking that was both toe-curling and heart-pounding. Sorcha couldn't remember the last night she'd spent at her apartment.

How was she supposed to keep concentrating on work when *after* work felt so good?

She rinsed her hair and turned off the water.

More troubling? Patrick and Aoife, the life they represented, had begun to feel like *home*.

A *family*.

Which was fine. Dreams changed and grew according to one's courage. But Sorcha had bucked against the idea of a family for one reason—they could be taken from her without any notice, a heartache she didn't think she'd survive twice.

On the surface, Patrick leaving her seemed impossible. As smitten as she was, he seemed worse. He always reached for her hand when they were out walking, sat next to her at staff meetings, kissed her when she least expected it, including at work.

But something nagged at her brain, making it impossible for her heart to fully let go.

Each time she'd inquired about the house in Dublin, he'd tell her it was still on the market, but that there weren't any hits. That alone wouldn't ping any flags, but in the beginning, his phone had blown up with house showing requests that had suddenly stopped earlier in the week. And ever since the basketball game, a shadow passed over his face each time she mentioned work, the expansion of the surgical wing, or how frustrating it was not to know anything about the trial yet.

It wasn't that she didn't trust him, but she'd begun to suspect he wasn't being honest with her about something.

Ask, then.

Her subconscious was meddlesome that morning, wasn't it?

Start with asking if he's still okay selling his house.

If he wasn't, she'd listen to why and they'd work through it. Because he was showing her in every other way that he was there for her. Every way that counted.

Still...

"Hey, Patrick?" she called from the bathroom as she layered on green eyeshadow. O'Shanahan's pub was having an Un-Patty's Day party, and it was the first time she and Patrick were getting a sitter to go out alone. It was nice getting ready as a couple, tucking Aoife in and reading her a book—about fairies, of course—together. One united front.

"Yes, love?"

Her stomach warmed at the moniker. They hadn't said they loved one another yet, but each time he called her "love" her heart screamed that it wanted to say it back. But if—when— she did, she wanted it to be *safe*. With no reservations or odd feelings. Nothing that could creep up and snatch away the sense of security she'd tucked around her like a blanket.

She walked out of the bathroom and let loose an audible gasp. Patrick sat on the edge of bed, shirtless. Each carefully defined muscle was on display; his biceps flexed as he slid on socks and the loafers he'd picked out. He was an Adonis, a biologically perfect specimen. And his thousand-watt smile was aimed at *her*. A flash of red-hot lust *almost* burned away her question.

"Can I ask you something?" She walked over to him, hoping proximity equaled courage.

"Always. But only if you take that towel off and get into bed. I want to answer whatever you're curious about with my mouth on your—"

"The sitter will be here in minutes," she argued, cutting him off with a finger over his lips. Which she regretted with every fiber of her body. Even though Mick had put a meeting on the books for the next day—hopefully to sign the trial paperwork— and they had this party to go to tonight, she'd be lying if she said she wasn't already looking forward to coming home later with Patrick.

Home.

He kissed the tips of her fingers, drawing one into his mouth and sucking on it.

"Fine. What's on that pretty, intelligent mind of yours?"

Her heart, actually, but she didn't correct him.

"I was wondering how your house sale is going back in Dublin. You haven't mentioned it recently."

The familiar shadow crossed his face, but it was gone so quick, Sorcha wondered if she'd imagined it.

Yet the pause in his answer was the same as other times she'd been brushed off.

He didn't meet her gaze when he finally answered. "I asked my folks to reach out to the agent and pause the sale for now. There's a downturn in the market, so I'll try again in a couple months when it's safer."

Sorcha's head and heart both issued pings of warning, and it took every cell in her body to calm the tremor in her voice. "Oh, I'm sorry to hear that. Just a downturn in the market? You're sure nothing else is the matter?"

He nodded, but his smile seemed forced. Her stomach flipped. Was it just her past, a lifetime of parents who didn't show up for her, that warned her of danger anywhere real feelings were involved, or was there an actual problem? She hated that she couldn't trust her own gut.

"Yep. Now get over here and let me kiss you while I button my shirt."

Sorcha obliged, letting the warmth and safety of Patrick's lips flush out the cold that had settled low in her chest. When his shirt was buttoned, she grabbed her own top—emerald lace with a sheer tank underneath—and slipped it on. His eyes followed her every movement. God, it was sexy having a man as alluring as Patrick watching her dress.

Patrick's cell phone buzzed on the table. He glanced at it, but then his gaze went right back to her. She felt it as if it were his hands and not his eyes tracing her body.

"This view never gets old. Real estate agents would make a killing if they just implanted you into every bedroom, putting on shoes and drying your hair, and—"

She stopped him with a kiss. "You're ridiculous. I look like a drowned rat."

"My drowned rat." He sat at the edge of the bed and pulled her on top of him, nibbling at the base of her neck. She squealed with delight. He knew just how to make her squirm in all the best ways.

His phone buzzed again and he flipped it over, ignoring it.

"Do you need to get that?"

He shook his head before diving into the crook of her neck, teasing her earlobe with his tongue. She wasn't sure if the goose bumps were a result of Patrick's seduction or a manifestation of her fears that he was hiding something.

When he patted her on the backside and gave her the space to finish getting ready without distraction, she decided maybe she'd just let it go and enjoy her night. All she wanted was to relax into this man and let him love three decades of neglect away.

Half an hour later, they were on the back roads of Boston, avoiding the I-93 at all costs. With the elevated train down for maintenance, Patrick had argued driving was the best option. He'd said since this was their first real date, he wanted to "pick her up."

It wasn't going well.

Patrick's knuckles turned white as he gripped the steering wheel tighter.

"Are you okay? I can drive if you're not comfortable—"

"I'm fine. It's the same as driving in downtown Dublin, just on the other side of the road."

"And car."

"Yeah, that." His jaw clenched. She swallowed a giggle,

supposing she'd feel the same if the roles were reversed and she was carting them around downtown Dublin.

His phone was hooked up to his car radio and Glen Hansard, her favorite Irish singer and songwriter, crooned over the speakers. Patrick stiffened as traffic stalled.

"We're fine. We've got plenty of time." She put a hand on his knee and his shoulders relaxed. She loved that she had the power to calm him with a simple touch. Heck, she loved him, period. Why had that been so hard to admit?

Because you're not sure why he's being so evasive all of a sudden?

True, but she was sure of *him*, and that was all that mattered.

"Does anyone use their indicators in America?"

Sorcha laughed, swallowing it when Patrick's brows pulled tight in the middle of his forehead. This man was the most competent surgeon she knew, and yet he was a nervous wreck in evening traffic. The disparity made him human, made him real to her. Made her heart beat a little faster, too.

"Um...hon, we call them turn signals. Or directionals."

"Well, they should be on, whatever they are. I mean—"

"Patrick?" she interrupted. He kept his eyes on the road, still tense, despite the smile he shot her.

"Yes, love?"

"I love you. I know this isn't really the time or place, but—"

He crept up to the stoplight, threw the car in park and leaned over, grabbing her cheeks and kissing her.

"Shh... It's perfect." He kissed her again. "In fact it's the only thing worth braving this mob of eejits for. I love you, too, Sorcha."

They sat there, grinning at one another until a car honked behind them. They laughed as he put the car in drive and inched forward.

"I've been wanting to tell you for a week now," she admitted, her cheeks flushed with emotion.

He pretended to scoff as they passed the bar, Patrick scanning the road for a parallel parking spot.

"Is that all? Wow. I don't know if I should be offended or..." He made a show of putting a hand on his chest as he backed into a spot two blocks away from O'Shanahan's. "I've known since the minute you and Aoife waved madly at each other across the room while I accepted this position the first time."

"You did not love me then," she said. But that didn't stop the loud thump of her heart as it swelled against her rib cage. "You'd just met me."

"Ah, but I did." She giggled, but was silenced with another kiss, this one deeper, more rife with meaning. "A woman so fiercely dedicated to her work, but who still finds time to chase fairies with my daughter?" Another kiss. "An Irish lass who kisses like she was born to do it? And who wants to save the world with the same passion? I'm head over heels, Sorch."

He kissed her again, and Sorcha didn't know how her body could contain all the happiness welling up inside her. If this was what love felt like, she chastised herself for avoiding it all these years.

"Why didn't you say anything sooner?" she asked.

"Ah, love. Would you have been ready to hear it?" he asked.

She shook her head. "Probably not. I mean, I think if I'm being honest I've felt it as long as you, but I don't have much experience in believing in love or family."

Patrick leaned in and kissed her, his forehead resting against hers.

"I hope you start, love. Because we'll have all that and more and anyone who tells us we're off with the fairies, we'll kick their backsides and prove them wrong."

He tangled his hands in her hair and kissed her yet again, teasing her lips open with his tongue. He tasted like peppermint, which sent Sorcha into overdrive. Lust *and* love? It was almost too good to be true.

"Do we have to go in?" she mumbled against his lips.

"Nah. I'm sure those folks headed to the theatre would be right as rain if I take this fine *ting* and make love to her on the boot of the car."

She giggled, about to lay into him about being medical professionals and all when his phone chimed again. This time, the text came through on her dash, since his phone was connected.

Hi, hon. You didn't answer my last text, but I have today on my calendar as the day of the meeting. I hope it went well and she's okay. Love ya, Ma.

Sorcha sat back against her chair, her lips still swollen from kissing.

"What is this?" she asked. Her pulse raced when he bit his bottom lip and frowned.

"Dammit," he muttered.

"What the hell is going on? And don't lie to me, Patrick."

"There's a snag with the trial," he whispered. She barely heard him over the music.

"A snag?" Her chest constricted, making it hard to breathe. "What kind of snag?"

"I'm not allowed to say more, Sorcha. Mick said—"

She let out a humorless bark of laughter. "I don't care what Mick said or didn't say. I'm asking *you*."

She shut off the radio and squared up to Patrick. He met her gaze, but what she saw there wasn't love. No, it was loss—*that* was a look she recognized.

The silence was punctuated by his deep inhale and exhale before he spoke.

"They're taking the money and moving it to the surgical wing expansion." He must have seen the way her cheeks drained of blood, heard the gasp that escaped her mouth. "Just for now. He promised they'd reallocate the funds and that your trial is first up when they do, Sorcha, but—"

"Is he coming tonight?"

"Mick? Yeah, but—"

Sorcha didn't wait for Patrick to stop her, to defend something as indefensible as knowing about this and keeping it from her. She stormed out of the car and ran toward the bar, the threat to her future—and the whiskey she'd have to consume if it was ripped from her—pushing her forward.

CHAPTER NINETEEN

"Dammit." Patrick undid the seat belt before attempting to chase after Sorcha. He ignored the traffic whizzing by him and ran toward O'Shanahan's.

Breathless, he caught up to Sorcha two doors before the bar. "Sorcha, stop. Please."

Tears streamed down her face, and any trace of the love-infused grin from earlier was replaced with pain. Her lips twisted into a scowl, her eyes wide and red.

"How could you keep this from me?"

He froze. It was a question that had plagued him every waking hour of the past few days and some of his nonwaking hours, too.

"Mick told me I couldn't tell you for legal reasons, so I tried to work on it from my end. I can fix this, Sorcha."

"That's not your job as my boyfriend. Honesty is."

"And as your boss?" He winced at the hurt on her face.

"Are you saying I have to pick between your roles in my life? If you make me make that choice, I will, but you won't like it."

"Sorcha, I'm sorry. I thought I had it handled."

"Rubbish. You were scared. You took part in covering this up because you were terrified about what my response would be."

Was that what had happened? It stung like the truth dragged over raw skin.

Patrick held her gaze. "The board voted, not me."

"But you could have told me."

He raked his hands through his hair, down his cheeks, which bore three days' worth of stubble. This had been killing him, too. Didn't she see that?

"I couldn't. The money isn't there for a trial this year, Sorcha, and we won't have an oncology floor in the surgical wing at all if we don't finish the renovation."

Sorcha's fingers trembled. She was furious and he didn't blame her. He was, too. Which was why he'd been working his butt off to get new funding, funding the hospital couldn't touch. If she could only see...

"If we don't get this trial, we'll lose more patients than any improved surgical suite will save in its lifetime."

He'd thought the same thing after Elsie's surgery. And somehow, he'd let the politics of the job sway his actions and hid the news from Sorcha.

"I know. I'm sorry, Sorcha. You have no idea how much. But if you'll just hear me out—"

"You want me to *listen*? To what? More excuses?" Her eyes didn't soften at his lame attempt at an apology. If anything, her gaze hardened like scarred skin after an injury. "Maybe if you'd told me straightaway—"

"Sorcha, I swear I'm this close to securing your trial funding forever."

"Are you staying in Boston?" she asked.

"Of course. I mean, I want to."

"Is the Dublin house really on pause until the market turns, or are you scared of being caught between Mick and me and needing a place to run to when everyone's lies catch up to them?"

He balked, his voice suddenly stuck on the sliotar ball-sized guilt lodged in his throat. She wasn't pulling any punches, was she? They didn't bounce off, either. They landed—*hard*.

"I—I don't know." If he didn't have Sorcha, and the job was going to be more of the same—him being used as a political pawn rather than being part of lifesaving surgeries, what was the point? "I pulled it because of this news, yes, but only so I could concentrate on the money, on getting it back."

Her laugh was without a hint of humor. "You weren't committed to staying for my sake, or it wouldn't have mattered, Patrick. Don't you think I recognize a family with one foot out the door?" He opened his mouth, a rebuttal at the ready. That's not what had happened, although he could see why she thought it was. She cut him off with an icy glare. "And even if that wasn't true, you *lied* to me. That isn't love, Patrick. Not even close."

God. After all she'd been through, he'd taken her trust and squashed it.

"I'm sorry, Sorcha. I wasn't lying when I said I wanted to move here, when I said I loved you. I hid the reason I paused the house sale because I knew you'd read into it, and I didn't want you distracted from working on the trial. When the time was right and the money came through, I wanted us to be ready. That's all it was."

"I can't believe we're here again. I've already told you—you don't get to decide how I read into things. It's your job as my partner to talk to me. *Especially* when it's hard."

"I'm not your parents, Sorcha. I'm not out to leave you or neglect you. I just… I just wanted you to have it all."

Patrick ignored the furtive glances of people heading into the Irish pub as they walked past the fighting couple.

"I *had* it all," she whispered. "I let you in, Patrick, despite my fears. I fell in love with you and your daughter and trusted that you wouldn't ever put me in the position my parents did when they froze me out, made unilateral decisions about our family without me."

"That's not what I did."

But didn't you?

Her glare said his subconscious wasn't far from the truth. Again.

"And what about you?" he asked.

Wait. No. This isn't the way to go. Don't get defensive.

He'd had enough truth, enough judgment. He'd messed up, yes, but he'd been trying to do the right thing. Didn't that count for something?

"What *about* me?" Her voice was cold, a steel scalpel's edge.

Fear flooded his circulatory system. Panic seized his chest. But his brain couldn't reach his heart in time to stop it from dumping his feelings all over her. "You keep me at arm's length and I'm willing to bet you wouldn't consider leaving Boston for me. But I'm expected to get it all right the first time I upend my and my daughter's lives?"

She took a step back as if she'd been slapped.

"No. That's not what I'm asking and you know it. I just wanted you to talk to me. I've discussed my parents with you. How I can be there for you and Aoife even though nobody showed me how. I might have been buried in my work, a little closed off, but I worked every day to let you and Aoife in, despite my worry you'd do the same thing to me that my parents did."

Her sniffle punctuating the end of her sentence implied *and you did.*

He grasped her hand, which trembled. "I know. And I appreciate everything you do for us. But do you realize you tell Aoife more about your past than you tell me? Look, I just wanted time to sort this out."

"How dare you talk to me about opening up more? It takes two, you know. I've asked you—twice—not to try to fix things for me. I don't need a white knight. I need a *partner.*"

Her tears had abated, but what replaced them—an icy calm—wasn't any better. He was losing her, and he couldn't let that happen. Not when he'd only just found out what love could look like, feel like.

Patrick groaned and leaned on the brick building. "I wasn't trying to be a white knight. I just wanted to make it right. As your colleague. Or boss, or whatever."

"The waters were muddled since we're dating, so it isn't totally your fault. But as a partner, you kept it from me." A shudder rolled through her, and he wished he could kiss her hurt away. "Maybe you're right. We're both still keeping each other at arm's length… It's got to mean something, and if I hadn't been so distracted by how good it felt to be with you, I might have noticed it sooner."

"What are you saying?" he whispered.

"I'm saying we had a good time, that I'm grateful to you for teaching me how to care for more than just my work, but that it was always going to be too complicated to work in the long run."

"You're giving up on us?" The jovial music coming from the bar and the laughter of the people inside was jarring—the wrong soundtrack for the scene.

He knew he could fix this, find the place the bleeding stemmed from and cauterize it. Couldn't he?

"What's there to give up?"

Patrick's heart was racing too erratically, his blood pumping too fast. He was losing control. "Sorcha, I know I messed up. I should have come to you no matter what Mick said. But please give me a chance to make it up to you."

For the briefest of moments, it looked like he'd said the right thing, stopped the bleeding. But the calm gave way to a sadness so profound, it was worse than death.

"I know why you did it," she admitted. Her lip was drawn between her teeth, but not because she was deliriously happy or focused on her novel like at home. Her voice quivered. He hated it—that she felt anything other than trusted, desired, loved, and in control of her life. "You were right. I *am* closed off. And my relationship with my parents is complicated at best. But I let you in. And Aoife. I gave you two time I could have spent working because you mattered to me. You mattered more than the rest. I… I just need time to think about everything."

He'd been a coward, afraid to let anyone in lest they break his and his daughter's hearts. Maybe that's why he hadn't gone to her with the truth, hadn't trusted that they could find a way to fix it together. Rachel hadn't let him be part of the solution when she'd been handed down her diagnosis, but Sorcha…

Sorcha wasn't Rachel.

His fears were well-founded, yes, but life wasn't going to just keep throwing beautiful, incredible opportunities in his lap. He needed to do the work if he expected the reward.

Patrick took her hand in his. "Then take the time you need. But don't push me out, Sorcha. I want to help you heal that relationship with your parents, as well as make the rest of your dreams come true."

"It's not your job," she whispered. "Maybe it never was. I didn't need someone to make my dreams come true for me. I only needed you to support me while I did that for myself."

He was nodding like he agreed with any of this, like they were already in the bar, celebrating Un-Patty's Day.

Before he could step out of that dream and into reality, Sorcha was walking toward a taxi, leaving him with the sound of an Irish drinking song to drown his misery. His impulse was to run after her again, to make this right if he had to suture every damned bleeder with rudimentary stitches until they healed.

Over the music, he heard a whisper.

Let her go. Find a way to show her the truth and then go to her.

Damn if a chill didn't slither up his spine and root at the base of his skull.

He hadn't had any whiskey he could blame it on, but he would have sworn the voice was one of Aoife's fairies. Maybe his daughter was onto something, thinking there was a force bigger than him guiding the way.

Patrick shook his head and headed into the bar to give Mick a heads-up.

He only hoped the voice—whatever it was—was right because watching Sorcha turn the corner out of sight, thinking it was the last time he'd held her, loved her, was enough to make him think he'd never be okay again.

CHAPTER TWENTY

SORCHA ROLLED OVER and glared at her beeping alarm clock. She unearthed a hand from the mountain of pity covers she'd burrowed under the previous night and snoozed it. Her bed moaned as she rolled back into the nook she'd made for herself, only an eye-sized peephole to look out.

The view was as bleak as the feeling that had led to the blanket fort in the first place. She found fault in every aspect she could see of her own apartment. The laundry basket in the corner was out of place—Patrick's basket nestled in the closet was much more efficient. Then there was the matter of her bedroom layout. The bed faced away from the window, which was fine and dandy if she didn't need a strong solar influence to motivate her on early mornings. But it also meant on rainy days—like that morning for example—she couldn't peer out at the gray landscape and use it as an excuse to stay cozy in her bed.

The most glaring fault with her apartment was its small bed and one bedroom. It meant there wasn't anyone beside her to kiss her awake, to snuggle against when the rain batted against the panes of glass behind her. There wasn't any padding of six little feet sprinting toward her from the back room, primed to jump into the middle of the blankets and beg to join her.

No Patrick. No Aoife. No George.

And it was all her fault.

The alarm rang loudly against the wall of cotton she'd erected. This time, she turned it off.

The silence wasn't any better, nor was the gentle urging of her mind to get up, get out of the house, and get to work.

"What's the point?" she mumbled. The trial was all but dead—the meeting to go over the details postponed by Mick until today—her relationship with her boss was fractured on both a personal and professional level, and her heart was broken. Patrick had messed up by not telling her about the trial, sure.

But something he'd said that night at the bar two weeks ago had nagged at her every time her mind quieted. Which, since she'd moved out of Patrick's apartment and taken herself off all his surgeries, was a lot.

I'm expected to get it all right the first time I upend my and my daughter's lives? he'd wondered.

No, that wasn't reasonable.

In the moment, she'd thought, *Well, yeah, for something this big, you should have done better.*

But every morning she awoke alone, every successful surgery where she turned around and found no one to celebrate the success with, she'd realized the truth. He'd done what he had to help her in the best way he knew how.

It wasn't perfect, but when the scalpel was put to skin the first time, it was rarely a clean cut. It took practice. All good things did.

It'd taken losing him to realize another hard-won truth—she wanted the risk that came with a family and love if it also meant experiencing the joy and fulfillment that accompanied them. Having Patrick and Aoife and losing them certainly shone a light on each and every error of her ways.

With a frustrated *harrumph*, Sorcha slid out of bed and went through her morning routine. Not that she liked a single moment of her solo shower, single bagel in the toaster, or the sole coffee mug that would sustain another long day, alone.

How did I live this way for so many years?

When she got to the hospital parking lot, she froze, unable to leave the car.

There, walking from the entrance, were Patrick, Aoife, and George. Maybe she could inch out to the back lot without them seeing her…

"Guess not," she muttered when Aoife noticed her and waved enthusiastically, drawing Patrick's attention. "I'll make it quick, and it'll be like they weren't here at all."

Her heart argued otherwise. She'd missed those three like a body in the desert missed water, but seeing them there, at work, might drown her instead of bringing her back to life.

She made her way to the family, her eyes carefully pinned to Aoife and the puppy so she didn't have to meet Patrick's gaze. Even so, she could still feel it sliding over her, pleasant and warm.

"Sorcha!" Aoife exclaimed. "I missed you."

"Oh, Aoife. I missed you, too." Flashes of heat burned behind Sorcha's eyes. "What's this guy doing in the hospital?" she asked.

George's eyes lit with recognition, but at a small cough from Aoife, he held back from bounding up to her. Sorcha was impressed with his training and size in just a few short weeks. He must've gained twenty pounds of solid muscle since Sorcha last saw him.

"We're training him to be a servant dog," Aoife said, her chest puffed with pride.

Sorcha glanced up at Patrick for clarification and was hit with the full force of the beauty of the man. His million-watt smile that could power an OR, the scruff on his chin she wanted to rake her hands across, the crinkle around his bright eyes when they were in on the same joke.

"A *service* dog," Patrick whispered to Sorcha, adding a conspiratorial wink. For a brief moment, she allowed herself to believe things were back to where they were, that they were a family. Her chest ached beneath her rib cage. "He had his emotional service certification today so he can volunteer in the peds wing from time to time as a therapy dog."

"Got it," she whispered back with a wink. "Aoife, that's such a great idea. It'll help George and the patients, and you."

"Dad said I couldn't be a doctor yet, but I was old enough for this. Someday I wanna help people like you do, Sorcha."

Okay, forget a dull ache. Her chest threatened to split down her spine.

"And you'll make a wonderful physician. Until then, you and George are going to be quite popular here."

Aoife hugged Sorcha's leg.

"Guess what, Sorcha?"

"What's that?" Sorcha wanted nothing more than for that little girl to hold on forever. On one hand, it was impossible having these small interactions with a child she'd hoped to help raise, but on the other, at least she had this. Not seeing her at all would have been catastrophic.

"Grandma Jo and Grandpa Dave met George," she announced, patting the dog that was now equal to her in height. In another month, the darling girl would be able to ride him like a pony.

"Is that right?" George gave a brief bark as if to say "yes."

"What a good boy. So, what did they think of George?"

"Well, I dunno, because we had to leave to take Da to work, but I think they loved him. Right, Georgie-Porgie?" She skipped away, George at her side, only a brief hop betraying him as the puppy he still was.

"They asked us to take him home after he knocked over three new pots of rhododendrons with his tail." Sorcha laughed. God, she missed Patrick. In time, she'd grow to appreciate the brief drive-bys of her almost-family, but right now, she hurt. "He won't be invited back, but at least we will be. They're joining us for a Celtics game next week."

"I'm so glad you mended those fences, Patrick. I really am."

He trailed a hand down her forearm until it reached hers, and then squeezed it once before dropping it. A shiver of awareness raced across her skin.

"We've got a long way to go yet, but the bridge is under construction at least, thanks to you. I was ready to tell 'em to get lost, but you showed me what Aoife would lose out on. Thank you, Sorcha."

She cleared her throat, which was suddenly thick and lined with heat. "Um…of course."

"I know I don't have any right to ask you this, but would you be open to doing the same with your folks?" he asked. "Not that it's any of my business right now, you know, what with…" He trailed off.

She nodded before an answer had fully formed in her head. "Yes, I would be. I can't give out that advice if I'm not willing to take it, and for the first time in my life, I feel like I'm ready. And I have you to thank for that, too."

"I guess we weren't all bad for one another," Patrick said. He rocked back on his heels. Was he nervous?

"No," Sorcha admitted. "We weren't."

"Anyway, I'm glad. I hope… I hope you can forgive your folks."

"I already have. I'm not mad about things anymore. Not about anything," she added. His eyes sparkled with understanding. "Life is too short and people mess up. But those who matter deserve another chance to learn from their mistakes, and also to hear about what they were doing well, too."

"They do?" The obvious hope in his voice buoyed her.

"Mmm-hmm. There isn't much that can't be forgiven when it comes to the ones we love. Especially when it was done with the best of intentions. Sometimes, emotions just run hot when there's something important at stake and—"

"And people say or do things they wish they could take back." He finished the sentence for her.

"Exactly." It was obvious they weren't just talking about her parents anymore, but where did they go from there? "I'm sorry, Patrick," she finally said.

"Me, too." The two words cracked down the middle.

"Will I see you at the meeting later?" Getting a call from Mick last night was the only reason she was in on a Saturday. Maybe at one point she'd have been there anyway, but that had changed the minute she realized there was so much more to life than working. Even if the work meant a lot to her, what good was it to give others their lives back, only to lose her own in the process?

She had Patrick to thank for that, too. And Aoife... Even Mick and the board had helped in their own way. The pulling of her funding and subsequent loss of what she'd thought was the most important thing in her life had led to a *real* loss, one she might never get over.

Her family. Patrick, Aoife, and George.

"You sure will." The sparkle in his eye made her pulse quicken. Why did he look so happy to be there on a weekend? "I'm just dropping these two off at the day care. Save me a seat?"

She nodded and made herself a promise—she would *not* read into Patrick's words. Hope was a fine thing to have, but false hope? Well, she knew better than anyone how fatal it could be.

No, she'd just be his friend and hope that someday he could forgive her for bailing on him for making a silly mistake. She'd blown his trust, and it was up to her to build it back.

She would, even if it took as long as she'd been working on her research.

Sorcha made her way to the boardroom, not surprised she'd

beaten everyone there. She had half an hour to kill so she scrolled through her email, deleting the junk and answering some from other hospitals she'd put feelers out to. She wasn't looking to move, but maybe there was a place she could sell the research, get the trial going again at least.

One email caught her attention. It was from her mom and the subject read Long overdue. Her pulse racing, she clicked it open.

Hiya, hon...

Sorcha choked out a small sob. She could hear the Irish greeting in her mom's brogue and she'd always thought it would break her, but it didn't. It was a healing salve, cooling a long-ago burn.

I wanted to start the conversation I should have had with you years ago. I love you, and I'm, oh, so sorry. I should have been a better mother. But that's neither here nor there anymore. I will be better, from here on out.

Sorcha chuckled and another hiccupped cry escaped.

I know it may be too late, but can we meet to talk? I hear you're up to some amazing things, and I want to know about them. I want to know about you, hon. You know my number, and I'll wait for you to reach out.

Sorcha responded.

Yes. I'd love that. I'll call you.

Then she closed the email, but only after reading it three more times, chewing on each word, savoring it, and swallowing it into her heart.

It couldn't be a coincidence that her mom had written today, after Patrick had asked Sorcha if she was open to talking to her parents. It'd been years since they'd talked. And how did her mom know about the work she'd done at Boston General?

She didn't get time to answer the questions because her phone rang.

"Hello?"

"Dr. Kelly, there was a change in venue. Can you come to the new floor in the surgical wing?"

"Of course. I'll be right—" The phone clicked off on the other end. "*Down*. Good talking to you, too, Mick," she mumbled.

She'd think through her mom's motivation in emailing her once the trial postponement was finalized. Why Mick had put it off so long when they all knew the outcome was beyond her.

She got up and made her way to the Thieves' Deck, which was what she called the oncology floor since it had stolen around ten million dollars of funding for something she'd spent a lifetime on.

Of course Mick would want to meet there to show it off. Jerk.

She walked around the corner, grumbling to herself, and stopped short. There, in front of her, was what looked like the entire surgical staff. Nurses and surgeons in scrubs, even the off-duty docs in plain clothes. At the center were Patrick and Aoife, Mick behind them.

"What's going on?" she asked. Patrick nodded above them. She followed his gaze and gasped. Her hand flew to her mouth just as the tears fell.

The Cara Kelly Oncology Center.

"What is this? Patrick? What—"

"I think there are other people who want to explain. I'll jump in at my part." Patrick pulled back Aoife—who couldn't stop bouncing on her toes—and somehow, the tears fell harder. Her mom and dad were there, smiling through their own tears.

"Someone, please. I... I don't understand."

Her mom crossed under the new sign, and Sorcha took a few hesitant steps toward her. They met in the middle and before she could overthink about how to react, her mom wrapped her in an embrace.

"Mo grá..."

"Hi, Mom. I missed you."

"I missed you, too. We both did." Sorcha gazed up through the tears at her dad beside them.

"Dad, Mom. It's so good to see you, but why are you here? Now?"

Sorcha nodded to the group of people waiting with bated breath as they watched the exchange. It was too public, too personal. She wanted everyone to disappear so she could have this moment with her folks all to herself. Well, maybe with Patrick and Aoife, if the circumstances were different.

"We donated the money to finish the build under one condition."

"What money? What condition?"

"When your sister passed, a tycoon in Dublin reached out to us," her dad chimed in. "He'd lost his daughter the same way and wanted to help. We were so lost in our grief, as you know. But we saved the money, put it in a trust in Cara's name, and it just grew over the years."

"I never knew," she whispered.

"We never found the right way to tell you, not when we'd made our relationship so fraught. To be honest, we were just mired in grief and hospitals weren't on the front of our minds."

"Until now," her dad said.

Her mom smiled up at Cara's name.

"Yes, until now. Until you and your work brought us back to what matters most. Family."

"I love it. It's perfect." And it was. But… "How did you know about the build in the first place?"

Her parents both looked back at Patrick.

"I guess this is my cue," he said. He and Aoife joined them. "I told them. Not specifically about the new floor, but about you, your work and why it mattered so much to you. In the beginning, I just wanted them to know what I was up to, but then they volunteered the donation, and it sorta solved everything. Except me not talking to you. That ends today."

Sorcha's emotions were all over the place. Joy at this moment she'd never expected to feel. Confusion at so much new information. Pride in seeing her sister's name above the door of the new center.

"What were you up to? I feel like I've been kept in the dark." Patrick took her hands in his.

"That was never my intention. I wanted to get out of your way and put you in contact with people who could actually help."

She nodded. "Thank you. Patrick, I'm so sorry for running out on you on Un-St. Patty's Day. I don't mind you being in my way so long as you talk to me while you're there."

"I'm glad to hear that." He took a deep breath and glanced at her parents. They nodded so he continued. "The good news is, all but two hospitals want to talk to you, meaning if you agree, the trial can start tomorrow and will be fully funded. It will also be in as many hospitals as you want to oversee, with a staff of your choosing."

Sorcha's breath stalled in her lungs.

"How? Why?" Then, glancing at Mick. "And you're okay with this?"

"If it solves our problem and makes it possible to pursue your dreams, of course I am. I never meant to hurt you, Sorcha. I was only trying to save the hospital. Forgive me?"

She nodded toward Cara's name.

"This is a good start," she said.

"It is," he agreed. "And I'll work to rebuild the trust I broke. I fully support this venture. We couldn't have done it without your folks, though. Their donation, coupled with the other hospitals' investments, covered more than we needed and allowed us to take the first batch of trial patients pro bono."

"Like I proposed," she whispered. Patrick nodded.

"Can I call them?"

Patrick laughed. "We invited the first round of participants here for the unveiling of the new center they will be staying in as you work to heal them. Want to tell them in person?"

Sorcha glanced around at the nurses, doctors, and her people. She'd kept everyone away for so long, but no matter what happened with Patrick, she could finally see that she already had what she'd secretly always wanted.

A family.

"I do."

"Good," Patrick said. "We were hoping you'd say that. So, get to work, folks, and give us a minute."

The crowd dissipated, everyone filing away to stations and rooms that would save lives. And she would be a part of it. Happiness threatened to overwhelm her.

When they'd all left, save Patrick, Aoife, and her parents, she exhaled.

"This is amazing," she said. "Thank you. All of you. I don't know what to say."

"Say yes!" Aoife exclaimed.

Sorcha chuckled. "Oh, I already did. This opportunity is too great to pass up. I think I'll need a few days to realize I'm not dreaming, but I'm definitely saying yes."

"Did you already ask her, Da?" Aoife asked. Sorcha's parents grinned at her, gesturing for Aoife to join them.

When she looked back, Patrick was on one knee in front of her.

"Patrick, what are you… You've already done so much."

"And I'm not done yet."

"You don't have to—"

"None of what I've done is because I have to, Sorcha. *You're* what I want, what I need, and what Aoife loves with all her heart. So only tell me no if you don't want me—not because you think my intentions are for any reason other than I love you."

Her face turned as red as the stethoscope band around her neck. "You… You still love me?" she asked. Her lips quivered.

"I've known from the day I met you in the bar and you almost threw your drink in my face."

She laughed. "I didn't—" He quirked a brow. "Okay. If it wasn't good whiskey, I might have."

He joined her, laughing. "Sorcha, from that moment, I knew you would challenge me, that anyone who earned your favor would have to deserve it every day for the rest of their lives. And Aoife reminded me of something the other day."

"What's that?" Sorcha asked. She sniffed, tears of pure joy falling. She didn't bother wiping them.

"That the fairies brought you to us," Aoife said.

"And we don't turn away gifts the fairies bring, do we?" Patrick asked.

"Nope." Aoife stuck out her chin, grinning. "So ask her, Da!"

"I am, I am," he laughed, taking a small box from his pocket. "Sorcha, will you do me the honor of practicing medicine alongside me, raising this little hellion with me, and letting me learn how to love you two ladies for the rest of our lives?"

"Will you marry us?" Aoife asked.

Sorcha looked at Aoife first. "I'd love that," she said. Aoife whooped and hugged Sorcha's parents, who squeezed her back. "Patrick," Sorcha said, turning back to her beloved. "I am so glad I met you, that you fought to get behind my barriers and made this life possible. Yes, I'll marry you both."

Everyone celebrated under the sign showing her sister's name.

"Now, who's ready to go save some lives?"

Everyone raised their hands and Sorcha laughed. The road ahead was bound to have some bumps, but with these wonderful people at her side, she knew she never had to worry about being left behind again.

* * * * *

*If you enjoyed this story,
check out these other great reads
from Kristine Lynn*

Their Six-Month Marriage Ruse
Accidentally Dating His Boss
Brought Together by His Baby

All available now!

MILLS & BOON®

Coming next month

NURSE'S TWIN PREGNANCY SURPRISE
Becca McKay

'What are you talking about?' Hazel asked.

But as she neared the urine specimen container set neatly on the side, alongside two testing strips, understanding quickly began to dawn on Hazel.

One strip to test her urine for blood, glucose, ketones…all the usual suspects. The other strip to test for a very specific suspect. The kind of suspect that Libby dealt with day-in, day-out. *Pregnancy*.

Hazel was hardly breathing as she approached the testing strip but even from a foot away she knew the result. She could see the two pink lines as clear as day.

'Libby is this a joke? Because…' but Hazel couldn't finish and from Libby's expression, and the vehement shake of her head, she knew this wasn't the kind of prank her friend would pull.

Hazel picked up the pregnancy test with shaking hands and tilted it towards the light as though that might change the result somehow. But of course, it didn't. Nothing would. Because Hazel was pregnant.

And when it came to the father, there was only one possibility. *Dr Garrett Buchanan*.

Continue reading

NURSE'S TWIN PREGNANCY SURPRISE
Becca McKay

Available next month
millsandboon.co.uk

COMING SOON!

We really hope you enjoyed reading this book.
If you're looking for more romance
be sure to head to the shops when
new books are available on

Thursday 27th March

LET'S TALK

Romance

For exclusive extracts, competitions and special offers, find us online:

- MillsandBoon
- @MillsandBoon
- @MillsandBoonUK
- @MillsandBoonUK

Get in touch on 01413 063 232

afterglow BOOKS

Afterglow Books is a trend-led, trope-filled list of books with diverse, authentic and relatable characters, a wide array of voices and representations, plus real world trials and tribulations. Featuring all the tropes you could possibly want (think small-town settings, fake relationships, grumpy vs sunshine, enemies to lovers) and all with a generous dose of spice in every story.

🎵 @millsandboonuk
📷 @millsandboonuk
afterglowbooks.co.uk
#AfterglowBooks

For all the latest book news, exclusive content and giveaways scan the QR code below to sign up to the Afterglow newsletter:

SCAN ME

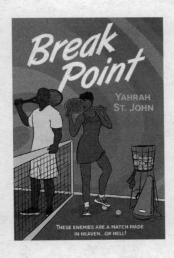

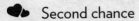
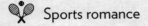